# THE ROLL OF Honour

By A. B. Reid

FriesenPress

One Printers Way
Altona, MB R0G 0B0
Canada

www.friesenpress.com

**Copyright © 2023 by A. B. Reid**
First Edition — 2023

Illustrator — Erik James Nelson
Photographer — Slyvia Pond

This story is a work of fiction, based on true events from my family history.

All rights reserved.

No part of this publication may be reproduced in any form, or by any means, electronic or mechanical, including photocopying, recording, or any information browsing, storage, or retrieval system, without permission in writing from FriesenPress.

ISBN
978-1-03-916946-3 (Hardcover)
978-1-03-916945-6 (Paperback)
978-1-03-916947-0 (eBook)

1. FICTION, HISTORICAL, WORLD WAR II

Distributed to the trade by The Ingram Book Company

*The night is alive, the wind sings its song, the stars are notes upon my heart. When I fall asleep, I will find you in my dreams.*

A.B. Reid

To my grandparents, who shared their stories of family, love, and courage. And taught us anything is possible. You are forever in our hearts.

To my mother, Catherine Johnstone Thomson Reid, who not only survived enemy bombing, but taught us the meaning of family and strength.

To my boys, Robert, Erik, and Nicholas: may you always know how much you are loved, and may you always have the strength and courage to conquer the world.

To my grandson, Jacob, my music maker, my storyteller, my heart.

# PROLOGUE

*POW Branch Camp 9, Amagaski, Japan*

A small drop of blood dripped from the inside tip of Nick's right-hand thumb. He watched as it fell, almost in slow motion, and it landed on his army-regulated red bandana. It dissipated, becoming one with the fabric. He licked his thumb; the blood was warm, and the taste distinct. He inserted the needle again, this time pushing it through using the corner of his worn blanket in an effort to save his thumb further puncture. The last piece of the letter Y was completed. Nick picked up the bandana and appraised his work of embroidery.

The little light available would soon shut off. The dirty light bulb above him started to flicker, a slight sound of depleted electricity humming as its last spray of light was extinguished and darkness fell. As Nick's eyes adjusted to the dark, he lay still, searching his mind for the vision that embraced him each night.

She is beautiful, almost a touch away, her soft pink cheeks, her deep brown eyes, her honey-coloured hair, her warm, inviting smile. She stands in a dance hall, poised for the camera, almost teasing its lens; her long red velvet dress hugs her curves, accentuating her beauty.

It's all he had to lay hold of: a possession that was his and his alone. They would not take it from him, nor would he let them. When darkness fell and cries shrilled through the night, he drew deep into the sacred corners of his mind and pulled the warmth of that memory he held so dear.

# PART ONE

*It's in the Still of the Battle
You Lose Yourself – Your Soul*

## CHAPTER ONE

# Far Away Frae Hame

*March 1941. Royal Scot 2nd Battalion: A company arrives in Hong Kong*

Nick Massaro was caught, blinded by the sun's direct ray, and he cupped his hand over his eyes in an effort to see the shoreline of the island. His mouth felt dry, his heart was racing. *This is what I trained for*, he thought. He had spent the better part of the last seven months travelling from Freetown down the beautiful western coast of Africa to Capetown, then venturing over to Lahore, Pakistan, and next to Bombay (Mumbai), India. This would be the Royal Scots' last stop.

Rumour was they wouldn't be stationed that long. According to the officers, the Japanese Army was inferior, their training sloppy, their equipment unsuitable, and they lacked skilled leadership. One officer blatantly expressed, "These short-ass yellow, comical-looking bastards and their imbecile behaviour will not beat us first-class lot, assuredly not the Royal Scots." The operation was to barricade and defend the borders of the new territories from the invading Japanese army. The directive seemed manageable and straightforward – all but for its fallacious judgment.

The men became restless as the ship crossed Victoria Harbour to set anchor at the Taikoo docks on the Island. The afternoon sun delivered a warm and familiar feeling of contentment. Nick dropped his kit on the deck of the ship, closed his eyes, tilted his head towards the sun, and breathed it all in. He took advantage of the halted crowd of men waiting to be unloaded and replayed the past months in his mind: the places travelled, the exotic countries, all so different from home. Hong Kong certainly wasn't a destination he had imagined and was definitely a slight delay in completing his arts program.

He had just turned twenty-nine on February 11 and felt he had the world by its tail. Soon enough he would be home, working towards all that he planned, all that he dreamed.

Before being stationed in Hong Kong, Nick had been home on leave in Edinburgh, Scotland. First on his list was to catch a football match; he was more than pleased when his team, the Hibs, had won. The favourable bet made for a good send-off. Second item was a night of drams and dancing. He was pleased to run into Emma Helliwell at the club, as they had dated occasionally. His sister Getna chummed about with Emma and always insisted they made a beautiful couple, but both Nick and Emma agreed they were just good friends.

It was Emma's younger sister, Alexandrena, that caught his eye. Rena, she preferred to be called, so Emma advised. She stood alone as if posing for a portrait. Her long, red-velvet dress hugged her slender curves. A twist of honey-coloured hair lay swept back, held by a silver comb dressed with pearls. Nick couldn't take his eyes off of her – she was stunning, no doubt. She looked neither happy nor sad; her expression was inscrutable. Nonetheless, everyone stopped and stole a stare. How could one not? Her beauty was captivating.

The band played Vera Lynn's rendition of "We'll Meet Again." During their dance, Emma informed Nick that she was engaged to a chap named Charlie and was very happy. Nick congratulated his friend, and they continued speaking of family and the changes the war had brought. They spoke of the atrocities that happened with the Italians in Leith. Nick had heard it all too well from his father; the hate was still largely alive.

He himself experienced a prejudice encounter one evening walking home. Two women, whom he knew, for they frequented his father's ice-cream shop, had spat towards him when they strolled by; one woman cursed out, making reference to his greasy Italian heritage. There was not even a riposte that Nick could devise – these women knew nothing of his Italian heritage. Christ! They had never been outside Leith. He had tried

3

not to let their closed-minded bigotry shake him. He gave a slight smile, tipped his hat, and continued walking along Henderson Street.

The music ceased and dancers stood in anticipation for the following number. "Nick, I must go and tend to my sister," Emma said as she brushed his arm.

"Your sister?" Nick asked.

"Aye." Emma pointed over to the beautiful woman dressed in red. "I literally had to drag her oot the hoose – she was desperately in need of a night oot." Nick now knew who she was. He suddenly felt embarrassed; how could he not have recognised it was Emma's sister? The resemblance was uncanny. He then felt fraught. They hadn't discussed the bombing, and he was prepared to give his condolences. It had been all over the news. Sadly, tragedy had fallen on his friend Emma's family when the German Luftwaffe released a spray of bombs over the Leith docks.

Emma, after kissing Nick's cheek and apologising for her hasty departure, made her way through the swingers and fox-trotters over to her sister. Nick watched as the two stood exchanging words, then Emma gave a point of her finger towards Nick and both her and her sister waved him a farewell. He stood caught amidst the dancers watching them leave, and at the last moment Alexandrena turned and gave him a warm smile.

The ship docked, and soldiers from all ranks began collecting their kits. Names of officers and battalions bellowed out over the loudspeakers, giving directions of who was to meet whom and where. The atmosphere was energetic, the harbour crowded with people from all walks of life and from all countries: Britain, Denmark, Australia, New Zealand, Portugal, India, Taiwan.

Along the coastline, hundreds of pans and junks swayed up and down, following the inward waves of the ships. The commotion was chaotic, and Nick found it hard to focus. Once off the ship, the air seemed less fresh; pungent smells of raw fish mingled with unfamiliar odours, and they filled his head, making his stomach feel unsettled; what he wouldn't give for a cup of tea and a scone right now. Laying left to the Royal dockyards, a row of tiny, makeshift stalls stood side by side, all staged to sell their daily catch of fish and strange sea creatures, which were foreign to Nick's observation. Trinkets of shells and beads were laid out row after row, accompanied by funny straw hats and bright-coloured fruits and vegetables, all to catch a soldier's eye. Children ran wildly and openly through the narrow streets, cupping their hands for handouts. Scrawny dogs weaved in and out of booths and pedestrians, their noses intently focused on the ground to snatch any expelled morsel.

Below the northern docks approaching the west coast lay a chain of mountains exhibiting rugged ridges and peaks. Victoria Mountain stood the highest, her tip rarely visible from the clouds; however, her stance was one of sheer intimidation. As the men crowded the docks, they all observed what was to be their new home for the next several months. Orders bellowed out for the 2nd Battalion to prepare loading onto the group of buses that lined up along the docks.

The Royal Scot battalions were divided up into three locations on the island. Nick's Company A Battalion would be lodging in Victoria, northeast of the island, just along Victoria Harbour.

"For Christ's sake, what I wouldna give for a fag and a pint right now." Pie Roberston was from Edinburgh, and he was at least a head taller than most of the men, his broad shoulders and thick arms displaying an intimidating persona. His flaming red hair added to his appeal. He was certainly opposite to Nick's shorter stature and dark hair.

"Aye, that, a warm bed, and one of those Chinese lassies to release my tension from the last few weeks at sea," Ian McMillan stated with a hearty laugh. Ian was a West Lothian lad, with a slender build, dirty-blond hair, and green eyes, a bonny lad. He was actually glad to be conscripted. "Saved me from the fucking pits, ye ken. A life at sea, a lassie at each port – all waiting for my Scottish charm."

A quiet chap Rab Stewart was, with a slight build, jet-black hair, and eyes to match. He was a Fifer, born and raised. "Lads, nae feeling the love here, ye ken." He lit his cigarette and inhaled deeply while viewing the harbour, then exhaled a cloud of smoke, masking the undesirable sight. "Place gives me the shites."

"I have to agree, Rab – not the same feel from Lahore, not at all," Nick replied, confirming his mate's prescient suspicion while he repositioned his army bag over his shoulder.

"Och, enough, the pair of ye, once ye get a few of those gin slings into ye, you will be fit as a fiddle," Ian confidently announced.

The bus arrived at the British barracks. Their colours flew high in the sky, welcoming the new arrival of Royal Scots.

The barracks ran parallel inside the compound, and each building was almost identical in shape and size. First orders were to unpack, organise their belongings, and meet in the central hall at 15:00 sharp. The men pushed their way into the building, all wanting to find a prime spot and a comfortable bunk. Nick claimed a top bunk directly at the back near a window, and Rab Stewart placed his bag on the bunk directly below. Jordie Ferguson and Danny Cameron claimed the bunk beside. Pie Roberston, Ian McMillan, Peter Taylor, Arthur Patterson, John Findlay, and Charles McGregor, all boys from the Lowlands, grabbed their bunks. Once all settled, the unpacking began.

Nick neatly placed his clothes in the small chest of drawers. Only one drawer was assigned to each soldier. He positioned his army-regulated glengarry on the knob of the headboard. The last item to be placed was a small, red-velvet box. Its contents were rarely viewed, however essential for Nick's safe passage, so his mother did advocate.

Once the men unpacked, a few decided to cross the harbour to check out the mainland before the scheduled briefing. They jumped on the ferry at Wan Chai, just north of Victoria, and arrived at the peninsula. At first sight of Kowloon, Nick was impressed. The city was beautiful, the air was fresh, and it seemed to be in a surprisingly prosperous condition. Many small businesses surrounded the area. The vast population lived and worked in Kowloon, although most of the local villagers lived within the most unruly, poor areas leading up into the mountains. Nick and the boys eyed everything with great fascination. All was foreign, all was new.

The city was congested and busy; people were dashing and darting everywhere, and smells of foods wafted through the streets from tiny huts that looked as if they had just been smacked together, effortlessly at that. Rickshaws dashed by. It was most impressive observing a slip of a man sprinting with great speed and agility while pulling one or more persons behind him. Nick learnt later that these working labourers were known as coolies.

Beyond the city, the terrain was thick and densely covered with denizens of foliage and forest, masses of fir trees prominently showcasing bright-green nettles.

"Fuck me, mate! I wouldna want to be fighting among that shite. Christ, ye canna see one foot in front of ye through that jungle," Rab voiced with considerable concern.

"We'll nae be fighting through that mess, Rab. Nae fear in that. Our station is to strictly hold and protect the border . . . and the island, if necessary," Nick countered, hoping his words spoke true.

South of Kowloon, in Tsim Sha Tsui, stood the prestigious Peninsula Hotel; its stature outranked any of its smaller, less-impressive buildings. Rumour had it that famous, big names frequented the hotel, Charlie Chaplin being one.

"I'll buy the first round of whiskey, boys!" piped up Jordie Ferguson.

"Aye, in yer dreams, mate," Danny Cameron replied with a chortle. "Ye couldna afford a glass of water in that place." Danny Cameron and Jordie Ferguson were East Lothian lads who grew up together, their fathers miners. Nick loved their patter, and the three formed an immediate friendship as they began their journey as Royal Scots.

"Nick, can ye picture us lot in that establishment, pished from whiskey, singing our Lowland Scottish songs . . . we'd be the belles of that fucking ball." Jordie slapped Nick on the back in a playful manner.

"Aye, they will know the Scots are in town . . . yer right there, Jordie," Nick admitted. The lads belted out hearty laughs, trying to find a morsel of commonality in this strange new place they were to call home.

The central hall was packed. A loud hum bounced around the room as hundreds of voices spoke in unison. The room was abruptly brought to command by Captain Ian MacGregor of the Royal Scots. Once the cordial welcomes and roll call were out of the way, the briefing of the pre-eminent operations commenced. All the men were to direct their attention to the presentation board positioned at the front of the room. First orders were a brief history of the recent activity on both the island and the new territories. Second was Japan's position and potential invasion. As the captain spoke, Nick surveyed the roomful of soldiers, more particularly the number of preceding Royal Scots. He couldn't discern exactly what he was looking for. He studied the men's faces, waiting . . . waiting for a sign or indication on what they were about to embark on. Like dedicated soldiers, their expressions were stern and focused. Nick turned his head slightly and noticed that John Findlay's curiosity, or concern, more likely, prompted him to do the same. John stared back at Nick with a contemplative eye. Intuitively, without words, they both shared the same disquieted apprehensions.

The captain outlined the map of the mainland with a long pointer, directing his troops through the geographical tutorial where two main roads and a railway crossed from north of the Chinese border at Fanling Village into the new territories. Hugging the west coast was Castle Peak Road, centre stage was Tai Po Road, and running parallel was the Tai Po railway – a vital link in transporting food, petrol, and other essential supplies. Their twenty-mile stretch ended at the harbour in Kowloon City. To the east was Devil's Peak, a peninsula of higher ground extending out into the Lye Mun Passage, its name just as intimidating as its densely fogged foliage.

The captain's pointer dragged in a leaden motion up to the centre position of the new territories, making an annoying vibrating sound. He gave a quick *rap tap tap*, arriving at the infamous Gin Drinkers Line and informed the men that the eleven-mile stretch was built in 1938 by the British Army. He described its zig-zag formation while the soldiers followed the drag of his pointer through its rocky terrain, precipitous hills, and densely covered deep valleys, where a chain of strategically built pillboxes lay, each positioned 200 to 400 yards apart.

A heavy thud startled the men, and the captain hit the map with great force as if rounding his troops to battle. The pointer remained still, as if introducing its leading character in a feature presentation, and that's precisely what the Shing Mum redoubt was. The concrete artillery observation post would play a significant key role in defending the mainland and repelling the Japanese Army from moving southward into Kowloon.

Below the redoubt, Smugglers Ridge and Golden Hill lay just outside the Gin Drinkers Line parameter. The pointer didn't reside there long, implying its insignificance.

As the following map turned over into position in preparation for its presentational tour, the room appeared to awaken; chair legs scratched along the floor as men stood to stretch their stiff bodies. The familiar smell of both sulphur and butane filled the air as soldiers lit their cigarettes. A tall, slim, uniformed gentleman entered the hall and surveyed the room with a keen eye and an affirmative smile. He was introduced as General Grassett. He had been in command of the Royal Scot battalions since November 1938. Nick overheard a couple of seasoned Royal Scots mention that Grassett, who was Canadian-born, was working assiduously to move some of the troops to another theatre of war. Some of the men had been stationed way too long in Hong Kong, and seemingly all the action was in the Middle East, fighting the Italians and Germans.

The short-lived commotion settled, and the captain jumped back into operation with his prestigious pointer, resuming the geographical lesson. Travel distance across the harbour between the mainland and the island was approximately a mile. The island in its entirety covered a thirty-two-square-mile range. The mountains stretched out like arms reaching across and touching each coast. Their formations broke into clustered sections; tortuous valleys surrounded the base of the mountains like a moat protecting its castle. The British headquarters resided southeast of Victoria Mountain at Lay Wanchai Gap. Farther east, taking up centre residence, was Mount Cameron, and four miles south was Mount Nicholson. Stationed below was the police station.

"We'll nae be wanting anywhere near that!" Pie whispered. Nick smiled and gave a nod. Both chuckled under their breaths.

The captain, a.k.a. Maestro, raised his pointer as if conducting an orchestra, swinging to the left, to the right, and bringing his written score to life. Southwest of the island was Repulse Bay, its inlet of water rolling into Aberdeen. Further southeast on the peninsula was Stanley View. He wielded his pointer central island where Jardine Lookout lay, another vital defence post. The northeast tip of the island played in andante, the tempo hitting allegro, travelling north to the Taikoo docks. The finale played in adagio, tracing slow and stately through North Point and Braemar Point, where a number of pillboxes lined the coast along Victoria Harbour.

Mercilessly the pointer struck down on Devil's Peak.

The captain delivered his proclamation as if each man's life depended on it. "Devil's Peak is a vital position, which must be secured and held at all costs. The Japs will utilise the peak to cross over Lye Mun straight and gain access onto the island, landing at the Lye Mun barracks, south of the Taikoo docks. The training you will receive in these zones is imperative to impede the infiltration of the Japanese regiments," the captain concluded, resting his fatigued pointer. "I understand you are all tired, and at this point hungry . . . we will have a quick briefing of the current conditions Hong Kong is under, then a break will be suitable."

Rab leaned in towards Nick, and with a low voice uttered, "I'm bloody famished . . . hope he moves things along."

Nick replied with a nod.

Before their dismissal and Captain MacGregor's orders for the men to return at 18:00 hours sharp, two newcomers arrived. The captain introduced them as Captain Douglas Ford and Lieutenant Colonel White, both with the Royal Scots Brigade. Both officials would conclude the military operations of the island where the Royals Scots would be stationed.

The patter of the rain hitting the roof was soothing, almost like a lullaby. Nick felt himself drifting. Voices tuned in and out like the weak frequency of an old radio. He had slipped the tiny red-velvet box under his pillow after he had opened it and viewed it. Sometimes he took it out and traced the gold pendant with his finger and thought of his mother. It was important to her that he carry it on his travels. He felt it safer tucked away, in case it became broken or lost – he would never forgive himself. The Saint Michael Archangel pendant, which once belonged to his dead brother, was now his. His mother had placed the red box in Nick's hand before he left for Africa. She had kissed his forehead, then prayed.

The lads' voices continued; they were discussing the last segment of the briefing. Without seeing their faces, Nick identified them by their voices and their dialect. Pie went on about China's civil war and something about how the hell they could trust any of them. Frank MacLeash and Harry

Graham, both Glaswegians, were trying to comprehend the order and outcomes of the Paris Peace Treaty, the League of Nations, and the Treaty of Versailles. Peter Taylor assured that Germany had wiggled their way out of the Treaty of Versailles unscathed, like the worms they were. And because Allied countries felt sorry for them, Germany was exonerated from paying further reparations from the Great War. Jordie Ferguson piped in only to take heed of the fact that Japan flipped sides like a pan of fried kippers. Patrick Munro, a Leith lad whose mother was Australian, laughed over the "White Australian Policy," saying, "The Japs are pissed over Australia's 'Racial equality Proposal.' No one wanted the bastards, and only Australia had the balls to tell them they weren't immigrating into their country."

Patrick lit a cigarette and inhaled. "One thing about us Aussies, we pull nae punches."

All the boys knew Nick was an Iti; he took a bit of flack, though always in jest. "No offence there, Nick!" was how Ronald Hughs, a Fifer lad, carefully phrased it before he prattled on about Italy flipping sides too. Charles McGregor mentioned that President Roosevelt – he couldn't remember his first name and wasn't too concerned – had heard talks that the US was withdrawing vital products, such as oil, placing Japan under heavy embargoes and sanctions.

Nick heard a match strike, and as Danny Cameron lit his cigarette, said, "It would take a fucking bomb to get those arrogant, self-indulgent Americans off their asses and support us over here."

Nick turned onto his side, nudging his pillow. The subject had now shifted over to the operations of the Gin Drinkers Line. This time it was Rab Stewart and John Findlay. They both took turns describing the line's concrete underground tunnel system and how it duly earned its name due to the amount of gin drinking that had taken place during its construction. Its zig-zag tunnels and connecting pillboxes stretched out from the west at Gin Drinkers Bay across the mainland to the east, covering nearly twelve acres of the mainland.

Nick chuckled, his eyes still closed when he heard John Findlay say, "Christ, they've even named the bay after the bloody drink."

And as Rab Stewart described, "This is the Brits' model of France's Maginot Line. Ye ken, a key land defence from a northern attack." He then described the number of Vickers 7.7mm machine guns that would be positioned inside the pillboxes and the redoubt.

"Well, the Middlesex lads are welcome to it," Pie bellowed.

Here they all were, the oldest and most senior British infantry regiment of the British Army. Proud of their unbroken service to the charter, bestowed by King Charles I since 1633. Most of the soldiers came from Edinburgh and the Lothian regions, some of the best lads Nick had had the pleasure to travel, train, and now possibly fight beside.

Topics of world politics, defence lines, and countries jumping sides became the topic of blonde bombshells, particularly Jean Harlow and Greta Garbo. Nick grinned as he heard Pie reveal what he would like to do with both lassies. As the boys joined in on Pie's aspirations, Nick thought of Alexandrena Helliwell, her warm smile, and that tantalizing red dress. Christ! He would get no sleep tonight.

## CHAPTER TWO

## *Full Moon, Gin Drinks, and a Gin Line*

*December 6–8, 1941. The Battle of Hong Kong*

The orchestra trumpeted "The Best Things in Life are Free" throughout the Peninsula Hotel's two ballrooms. Champagne, whiskey, and now Nick's favourite bevvy, the Singapore Sling, were being served around the room on round trays carried by the most beautiful, exotic Chinese women Nick and his mates had ever laid eyes on. This was their first night within all the months they had been stationed in Hong Kong that they had the privilege of attending the prestigious hotel.

The boys from the Royal Scots had a bit of a reputation among the English battalions for becoming rowdy after indulging in drink. "Rowdy!" Pie yelled out over the music and loud hum of voices. "They havna seen us at a football match." Pie's laugh was deep and contagious.

"Well, let's try to have a wee bit of dignity tonight, shall we, lads?" Rab pleaded. "I'd like to enjoy the entire evening with nae interruptions of being kicked oot, ye ken."

Nick slipped away from the group, leaving them in contemplation over their questionable behaviour. Nick grabbed the last gin sling drink from the young girl's tray. She smiled and slightly bowed.

He had learnt her name was Pan Lingyu; she was twenty-five years old and was from Shanghai. She and a couple of girlfriends had moved down to Hong Kong to work. The sex trade was booming throughout the Japanese-occupied territories; girls, no matter their age were being abducted and used as "comfort women." Even young boys were in demand.

Pan's father, with his military connections, secured her a job and accommodations at the hotel, all to keep her safe from the Japanese gestapo and out of the turbulence Shanghai was facing.

Pan and Nick spoke for hours. Her shift had ended, and they had found a quiet retreat on one of the terraces. She talked about her family and how her father supported the Republic of China and was a nationalist. Pan was uncertain where her loyalties lay. While some of her friends were in support of the Communist Party, she could not choose. How could she? Both parties had rallied together to resist the Japanese. It was all so overwhelming. At one time, China was divided and at war; now they had joined in alliance. Shanghai had changed so much from the time she was a little girl. Opium and gambling enticed a whole new world of people, and the city became known as "The Paris of the East, the New York of the West." There was an influx of Russians, who found refuge after their country's political revolution. And thousands of Jews escaped Nazi Germany only to find themselves victimised all over again by the Japanese.

Pan continued telling Nick the horrific scenes she had witnessed as the Jews were rounded up and placed in the most terrible of slums, known to her people as the "Shanghai ghetto district." With all this evolving, her father moved her south against her mother's wishes. It was a confusing time for many of the youth in China, especially girls. Nick listened attentively, intrigued by her story. Even in worlds apart, everything to everyone seemed uncertain – lost. Nick didn't share much about himself, his attention strictly on Pan. Although he decided to share that he was an artist and would love to draw her portrait. He had packed a few charcoal pencils and a sketch pad before he left Scotland and when time allowed, he drew. Hong Kong provided beautiful landscapes, and the island's shoreline along the China Sea was an artist's paragon.

Pan smiled, and a dainty laugh escaped. "I would like that much, Nicholas," she said shyly as she gazed directly into Nick's blue eyes. Her exquisite porcelain skin and large dark eyes captured Nick's heart. He bent in and stole a kiss; her sensuous red lips did not protest.

"Nick, here ye are, for Christ's sake! Did ye nae hear the announcement?" Danny breathlessly summoned. "We . . . all battalions are to report at once for duty at the harbour. You must come now!"

Nick and Pan entered the first ballroom, and it looked like a bomb had already dropped. People were running everywhere. The dance floor was covered in debris of broken champagne glasses, stomped flower arrangements, and articles of clothing – even lit cigarette and cigars lay strewn about.

A few of the lads had waited for Nick, while others made their way outside, eager on operational orders and combat positions.

*This is it*, Nick thought. His stomach turned slightly, perhaps from too many gin slings, or maybe it was just good old-fashioned fear. A couple of Pan's friends frantically grabbed her arms, pulling her away. Nick loosened his grip from her hand. She looked frightened and disoriented, and her dark eyes darted back and forth between her friends and Nick.

"Be safe, Pan!" was all he could think of saying. He should have said more, but what? He himself was lost in his own trepidation.

Nick wasn't certain of the time, but he knew it was after midnight somewhere in the early hours of Sunday the 7$^{th}$. The moon was perfectly round, and its bright palette of yellow shone full and bright. Shadows danced across the sky as clouds swiftly swept by. North of Kowloon lay prepared; the Royal Scots had dug trenches and positioned wires strategically around the Shing Mun Redoubt. They were to impede the Japanese regiments infiltrating from the northern territories. It was crucial that they control and stronghold the redoubt.

The Punjabis and Rajputs had been assigned their stations along the Gin Drinkers Line, each battalion instructed. It was now a waiting game. Nick befriended a few of the Indian lads, one in particular. Amik Singh was a Punjabi soldier, and a hell of a football player. Nick and Amik spent many an afternoon playing on the lush green lawns at the jockey club at Stanley. And if luck felt on their side, they would enjoy a few gin slings over bets of a card game, or a horse race at the track just outside of Leighton

Hill. Many a fine breed of horse resided at the stables on the island. Nick couldn't account for why that specific memory erupted; nevertheless, it did.

Everything before the strike of midnight seemed distant. Time elapsed. Reality settled in. "I hope we're fucking ready for this," Nick spoke under his breath.

But Percy Miller, a Fifer lad, heard him and replied. "Aye, Nick! Canna agree mair."

The bulk of the Royal Scots' training and defence strategies were carried out strictly on the island. The Middlesex battalion was to secure the redoubt and Gin Drinkers Line, that is, until the Canadians arrived and all that changed. General Maltby was in a position to alter tactics, and two infantry brigades were formed, each being assigned three battalions. Nick's outfit, Company A Royals Scots, along with the No. 8 Platoon would cover the southern slopes of Mount Tai Mo Shan along the west of Gin Drinkers Line and fortify the Shing Mun redoubt, which was strategically placed between a narrow piece of land at Shatin Cove and Gin Drinkers Bay in Kwai Chung. Company B and C Royal Scots lay lower ground at Jubilee Reserve; D Company would cover the southern slopes of the redoubt. The Punjabi spread throughout the GDL centre stage, and the Rajputs would defend the east of the line, north of Devil's Peak at Tai Po Road.

Brigadier C. Wallis, who previously commanded the 5/7 Rajputs, had now been appointed to lead the mainland brigade. He had lost his left eye during World War One and wore a shaded monocle, which added to his authoritative persona. Nick thought back on the weeks leading up to December 6, before his battalion was summoned for duty. The brigadier's orders had the men working intensely by digging trenches and establishing defence holds around the parameter of the GDL. Malaria was prevalent in the heavily dense area, and the Scots took the brunt of its infectious disease. Nick witnessed close to 200 Scots hospitalised during that time. Due to overcrowded beds, the poor sods that experienced lesser symptoms were sent back out to dig trenches, shivering with chilled fevers.

Nick's mind reeled uncontrollably, his thoughts heavily afflicted with what he considered the unfavourable circumstances he and his battalion found themselves in. He learnt that almost a hundred soldiers stricken with malaria were determined unfit for battle. The remaining infected men could hardly stand up, let alone fight. That left fewer than 600 men to fortify the area. This was their first dilemma. The second was the Scots were discordant and concerned, defending an area of disadvantageous terrain that they had little time to train for and become familiar with. The last, though most vital, dilemma, was the odds. Nick, who enjoyed a good bet, ascertained the numbers. Typically, an area of a battleground for a battalion of 700 soldiers would hold a range of half a mile; these men would be covering three miles, leaving many gaps exposed to enemy infiltration.

Pie caught Nick's discomposed expression. "You've nae lost a quality bet yet, Nick!"

The redoubt's shape was unique, almost a trapezium, with an elongated triangle placed inside. Its observation post housed five machine-gun pillboxes.

The pillboxes were numbered by a 400 series: Pillbox 1 was PB400, Pillbox 2 was PB401, and so forth. Nick and forty of his regiment would call the redoubt home for at least the next ten days, as that was the objective of the defence plan.

Steel looped hinges protruded inside the cement walls, where netted hammocks hung for sleeping. Built-in cavities held burners, pots, dishes, and utensils – all the necessities of home. The men had enough food and water for at least three days, possibly four, until the Chinese volunteer runners would resupply them.

The boys, in an intoxicating spirit of adrenaline, laughed and made jest at the Middlesex regiment inscribing names in each of the cement tunnels that ran through the zig-zag line, after renowned streets from back home in London.

"Christ, the bloody English had the cheek to name the goddam tunnels after their fucking streets!" Pie wasn't partial to the English and found himself in many a scrimmage with a few of the Middlesex chaps, keeping the Wan Chai police on their feet. Nick was happy to have Pie along; he was built tough, and one of the strongest out of their unit. More so, his heart was as big as the oceans.

The men had split up. Some entered Oxford Street tunnel, some Shaftsbury Ave., others through Piccadilly, Haymarket, and Charing Cross, arriving and settling into what Pie characterised as the English-knighted pillboxes.

The afternoon's sun was intense, and it shone beautifully. It was hard to believe that such a peaceful sunny sky was outperformed by an explosive surge of black and grey smoke from anti-aircraft and descending bombs. The loud, piercing sound of machine guns disseminated all around, cracking up the sky like a thousand fireworks. Streaks of flashing light bounced in all directions, like lightning waiting to strike. Two heavy explosions reverberated, alarming Nick and Jordie. Both jumped and joined Patrick, Harry, Ian, and Percy to assist in priming the Vickers. Shamshuipo was hit. The second blasted the skies, and blazing fires ravaged through Kai Tak airport, destroying a number of unprotected Allied aircraft, including a group of Vickers Vildebeest bomber planes. Hundreds of Japanese A6M fighter aircraft liberally charged the skies. Nick could hear the engines scream as they flew above him.

The news was spreading fast, the men all stood around intently, trying to listen. The high-pitched frequency of the two-way radio line crackled, and between the piercing screams of the air-raid sirens and exploding bombs on either end of the wire, the message was almost unintelligible. Nonetheless, it was enough to cheer the lads on. The United States had now joined the war. Japan had bombed Pearl Harbor early Sunday morning, December 7. The catastrophic attack shook the US, and President Roosevelt declared war on Japan.

Danny sarcastically responded, "I kent it would take a fucking bomb to get the arrogant Yanks off their arses."

## CHAPTER THREE

# *The Abyss*

*December 9, 1941. Mainland, Hong Kong*

Nick stood leaning against the cold, damp cement wall. His tin cup of once-hot tea had chilled quickly. He swallowed the last mouthful, contemplating last night's orders. He dragged on his cigarette and blew the smoke in the direction of the redoubt's opening, where the Vickers' long barrel rested, waiting for action, waiting to unload its 500 rounds of fury in just under a minute. *At all costs, hold the redoubt.* The barked command was a constant. It rang in the men's heads like a church bell; loud, reverberating, never letting you forget its intimations, its principle. It was crucial that the Japs did not breach the Gin Drinkers Line, gain access into Kowloon, and cross the harbour over to the Island.

"What day is this, Nick?" Jordie asked, lighting his cigarette.

"Tuesday the ninth," Nick replied, extinguishing his butt under his heavy black boot.

"Oh, aye. It still feels like yesterday." Jordie rubbed his hands up and down the length of his arms. "Christ, it isna half damp in here."

Nick laughed. "No fear, Jordie, it won't be for long. Once these old Vickers start up, we'll be faced with one hell of a blast of heat."

Jordie gave a huff. "I'd rather have a lassie keeping me warm, mate."

"Aye, you have a point there," Nick replied. "By the sounds of things, it won't be long. I overheard a few officers talking that this scrummage should be over in a week or so." Nick, now thoroughly chilled, moved away from the wall's damp hold.

Harry and Danny appeared out from Shaftsbury Ave. tunnel, leaving PB400. The men had been given strict orders to man their stations and stay alert. "Christ, you can no half hear Pie throughout the tunnels; his voice is loud as a bloody bomb," Harry stated. When Nick asked Pie's location, Ian answered, saying he was causing havoc at PB402, Piccadilly. They all laughed with great vigour.

"I pity the Jap soldiers who get in Pie's way!" Nick responded.

Harry agreed, relaying the last commentary he and Danny heard Pie yell out as they were running down Shaftsbury. "This is Pie's words nae mine, 'Let's kill some fucking Japs!' Though I must concur," Harry concluded.

Patrick and Percy made their way in from Haymarket, leaving a unit of men at PB403. Patrick updated the now-occupied redoubt of about forty Company A Royal Scot soldiers that a Japanese infantry was detected north of Gin Drinkers Line late yesterday crossing through Laffain's plains down Fanling Road, centre mainland, and they had reached Tai Po Village. And farther west at Gin Drinkers Line, a division of Japs seized Shatin, though not before the HMS *Cicala*, which was positioned in Gin Drinkers Bay patrolling the shoreline, launched a frenzy of gunfire detaining the enemy, at least for a short time, allowing the Chinese defenders, Z Force, to retreat south, closer to the Gin Drinkers Line. Percy mentioned that the efforts of Maltby's orders to blow up the bridges over the Sham Chun River and along the railroad and northern border at Fanling were ineffective. The Japs bulldozed through with great speed and efficiency, setting up their own replacement bridges. It was expected that the Japs would make their way down Castle Peak Road, along Gin Drinkers Bay, and blast through the western line to attain access into Kowloon. They had not heard a word from the eastern side of the GDL, where the Rajputs were stationed. Although they knew they would, soon enough.

The sun had risen, though it lay hidden behind black clouds and a thick cloak of fog. The faint cries of air raid sirens were outranked by the incessant whirring of Japanese planes unloading bombs throughout the mainland and harbour. Nick, Jordie, and Ian manned their Vickers, waiting. Reports were coming in over the wireless that a flotilla of Japanese ships, led by a flagship called the *Isuzu*, had strategically deployed a naval blockade around the island of Hong Kong. A bit of relief was emitted from the broadcaster's voice when he contentedly reported that two British destroyers had managed to escape.

The next dispatch wasn't as affable: hundreds of Japs had been observed east of the Gin Drinkers Line at Tai Po, where the Rajputs found themselves thrust into full combat.

Nick knew the knowledge the men received was on a need-to-know basis; perhaps a tad concerning, but who were they to question? What seemed like an extemporizing chain of orders was delivered in intervals, announced with a sharp edge of urgency. What now echoed throughout the confined tunnels was that the Japs had penetrated through the northern territories with great speed and were rapidly advancing south, flanking from the west to the east. The men learnt three Japanese regiments would be their adversaries. The 230 Regiment, the 228 Regiment, and the 229 Regiment. Not that this morsel of information was valuable or even necessary to the men: what was and would be of value to the Royal Scots was targeting areas the Japs were encompassing, regardless of the sequenced number their units were issued.

Castle Peak Road was a vital link running down the west coast into Kowloon. Fanling Road, running centre stage along the railroad, would hit head on with both Jubilee Reserve and Pineapple Ridge, north of the GDL. South of the redoubt was Smugglers Ridge and Golden Hill, where the Royal Scots Companies C and B remained positioned. The other targeted area of attack underway was to the east, at Tide Cove and Tai Po, a vital artery to Devil's Peak. The enemy without doubt would cross the Lye Mun Passage of water and land at Sau Ki Wan, an ingress onto the island where the Lye Mun British barracks lie.

It was a waiting game; even the communication wires crackled impatiently, waiting for the ensuing chain of commands and the next set of ordinates.

Nick's adrenaline was surging; he could feel his blood racing back and forth from his heart to his head. The pressure, pumping inside his ears, was waiting to explode. His thoughts drifted aimlessly, bolting like a stray bullet, and he was not entirely sure where they would land. When they did, he reflected on whether the four weeks of preparatory measures the Royals

Scots took, (taking into consideration the men stricken with malaria) strategically positioning coiled wires and, with great exertion, digging trenches. Would it be enough to hold the enemy from penetrating through the infamous line of tunnels? "Christ!" Nick said aloud. "Not sure how many Japs are coming at us, boys."

Ian yelled above the constant noise of sirens and bombs. "How the fuck will we ken how many Japs are oot there? Ye canna see a fuck'n thing in front of us." He continued to load the canvas belt of 250 rounds into the Vickers' mouth.

The men all appeared to exude the same apprehensive feelings: concern foremost on the list. They had all looked down the extended barrel of the Vickers gun, navigating its reach from the tripod it rested on. After eyeing into the gun's clinometer, it was evident and most discernible that the scope of angles and elevations were dependent on the reach of the barrel itself. The Vickers' barrel was held hostage, as its downward throttled angle was trapped by the height of the cement wall on which it was perched. The range of firing would only reach above the descending terrain.

"How the fuck are we to see the Japs at this angle?" Jordie was fuming. "We canna even shoot the bastards at this range." The terrain fell over a thousand feet below the redoubt, spilling down into Smugglers Ridge and Golden Hill. Turbid sloughs twisted in between deep, dense bowls and precipitous hills, like a bed of snakes gesturing an act of intimidation. The entire presentation appeared impenetrable.

Nick's blurred vision bounced in and out as he again tried focusing a steady eye through the clinometer, as if repeating the same visual exercise would change the outcome. He stood, arching his back, holding his hands firmly against his hips. "Christ, it's all starting to look the same. Ye canna tell if we're up, doon, or fuck'n sideways."

"Mind the fuck'n gaps, boys!" Pie's voice bellowed over the crackling line. He was calling out from PB402, Piccadilly, his station. "We have open gaps between Piccadilly over to PB401A and PB401B, Oxford. I can see movement coming out and around the southern slopes at Jubilee Dam, and ..." The signal was lost. A high-pitched scream shrilled out from the field phone, oscillating between the cement walls. The men were trying to listen for its recovery.

Captain CR Jones, commander of the Royals Scots A Company, had set up his command post within the perimeter of the redoubt. A few days prior to the battle, a mock attack was carried out. Brigadier Wallis emphasised that a constant patrol between the line and the redoubt was critical. And to all, with a great sense of distress, the featured performers breached through the wired perimeters unobserved. It was evident that there was not an adequate number of soldiers to patrol the terrain. The redoubt had occupancy for at least another hundred or so soldiers. The men knew they were stretched thin. They could not conceal their stately, doleful facial expressions. Even the lieutenants, first and second, and the captains of the battalions bore pensive guises.

"Quiet doon, lads, there is a broadcast coming through." Harry raised his hands in an effort to silence the men, while holding the wireless high out the opening. With poor reception, the voice of the commander-in-chief of the Far East, Singapore, waned in and out. Harry turned the volume, again yelling at the lads to quiet down. *"We are ready . . . we've had plenty of warning . . . our preparations made . . . and tested . . . we are confident . . . defences are strong and our weapons efficient . . . defend these shores . . . destroy the enemy . . ."*

That was the order of the day, its delivery emotional – riveting. Nick felt his heart beat heavy as each word was expelled.

General Maltby's order of the day also motivated and compelled the lads: *"Stick it out unflinchingly, and that my force will become a great example of high-hearted courage to all the rest of the empire who are fighting to preserve truth, justice, and liberty for the world."*

Heavy explosions detonated all around, and machine-gun battery charged the skies. Nick stood aside the Vickers' barrel, his hand firmly gripping the firing lever. Both Jordie and Ian held the canvas belts, ready to feed the machine. The gun's recoil was solid, unforgiving. Nick felt the power of the muzzle booster, expelling its 2,440 foot-per-second reach. He heard other Vickers batteries along the line discharging in sync. The rain was heavy and relentless. The high winds howled, circling within the cement tunnels, causing debris to uplift and twist like a tornado. Reports were filtering through from several sentries positioned outside the cement tunnels.

All five pillboxes remained secured by the Royal Scots and two Indian infantrymen. The fog was still heavy; nevertheless, the men could hear the Japanese regiments moving. The final report was not what the boys wanted to hear. The enemy was advancing towards the GDL and redoubt. To all appearances, the Japanese were quick. They moved with great speed and furtively. They used a camouflage of rolled nets carried on their backs, which when released, uncloaked a patchwork blanket of reinforced twigs and long grasses, concealing their heads and shoulders. They could skulk through the treacherous terrain with ease, guided by the moonlight.

Nick's hand felt stiff, his hold on the lever rigid, and he dared not withdraw his stance. Ian and Jordie were replacing the belts consecutively. Shells were piling up in heaps. The men dodged back and forth to avoid either tripping or being shot by the return of enemy fire. It was difficult to see through the unbroken fog, and the clouds of black smoke that discharged from the Vickers' blitz of rage hung in the air thickly. Adding to its appeal was the heavy stench of machine oil. Nick was choking, gulping for any oxygen that could be had. He heard men yelling beyond his station, and throughout the tunnels machine guns performed top-notch. Bombs were dropping in the near distance and over the harbour. The skies resonated with the sound of war. The thick fog obscured any visibility out the opening of the redoubt. Nick squinted his smoked-watered red eyes, throttling the barrel as low as he could, firing out to the abyss.

## CHAPTER FOUR

# *London Bridge is Falling Doon*

*December 9–10, 1941. Mainland Hong Kong*

By dusk, all defence lines had moved south to the Gin Drinkers Line. All except for the Punjabis to the east who were holding off the aggressively advancing Japs at Tai Po. A Punjabi sentry described the chaotic scene after his platoon had blown several bridges and railroad tunnels along Tai Po Road. The information, necessary as it was, held no confidence with the boys at the redoubt. Nick felt his gut fall out of his ass. Ian and Jordie and the other surrounding infantry, without doubt, were unanimously distressed over their positions. At first, the news sounded favourable, indicating perhaps the first in a chain of small victories. Lamentably, that was not the state of play. Regardless of the Punjabis' pathway of destruction, Nick feared the impetuous Japs would press forward – relentless and tireless, like a pack of rabid dogs.

The Punjabis watched a group of Jap soldiers struggle to carry their heavy guns across the murky rivers where the bridges once stood just hours ago. Hundreds more were spotted crossing in Sampans. The Punjabis took advantage and released a madness of ammo out to the tiny boats of sitting ducks. A celebrated choir sang out across the wires.

"They're coming our way, boys!" an officer shouted out. The surviving Japs reached the defence line, and A and B companies of the Royal Scots held them off for a couple of hours. Another choir of singing spread, affirming that the Japs had suffered many casualties between the Punjabis and the Royals Scots. To the west of GDL at Shatin and Tai Mo Shun, the enemy had already infiltrated the defence line, and now the latest commentary was they were heading south to the redoubt, towards Pineapple Hill and Jubilee Reserve. The artillery was incessant from both sides. The Royal Scots were now tossing grenades from their pillboxes, out into the southern slopes.

Nick dropped the Vickers barrel as low as its reach would allow, unleashing as many rounds as mechanically possible, shooting out and across and all around to kill the Japs before they climbed up the steep terrain. By Nick's assessment, they could clamber up the slopes with ease given their forging ability. And more unsettling, without notice.

The rain was easing, and a light mist remained suspended; it hung dense, refusing to subside. Nick could now only see the harbour on account of the weather slightly clearing. It was his first sighting since they all were assigned to the GDL tunnels three nights ago. The reflection of lights, bombs, and machine-gun artillery rippled across Victoria Harbour. It was eerie, and at the same time beautiful, like a painting. Nick stared out at the showcase of fireworks – its performance of death.

He thought of the fallacious judgemental comment that was made when he'd arrived to Hong Kong. It stung inside his head like a swarm of angered bees, waiting . . . waiting to land, waiting to inflict a sundry of stings. Nick visualised the officer standing with an arrogant lean, his long fingers wrapped around the chamber of his pipe, talking while he exhaled a cloud of smoke. "These short-ass, yellow, comical-looking bastards and their imbecile behaviour will not beat us first-class lot – assuredly not the Royal Scots."

Nick shook the echo of words from his head. "Christ, what the hell are we in for?" He mumbled the words as it was useless trying to yell out to Ian and Jordie; the scene was chaotic. His sense of audio became muffled, vibrating in muted tones, like he was trapped underwater.

It took everyone by surprise. It was quick, precise. The blast from the explosions roared through the tunnels with a violent force. Its turbulent pitch was ear-piercing, rendering moments of complete deafness. Debris of cement and wire, remnants of dismantled weapons, and fragments of battery shells blew through the tunnels at a severe velocity. Nick felt each and every hair stand on end. The blistering, airless waves blew over, around, and through him. Voices were rumbling, men were yelling loudly and threatening. And not only in English.

It was just before 11:00 p.m. on December 9. A group of Platoon 8 Royal Scots were ordered to parade the redoubt and check the wires. It was at that perilous moment when the disadvantageous news dispatched across the field phones. The British Army was severely outnumbered. Hundreds of Japs were surrounding the redoubt and hundreds more were observed combing the defence lines. The men couldn't secure all the gaps around the line; it was impossible. They were stretched considerably thin. And shortly after 11:00 p.m., over a hundred more Japanese soldiers surrounded the eastern corner of the cement tunnels at Oxford PB401A and PB401B. Grenades were tossed into the air-ventilation chimneys. The Japs were in!

On the outside of the tunnel defence line, Royal Scot Bren gun carriers aggressively bulldozed around as much as the perimeter of the rutted, uneven terrain would allow, causing menacing havoc. Nick knew these tactics wouldn't stop the Japanese, only slow them down, causing several casualties. Captain CR Jones ordered the men to keep fighting and hold the redoubt. To the east, at PB401A and 401B, hand-to-hand combat was at large. Some of the Royal Scots were making their way through the zigzag centre tunnels by way of Regent Street and Charing Cross to reach Oxford and support the men.

Nick heard the disturbing news over the wire. The first casualties reported were two Indian signallers. Both had died instantly from the grenade blast. It was apparent that the Royal Scots needed reinforcements. The Rajput Company D would have been a likely candidate if timing and distance were not foreseeable issues. However, that morning Captain Newton of the Rajput Company D had been ordered to move his troops closer to Devil's Peak. Strategic positions changed quickly, and improvising became a critical manoeuvre. The Peak was considered a key defence zone, just as significant as the redoubt. The Rajput's post would be to fortify the southern point, to repress the Japanese regiments crossing the Lye Mun Passage and docking at the Lye Wun Barracks. Word was the Japanese cruisers and destroyers waited patiently near the island's ports of entry.

Nick's head was reeling. Orders were being bellowed out by both commanding officer Gray of the 2/14 Punjabis and Lieutenant Colonel White of the Royal Scots. The instructions were explicit: Hold the Japs! Hold the redoubt!

Ian picked up the last ammo belt. "Nick, nae getting a good feeling about this, ye ken."

Jordie chimed in as he fed the belt into the Vickers. "We canna stay in these fuck'n tunnels. The Japs have surrounded us, we'll all be killed." A few other Royal Scots expressed the same disconcerting sentiments. Supplies were running low, and the men knew it would be impossible for the Chinese volunteers to reach the defence lines with any provisions.

Nick was not hungry, only thirsty, and that was from the mass of surrounding smoke and machine oil lingering within the confined cement pillbox. It lingered inside his throat, his lungs. His adrenaline had long suppressed his appetite.

The lights in the tunnel flickered, and shadows jounced up and down the walls. Grenades sounded all around. Loud explosions and men's raging voices pulsated within the cement barrier. Hours had passed, and Nick guessed dawn was breaking, although it was hard to be sure. They had no sleep, no time to eat, only quick gulps from their canteen, and when attainable, a piss.

And then, there it was, like a volcano erupting. Sure, pandemonium hit. The blast came out from the east, at PB402 Piccadilly and PB403 Haymarket. Like a chain reaction, both collapsed. The Japs gained access at PB400 and demolished it before heading into Shaftsbury Ave. tunnel. The Royal Scots that were in hand-to-hand combat at PB401A and PB401B were ordered to evacuate and join the Rajput company on the right flank. Nick, with great apprehension, looked around. There was just over twenty Royal Scots, along with their officers and platoon commanders and lieutenant. You could see it – the determination, the courage, the anticipation, waiting for the next set of orders. It was distinct in the eyes of all the men. They would fight to the end if necessary.

In what seemed like a count of a handful of heartbeats, it was over. The men were instructed to reorganise, exit the tunnels, and head south towards Golden Hill, an area that had been determined insignificant during their briefing.

Nick's handful of heartbeats in time amounted to eleven hours of combat. He contemplated his answer, his acknowledgement of what had just transpired. If he were ever questioned, he was unsure of what his response would be. The entire interval from its onset to its cataclysmic finale was obscure, uninterpretable. It was best cast aside, easier not to think about. The less-forgiving course of action was to march forward, a gambit Nick and his comrades would quickly adapt to – to remain focused. To survive.

To the east of GDL, the Royal Scots section remained in a state of incessant fighting until it was no longer sustainable. The Japanese hurled grenades, destroying the main steel shutters.

The lieutenant of the Royal Scots ordered artillery fire down on the redoubt to save his own men and push the enemy back. That action caused their pillboxes to collapse. Four Royal Scot soldiers had been buried alive under the rubble. The field phone's frequency was weak and waned persistently. The best the men could discern was that the Japs had dug them out. Nick and Jordie locked eyes, and the same inconceivable notion crossed their minds – becoming prisoners.

A fury of shelling and explosions prevailed. The Gin Drinkers Line and operational post was overpowered and broken.

It was now after midnight on December tenth. A new strategic pursuit was in motion. The Winnipeg Grenadiers, under Brigadier Lawson's command from the island, were on the move to join Brigadier Wallis's brigade on the mainland. A unit from the Grenadiers moved into Kowloon. What peeved the remaining Royals Scots was there were not any forward troops that could rush in for a counterattack. The D Company of Rajputs had been moved closer to Devil's Peak two days prior. And the other Royal Scots reserve unit was over a mile away. Neither company could have arrived in a timely fashion, and even if they could, meandering at night through the hazardous terrain was not a plausible course of action. And so here they were, hungry, thirsty, tired. Some were still encumbered by symptoms of malaria as they were stealing away in the night, climbing up to their subsequent line of defence towards Golden Hill.

Above all, the Scots were well known for their sense of humour, their brilliant patter. And it was no better needed than within this hour of defeat. A Scot's loud rumble could be heard as they marched onward in the dead of night. "Well, lads, London Bridge is falling doon." The men laughed, for what else could be said?

## CHAPTER FIVE

# In the Still of the Night

*December 1941. Mainland*

After leaving the fall of the Gin Drinkers Line tunnels a.k.a. English knighted tunnels, they reached their destination.

The climb was appallingly strenuous, and the thought of reassembling for battle siphoned the last remaining fragments of morale the men had been holding onto. Captain Ford had been ordered to assemble the men to the highest site on Golden Hill. The D Company remained positioned at Smugglers Ridge to intercept the Japanese soldiers that had broken through the redoubt.

Nick felt sick to his stomach and thought he could vomit. He ran through the list of malaria symptoms: fever, chills, headache, diarrhoea. He didn't seem to be afflicted with those – not yet, anyway. He hoped his body was only reacting to the strain of carrying his heavy equipment. Most of the climb had been on his hands and knees, crawling through rocks and shrubs in total darkness. His hands bled from cuts and abrasions, and his fingertips felt numb. John Findlay whose unit had now joined the battalion was behind Nick. He'd fallen flat on the ground a few times, face down, trying desperately to push forward. Nick could hear his comrade's breathing, and it was erratic, which was concerning. The men were exhausted, and those that were still affected with malaria barely made it up the vast hill. Nick shook away the thought that he too may be infected. He was sure no quinine was available, and if there was, John required the malaria medication most.

The men had not said a word during the entire climb, not even Pie. All were head deep in their own trepidations. They had no food, only canteens of water. Rumour had it the lieutenant had a jug of rum; something the men eagerly anticipated upon their arrival.

Once to the top, orders were made and sentries posted. The men stumbled across a few empty weapon pits, and it was obvious by the lengths of rusted wire that they had been abandoned for some time. The men settled in and around the trench, trying to find comfort. Nick curled up alongside his equipment and prayed for sleep. The night was insufferably silent, except for deeps sounds of snoring and exhausted moans escaping into the darkness.

The men woke early. They were stiff, still tired, and hungry. Each received a tot of rum for breakfast. They welcomed the warm, smooth liquid. Nick savoured it, holding it in his mouth as long as he could before swallowing. The men stood, erect and ready, though too overwrought to listen to the lieutenant give orders. Their tormented thoughts lingered while waiting for the Japanese to attack. The boys had discussed it the night before, before they fell asleep. Jordie first mentioned the inevitable outcome. "There is no fuck'n way oot of this! The Japs are pushing southward in great numbers, and they're surrounding the southern ports of the island. If we're forced to the island we will be nothing but sitting ducks."

"Aye, that's if we even make it to the island," Nick replied, short of believing they would make it off Golden Hill.

"Lads! If we're forced to the island, we've lost! There isna anywhere to go but out to sea. I ken one thing – I will be taking as many yellow bastards with me." Pie rolled over, adjusted his bag under his head, and before falling asleep said, "Christ, let's get some shuteye, there is plenty of killing tae be done come morn."

Morning arrived under a rage of heavy mortar. Nick was grouped with Pie, Ian, and Danny, Rab, Jordie, and John. It was 10:00 a.m. and they had been under fire for three hours; the Japanese were closing in. The men learnt that C Company had suffered heavy casualties and it was imperative two units of A Company reassemble and hold the line. The commanding officer of the Royal Scots stressed with great empathy that the good name of the battalion was at stake and further withdrawals must be avoided to prevent the Japanese reaching Tai Po Road.

Nick and his platoon occupied the left flank of the hill. He caught sight of the Japs meandering upward, and he stayed as low to the ground as possible, signalling to Pie. In a matter of seconds, the Royal Scots rained down a fury of gunfire.

The first row of Japs fell, though more rushed up and over. The Royal Scots resorted to throwing grenades, causing chaos and pushing the Japs back down away from the left flank. It seemed they had succeeded, and the same orders were discharged to hold the line.

The still of the battle unnerved Nick. Its eerie silence messed with his head, breeding uncertainties and apprehensiveness. The reprieve of no gunfire from either side was unsettling; it was like waiting for a time bomb.

"Red Rover, Red Rover, I call you fuck'n Japs over!" Pie's intonation was severe.

Ian raised his gun, panic riddled across his face. "They're back!"

The silence did not last long; the sound was deafening, and gunfire blazed upward, reaching the height of Golden Hill. Nick dropped to the ground. The men in front of him had been hit; he could hear the screams, he could smell the blood. He crawled over to the injured soldier, and the urge to vomit rose in the back of his throat as he removed the soldier's hands from his stomach to assess the wound. The soldier's legs flailed uncontrollably, his screams bellowed, and Nick placed the man's hands back over the torn, mutilated flesh and exposed organs.

Nick yelled for help. It seemed pointless; who would hear? Within seconds another fell, and Nick heard the spray of bullets lacerate through the soldier's thigh, blood and pieces of flesh flying skyward.

"Nick, Nick, we are to pull back," Ian yelled out.

Nick could never calculate time. Sometimes minutes felt like hours, or sometimes hours felt like minutes. Time seemed to have no stability, it held you hostage and you functioned through the narrow passage of an hourglass, never knowing which globe you would arrive in.

"Nick!"

"Aye, Ian, I hear you!" The two soldiers were D Company, and both died within minutes, or perhaps it was hours, Nick couldn't discern.

It was late afternoon and they had been in combat since early that morning. Nick felt it was days, not hours. Hunger had set in, the air was dense, and it was hard to breathe in its despaired offering. Their efforts had been unsuccessful. New directives found the Royal Scots joining a company of Winnipeg Grenadiers. They were to withdraw and form a new defence line closer to Shamshuipo in Kowloon. The two Indian battalions remained to the right flank at Gin Drinkers Line; it was imperative the Japs did not infiltrate Devil's Peak, cross Lye Mun Passage, and invade the island.

As they made their way towards Kowloon, Nick thought of the two soldiers left behind on Golden Hill, their bodies left to rot, with no service, no family. He had managed to remove their discs and would find an officer to leave them with; that was the least that could be done. It was his first encounter witnessing comrades blown apart on the battlefield. Nick shook away the image of their desperate expressions pleading to survive, and like everything else, he had to lock it away and push forward.

The stench hit them first. "Christ! What in God's name is that smell?" John, still grappling with malaria, covered his face with his bandana.

"That is the smell of death," Pie answered, doing the same and covering his face. Jordie and Nick tucked their faces inside their arms, hoping when they came up for breath the stench would be gone. All the lads coughed and choked, rooting about their persons to find a face covering. The afternoon sun preyed upon the piles of dead bodies that lay scattered. Raw sewage flowed throughout the bomb battered streets, as water mains and electrical power circuits had been damaged. Smells of human remains and faeces charged the skies. It gave the soldiers no confidence that Kowloon was any better of a position to be in.

The city was in chaos. Riots, fires, and looting turned Kowloon into a frenzied pit of destruction. Enemy shelling destroyed the main street, leaving dozens of shops exposed to looters stealing food and medications. Chinese civilians ran through the streets as if deranged. To gain order, looters were shot, though the mayhem continued.

A refugee camp had been set up, and villagers came in droves, escaping from the battle zones. Queues of civilians swarmed the wharves of Kowloon, trying to get into the camp or make their way across the harbour to the island. Nick watched thousands of evacuees push and shove, scream and cry, all desperate to survive. Their expressions of terror crushed Nick's soul; he felt paralyzed and powerless. It was the mournful cries of a woman that caught his attention. She sat at the side of the road, barefoot, her clothes tattered and filthy, tears streaming down her soiled face. She clung to a torn, bundled blanket, the infant's lifeless face exposed to the harsh reality of war.

Jordie caught the same horrific scene and signed the holy cross. "Fuck'n Christ, let's get the fuck out of here!"

Nick collected his equipment and, against his better judgment, looked back. The grieving mother hadn't moved; she remained hovered in a ball, clutching her dead baby, while people rushed by as if she was invisible. Nick's heart dropped; this was a side of war one was not trained for.

The Japanese were storming south, leaving Golden Hill and Smugglers Ridge. Again the British battalions found themselves establishing new defence lines, this time across Tai Po Road, closer to Kowloon. Wire reports circulated, and their news didn't win any assurances; the enemy had landed on the isle of Lantau, southwest of Hong Kong Island. A platoon of Winnipeg Grenadiers and a battery of volunteers had been under heavy gunfire and managed to keep the enemy at bay. However, when the news came that HMS ships *Prince of Wales* and *Repulse* were reported torpedoed and sunk off the shores of Singapore, it shattered any hope of reinforcements reaching Hong Kong. And adding to the dispirited, heavy hearts of Hong Kong's garrison, the communication cables from the Eastern Telegraph Company linking Hong Kong to the outside world had been cut by enemy action. Also, the bombing of Kai Tak aerodrome's runway a week earlier had left Hong Kong civilians and troops totally isolated.

The entire night had been a constant charge of gunfire and grenade flinging. The Japanese suffered many casualties at the hands of the Royal Scots and Grenadiers. But from the men's earlier experience the night before on Golden Hill, they knew the Japs would not give up. More disconcerting was the number of soldiers the Japanese regiments consisted of.

"Christ! Where in the hell are they all coming from?" Charles yelled out while releasing the pin and tossing out his grenade. The men crouched down in the trench, allowing the blast to penetrate. "We'd better receive reinforcements soon or we will be blown to Kingdom Come." Charles reached for another grenade, waiting for the next signal.

Nick swallowed the little saliva his mouth had. They were now rationing the last drops of canteen water. Their concern of not having enough food quickly changed to a fear of not having enough ammunition. Pie stopped to reload his Bren machine gun. "At this rate, we'll all be fucking killed."

The numbers were staggering, and with ease the Japanese forced through the dense terrain like a pack of wild dogs. By the time night fell, the Japanese 230 Regiment had broken through Tai Po Road into Kowloon. The Royal Scots and Winnipeg Grenadiers had been ordered to withdraw to the peninsula. There, they would be ferried across Victoria Harbour to the island and join the Middlesex and Royal Rifle regiments. The last stronghold remained at Devil's Peak, where two Rajput companies continued to fight.

As Nick and his battalion loaded into the boats, he thought of the Indian regiments. He thought of his friend Amik and prayed for his safety. It was 10:00 p.m. on December 11, the night air was cool, and it was pitch dark, but for the blaze of gunfire lighting up the sky and reflecting off the water. The Japanese regiments stormed the coastline of the peninsula, shooting out and across the harbour. Nick bowed his body as low as possible. In the distance, cries of men being shot echoed across the water. The evacuation of the mainland had begun, and pandemonium settled in and all around.

## CHAPTER SIX

## *A Vision in Red*

*December 1941. Hong Kong Island*

The energy on the island differed from the mainland. Nick couldn't decipher the shifting effect of its energetic atmosphere. Was it fear? Or self-assured optimism that the British could hold the island?

Pie's pragmatic comment brought the atmosphere back to an austere reality. "Well, there's nae fighting our way off this fuck'n island!" His laugh didn't have the usual bluster of humour; it was more hesitant, with tones of cynicism. Pie received a perturbed eye from a sergeant who was standing within earshot; it wasn't the most auspicious moment for negative commentary. Already over half the Winnipeg Grenadiers lads were unnerved from the battle they had just left behind. And it wouldn't be long before the Japanese would make their move to infiltrate the island. Nick glanced at the young Canadian soldiers. He could see the efforts of valiant patriotism wielded across their young faces. It was their eyes that betrayed them; frightful, ambivalent pools of innocence staring into a realm of uncertainty.

Orders were discharged and the men filed out carrying machine guns, equipment, and army bags. They were right back at their barracks in Victoria. Nick couldn't help but feel they'd just undergone a severe army drill and now had returned for the evening. At least the surrounding wooden structure offered some order and some respite.

Most of the men decided on leaving their personal belongings, hiding them under floorboards and mattresses, just in case. Nick tucked his charcoal sketches of the mainland and island, and the tiny red-velvet box, inside his kit bag and placed it under his mattress. Each item, regardless how small or insignificant they seemed, became the men's entire worlds. Pictures of loved ones, girlfriends' hair ribbons, a worn Bible, a chain bearing the Holy Cross or a saint... they were keepsakes, reminding them of home, of loved ones.

The short reprieve of rest and reorganization did the men good; Scottish songs were sung and tall stories evoked laughter. Nick smiled when he heard Pie's hearty laugh roar through the barrack. He lay on his bed, appreciating its warmth and comfort. It had been several nights that the men had slept in either the damp tunnels of the Gin Drinkers Line or the unforgiving solid earth on the slopes of Golden Hill. This would be their last few hours of encountering such luxury. Food and supplies were scarce, and now that the Japanese had the mainland under siege, there would be no transporting of goods.

Nick and the other men pushed the thought of food, supplies, and foremost, reinforcements, out from their minds. Nick overheard an officer stating that the 212 vehicles that were to accompany the Grenadiers to Hong Kong back in November were still held up in Manila. That meant advancing around the island on foot. Most of the roads were inadequate to drive on anyway, but regardless, the vehicles could have been of some use. The steep slopes and hazardous mountains were another story. The terrain was a challenge during training; it would prove to be more deadly during battle.

General Maltby commanded that the battalions be divided and positioned around the island. The Royals Scots, Punjabis, and Grenadiers made up the West Brigade covering Victoria, Mount Davis, and the north shoreline of Wanchai. The East Brigade was the Rajputs and Royal Rifles. Centre was the volunteers and Middlesex. Pillboxes lined the northern shoreline, looking across the harbour into Kowloon Peninsula and Devil's Peak, where just hours ago the Rajputs had made their evacuation.

It was anticipated that the Japanese would hit Victoria first, given the narrow waterway from Kowloon peninsula over to North Point and Wanchai. There, a unit of Royal Scots from the West Brigade would be waiting.

It was mid-morning and the air was cool and the sky overcast. Shell fire was continuous, and the waterfront was a blaze of artillery warfare.

Clouds of grey smoke obstructed Nick's vision, and he wiped his weeping eyes, which at this point had a steady stream. Thick masses of black smoke from the petrol and oil storage tanks at North Point wafted through the air, hanging densely, and its hydrogen and carbon compounds stung Nick's eyes and choked his throat. He was thankful for being stationed away from the tanks, because God save the men if enemy fire should hit North Point, they would be blown to kingdom come.

It had been two days of steady bombing and heavy artillery. The fortress headquarters was stationed centre island in Wong Nei Chong Gap. Communications were distributed out in what seemed like every hour. The last dispatch informed the men that Mount Davis, on the coastline west of Victoria, had been blitzed by seventeen bomber planes. Hundreds of Chinese civilians were killed. And to the north, the bombardment remained incessant. The shoreline of Wanchai, west of North Point, suffered severe air attacks. Over half the British pillboxes along the shoreline were destroyed. To add insult to injury, cable routes were hit, rendering communication from the northern point of the island down through Victoria and south of Wan Chai Gap. Over half the repair crew were killed, Nick could hear the death rattle of machines guns and the tormented screams of men being pumped with lead bullets. The next report, although inevitable, proved to be alarming: the Japanese had landed onto the northern shore at Wanchai. This propelled the battle to new heights.

Little food was available. It had been two days since the men had eaten, and that amounted to a small piece of bread and a ladle of stew – hardly enough to sustain one's body under the constant strain of battle.

Jordie and Danny both lit their cigarettes. "Pass me a fag, will ye?" Nick said, reaching his hand towards Jordie.

"Aye, mate!" Jordie pulled the cigarette from its pack and handed it to Nick. "It's the only bloody thing keeping me sane," Jordie said, striking the match.

"Aye, and thank God we have plenty of them," Nick replied.

"Well, fuck me!" Danny pointed towards a group of questionable ladies darting through the mud road between the trenches and pillboxes. A few of the other lads crowded around, curious of the unannounced visit.

Patrick bared a grin. "What do we have here, then?"

"They'll no be wanting our business today." Pie released his usual heartfelt laugh.

They arrived in a group, skin and bone, dressed in what was once apparel of vibrant colours, now tattered and dull. Nick studied their pretty faces that lay concealed under patches of grimy dirt and stains of black smoke. Their timorous eyes darted back and forth between the men. The first prostitute handed Nick a flask. Her English was broken, but comprehensible. "Dis green tea for ya Scots." Patrick laughed at the girl's reference to the group being Scots. "She knows her client base!" They all laughed.

The other girls handed out flasks of hot tea and some gave packs of stale biscuits. The men thanked them and hustled them off quickly, as the shelling never ceased and they would not have the girls' blood on their hands. Nick remained crouched in the trench to avoid shell fire, and he watched as they scampered off into the clouded backdrop of destruction. He prayed they would all be safe, but he knew that was unlikely.

Nick nearly shit himself as a shell landed some ten feet away. Quickly he spread his hands out and over his body, checking for blood. Shock had a way of masking pain. Nick recalled watching one soldier frantically running wild; the poor sod didn't know he had been hit until he noticed his arms were missing. He then fell and died instantly.

Jordie, clutching his hand over his heart, yelled over to Nick. "I kent . . . either Christ himself or the Virgin Mary has saved your ass, pal." Nick gave a weary grin. At that, both Royals Scots released a fury of bullets.

It had now been seven days they'd endured heavy artillery on the island. The Japanese raised hell from across the harbour out from Kowloon. In addition, enemy aircraft were precise in their bombing, destroying the defence lines along the island's north shore. Reports wailed out and runners were relentless in their back-and-forth efforts to dispatch changing orders. A regiment of Japanese penetrated through the Rajput outposts and gained access out of Devil's Peak across Lye Mun Passage onto the northeast shoreline of the island into Braemar Point and Lye Mun Barracks.

Further disturbing news had reached the men, which caused a wave of claustrophobic panic. The Japanese, by way of Repulse Bay, southwest of the island, had crossed up and over into Aberdeen. It was predicted they were moving towards Jardine's Lookout. It was imperative they did not siege the centre island at Wong Nei Chong Gap, where Allied information resided at the HQ of Brigadier Lawson.

Victoria was lit up, and fires had broken out everywhere. Oil tanks and paint huts exploded, and shelling and bombing remained incessant. The Japanese battalion that stormed ashore through Braemar were moving inland. One young runner told Nick and a few lads that the Japs had suffered many losses from the Rajputs while crossing the harbour. Nick hoped the depleted number would be somewhat favourable. Most of the Canadian troops were scattered inland between the Gap, Jardine's Lookout, and Mt. Butler. Pie had heard that the Canadians were in rough shape. "Christ! Those lads are still shell-shocked from the battle on the mainland. Ye ken, it canna get much worse!"

Nick gave a nod of his head and reloaded his machine gun.

John, who with great ferocity forced himself each day, each hour, to fight on, disregarded Nick's plea for him to lie low and rest. John responded with such great zeal and intensity that Nick saluted his comrade with the utmost respect. John said, "Nick, I'm no the only soldier here inflicted with malaria. I have a duty to my king and my country. I will fight to the end." And the way things were going, it seemed they all would be fighting to the bitter end.

It was December 18, and evening was closing in. The trench's putrid stench had become almost a blessing, as it inhibited any thoughts of food. Cries and screams bellowed out, reaching across the skies; civilians were mercilessly being killed. They had nowhere to flee and forging for food became a race of life or death. A rice line of civilians stood thirty feet away from a string of standing pillboxes and trenches where Nick was. He watched as they stood with tarnished, rusted tin cups, hoping to make it to the large steel barrel of steaming rice before they were shot. What should have been sounds of laughter and footballs bouncing in the streets were sounds of children and babies crying and wailing, plagued with hunger and disease. One mother carried her baby on her back, bound around her waist in a blanket that was stained with urine and shit. Nick closed his eyes and turned his head. These were the atrocities that made his gut wretch more than the shelling and bombing.

Come the morning of December 19, Lieutenant-Colonel White, leading the Royal Scots, had been instructed to assemble a unit to infiltrate enemy action at Brigadier Lawson's HQ.

Distressed dispatches were communicated throughout the night stating that Lawson and his men were surrounded, and it was crucial that a rescue operation reach Wong Nei Chong Gap and fortify the HQ. Nick and his company remained entrenched in severe battle, holding the defence lines between Jardine's Lookout and the north shore. Their orders reverberated in severe tones of desperation from their lieutenant: *"Your bravery is an inspiration, the world's eyes are upon you. We must fight to the end."*

Patrick groaned as he slid down the cool, muddy incline of the trench. Keeping his machine gun in an alert position, he slipped off his boots and began unloading clods of mud that lay caught inside. "Christ, if I don't get one day with dry feet, they will bloody rot off."

Nick joined Patrick, squatting in the bowels of the trench while he reloaded his gun. "Christ, they're a right mess!" Nick caught the dreadful condition of Patrick's feet just before he yelled, "Reloading."

Every action during battle was systematic. Drill practice and training were one thing, but existing under continuous gunfire, shelling, and grenade blasting escalated one's artillery performance. Nick was certain he could load his weapon while asleep.

Pie crouched down between Nick and Patrick with the same intent to reload. "Fuck, mate, if ye dinna get your boots back on and start shooting, you'll nae have yer head!" Pie was back in shooting stance within seconds, yelling out towards the enemy. "Come on, you bloody yellow fuckers!"

Patrick, ignoring his pain, slipped his socks and boots back on, reloaded his gun, stood his position, and joined the line of artillery warfare. Trench foot was becoming a common affliction, and the men tried airing out their feet when time permitted. And time was nowhere to be found on the battlefield.

The onslaught continued. Defence lines were being pushed back and forth like a ball in a football match. The commentary from the field radio resorted to crackled voices of uncertainty and confusion. The men were completely exhausted, and to make things worse clouds of fog rolled in and hung just above the ground's surface, masking any visibility the men may have had. Nick prayed that it wouldn't rain.

Jordie crouched down and yelled, "Reloading" and looked up at Nick. "This is a fine fuck'n mess!" Once reloaded he stood and fired out into the grey dismal pit of hell and concluded, "The world's eyes are upon us, my arse! If they were, we would have reinforcements fighting by our sides this very moment."

The brave unit of Royal Scots that had trudged through Jardine's Lookout into Wong Nei Chong Gap to fortify the HQ were reported missing. Many were shot and killed along with all the officers, including Brigadier Lawson. The Japanese overpowered and sieged the area. Rab Stewart informed the men that the enemy were in possession of much of the higher ground and were forging inland. Enemy snipers had been spotted along the mountain ridges, making movement for the British battalions troublesome. Sentries and platoons spread out to determine enemy positions and to cut down the Jap snipers.

The disheartening news of Brigadier Lawson's unsuccessful rescue mission came through the wire like a grenade. The attitudes of the men had been on a steady decline since they'd evacuated the mainland. Nick sunk lower into the trench and watched a patch of grey fog waft by, and he could feel the tiniest of droplets fall onto his face. As gunfire and grenades charged the skies, he closed his eyes, searching for a suitable prayer, and out of nowhere he heard the sweet-sounding melody, "We'll Meet Again."

And there she was, standing amidst the fog in her red velvet dress, the only palette of colour against the dismal grey backdrop. Her smile caught his heart and possessed his mind. It was only for a moment but was enough to surrender himself into a state of calmness and peace. He thought back on that night at the dance when his friend Emma drew his attention to her sister Alexandrena. And for whatever reason, perhaps it was God that sent him the vision, but nevertheless, he knew in his darkest of hours he would reach out to her.

# Part Two

*The Pulse of My Mother's Heart*

## CHAPTER SEVEN

# *It's Your Name – Your Clan*

*July 1925. Edinburgh*

Today was to be a most exciting day. Alexandrena and two of her sisters would be accompanying their mother up to Ardersier in the Highlands. The three girls danced around the kitchen in anticipation. The Highlands always offered adventure, and of course the train ride itself was half the fun. It was the perfect time to travel. The heather in the summertime would be in full bloom, painting the rolling hills with shades of purples and mauve. The snow-capped mountains, no longer captive under the frigid winter months, released their locks of rushing blue, winding down between the lush, deep glens and Scottish-thistle-cloaked moors. It was a sight that would take anyone's breath away.

Alexandrena Johnstone Helliwell was one of ten children: nine sisters and one brother. She was the second youngest and had turned seven on March thirty-first. Her younger sister, the baby of the family, Margaret, was two years her junior. Her older siblings all two years apart. Her two eldest sisters, Jessica and Betty, were out on their own and married, and her remaining siblings living at home were Catherine J, William, Emma, Mary, Lily, Hannah, and of course, wee Margaret. Their home on 8 George Street, Leith, was by no means large, but comfortable enough to sustain ten births and the raising of ten bairns.

Alexandrena's parents, John and Catherine Helliwell, maintained an orderly and disciplined household. Of course, that was not always an easy feat with such a large clan. Outside of regimented time schedules of schoolwork and a daily list of ongoing chores, the Helliwell family always found time for fun and entertainment. And travelling up to the Highlands to visit their grandparents was considered a bonus.

Alexandrena's sister Mary Helliwell turned thirteen on April thirteenth, a couple of weeks after Alexandrena's seventh. Both girls were delighted when their mother chose them for the Highland holiday. They could celebrate their birthdays all over again with their grandparents. Naturally, Margaret would tag along, for she was never far from her mother's sight. There was no doubt that both Alexandrena and her wee sister were spoilt by the older children and most times both fought for the limelight. Outside of their sisterly rivalry, they shared a special bond. Alexandrena was present at the time of her sister's birth and proudly told the tale that she was the first to see her sister enter the world and the first to hold her.

Alexandrena's father was at sea the day Margaret was born. Most nights when her father was away, she would crawl into bed with her mother, snuggle in tight, push her face right up close and yell, "Hello" into the swell of her mother's belly.

"Lass ye dinna need to shout, the bairn can hear you," her mother would say.

Alexandrena would switch to a whisper, though concerned whoever resided inside could not hear her.

The morning of November 13, 1920 was dismal and rainy. Alexandrena hadn't slept much, as her mother kept her up all night with her persistent tossing and moaning. It wasn't until the wee hours of the morn when the big event took place. Alexandrena heard the bustle of her older sister Emma racing to leave the house to fetch the midwife. It hadn't taken long. The midwife barely arrived in time, grabbing the screaming, wet, pink infant and handing it over to Alexandrena while completing the process of collecting the placenta and cutting its cord. Alexandrena, just two, had sat at the end of the bed, astonished how her wee sister had been crammed inside her mother all this time. And now she looked down upon the pink, wrinkly face, amazed at the miracle she had just witnessed.

Alexandrena was born four months after World War One had ended. Her father, who had fought in the Sudan and Khartoum wars in Africa as a young man, served as a merchant marine during the Great War. Most of his time during those turbulent four years was spent at sea, supplying Britain with defence materials such as ammunition and arms. In later years, it had become a poke of jest towards Alexandrena's parents that even through a war, the birth of bairns remained a constant.

Her sister Lily was born in 1914, the year the war broke, and Hannah in 1916 in the midst of war. Now wee Margaret made her way during the world's reprieve of bombing and destruction.

As the girls collected their items to pack, their sister Jessie popped in to wish them bon voyage and handed them each a bag of sweeties for the train ride. Margaret gave a wide smile, accentuating her chubby pink cheeks, and her chestnut-coloured eyes gleamed as she ruthlessly rooted through the brown paper bag. "Soor plooms! Ta, Jessie."

Jessie bent over and gave her wee sister a solid hug. "Now, dinna be eating them all at once, ye ken."

"We're gonna see Grandad and Grannie. She has your name, Jessie," Margaret mumbled as slavers of green ran down the corner of her mouth.

"Margaret, what did Jessie tell you!" Mary scolded her sister, grabbing the bag away.

"Dinna fash Mary, she's fine." Jessie turned her attention back onto Margaret. "Truth be told, Margaret, I have Grannie's name. Just like Catherine J has our mum's name. Your name is important; it's chosen not only out of tradition, but it's regarded with great respect." Jessie tousled her sister's head of brown hair and gave her plump cheek a soft pinch.

"Dinna dae that!" Margaret pulled back in protest.

Jessie laughed. "Yer grannie will be grabbing yer fat wee cheeks, so be prepared."

Alexandrena piped in, "I have Grandad's name."

"Who am I named after?" Margaret asked, still sucking on her green soor ploom.

Their sister Lily had entered from the back garden and just caught wind of her sisters' inquiry. "Yer named after a dead auntie," Lily replied with a goading grin.

"Lily! That's enough," Catherine chided her daughter.

Lily gave a wee snort and laughed out in consensus to her sister's exposé on family names. "Mum, ye ken most of us are named after dead aunties." With that, the girls broke into laughter, including their mother.

The younger girls fled from the kitchen, candy bags in hand, prattling on about their namesakes. Catherine gave her daughter Jessie a hug and placed her hand on her daughter's belly where her first grandchild resided. "How's the morning sickness?"

"Och, nae bad, Mum," Jessie replied, placing her hand on top of her mother's, which was still in place.

"Take yer tea with peppermint leaves. I lived on that for nearly twenty years." Both chuckled.

Jessie knew she was pregnant, even if it was only just weeks, as her mornings had been spent in the privy. She was filled with admiration, imagining how her mother persevered through ten pregnancies, ten births, and nursing in between. And the nappies! *Christ*, she thought. She and Ralph had discussed only having a couple of bairns, and they both agreed that would be plenty to handle.

"You will be fine come yer second term, lass."

Jessie nodded, trusting her mother's expertise. "I really must be off, Mum, Ralph will be waiting for me." Jessie yelled out to her sisters to enjoy their Highland holiday, and before departing, said, "Give Grandad an extra hug from me, and wish him well."

"Aye, lass." Catherine squeezed her daughter's shoulder and turned to finish preparing their packed lunch for the journey.

The train's iron wheels screamed below, and Alexandrena heard her mother give out a sigh and watched as she gazed out the window, bewitched by the countryside. Catherine missed the Highlands; all her children knew that, and she often shared childhood stories with them. Their grandad, Alexander Johnstone, was a baker, and both he and his wife Jessie crofted a small piece of land. It wasn't an easy life, and Catherine and her siblings had worked hard. Two of her older brothers emigrated, and it broke both her and her mother's heart. Her brother Donald packed up and moved to Australia, as seemingly sheep farming was booming Down Under.

It was when her brother James announced he was leaving for Toronto, Canada, that she felt her world fall apart. Out of her six siblings, she was the closest to James. And the thought of never seeing him again tore at her insides. Both brothers wrote home. Donald wrote mostly to his mother, and on occasion he wrote to Catherine. James wrote regularly to Catherine, and with great anticipation, she waited eagerly for each letter. She kept a box of all the letters, and as the years passed, the pile of stories from far-away places and sincere expressions of loved ones that were dearly missed grew.

Alexandrena was disappointed her grandad, Alexander Johnstone, her namesake, was not at the train station to greet them, though her grandmother, Jessie, and her brother, Erik James McKay, the girls' great-uncle, were there to welcome them.

Alexandrena had only met her great-uncle a couple of times, and she struggled to understand his Gaelic. He was tall with a solid build, he wore his thick dark hair tied back, and his eyes were as blue as the sea. McKay was a popular name in the Highlands, and everyone knew Erik James. He was the lightkeeper at the Talbat Ness lighthouse near the tiny fishing village of Portmahomack, north of Ardersier. The villagers called him *gaisgeach stoirm*: Gaelic meaning storm warrior. Where most fishermen would flee at the sight of a brewing storm, Erik positioned himself, adrenaline soaring like the preeminent sea eagle pursuing its prey, standing vigil over the fishing boats and ships making their way home across the tempestuous North Sea.

Margaret giggled as her uncle swung her up high in his arms while she reached her waving fingers, tickling the low-hanging clouds that hung suspended within the blue sky.

Later that evening, after everyone was settled, Erik suggested he take the lassies on a tour of the lighthouse in the morn. "That is grand, the bairns will love that," Catherine said and reached out and gave her uncle a hug.

Morning could not come quick enough for Alexandrena and Mary, and both jumped up and down with anticipation. Poor Margaret sobbed uncontrollably – not that she couldn't tag along, but because of an earache that came on through the night. Her earaches were notorious and seemed to come on at all the wrong times. Alexandrena didn't mind Margaret not joining them up to Portmahomack, as it gave her and Mary a chance to be on their own and allowed them to become more acquainted with their great-uncle. And that they did.

Their uncle didn't treat them such as silly bairns; he regarded them as grown lassies. He showed them around the lighthouse and explained how all the mechanical pieces worked. They toured the grounds and the tip of the peninsula. The view reaching out to the North Sea was spectacular, and even Alexandrena, being only seven, appreciated the majestic seascape.

Their uncle also taught them some Gaelic phrases and told the girls they should be more familiar with their heritage and learn the common tongue. For fun he slipped in a Gaelic curse, and he made the girls promise not to tell their mother or granny. Both girls found this devilishly exciting, and to seal their promise, they traced a cross upon their chests and pledged, "Cross my heart and hope to die, stick a needle in my eye."

The train ride back home to Edinburgh was uneventful. Dark clouds hung low, hugging the hilltops. Shades of grey replaced the Highland's vibrant colours that lay hidden between the fog and heavy rainfall. Alexandrena fought for the window seat, but Mary promised her sister they would switch closer to the city. Mary leaned in towards the window, lost in her thoughts; she so enjoyed spending time with her grandparents, and she could appreciate her mother's pining spirit for the Highlands. She herself could sense its history of clanship. Hundreds of years of ancestry bewitched you; they howled your name amidst the Highland gales. Mary traced her fingers through the moist droplets of breath she formed on the window and watched her initials, MGH, evaporate, picturing herself one day among the howls of the wind.

Margaret was snuggled up in her mother's lap on the opposite seat. Her earache had surrendered, though she was still weary. Alexandrena sat quietly, swaying back and forth with the motion of the train, thinking back on all the fun she and her sisters had (outside of Margaret's earache). But their visit had been more than a Highland holiday. They had stayed a fortnight, longer than any other visit. And from the day they arrived, Alexandrena had sensed her mother's apprehensiveness.

Her sister had become intolerant of her continual questioning. "Stop asking what's wrong, Alexandrena. Mum does nae need you bothering her," Mary said, clipping the side of her sister's head.

"Ouch!" Alexandrena yelped.

"Don't be daft. I didna hit you that hard," Mary responded.

Jessie, exasperated with her granddaughters, had clipped them both. "Hauld yer wheesht, the pair of ye." Both girls stood dumbfounded.

Jessie McKay Johnstone had been raised hard and strict, although she had softened in her role as grandmother. Her husband's illness had been hard on her, and as much as she depended on her daughter's stay, she found she had little patience for her granddaughters.

"Sorry, Gran, we didna mean to upset you," Mary said, regretting her behaviour. Alexandrena wrapped her arms around her grandmother and offered an apologetic hug, with flowing tears.

"There, there, lass, stop yer greetin," Jessie replied, petting the top of her granddaughter's head.

It wasn't until weeks later, when they arrived back home, that the children learnt of their grandad Alexander's heart attack and the reason for their mother's required presence.

Unbeknownst to Alexandrena, she wouldn't travel back to the Highlands for another year, and that was for her granddad's funeral.

Once home, the three girls raced through the front door, all excited to share their tales of the Highlands with their sisters and brother. Catherine, at this point, was exhausted, and only wanted to fall into a chair with a cuppa. Her husband, John, poured her a cup of tea, and at the same time handed her a letter. "This came while you were gone. It's from Canada."

"I will take it oot to the garden with my tea," Catherine said as she rose.

John joined his children and the commotion of laughter and storytelling in the sitting room. Mary was offering her newly acquired knowledge of how a lighthouse operated to her attentive audience. Her sisters Emma, Hannah, Lily, and Catherine J were all ears; her brother William, who not that long ago had experienced the same tour with his great-uncle, fancied the need to join in on the tutorial.

"William, let our Mary finish," Catherine J strongly demanded. In unison, her sisters gave expressions of agreement. William was left silenced and considerably outnumbered. Mary gave her sister a smile and continued.

Catherine J (Johnstone), the third eldest, was named after her mother and it was quite apparent the name befitted her. At the age of eighteen, her looks were identical to her mother's, boasting her long dark hair and chestnut-brown eyes. When Catherine J completed her schooling, she worked as a nanny for a family in Edinburgh. Her desire to travel had broadened, and she took it upon herself to write to her mother's brother, her uncle James in Canada, but she had not yet had the nerve to approach her parents.

During Mary's explanation of the importance of maintaining the wicks and lenses of the Argand paraffin lamps of the lighthouse, their father's loud voice reverberated through the house like a Highland storm. Catherine J jumped at the sound of her name. They had all noticed their father's departure and assumed he had joined their mother in the garden to smoke his pipe. There were never dull moments in a household of ten bairns: fighting, crying, yelling, and laughing were commonplace. Catherine J was the quietest and most well-mannered out of the clan, and rarely did they hear their father holler her name. So, when Catherine J was summoned out to the garden, the seven stood in silence, curious about what possible trouble their sister was in.

That evening, their parents were uncomfortably quiet, and Catherine J too; she never spoke a word; only to pass the tatties at teatime. Even the bedtime ritual of hugs and kisses and wishes of bonny dreams were skirted over.

Alexandrena lay awake even though she was tired from the day's travel; she could not sleep. Margaret lay sleeping beside her, faint sounds of tiny snores escaping through her stuffed nose. Alexandrena hoped her sister was not coming down with another ear infection. Hannah and Lily were sleeping in the next bed. Alexandrena was sure her parents and brother were in their beds and asleep; she only heard Emma's, Mary's, and Catherine J's voices.

"Mom crumpled it all up. Open and read it, Emma. Both her and da are beside themselves. But I still must go," Catherine J stated.

"Read it aloud, Emma," Mary urged, her interest now piqued.

Alexandrena heard Emma straighten the paper and begin to read. Her sister skimmed through what must have been unimportant bits and pieces, because she heard Emma mumble, "And . . . and so on and so on."

"Emma! Skip to the last paragraph," Catherine J urged impatiently. Emma cleared her throat and read aloud.

> "Your Lass Catherine J is a smart young woman and has expressed an interest in coming to Toronto. She and I have been in correspondence these past few months. We would love and encourage her to come live with us. Martha has been desperate for a nanny, and Catherine J could fill this role as she attends university. I am making a good living, and she will be well cared for; Toronto has a lot to offer a young woman as smart as your lass. We've gone so far as to discuss her joining me at my company when she completes her education. I can promise you, dear sister, I will take great care of your lass. I have paid her passage, and her ship sails from port Friday, July 30. I hope we have both your and John's consent."
>
> *Your loving brother,*
> *James A Johnstone.*

## CHAPTER EIGHT

# A Letter of a Promised Life

*Tuesday, April 6, 1926*

It was Mary's responsibility to collect her sisters at the end of each school day. And when her sister Lily made a fuss and was adamant she would walk home with her mates, Mary shrugged her off without arguing. Her mind was preoccupied. It was coming up to a year that her sister Catherine J had been living in Toronto. She wrote to Mary regularly, and because Mary had not received a letter since December, she couldn't help but feel concerned. When she would mention it to her mother, she always received the same reply: "Och, Mary, dinna fash, our lass is busy with school. And Uncle James will be taking her oot places. She will write when she has the time."

The response was not enough to convince Mary, though she would never admit that to her mother. It was still a sore topic in their household. And when mentioned, her father cursed his brother-in-law's name, distressing her mother.

Mary's thoughts were interrupted by Alexandrena's attempt to keep Margaret in line.

"I'm nae a baby," Margaret scoffed at Alexandrena.

"I ken, but I'm yer older sister, and you must listen."

Alexandrena tried asserting her rank of sisterhood by using the same declaration her older sisters did practice on her. Margaret effortlessly tried to release her sister's grip.

"Haud yer wheesht, you both are acting daft!" Mary lost her patience at this point.

Hannah, oblivious to any of her sisters' exploits, teetered behind, swinging her lunch box and singing.

> *Three craws sat upon a wa',*
> *Sat upon a wa', sat upon a wa',*
> *Three craws sat upon a wa',*
> *On a cauld and frosty mornin'.*
> *The first craw was greetin' for his maw,*
> *Greetin' for his maw, greetin' for his maw,*
> *The first craw was greetin' for his maw,*
> *On a cauld and frosty mornin'.*

Mary, Alexandrena, and Margaret joined in on the third verse, singing in unison.

> *The second craw fell and broke his jaw,*
> *Fell and broke his jaw, fell and broke his jaw,*
> *The second craw fell and broke his jaw,*
> *On a cauld and frosty mornin'.*
> *The third craw couldnea caw at a',*
> *Couldnea caw at a', couldnea caw at a',*
> *The third craw couldnea caw at a',*
> *On a cauld and frosty mornin'.*

With conviction, the girls belted out the final verse, their voices carrying through the street:

> *An that's a', absolutely a',*
> *Absolutely a', absolutely a',*
> *An that's a', absolutely a',*
> *On a cauld and frosty mornin'.*

A couple of magpies, startled by the performance, fluttered off their perch, leaving the old wrought-iron fence entangled with ivy behind. The girls laughed with delight as they made their way up to the front door.

Lily was standing by the iron gate waiting for her sisters' arrival. Once inside, the girls unloaded shoes and lunch boxes. Margaret continued her defiance with Alexandrena, arguing about who would be first to share their school day events with their mother. Lily and Hannah raced into the sitting room, wanting to be the first to select a music channel from the family's brand-new radio, their father's prized possession.

Mary stood in the kitchen entrance, trying to decipher what she wasn't smelling. No earthy scents of broth or stew, no buttery smell of scones, nothing, not even her father's fry up of kippers. All the vacant smells disconcerted her gravely. Mary never recalled the Helliwell home to be absent of such aromas.

The house was unsettling still. She jumped, startled by Brodie's sudden rush towards her, his black, wiry figure chasing around Mary's feet as if in pursuit of a rodent on a ship. Brodie was the family's black Scottish terrier, and at the age of three he was still wild in manner. Her mother had been against having a dog; however, her father insisted a dog was necessary to accompany him on the ships to keep the rat population down. Mary now questioned the dog's timely presence; should he not be at sea with her father? On his final lap, her eye caught notice of the spurtle clenched tightly in his jaw. Her mother would never allow the dog to play with any kitchen utensil – certainly not one of her wooden spurtles. She felt her hair bristle along her arms, ascending to the nape of her neck.

At first, the sounds seemed muffled – deep sobs carried through from the sitting room. Mary entered, not knowing what to expect. It was unusual for William and Emma to be home this time of day, they should be at work, she thought. They stood quiet, not even a crack from her brother. Mary glanced around the room of swollen eyes and wet faces. Her sisters Alexandrena and Margaret sat in front of the fire, heads hanging; they gave no acknowledgment of her entrance. Lily and Hannah were standing side by side like statues, no movement, no sound. Solemn the look on all their faces. She directed her gaze towards her mother, who was sitting on the settee, and her grave expression tore through Mary's heart; she felt as though she'd been struck by a tram car.

In that desperate moment before words were spoken and sorrows unleashed, Mary's mind uncontrollably began playing the second verse of "Three Craws":

> *The first craw was greetin' for his maw,*
> *Greetin' for his maw, greetin' for his maw,*
> *The first craw was greetin' for his maw,*
> *On a cauld and frosty mornin'.*

She shook the words from her head, along with the indignant feeling of letting such nonsense enter her mind at such a perilous moment.

Her father spoke first. Finally, she thought, as the unrevealed silence was unbearable. He approached, his eyes filled with tears, his cheeks rouged and damp, and he softly wrapped Mary's hands in his.

"Lass, our Catherine J has passed."

Mary remained still, expressionless. As if on queue, the entire room wept. She felt her father's grip tighten, a sign Mary believed was letting her know, *it's okay, you can cry now.*

*The first craw was greetin' for his maw, greetin' for his maw, greetin; for his maw.* Mary shook her head. *Bloody Hell,* she screamed to herself. Without realizing it, she continued to shake her head back and forth to erase her father's words.

Later that evening, Jessie and Betty arrived. They had already received news of their sister. Betty travelled home from Aberfeldy and was dependent on train schedules. Jessie and her husband, Ralph, lived close by and arrived by way of tram. All the Helliwell children were home; all had come home to grieve for a sister they lost – lost for a second time, lost forever. Tea was in the middle of being prepared. *What do you make for tea when you lose someone?* Mary thought as she watched Jessie, Betty, and Emma rummage through the icebox and cupboards.

Everything seemed so mechanical. Mary recalled her brother's wind-up toy soldier he'd received one Christmas as a young lad: you just turned the key, which protruded from its back, and it marched, stopped, and waited to be wound, then proceeded. A placid expression was painted on its tin face. Her sisters marched around the kitchen with that same look. They prepared tea, set dishes – when would they stop? When would they need winding?

Tea was served, and all gathered around the table, except for Margaret. She fell asleep in front of the fire with her ragged doll secured in her tiny arms, Brodie nestled in beside her.

A few morsels of food were eaten, but mostly silverware scratched across plates. Mary watched her mother push her food back and forth, her eyes still swollen and red. *How must she feel?* Mary thought. The pain herself as a sister was enough to bear. She could not conceive her mother's grief.

"Jessie, how are you feeling? You look as if yer about to explode," Betty asked.

"Nae bad, I think it will be a laddie . . . he kicks like a wee football player," Jessie replied as she rubbed her stretched belly.

"Aye, a laddie it will be, a Hibs supporter like his father," Ralph said in an effort to lighten the mood. A few soft laughs escaped.

*Was it fine to laugh after someone dies?* Mary thought. She didn't like Ralph making such a heedless comment. *Who cares about your football or your Hibs, who even cares about your baby?* Her tears welled until the point of overflowing, streaming her cheeks.

Emma sat stationed between Mary and Alexandrena, and she reached over and caressed Mary's back.

"Jess, you must soon be ready to birth this bairn, are you not?" Emma asked as she continued to soothe her wee sister.

"Aye, any day now, any day," Jessie replied.

The remainder of the evening consisted of small chatter, mostly about the baby. It drove Mary mad, and she wanted to scream *STOP! Stop talking about the bloody bairn – our mother has just lost hers.* She felt choked, and all she wanted was her sister Catherine J.

Unsettled goodbyes and kisses placed on moist cheeks brought the evening to a close; this was their farewell to their sister. No body to bury, no service to be had, just a simple meal of leftovers and irrelevant conversation. Mary collapsed in bed after her rendition of the evening played over in her mind. She thought about how things had changed over the past few

59

years. The household was now downsized to six children: Jessie, Betty, and William grown and gone, one dead child, two heartbroken parents.

Lily was sound asleep in the next bed, and soon Emma would retire for the evening. Hannah, Alexandrena, and Margaret would all be asleep in their bedroom across the hall.

As tired as Mary was, she could not sleep; her mind would not turn off. She had kept all Catherine J's letters; her sister had been studious in writing to each family member. Even Margaret and Alexandrena would receive the odd letter. Mary reached for the box from under her bed, untied the ribbon, and released the lid. She pulled out the last letter received from her sister.

*Saturday, December 19, 1925.*

*Dear Mary,*

*First, I can't recall when I last wrote you? And I do hope I am not repeating myself in some of the events I am about to share with you.*

*I've learnt to ride horseback. Uncle James's friend Mark has a ranch just outside of Toronto. It's beautiful; you would so love it, the stable houses twenty horses. At first, I was nervous. They are such large creatures, and so unpredictable. Mark advised me never to walk behind a horse and always make my presence known; never, never sneak up on a horse. You remember me mentioning Mark? He was born in Toronto. He and Uncle James attended Edinburgh University. It was Mark who convinced Uncle James to immigrate.*

*I've finally finished my first set of exams. And between you and I, I'm relieved they are over. I actually threw up during the week of my studies. Each evening Aunt Martha made me a pot of peppermint tea and prepared a hot water bottle, both to settle my nerves and stomach. She is so kind, Mary, you would love her.*

*My, or I should say our, wee cousins have grown and are quite active. James and Martha are not as steadily strict as our parents. I assume raising ten bairns compared to three has its vast differences. I do not tend to the children as I did when I first came abroad. Martha hired a new nanny, who also does some housecleaning and cooking. Thank goodness; I couldn't have completed my studies and cared for the children. Could you picture our mother letting someone run her kitchen or raising her bairns? It certainly would not happen.*

*The boys are a wee handful. Jacob is now six, and Benjamin is four. They both ride horses with ease; it's truly something to see, I assure you. Of course, they ride only ponies. Bonnie has just turned eight. Her birthday was on December 12, the same age as our Alexandrena. Oh, how I miss my sisters. Some days it hurts; at times, I feel a pain in my heart. How is our wee Margaret? I miss her pudgy face and her wee laugh.*

*I received two letters in November, one from Emma and the other from William. It was so good to hear from them. Emma mentioned taking up college, she just hadn't chosen which courses. William would love to come to Canada. He wrote that he would try to save and visit me. That would be splendid. I miss his patter. And isn't it wonderful, our Jessie is going to have a bairn? She wrote to tell me the good news. The first grandbairn, how lovely. Mother and Father will be pleased.*

*I must go now, Mary. I promised Bonnie I would teach her to braid her hair. Remember how Betty spent hours braiding ours? Which reminds me, I owe Betty a letter. She tells me she loves Aberfeldy and plans on opening up her own hairdressing shop. She will do well, ye ken she has a head for business and is lovely with people.*

*Uncle James and Aunt Martha are putting on a Christmas party this evening. Oh, I must tell you before I end my letter. Aunt Martha took me shopping on Bloor Street and bought me a beautiful emerald-green party dress. I told you about Bloor Street in my prior letter. The shopping is brilliant. Don't tell Mum, but Uncle James has a surprise parcel for her. I know she will love it.*

*I will try to write after Christmas, once things settle. I find lately that I become overly tired and feel drained.*

*PS. Hugs and kisses to Mother and Father.*

*PSS. Father has not yet written. I know he is still upset I moved abroad.*

Love, Catherine Johnstone Helliwell.

## CHAPTER NINE

## *Wedding, War, and Weeping*

*Edinburgh, 1929*

It had only been a few years and John and Catherine Helliwell still grieved the loss of their daughter Catherine J. Both had been devastated and shocked to learn that their twenty year old daughter died of heart complications. She was so young, and in perfect health when she left Scotland, her death was inconceivable. And when Mary announced she was moving up to the northern tip of Scotland to the small village of Dunnet, they both were disconcerted.

It was in March, the month Alexandrena turned eleven, when Mary informed the family of her engagement and plans to leave Edinburgh. Alexandrena didn't take well to her sister's news. She felt it a betrayal, because the day they learnt of their sister's death, Mary made a promise to her younger sisters that she would never leave them.

Mary was torn. It was bad enough that her father had lost his English temper and her mother cried into her cup of tea. But when Alexandrena hugged her waist and pleaded for her not to leave, it tugged at Mary's heart something awful. But she was young and in love, and Morogh McIntosh was her entire world. Even when her sister Emma told her she was daft and far too young and that she hardly knew the lad. Daft or not, Mary accepted Morogh's proposal of marriage.

Mary met Morogh clam digging during one of his visits to Edinburgh. They hit it off straight away. Morogh described his family farm and how an unruly set of hens ran the house, but their daily fresh eggs well enough compensated. His herd of woolly sheep's fleece made a good bob or two.

And he told how a handful of border collies, with coats as thick as the sheep, keenly guarded them had made up his family. And last but not least, there were a couple of old highland ponies, which he and his brother rode as bairns.

Morogh's mother travelled into Edinburgh often to visit her sister, and Morogh and his brother Maxwell usually trailed along. After his mother had passed away, he continued the traditional visit, more out of respect for his mother.

His aunt begged him to sell the family cottage and move to Edinburgh. "It's in your best interest to attend university, further your education." That was his aunt's contention during each visit. He eventually learnt to ignore her, as most conversations led to arguments.

Morogh felt claustrophobic when visiting Edinburgh. The air felt thick, and he couldn't breathe. He once described his apprehensiveness to his friend one morning as they were repairing broken fence poles along the property line on the farm.

"The city suffocates me, ye ken, I feel trapped. I head straight to the seaside to harvest clams and try to stay clear from my aunt's badgering. I remember one time looking into a bucket of clams I had collected and thought how crammed they all looked; no space, no air, no way out. That's how I feel away from my farm."

Later, he only found solace in his visits after meeting Mary Grant Helliwell. He fell in love with her immediately. They both spent hours by the sea, clam digging and talking. Morogh loved listening to Mary's stories of her family and that she was the sixth eldest out of ten siblings and perhaps the most unruly out of the brood. Well, next to her younger sister Lily, she confided with a wee chortle.

"I was around fourteen, and Lily twelve, and we were caught smoking fags out behind the coal shed. Our da was home early from work and surprised us. Lily and I couldna find a spot to hide the fags – our da was quickly approaching, wearing a suspicious grin. We quickly tucked our hands behind our backs. Lily had just taken a drag and she tried so hard not to exhale. Our da was nae fool – he kent what we were up tae. He just stood there eyeing Lily until her cheeks blew up like balloons and her eyes watered. When she finally exhaled, she gasped, choked, and nearly fell over. I was trying nae tae laugh. We were both banned from any social life for a fortnight. Of course, we dared not divulge how we came across the fags – our brother William would have been battered." Mary laughed, accompanied by a wee snort.

"I love yer laugh and how your upper lip does a wee quiver when you snort." Morogh grabbed Mary, pulled her tightly against him, and kissed her. "I want to marry you. I want to lie with you every night, feel yer bare arse next to me, smell your honey-and-oatmeal-scented hair each and every night before I fall asleep."

"Are you saying I smell like a bowl of porridge then?" Both laughed. Morogh kissed her harder and placed his hand firmly on her round bottom. Mary let out a small sigh and let herself go, both into his embrace and his soul.

"I want a simple life, Morogh, a few bairns, a husband to love, and him to love me."

He held her tighter, and she became lost in his broad chest. She loved everything about him, his soft nature, his laugh, his mass of red hair. She reached up and ran her fingers through his curls. "We will have bonny laddies, Morogh, with messy red hair and faces painted with freckles." Mary gave a chortle, stood on her tiptoes, and kissed his lips deeply.

"And a lassie as beautiful as her mother." He smiled, setting off a crinkle at the bridge of his nose. Mary traced her fingers over his face, where a spray of soft red freckles lay scattered across his cheeks.

Against her parents' wishes, she left the city and moved north. Without her family knowing, Mary was with child. Both Morogh and Mary were thrilled.

Morogh had been living in Dunnet alone after his brother had moved to Edinburgh. He felt it necessary to tell Mary of his mother's death, and that he feared the tough lifestyle had taken her too soon. And when his father died, he had never felt more alone until he met Mary. He wanted Mary to understand the lifestyle she would be exposed to. He loved her so much, yet he felt guilty of that love by asking her to live a life that presumably killed his mother.

Mary cupped Morogh's face in her tiny hands and searched inside his ocean-blue- coloured worried eyes. "Morogh, the choice is mine. I would follow ye tae the ends of the earth. Besides, cancer killed yer mother, not the Northern Highland life. Our ancestors have been living and working these lands for centuries. And remember, I'm from Highland blood myself – my own mother's clan is the McKay. I'll hear nae more of yer talk." She kissed him again.

Morogh tried to heed Mary's words; however, a wee tug lay in his heart, one he couldn't discern.

*Saturday, June 8, 1929, Dunnet*

The wedding was small, with immediate family only from both sides. The Helliwells, who travelled by train, outnumbered the McIntosh's. Everyone was dressed and ready for the celebration. Alexandrena was still sour on her sister leaving her. But she was anxious to see Mary, to hug and hold her. And she would consider asking her if she'd had enough of living in the Highlands and would come home where she belonged. Irritated by the sounds of laughter, she moved away from her brother where she could think in peace.

William was playing with his sisters Jessie and Betty's bairns. Jessie now had two children. Ian was three and wee Catherine Ann was one. William was tossing Betty's son Nichol in the air – he had just turned two. His soft blond hair was now a static mess, and his steel-blue eyes were lit with excitement, anticipating the next toss.

"Do be careful, William, he's only wee, ye ken," Catherine warned her son.

"Aye, Mum, of course, but he needs a bit of roughhousing," William retorted.

Betty interrupted and strongly advised her brother that he would be taking care of any scrapes wee Nichol might endure under his watch. William continued to toss Nichol, and Nichol continued to giggle with delight.

Jessie grabbed her three-year-old son's hand and directed him away from her brother. "Ralph, grab wee Catherine Ann ... she thinks her uncle is going to toss her aboot as well."

Ralph bent down and swooped up the one-year-old, who immediately showed signs of defiance. "Jessie, the bairns are just seeking some fun ... ye ken, and William is keeping them nicely occupied." Ralph realised as soon as he delivered his commentary that his wife Jessie would be contrary.

She gave him a stern look and replied, "I didna spend all my time sewing our Catherine Ann's dress for her to be tossed and soiled before the ceremony."

With that, William lowered his nephew Nichol, patted Ralph on the back, and chuckled. "Ye canna argue with a Helliwell woman. Come, we will have plenty of time for pints and child play after my sister is married."

Wee Ian escaped his mother's grip and ran after his uncle. "But Unca Willie, I didna get me turn."

John, still not convinced of his daughter's decision, one he thought that was made hastily, took a moment to admire all his lassies while they stood chatting and laughing. All fathers considered their daughters beautiful, simply without prejudice. John not once but a thousand times over received compliments from friends and neighbours, who said things like, "You have beautiful lassies, John. Very blessed, you and yer Catherine."

He observed each one, from Margaret, Alexandrena, Lily, Hannah, Emma, and Betty, to the eldest Jessie. And, of course, Mary, who at seventeen was already the spitting image of his wife, with her dark hair and engaging, chestnut-brown eyes. John thought how bonnie she looked.

A hearty laugh caught his ear, and John turned with an amused smile. His son William stood tall and proud, his chiselled features and blue eyes a reflection of John himself.

The afternoon was blessed with the sun's warm rays. The tiny Dunnet Church lay perched along the seaside, soft sprays of droplets from the crashing waves dancing through the air, shining like diamonds as the sun cast its veil. The ceremony was to begin at 4:00 p.m.

As both families made their way into the church to be seated, Mary and her father remained in the back of Morogh's family car. Morogh's uncle had volunteered to drive the bride-to-be and her father to the church. Once parked, Morogh's uncle advised he would head into the church and leave them to a bit of privacy before the ceremony.

After a few moments of silence, Mary spoke first. "Father, yer nae losing me, I will be right here, a train ride away, that's all." She took his hand in hers and squeezed softly as a reassurance of her promise.

"I know, lass … it's … it's … just that your mother will miss you something fierce." His voice caught and struggled. Mary saw him fighting back his tears. She had only ever witnessed her father cry a couple of times. The first was when he received news of his mother's death. The second, for his daughter, Mary's sister, Catherine J. She knew how difficult this was for him. He tightened his grip on her hand, pulled it towards him, and lightly kissed the back of it. "This will nae be an easy life, Mary … farming is a hard business, and the winters here can be brutally harsh."

"I ken, but I love Morogh, and I know I will be happy here. I've already met one of the local lassies from the next farm over. She comes from Glasgow and has been living here for a few years now. Morogh and her husband chum aboot and support each other with the farming."

"Lass, I canna convince you not to marry Morogh, nor do I wish to … I … I just need you to promise you will take care of yourself."

"I will, Father, I promise."

John looked away from Mary and stared out the car window, and he kept a strong hold on her hand, just as he had three years ago. A rooted memory emerged, rising to its fragile surface. "It was hard on your mother and me losing our lass … bad enough she was gone for nearly a year with only letters to remind us of how much we missed her. I always hoped she would travel home, perhaps for Christmas or Hogmanay … never did I imagine we would lose her to a far-off country never to see her again." He wiped his damp cheek then added, "I will never forgive that man." Mary knew he meant her Uncle James, and she was about to console her father, to reassure him she would be safe and only a train ride away – not in a far-off country, but home, home in Scotland, when a tap on the car window interrupted her assurances.

"I just came out to check on you both. We've all been in the church for a wee bit now." Betty opened the car door to speed up the process. "Unless you are in doubt of the marriage, Mary?" She gave a small chortle.

"Absolutely not!" Mary sharply responded.

John and Mary climbed out of the car, and the three stood in a moment's silence as though they were in contemplation.

"Oh Da! Ye havna been greetin', have you?" Betty remarked. She gave a warm smile and wrapped her arm around her father's shoulder, trying to lighten the mood.

"Now come on, the both of you, this is a day of celebration." Betty stepped towards Mary and re-positioned a stray curl that fell loose against her cheek. "You look lovely, Mary."

"Thanks, Betty, and thanks for doing my hair. I don't know how I would have managed without you."

"Da, can you give Mary and I a moment?" Without questioning, John strolled towards the church's cemetery.

"Mary, we all know how hard this is on Da and Mum, but try nae tae worry, they will be fine. They still have Margaret, Alexandrena, Hannah, and Lily at home. They will fare well."

"It's nae so much that, it's father's eyes. He's aged, Betty. I dinna ken how often I will make it home; it's a long journey and an expensive one. My heart is here in Dunnet with Morogh, but my emotions are all over the place. Christ, I'm crying at a drop of a tuppence."

Betty smiled and reached out to stroke Mary's belly. "How far are you?"

Relieved, Mary answered, "A couple of months, but how . . ."

"You show all the signs . . . yer soft pink glow . . . the sparkle in your eye . . . and now yer emotional state."

Mary smoothed her dress and laid her hand on her belly. "Oh dear, it's that obvious?" Betty laughed. "Only to another expectant mother."

It took Mary a moment. "Betty!" she yelled out. "That is wonderful news. Percy must be thrilled."

"Aye, he is, Mary, he is . . . he's hoping for a lassie. I myself would prefer another laddie; wee Nichol is a going concern and could use a wee brother to share in his energy."

Before Mary had a chance to tell Betty to keep her pregnancy quiet, she heard her father. "Betty, you best get in. Mary and I will follow. I'm sure they are wondering what the hell is going on."

"Oh, Da . . . tis good to keep a man waiting," Betty said as she aimed a wink at her sister.

"Enough of your cheek, lass, get a move on."

Once the vows were promised, Morogh leaned in and whispered in Mary's ear. "Yer beautiful, Mary, I canna believe how lucky I am to have found someone as bonnie as you, my heart bursts." He brushed a soft kiss on her cheek. With that, the families cheered. Once the ceremony finished, everyone but Emma and her mother headed to the Dunnet Inn for the celebration.

"Emma, where is yer father? I've looked everywhere and I canna find him." Catherine was fervently searching the church grounds for her husband, but to no avail.

"He said he was going to the graveyard just on the other side of the church. He'd found something of interest. I will fetch him, Mum, you head over to the inn with the girls, it's nae that far. Da and I can walk over, it's a beautiful day."

"Hurry him along, Emma, you ken what he's like . . . he's found some war monument or gravesite of someone he's fought with. And he'll be gone for hours." Catherine placed her handbag over her arm and made her way towards the wedding crowd.

Emma chuckled to herself. One thing was certain. Her mother knew her father inside and out.

Her father was standing beside the stone wall that ran alongside the back of the church.

"There you are, Da, what have ye been doing? Everyone is heading to the inn. Mother asked me to track you down." Tombstones all stood at attention, calling out to the living. Emma then noticed the plaque he was reading. It identified the Caithness soldiers who had lost their lives during World War One. She knew with just one look, one small keek, he would consider a historical tutorial. "Ye ken, lass . . ."

"Oh Christ! I had to look," Emma chastised herself.

" . . . many a young lad from this northern region lost their lives. Unnecessarily, may I add. June 15, 1915, Caithness Blackest Day. The first Highland soldiers left for France in November 1914. Destination Flanders. Just laddies, full of heart and vigour . . . all to keep the bastard Huns from crossing the Rhine. It was inconceivable. Christ, by the end of 1914, only months into the war, there were already over a hundred thousand deaths. Herbert Kitchener had just been sworn into office as secretary of State of

War. Did I tell you my regiment, Cameron Highlanders, fought under him when he was the British general during the Omdurman War in Sudan?"

"Aye, Father, many a time," Emma answered impatiently.

"Ye ken, he was born in Ireland, won't hold that against the bastard ... at that time he was a fine leader ... however, wasn't too impressed with his onset leadership into the Great War. He established a deceitful plight of recruitment. He sent recruitment sergeants to comb the Caithness region, receiving payment for each lad enlisted, no matter the age. Some lads not yet sixteen ... downright blasphemy ... between a war-hungry press and blind patriotism, those poor lads were rounded like lambs to the slaughter."

"Da, we really need to be heading," Emma stated as she moved a few steps away from the war plaques.

"Then in May 1915, lads from Thurso – Wick – Lybster suited in kilts and crowned in their Glengarry, all improvising as infantrymen of the 1/5th Seaforth Regiment, were shipped off to the Western Front. And there they were in Givenchy, the fourteenth day of June. Pointless, tragic deaths."

Emma took another few steps.

"Right across the way from where we are standing, one Wick family suffered unimaginably – they lost five lads in one household. All perished at the front within fifteen months."

"Aye, Da, tis very sad. We really must be going." This time Emma stomped her foot while she stepped back, but her father paid no attention.

"Kitchener was responsible for the slaughter of those enlisted lads ... Caithness troops brimming with courage and passionate ignorance running into a battlefield of barbwire, bombs, and machine guns, running into no man's land, running into hell."

"Da! Please!"

"Back in Egypt, he was called a flaming poof. 'Kitchener and his band of boys.' Poor sod died before the bloody war ended, drowned as the HMS *Hampshire* sank off the Orkneys."

"Da, I'm heading back." Emma raised her arm and waved the white flag, surrendering. There was no persuading her father.

## CHAPTER TEN

# An Outnumbered Englishman

*June 1934. Edinburgh, Scotland*

John sat in the sitting room enjoying his cup of tea and reading the paper. He heard his daughter Alexandrena shouting out that she couldn't find her wellies and was convinced that her sister Margaret had taken them. He took a deep breath and waited. At last she was out the door, and he could now finish his paper in peace.

At times John wondered what his life would have been like if he had stayed single. He had never planned on marrying. His intent was to travel the world with the Cameron Highlanders. But his once predetermined path strayed wayward without warning. And after he had fought in the African and Sudan wars, and before the wrath of the Great War, he found himself hopelessly in love with Catherine Johnstone, a Scottish lass, a Highlander at that. And he could only admit that outside of their stubbornness were a people who breathed a determined strength, an inspiring passion, and a spirited patriotism towards their country and heritage. He came to understand why the Scots despised the English. His wife's tales of her family clans, the Johnstone and the McKay, portrayed a people fighting for their independence – their freedom. And at times somewhere deep within, John felt ashamed of his English heritage.

John, like his father, William Helliwell, was born and raised in Yorkshire, and according to John's father there was not a better breed in the world but the English. He despised the Scottish and was more than happy to distinguish the differences between the two countries and their people. He would say, "The Scots are a different breed, savage-like almost.

You are better to walk away than satisfy their barbaric ways. They believe that a good brawl is essential in any a quarrel."

John never argued with his father; he simply would not win. It was indubitable that John follow the same career path as his father, and his father's father, a member of Her Majesty's Cold Stream Guard for Buckingham Palace.

John, however, started planning his own future, without his father's knowledge.

Of course, he had loved living in Yorkshire; the Yorkshire it had once been, that is. The nineteenth century was influenced by the Industrial Revolution. A rapid growth of skylines, collieries, and factories led to an influx of working-class inhabitants. And unfortunately, this institutionalised slums and poor living conditions.

He recalled the day he announced to his family he was leaving for Scotland. He had completed his last year of secondary school and was very much intrigued with the Cameron Highlanders. The collaboration and brotherhood of the Highlanders intrigued him, and he would quickly come to learn that the Scottish chaps he served and fought alongside with were spirited, passionate, and displayed patronage to their country and king, which commanded great respect. Most certainly the opposite of his father's prejudiced views and distasteful remarks against the Scots.

With great reserve he broke the news to both his mother and father. The whole time, his eyes were fixated on the family clock. He studied the wooden structure. It was square in dimension with two small ledges protruding on either side. The centre displayed a square face bordered in gold, and a range of roman numerals occupied its space. A long and tarnished silver key protruded out from the side of the clock. He didn't recall anyone ever winding the key, or recall the key, for that matter. Obviously, someone performed the daily task. And once he delivered his well-prepared speech of moving to Scotland to become a Cameron Highlander, the room fell silent.

The uncomfortable moment bounced around the room until John's father spoke. "I see." The answer was short and it sounded impartial – not at all what John expected. And for now, that was good enough. His father lit a match to his pipe, and the smell of sulphur filled the air.

And as the years passed and paths altered, he had nicely settled into working as a merchant engineer at Leith docks and found the life of a family man quite pleasant and rewarding. At times a household of ten bairns was chaotic, and he often felt outnumbered by ten lassies, if he included his wife. But by the grace of God he had his son, William. Finally, after three lassies – a laddie! Shouts of joy rang through the Helliwell home, not to mention the streets, the Leith docks, and lastly the local pub where Father Helliwell arrived triumphantly rejoicing in the success of producing a male to carry on his name. "Drams all around, this is a night to celebrate." John rounded his mates.

"Congratulations, John, ye did a fine job, a laddie – here's tae many maire," the bartender toasted, pouring drams of whiskey for the men positioned along the bar. All lifted their glasses, saying, *"Slainte mhath."* After all, John had finally planted the correct seed.

John loved that his son had ambitions to join the Royal Regiment and travel the world. It was something he and William often spoke about – how could you not when you lived under the roof of a Cameron Highlander who'd fought under the duly decorated Herbert Kitchener and alongside a young Winston Churchill in the Egyptian War. On occasion John would hear his wife mockingly express, "Lassie, I am thankful to God I didna have all laddies. Yer father would have conscripted an entire army by now." It was not directed to any particular daughter, but nevertheless, never a truer statement.

Not that he regretted having a houseful of lassies; he loved them all and found them quite fun and entertaining. Many an evening he stoked a full fire, and after hours of storytelling he lined up his lassies and made them sing for his delight. The fires full blaze cast shadows of dancing bodies darting across walls, reaching as high as the ceiling. John, out of tradition, chose an old favourite, "Onward, Christian Soldiers."

He always appointed Alexandrena and Margaret to sing the old hymn. He knew they disliked it and only pushed through it so they could sing their favourite songs. Margaret always rushed through the final verse, then without pause started singing "Ally, Bally Bee." Her cheeky smile lit the room while she belted out the first verse:

*Ally bally bally bally bee*

*Sittin' on yer mamy's knee*
*Greetin' for a wee bawbee*
*Tae buy some Coulters candy.*

She loved the attention, and as the last verse closed in, she danced around the room, circling the settees as her audience applauded.

"Well done, lassie, you are a fine singer, you are," John complimented his daughter as she jumped into her father's lap for a wee snuggle. Alexandrena sang her favourite, "The Bonnie Banks of Loch Lomand," and once all his daughters' performances ended, his son William showcased the room with his rendition of "I Love a Lassie." A dedication to his mother.

Some evenings were more cultured and pedagogic or filled with historical family tales. His wife loved to share about her adventurous childhood growing up in Ardersier with her brothers. His daughters shared in the ancestral tales. Alexandrena especially loved the stories of her grandparents, Jessie and Alexander Johnstone. Hannah loved the story of how their parents met. His wife never grew tired of telling the tale, perhaps a wee embellished, but weren't stories meant for such? She always began when she moved to the Lowlands to care for her grandparents on her father's side, the Johnstone. She found employment at Edinburgh Castle, thus meeting her dashing Englishman. John at that time was in training with his regiment at the castle.

"Was it love at first sight, Mum?" Hannah asked.

"Well, lass . . . aye, you could say that," Catherine replied.

"Hannah, always the romantic," Lily said with a chortle.

As much as John enjoyed watching his family carefree and happy, he couldn't help but contemplate over the news coming out of Europe. War was the hot topic. Rumblings of a new political party in Germany were steadily growing. Adolf Hitler had advanced from chancellor to führer, positioning himself with the intent to aggrandise the Nazi Party. The signing of the Treaty of Versailles in 1919 imposed harsh terms on Germany, forcing them to relinquish their occupied territories and assume full responsibility by paying large amounts of reparations. John's fear was that another war was evolving, kicking off the heels of World War One. He did not believe or trust that this young idealist leader would honour any of the terms set forth by the League of Nations, and it left an unsettled feeling in the pit of his stomach.

Papers and radio broadcasts continuously reported that European countries were seeing division within their own people, and heavy resistance and rebellious behaviour were forefront. Revolutionary groups were forming, all to undermine their own governments. Mussolini had been in power for the past twelve years, and Fascism was on the Rise. Scotland saw more and more Italian immigrants. The talk in the Italian sector of Leith was that Mussolini was preparing to widen his empire into North Africa. Italy was a late contender to the colonial project; in the late nineteenth century, they overpowered Eritrea, Somalia, and Libya, and they were defeated in taking Ethiopia in the Battle of Adwa. But now their plight was to storm back in.

Russia's anti-communist White Army was struggling to overthrow the Red Army. Japan invaded Manchuria in 1931 and rained terror on Northern China in 1933, killing thousands of civilians; this left a very sour note in the mouths of the British, as Hong Kong was a British colony. The world seemed as it was preparing to explode. John felt it was his duty to prepare his children for what he perceived was inevitable. Yet he felt helpless about where to begin to protect his family. And when he would try to broach the subject, his wife shot him down. Once she said, "John, enough talk of war, it's behind us, the bairns will have nightmares." Discouraged by his wife's curt interruption, he gave a slight nod in agreement, tucking his medals, which he had brought out to show his children, away. When the last medal from the African wars was placed in its pouch, he felt compelled to make a final appeal.

"That's all fine, Catherine, we've been through a war, a wee history lesson and points of preparation will not hurt."

"I assure you, John, they're well versed." Catherine shot her husband a severe persuasive glare. Indicator received, subject aborted.

## CHAPTER ELEVEN

## *Dead Man at Sea*

*June 1934. Edinburgh, Scotland*

Alexandrena had planned a morning out with her mates to dig for clams by the sea. Annoyed, she rushed around yelling out that her sister Margaret had taken her wellies. Hastily, she grabbed the next pair and slid them on before she greeted her friend Mirren at the door.

Mirren Wilson was one of Alexandrena's three closest friends. She had mousey-coloured bobbed hair which always looked dishevelled, or the back anyways, as if intentionally missed when brushing. She was short and heavyset with broad shoulders. At times she was loud and brusque, perhaps a pretence to compensate for her less-than-feminine features.

Mirren's family lived a street over from Alexandrena in a run-down tenement building. She was the eldest of four children. Her father worked as a miner and was absent most of the time.

Alexandrena slid her raincoat on and yelled out to her mother, "Mum, Mirren is here, and we are off to the seaside. Mrs. Wilson is here for a cuppa!" Alexandrena gave a wide impish grin, shutting the door behind her, picturing her father's reaction at Maggie Wilson's arrival.

Mirren's mother, Maggie, frequented the Helliwell household, and her appetite for gossip was considerably renowned. Alexandrena's father couldn't stomach the woman, and against his better judgement, he found himself tangled in the most ridiculous of conversations. Alexandrena's mother felt obligated by her Presbyterian ways to look beyond Maggie's ill-mannered and offensive conduct and try to find the good. Before each visit Catherine pleaded with her husband to keep his English temperament to himself. "John, there is good in everyone. Now please, she's only here for a cuppa and blether. Try to hauld yer wheesht."

"Catherine, she is a hypocritical gossipmonger." He caught his curt tone. "She's not worth your efforts," he said, his approach lightened. With that, he said he would retreat to the sitting room, glad to be out of harm's way before the old battle-axe showed up.

After a large gulp of tea, Maggie placed her cup on the table and wiped a few scattered scone crumbs from her lap. "'Tis disgraceful, bloody Iti's tak'n over Leith, open'n up fish and chippies and ice-cream parlours. They is stealing fae er own, ye ken pluck'n er livelihood right from under us. Steal'n guid jobs fae er folk." Maggie paused, took a deep breath, and tore another bite from her scone. "And what is tae become of Scotland? Ye canna tak' a stroll along the walk wi'oot seeing Mother Mary glaring at ye fae their front gardens. Very strange these Iti Papists . . . and a strange language they speak, ye canna understand a bloody word they're saying." Once her exasperated rant ceased, the last bite of scone was mercifully shoved into her mouth as if the action was imperative to its ending.

John held his newspaper high, as not to draw attention: it would only take one glance through the doorway to the kitchen, and old Maggie would consider it an invite. "John, what do ye think of all the Iti's tak'n over Scotland?" Maggie more or less demanded an answer. Crumbs of scone spewed across the table as she spoke and spat in unison.

It hadn't even been a leer, just a keek over, but there he was, caught. The sniper was precise; she had engaged her target, and mercilessly at that.

John slowly dropped his paper just slightly under his glasses where they rested on the end of his nose, and he peered over the rim. He couldn't respond in the manner he would have liked. He knew his wife would have words with him over tea. John was well-read and educated. He had experienced many interactions with all races, religions, and cultures, on and off the battlefield. He himself wasn't particularly fond of the number of Scottish local businesses competing to survive, whether it was with the Italians, Jews, or any other immigrant.

To some degree, he had empathy for the immigrants, who endured name-calling and crude snide remarks as they passed by in the street. John himself felt the sting of prejudice on the account that the Scots were not particularly fond of the English. The treacherous history between Scotland and England has remained a constant over the centuries. The Scots had no more trust in the English than they would a perfidious lover.

"Aye, Maggie, it is true there is an influx of Italian immigrants, the world is evolving, and travel has become more prevalent. Opportunities for success and independent business are forefront. The ending of World War One created great loss and poverty. Rebuilding the country's economy has opened up passage to neighbouring folk. Scotland is no stranger to foreign intrusion. The Scots have survived the Vikings, the Spanish, and the English. I'm sure it will survive the Iti's."

With that said, Maggie quickly turned her head in a manner of disapproval, making a snuffled sound through her nose.

John shot a wink towards his wife and raised his paper to face height. *Christ*, he thought, *I will hear about this come tea.* Nevertheless, he couldn't help but snigger.

♣♣♣

Muffled sounds of shouting and laughing could be heard across the shore of the seaside. The sun's subtle rays peeked through the low-hanging clouds, promising a send of light showers. The misted sea air circled Alexandrena's rosy cheeks, and the taste of salt settled upon her lips. She licked around her mouth as another gust of wind surfaced, almost knocking her off balance. She struggled to keep up with the other three girls, bucket in one hand and a clam shovel in the other.

"Hurry, Alexandrena, hurry, we'll no find a spot," Mirren yelled as she ran forward with her head slightly turned in hopes Alexandrena would hear her over the wind's loud whistling howls.

"I canna run in these bloody wellies," Alexandrena hollered. The force of the wind carried her words away, never reaching her friend.

The race was on as clam diggers combed the sandy bed to find a prime location along the shoreline of the North Sea while it lay exposed, flaunting all its hidden treasures. Time was of the essence to dig for an abundant hull before the sea washed in, protecting the clams from heaving shovels.

Alexandrena finally reached her mates and was still feeling a bit perturbed that Margaret had taken her wellies. She was sure she'd grabbed

Lily's in her haste. They were a tad bigger than hers, and her heels rubbed up and down inside the loose-fitting boots, causing her to run clumsily and trail behind.

Mirren had already dropped her bucket and fallen into position. Her body was slightly arched, and she was moving her head slowly back and forth in a sweeping motion, eyes focused on the seafloor in search of dimple marks where razor clams lay burrowed. Elizabeth and Kitty dropped their buckets and followed suit.

"Alexandrena, are you going to the dance tonight?" Kitty asked without moving her curved stance, eyes sternly focused downward.

Kitty Haggan and Alexandrena Helliwell grew up together, and their fathers worked together at Leith Docks as merchant marines. One thing the girls had in common was they both came from large families. Kitty was one sister out of eight brothers, all gingers. She had a head of red curls and a mass of freckles that splashed across her cheeks and over the bridge of her nose, intensifying her brilliant blue eyes.

A high-pitched shriek interrupted any thoughts Alexandrena had regarding the dance. All three girls quickly turned towards Elizabeth. Elizabeth Graham, the youngest of the circle of friends, although by far the tallest, was thin built, but not without a figure. Her straight, jet-black hair fell in a neat bob below her earlobes. She had fine, delicate features and emerald-green eyes.

Her parents had moved from Glasgow the year she started secondary school, and she and Alexandrena became friends straightaway. Her father was a pharmacist and ran a drug store along Princess Street. After the death of her mother when Elizabeth was nine, her father became very protective of her. Her mother had died giving birth to her brother. She'd had complications carrying Elizabeth and was diagnosed with placenta previa. The doctor ordered strict bed rest. She had lost quite a bit of blood delivering Elizabeth and took months to recover. Cognizant of the risk, Elizabeth's parents decided to try for a second child, against doctor's orders.

Elizabeth didn't talk much about her mother or the death of her wee brother: only that she recalled neighbours and friends dropping in with baskets of food, offering condolences. She had resented each and every one standing at the stoop, faces long and sad, staring past her father to catch a glimpse at the motherless child. She met their pitiful scrutiny with a hateful glare, willing them to go away. She did not want their sympathy or words of endearment; she wanted her mother.

Her father worked hard in his practice to afford Elizabeth a sound education. He saved diligently in preparation to enrol her into university to become a doctor.

Elizabeth promised herself and her dead mother she would pursue a career in the field of obstetrics and save the lives of mothers and babies. Save young girls such as herself growing up motherless.

The three girls dropped their shovels and ran towards Elizabeth.

"Christ! What are ye screaming aboot?" Mirren cried out. Elizabeth, speechless, slowly looked up at the girls, keeping her head still. She used her eyes in a directional motion, moving from the area she was digging and back up again, drawing their attention to look down at the seafloor. In unison, all three looked. At first, they couldn't make out what they were eyeballing. Then like a fall of dominoes, one by one, it registered.

"Oh my God!" Alexandrena shrilled. She stepped back and lost her balance. Instinctively her arms flung out as she took a solid land. She cringed, feeling the sharp pain tear through her right arm, which took the brunt of her weight. She blamed her sister's loose-fitting boots preventing her from a quick recovery.

"Jesus Christ," Mirren spurted out. "What the hell!" Mirren could swear like a sailor without even a blush. All four girls stood paralysed and speechless. They'd all seen dead animals: dogs, cats, numerous types of fish and birds along the shoreline, but never a human.

Mirren began to tremble, her legs turning weak. "I'm going to be sick!" she said, and with that said, she bent over. The wind caught her morning intake of blood pudding and buttered scones.

"Jesus Christ, Mirren," Kitty yelled, feeling the splatter against her legs. "Ye couldna have turned the other way?"

"Bugger off!" Mirren shouted back, wiping the hanging strings of vomit from her mouth.

Elizabeth bent over the body and using her shovel carefully pulled the dead man's shirt away from the side of his face. This action unsettled a nest' of tiny sea crabs; each creature scrambled from various parts of the corpse, one pushed its way out through the man's mouth, thus sending Mirren back to her vomiting stance.

Alexandrena swallowed, trying to contain her breakfast in its rightful place. "We need to get help!" she urged.

Within no time, the girls were surrounded by neighbouring clam diggers. A buzz of voices and alarmed gasps grew louder. Alexandrena found herself being pushed out the way by a few lads eager to view the dead body.

The walk home was quiet. The girls swung their empty buckets, the hunt unsuccessful. The seashore was now vacant of diggers and spectators; all that remained was Scotland Yard. They worked quickly but accurately to collect any evidence before the sea made her way back in.

The girls arrived at the corner of George Street, still shaken from the image of the dead man's body. "Alexandrena, are you coming to the dance tonight?" Mirren asked, desperate to switch topics. Every Friday there was a dance in Leith, and every teenage lassie and laddie who lived in the area attended. It was the highlight of the girls' week.

Alexandrena set her bucket down and tried adjusting her wellies, which at this time were causing a burn along her heels; she suspected small blisters had surfaced. "I need to check with my mum. My Uncle Geordie and Auntie Lizzie are coming doon from Ardersier. My mum will be delegating jobs oot, left, right, and centre. Ah dinna ken if I can sneak oot."

"You must come, Alexandrena!" Kitty begged. "We have so much more fun when it's the four of us . . . and ye ken Robert Thomson will be there, and ye ken he canna take his eyes off ye." All three girls teasingly laughed, leaving Alexandrena with a warm flush upon her face. No denying, she certainly had feelings for Robert. They met up quite a bit – nothing serious, but Alexandrena could feel herself falling in love with him.

Robert Thomson worked for his father in their family bakeshop. There were never conversations between Robert and his parents regarding his career path, and even if he could broach the subject, he already knew the answer. It was indisputable that once school was completed he would start full time at the Thomson Black Bun Bakery.

"This will be a profitable business for you, Robert – good standing in the community, a good provider for a wife and wee yins. A tradition to hand down to yer sons." His father always sounded convincing when selling the idea of the family business.

Robert didn't dislike the idea. For the most part, he enjoyed it and felt a sense of achievement. His sister Meg certainly was not interested, not at the fault of his parents persistently coaxing her every Saturday to mind the cash counter. She was only focused on marrying her childhood sweetheart, Sandy.

The bakery proved to be popular, with heavy traffic from the early morning to teatime. Robert Thomson Sr. and his wife, Margarie, were both well respected in Edinburgh; everyone knew the Thomson name, and their black buns were famous. Robert Sr. inherited the bakeshop after his father had passed away, and it was apparent the intent was to continue the family recipes of buns, pies, and everything sweet and creamy over to his son.

The first time Robert saw Alexandrena was when she and her younger sister Margaret entered the bakeshop. There was no denying they were sisters – both had honey-brown-toned hair, chestnut-coloured eyes, and beautiful complexions, which showcased a soft rouge across their cheeks. Margaret was slightly shorter than Alexandrena and a wee bit plumper.

Margaret leisurely walked around the shop assessing the different baked goods, tossing her hair with the back of her hand, cocking her head to one side and looking directly into Robert's eyes, her smile provocatively playing with him. Robert noticed Alexandrena poke her sister in the side. He couldn't hear what she said but knew she chastised her sister, as Margaret's smile subsided with a twist of a tongue. Robert smiled under his breath; he found it quite entertaining.

"How much are yer custard squares?" Alexandrena asked.

"Six slices for a shilling. Would you like them wrapped?" Robert watched her as her eyes inspected the other baked goods.

"How much for the jam scones?"

"One dozen for two shillings." After a few price inquiries, Robert now sensed that Alexandrena was playing with him, not that he minded in the least.

The last inquiry was wrapped and tied with twine. He handed Alexandrena the box in exchange for a sterling note. He finished counting out her change and asked, "Do ye attend the Friday night dances?"

Alexandrena felt her cheeks flush, and shyly she responded, "I havna been as yet but am interested."

"Da and Mum will nae let ye go, Alexandrena . . . yer nae auld enough!" Margaret chided. Alexandrena ignored her.

Loud chiming rang through the bakery when the brass bell above the door set off as the girls left the shop. Robert Senior came out from the back room after pulling a tray of black buns out of the wood-burning oven; an aroma of ginger and cinnamon infused the room. "Was that the Helliwell lassies just left?"

"I dinna ken their last name . . . the one is named Alexandrena."

"Aye, that's John and Catherine Helliwell's youngest lassies. Nice family, usually Hannah or Lily stop into the shop. It's been a while since I've seen the younger two. Bonnie lassies they are . . . especially Alexandrena. Dinna ye agree, Robert?"

"Och awa' with ye, Da!" Robert felt a bit embarrassed at his father's remark. But for the rest of the day, he couldn't stop thinking about Alexandrena Helliwell.

Alexandrena found herself popping into the bakeshop quite often and purchasing a vanilla custard, or her favourite, a raspberry fern cake, whether she desired one or not.

She was relieved when she and Robert started dating. Not at the prospect of their relationship, but rather for the sake of her knickers. *At last, I can stop eating all those cakes; my arse is the size of a hoose,* she thought.

Her adolescent crush had long passed, and a new and exciting passion surged, wanting more of him. Her first attraction was undeniably his looks; he was tall and lanky with thick, dark, wavy hair. His rich brown eyes flitted under a lush mass of eyelashes, which many a lass would have died for. Her second attraction was his quiet nature, always polite and ever so gentle.

She admired him even more after he endured his first family dinner with the Helliwell household. Alexandrena was thankful Robert's first encounter would not be with the entire clan, as that would be a force to be reckoned with. It was only the four youngest living at home now: herself, Margaret, and her two older sisters, Lily and Hannah. Hannah, at eighteen, was toiling over life decisions. Lily, twenty, was recently engaged.

Alexandrena could feel the flush of prickled heat rise from the base of her neck and seep across her cheeks as she watched Lily and Hannah be relentless in their teasing performance, playing on Robert's already bashful disposition. And steady with his banter was her brother William, who hadn't lived at home for some time. He showed up miraculously, unannounced. Margaret was incessant with her flirtatious manner.

"That will be enough! The lot of ye. Do leave poor Robert alone to eat his tea. Ye are embarrassing yer selves." Catherine shot her daughter a wink and patted Robert's shoulder as she passed by to put the kettle on.

*Thank God for mothers*, Alexandrena thought. Her father, of course, questioned Robert on his education and work platform. That too was cut short by the saving grace of a mother.

The remainder of the evening was pleasant, and easy conversations and cheerful laughter flowed around the table. Without Robert realizing it, this was his initiation into the family.

Alexandrena looked forward to the next chapter in her life, though she wasn't entirely sure what that looked like. One thing was certain, Robert Thomson would play a significant role. And for now, she intended on working at Scott-Lyons Bakery until she chose a college. The end of her final school year was fast approaching. Turning sixteen was a pivotal year. Decisions were to be made on future endeavours such as choices of colleges or universities, or perhaps neither.

Her mother had other plans, naturally. She suggested her daughter move north to Ardersier and work for her Uncle Geordie, her mother's younger brother. He and his wife, Lizzie, owned a bake shop and were desperate for a bookkeeper. And on one of their visits to Edinburgh they mentioned that Alexandrena would make a fine addition in their shop.

They did not have children of their own. And when Alexandrena asked why, her mother simply replied, "Lass, it wasna God's plans."

## CHAPTER TWELVE

# *Tears, Flummery, and the Death of an Irishman*

*June 1934. Edinburgh, Scotland*

The smell of homemade soup and freshly baked rolls greeted Alexandrena as she entered through the front door. Both the sea air and excitement of finding a dead man was enough to stir her appetite, and her empty stomach growled in protest.

She could hear her mother singing, and the clanging of soup bowls.

"Lass, keep those wellies outside, I can smell the seafloor from here. And when yer done, wash up and set the table." Her mother's voice appeared pleasant, and her mood pleasing.

If the tragedy of losing one daughter wasn't enough, the death of another had devastated the family. On November 8, 1932, six years after losing Catherine J, their Jessie died. She was twenty-nine years of age and pregnant with her third child. The doctors could not save her. She suffered from complications of mitral stenosis, an undetected heart condition that sadly erupted during labour. Alexandrena's heart was heavy, not only for the loss of another sister, but the sorrowful affliction of pain and despair her parents endured, silently battling through each day. Her mother encapsulated herself within the house, and she clung to Margaret, never wanting her out of her sight. Her father dealt with his grief in the only way he knew how – he left for sea. The family gatherings were her mother's salvation, and they had become her lifeline.

Alexandrena slid off the boots and placed them on the back stoop. She felt immediate relief; at last her blistered heels were set free from their rubber bondage. She entered the kitchen to wash up before placing the soup bowls around the table. Alexandrena and her sisters spent a great deal of time in the kitchen. Some of her fondest memories were of them all gathered around the long wooden table, hands kneading and rolling, slicing, and chopping, whichever task was at hand. It wasn't only a place for dutiful performance; it was a place of sisterhood. A place of storytelling and secrets. A place for laughing and sometimes crying.

The kitchen was small, although set up for functionality. The large sink under the double-hung window served as a bath at one time for wee bairns. Below the sink, two cupboards lay jammed with pots, pans, and various baking dishes. Across from the sink, a large hutch (as if no room could be spared) was tightly pressed against the wall. Its contents varied from dishes, silverware, linens, and crystal: all Alexandrena's mother's prized possessions. Her mother took pride in her meal preparation and the manner it was served. An embroidered tablecloth lay the foundation, with china plates and silver cutlery placed in succession. And when available, a centrepiece of fresh-cut flowers from the garden crowned the presentation.

Each tablecloth was hand-embroidered, a ritual in which all the Helliwell girls partook. Once the evening dishes were washed and put away, her father built a fire in the sitting room. There they all gathered, selecting their favourite seats. A large wooden box with a leather handle sat by the fire with the initials CAJ, for Catherine Alexandra Johnstone, embedded in gold letters. It was Alexandrena's mother's cherished gift from *her* grandmother, *her* namesake Catherine McKay. The box was filled with knitting and embroidery needles, and an array of coloured wool.

The sitting room was through from the kitchen. And when the bustle of the day had settled and the kitchen retired after what seemed like an endless list of chores, only an entrance away lay a pleasing retreat. Not a large room by any means; nevertheless, its elegance, warmth, and comfort welcomed its weary household.

Alexandrena placed the last bowl and proceeded with great caution. "Mum, my mates have asked me to the dance tonight. Would you mind if I slipped out after tea?"

Without missing a beat in her kneading, her mother replied, "I dinna ken, lass. Ye ken, yer Uncle Geordie loves when all ye bairns are home when he visits."

"But mum, I must go, my mates are counting on me. We have much more fun when it's the four of us. Please!" A tiny grunt escaped from the family room.

"Catherine, surely once the dishes are cleared, Alexandrena can have her night out. After all, Geordie and Lizzie will be here until the morn. I don't see any harm in her leaving. Besides, everyone else will be here." John gave his daughter a wink as he looked over his paper, and he commented, "Besides, after dinner and a few nips, Geordie's asleep by the fire."

"Da is right, Mum." Alexandrena smiled back, agreeing with her father's assessment.

"Aye, fine. You can go, as long as you speak to your Uncle Geordie about taking the bookkeeping position in Ardersier."

Alexandrena hesitated, but she knew better than to jeopardise her night out. She had no intentions of moving to Ardersier and working for her uncle. She would rely on her father's support when the time came. A simple nod and smile had been enough to satisfy her mother's intent.

Margaret entered the kitchen with the same tactic for slipping out for the evening. She knew the evening would be nothing but boring discussions of business by her uncle and an endless list of unwelcomed advice about school and dating from her aunt.

"Can I go to the dance with Alexandrena?"

Her father responded without removing his study from the paper. "No, you're just a wee bit too young."

"But Da, I'm fourteen. Girls my age go, ye ken!"

"Enough! Help yer sister set the table," John interrupted.

Margaret continued to plead her case. No sooner did she finish her last conviction, when John threw his paper down. "Christ, lass! You're staying home, and I will hear no more of it."

Margaret couldn't contain her anger. She kicked the sideboard and headed out the back door. Brodie quickly jumped up from his position by the fire thinking this a good time to head outside. Regardless of Brodie now being eleven years old, he had the energy of a pup. As the years passed, he spent more time in the family home than he did at sea.

"No, Brodie! Stay! Yer no coming with me, ye wee toe rag that ye are!" The slam of the door was the last to be heard from Margaret and her bluster.

Everyone knew Margaret was spoilt; being the baby of ten bairns has that effect. But it wasn't only her birth order that aggrandised her cheeky, indulgent manner. Margaret became their mother's salvation, all entwined among love and grief. Catherine indulged her daughter's every whim, all in an attempt to save herself from drowning in a pool of despair. And perhaps in the end, Margaret became everyone's anchor.

"She's no half your lass, Catherine, the Johnstone temper she has," John stated as he collected his paper to finish the last piece of unread news.

"Aye, that may be true, John, but that performance has Helliwell written all over it!" Catherine gave a quick slap against her thigh, then retied her apron. That about ended the conversation, leaving Alexandrena relieved she came out unscathed.

Hannah had just arrived home and was exhausted from her studies. She was studying at Edinburgh University in the nursing program.

"Hannah, have a bowl of soup. You look like you could use some sustenance," Catherine insisted with a concerned tone.

"Aye, Mum, I will take a wee bit." They all sat down to enjoy the soup, which had spent most of the day simmering, tantalizing their senses with its hearty aroma.

"Hannah, have a hot buttered roll," John coaxingly suggested.

"I'm fine, Da, honestly. The soup really is enough," Hannah replied.

"Well, lass, I do believe you are not eating enough, or sleeping enough, for that matter." John expressed as he slathered butter onto a warm roll. "Here, take this down with your soup." John passed the dripping, buttery roll. She took it reluctantly, forcing it down. "Now, lassie, what of your studies? Are they going well?" he asked.

"Aye, Da, very well. I canna get behind. Lots of reading and exams, but I am so enjoying it."

"And what of this Victor Ainsworth you've mentioned. Does he occupy your time too?" John raised his brow, searching for an answer.

"Da, I've told you, his sister Grace and I are schoolmates. Her brother merely chums aboot once in a while, that's all."

Hannah's relationship with Victor was much more than she cared to divulge – to her parents, anyway. The only one she confided in was Alexandrena, and she knew her sister had her confidence.

Alexandrena began clearing the lunch dishes. It may have been the water's rise and fall as she placed the bowls into the hot soapy water: tide in, tide out, or simply a vacant moment, but regardless, her memory triggered.

"Da! I canna believe I almost forgot to tell you of the dead man we found by the sea while clam digging!" Her voice was pitched high with excitement. She described the scene to her parents in great detail and how Scotland Yard scrambled to collect evidence. John, being a merchant engineer, had seen his share of deaths between man and sea.

"Lass, it will be some sailor or fisherman heavy with drink. He's most likely fallen overboard. He isn't the first and I suspect won't be the last."

Catherine poured the leftover soup into a large china bowl, and she paused, lid in hand, contemplating the news. "I hope it isn't someone we know, John, and I pray it's no Mr. Doyle. He's nae been the same since Iona's death." The lid slid from Catherine's hand with a clink – a perfect landing atop the bowl.

Mr. Doyle had left Belfast at the age of forty-two. He began working at Leith Docks as a merchant engineer alongside John. The two hit it off straightaway. John loved his patter.

"Cian, you're not half bad for a bloody Irishman," John would say in jest.

John and Catherine entertained Cian and his wife Iona often. The Doyles never had any children. Cian had met Iona a few years after he moved to Scotland. He was nearly fifty when they married. Iona was a widow with no children.

"Ah, would have loved a cupla leanbh," Cian expressed. He did love the bustle of bairns when visiting the Helliwell household; he always arrived prepared, a pocket full of sweeties, from tunnocks to soor plooms.

After thanking Catherine for a grand meal, he always pulled a bottle of scotch from his overcoat. "Old Highland whiskey – Johnnie Walker it tis tonight."

They all adored Mr. Doyle, especially Margaret. "Ye talk funny, Mr. Doyle – did ye bring us some sweeties?" She would ask, reaching in and searching his pockets. The children would sit around, all eager to learn how the SS *Titanic* was built. Alexandrena and William were most fascinated.

"How many rooms?" Alexandrena asked once.

"Eight hundred, Rena." Cian always called her Rena. She didn't mind; she loved how he spoke her name with his Irish lilt.

"How many decks?"

"Ten decks, Rena."

"Tell me aboot the grand staircase again, pleeease, Mr. Doyle."

William's questions were geared more on the engineering side.

"How many coal furnaces?"

"Twenty-nine, lad."

"What speed could she go?"

"Twenty-three knots, lad."

"How many engines?"

"Three magnificent engines, William."

No show without punch, Margaret had butted in. "Were there soor plooms, Mr. Doyle?"

"Don't be daft!" William cut in.

Mr. Doyle laughed and tousled Margaret's brown mane of hair. "Of course there was." Margaret quickly turned her head and stuck her tongue out towards her brother.

"Enough questions! The pair of ye, leave poor Mr. Doyle in peace," Catherine had interrupted.

Apart from the ship's details, her tragedy was more fascinating. A few nips of Highland whiskey and Cian journeyed back to Belfast at Harland & Wolf shipyard, where during a three-year period, some 14,000 men worked for the White Star Line company erecting the monumental ship. Nearly 300 men were injured from the point of keel laying to her launch. Eight had died. Cian's best pal was crushed during the installation of one of the sixty-ton funnels.

"It's sad to bear thinking, if only there had been a sufficient number of lifeboats, lives would have been saved." His closing remark had remained steadfast.

Alexandrena continued clearing the kitchen in preparation for the next meal and prayed it wasn't Mr. Doyle. Wouldn't she have recognised him? No, how could she?

John packed his pipe with tobacco and stated, "We will find out the dead man's identity soon enough. News runs rampant in Leith." Catherine turned on the radio, also praying it was not their old friend.

Aromas infused the Helliwell home, and each one inspired a memory. Earthy scents of homemade soups, steak and kidney pies, leg of lamb, baked haddock, and clams. Even the smell of smoked kippers. Tonight's tea consisted of a leg of lamb rubbed with butter and fresh herbs. Scrubbed potatoes, turnips, and carrots, were all tucked in, slowly roasting, stimulating a new memory of the day's events. The finale was the dessert. Alexandrena and Hannah were up for the challenge to make their grandmother Jessie's recipe of flummery, a recipe handed down to their mother. The oats had been soaking for the last couple of days, the liquid of starch now thick enough to prepare the rich and creamy dish filled with caster sugar, honey, cream, orange, and of course Scotch whisky.

"Da, leave some whisky for the flummery," Hannah protested as her father pinched the bottle for a dram of the single malt.

"Aye, and dinna let Mum see you," Alexandrena added.

"Haud yer wheesht, lassies." John poured another dram and placed the bottle down, shot the girls a wink, and made his way back to the sitting room.

The dish of flummery was complete, and Hannah retired into the sitting room to study. Alexandrena volunteered to clean up the sticky mess. She thought of the dance, and of Robert. Her insides fluttered just thinking about him. She was so in love with him, and she knew she wanted to marry him. She was sure he felt the same.

*A whimsical image danced, advantageously dressed in a romantic white parchment satin gown. A sweetheart neckline embellished with Chantilly lace and a line of pearl buttons cascaded down her back, complemented by a sable stole, or perhaps silver fox.*

A heavy thud sounded. Alexandrena's image adorned in her wedding dress lay shattered as lace and pearl buttons exploded into fragments of dream dust.

"Bloody hell, dug, get oot the road!" Lily yelled as she dropped her parcel.

A black, wiry mass wearing a tartan collar ran through the kitchen and into the sitting room. "That bloody dug is always in the way!" Lily picked up the parcel and continued her huff into the kitchen.

"Lily, he's just happy to see you," John's voice rumbled through from the sitting room.

"I dinna care . . . he's a right pain." By this time, Brodie was curled up in front of the fire, enjoying the warmth, oblivious to the disruption he had caused.

"What's in the parcel?" Alexandrena asked.

"A new dress," Lily replied. She pulled it from the box. "Jock and I are having dinner with his parents next Sunday; we are announcing our marriage plans, and I needed something a wee formal."

"I canna believe yer getting married," Alexandrena said. Lily held up the dress for her mother and sisters to appraise.

Hannah had come through from the sitting room, her study interrupted from the commotion. "It's beautiful, Lily . . . the blue matches the colour of your eyes," she complimented with a smile.

"Do you think his parents will approve?" Alexandrena asked with a wee chortle.

"Don't be daft, lass, they should be so lucky to have a daughter-in-law as bonnie as our Lily," Catherine expressed.

Margaret made her way back into the house and evidently was over her outburst and back to her clever self. "Aye, she's as fitting as a queen, she is."

They all began to laugh. "Alright, enough, the lot of ye, Christ sake!" Lily replied while positioning the dress on a hanger.

"Lily, dinna use the Lord's name in vain," her mother countered.

The family clock chimed twice. Alexandrena's sister Betty arrived alone this trip, leaving her two laddies at home in Aberfeldy with their father, Percy. Her sister Emma and her two-year-old daughter June would be arriving shortly.

Alexandrena was eagerly anticipating some one-on-one sister time with Emma. *I hope June goes down for a wee nap, or Father keeps her entertained for a bit. He does love to fuss over the bairn. Or Auntie Lizzie, aye, she loves to spoil June*, she thought. Alexandrena was bursting to tell Emma all about Robert.

How could she predict a dead man would alter the course of a conversation ... the course of a day?

The afternoon was delightful. Betty, Emma, and wee June had comfortably settled in. William showed up with a bag of soor plooms and Turkish delight, anticipating his nephew's attendance.

"Sorry, William, I needed a wee break from the laddies, including my husband. Today I'm here as a free woman," Betty stated with a wry grin.

"Right then, take the bag hame for the lads."

William tried handing the bag over to Betty, but Margaret chimed in, "I'll take some soor plooms, William, the laddies canna be eaten all that!" Betty laughed and agreed with her sister's verdict on the plenitude of candy.

"You are needing yer hair cut, Margaret," Betty stated while she seized a handful of unruly long strands.

"Noo, I dinna want my hair cut." Margaret pried her sister's hand from her hair, grabbed the candy bag, and made a dash.

"Still impish as always," Betty said with a grin.

"Och now, Betty, she's just a bairn, leave her be," Catherine responded defensively.

"I wouldna have it any other way, Mother, I love her robust nature," Betty stated apologetically.

Catherine turned towards the sink and began washing the remaining dishes. Alexandrena noticed her mother's shoulders rise and tighten, tears streaming her flushed cheeks. Alexandrena picked up a tea towel, moved in close, and offered a hug. "Mum, why the tears?"

Catherine hesitated, and her gaze remained focused beyond the window. "Oh, lass, I'm losing another bairn ... Lily will be off married to Jock soon. And I know Hannah has plans, though she has never said. The hoose is becoming very still." Catherine wiped down the sink and carefully hung the dishcloth. "I'm fine, lass, dinna fash, just emotions of an old woman." She smiled and hugged her daughter.

The dinner table was fully attended, blessed with family and a meal fit for King George.

Geordie and Lizzie arrived just in time for dinner, with apologies all around for their tardiness.

The patter was brilliant, and the laughing never ceased.

John stood first and stretched himself as if to touch the sky. "Fine meal, Catherine. I'll need a wee rest before plating a dish of that delicious-looking flummery. Geordie, how about we stoke the fire and have ourselves a wee dram?"

"No argument here." Geordie excused himself from the table. William followed, as not to be left with the women.

Emma gathered her daughter from the table and turned to her sister. "Margaret, why don't you take wee June in beside the fire and read her a story? She loves the book *The Story about Ping*."

Margaret wasn't too enthralled to be left babysitting her wee niece but thought better of it. *Perhaps this is my ticket to the dance*, she thought. "I would love tae, Emma!" Margaret gathered June and her bag full of books and made her way into the sitting room.

"She's so good with children," Lizzie indicated. A wee tug erupted within her heart: heavy the burden, walking the barren path of motherhood.

Alexandrena rolled her eyes, thinking. *The wee scunner is looking for a way to the dance.*

"Emma, put the kettle on, will ye, love," Catherine asked her daughter as she pulled china teacups from the hutch.

"Auntie Lizzie, those molasses cookies look simply divine," Hannah observed.

"I brought a couple of dozen . . . for everyone tae try. It's a new cookie I want tae sell at the bakery," Lizzie replied, smiling at Hannah's enthusiasm. Lizzie always liked Hannah. She had a real soft spot for the lassie and would have loved her to fulfil the bookkeeper position at their new shop. However, Hannah's vocation was nursing. Alexandrena was a suitable runner-up. A wee rambunctious, but just the same, Lizzie thought she would make a fine addition to the Johnstone team.

"Go ahead, Hannah, take one, we can all enjoy one with our tea . . . of course, it won't be as grand as yer flummery," Lizzie acknowledged.

"It's nae just mine, Auntie, Alexandrena had a hand." Hannah flushed with embarrassment. She hated that her porcelain skin took on the colour scheme of an entire palette; soft hues of pink brushed the tip of her nose, painting broader strokes of crimson red across her cheeks.

Betty grabbed a cookie, but before biting asked her mother if she had heard from Ralph or had seen her grandchildren. She knew it was a delicate subject, but regardless, it needed to be broached.

Emma shot Betty a glance – if glances could kill. Betty paid no heed to her sister and carried on. "Mum, do you want me to ring up Ralph? I will!"

"Betty, love, leave well enough alone . . . he has a lot to attend to . . . he's still mourning the loss of his wife, ye ken."

"And what about you? Yer mourning a daughter! He canna keep the wee yins from you. Christ, you need your grandchildren more than ever." Betty's voice shook with vigour, and she could not control her anger.

"Betty, please do not use the Lord's name in vain."

"Mum, ye took those bairns in and practically raised them, while Ralph ran off trying to sort his bloody head oot. Ye didna have time to mourn yer own daughter, for Christ's sake. And ye havna seen the bairns in two years. Ye ken he has found someone."

"Betty! Enough!" Emma piped in, and this glance killed.

Betty left well enough just where her mother and sister wanted it: alone.

"These cookies are delicious, Auntie," Alexandrena interrupted with good intentions: first to save her mum further heartbreak and second to move the night along so she could get to the dance. Christ, she hadn't even had time to speak with Emma about Robert.

"Thank you," Lizzie nervously replied. She hated conflict.

Alexandrena watched her aunt struggle to avoid one of the Helliwell family complex moments and felt her timidness excruciating. *Thank God I'm nae moving to Ardersier*, she thought.

"It is tae bad our Mary couldna make it." Again, Lizzie tried to circumvent the situation.

"Aye Lizzie, her and Morogh are busy this time of the year . . . hope to see them come summer. I would love to have seen the bairns, especially Avril. She must be toddling by now." Catherine stifled the tears that lay balanced on the bottom of her lower eyelids. She missed her grandchildren. After her daughter Jessie died, she and John took the two little ones in until their son-in-law sorted out his grief. It had been a chaotic year, but the family learnt to settle. Catherine knew the children's father would come for them, and she prepared herself for that very day. However, she was not prepared *never* to see them again. There was no explanations or reasons why; they were just gone, and she broke down and cried. And when her husband lost his English temper, roaring through the house, voicing his intentions, Catherine wiped her tears and begged her husband to leave well enough alone. There had been enough grief, she said.

As a mother of dead children, you learn to survive; apart from the essential elements, such as food and water, there was the daily routine of survival – the more structured. Laundry, errands, and cooking were all mechanical performances. Although, it was the emotional element that tripped you up. It hid, then stumbled when you least expected it: you saw that familiar smile or heard that familiar laugh, making you look beyond one child, searching for another, as if misplaced. Yet knowing it was lost forever.

Eight years had passed since she received the expedited telegraph of the unbearable news of her daughter Catherine J. Weeks later she received her brother's post. Words hung from a tear-stained letter, a letter she could not bear to finish – a letter she could never reply to. Inside the fold of the letter lay a picture, carefully wrapped in crisp white tissue paper. And such as her heart, she kept it tucked away. Unbeknownst to Catherine, her husband John wrote his only letter ever to Canada, a fervid intensity of words unleashed under a year of self-restraint. And the intended recipient was his brother-in-law, James Johnstone.

On the brink of learning to survive – survive most elements, that is – a cruel tragedy imprisoned you, this time rendering the art of survival powerless. A dead daughter was accompanied to the heavens by a dead granddaughter. *Bye, wee lamb. We never met, yet I miss you.*

Catherine accepted the cookie Lizzie offered and merely smiled, catching her unbalanced tears. After all, she was with the living.

Bellies were full. Accolades rang out to Alexandrena and Hannah; the flummery was a huge success. Not one morsel left. Betty poured the last bit of tea into her cup. She announced she was staying the night and would travel back to Aberfeldy in the morn. She looked forward to a late night with her sisters, and to catch up on the news of Lily's wedding plans.

"You must show me yer new dress, Lily. I hear it's bonnie."

No one heard the knock, not even Brodie. How could they? *The house was alive.*

"I say! Excuse me! Catherine! Excuse me!" Maggie Wilson stood in the doorway like the infamous Cheshire cat eagerly waiting to divulge her tale. "Sorry tae intrude, but I came as fast as I could, ken." She was out of breath, puffed cheeks steaming red, and Catherine thought old Maggie would fall over with heart failure.

"What is it, Maggie?" Catherine implored. It was not like her to barge in like this, though John would disagree.

"Tis the dead man, ye ken, the one the lassies foond by the sea. My Mirren told me all aboot it. Bloody awful it is." Maggie, now bent over clutching her knees, managed to gasp out the last words. "I knew his drink would be the death of him."

Catherine urged her to answer. "Who? Maggie . . . who are you talking aboot?"

John made his way into the kitchen, the commotion enough to discharge him from his comfortable chair and dram. "Maggie! What the hell are you blethering on about, woman?" John's petulant voice quieted the room of its disorderly prattling.

"I'm trying to tell ye, poor Mr. Doyle droon, he did, drunk off the docks he was, fell into the sea and swept in with the tide."

The room's prattle ceased. It was dead quiet except for old Maggie gasping.

A scented melody of herbed lamb, honey, orange, and whiskey would forever trigger a memory of their old friend: for Margaret, it was soor plooms.

♣♣♣

It had rained heavy all night, tapering into a soft morning shower, provoking the deepest of earthy scents. There was a rouse of maternal instinct when you drew a deep breath from misty drops and dewy soil, imbuing the most passionate of emotions you did not know existed. It was familiar – it was comforting.

Alexandrena didn't hear her friend, as she was focused on everything around her that was rousing her senses. The girls walked along the wet glistened cobblestone street, making their way towards work.

"I said we missed you at the dance." Elizabeth shot Alexandrena a glance, this time raising her voice.

"Sorry, Elizabeth, I didna hear you."

"I can certainly see that."

Once Alexandrena shared the news, revealing the dead man's name and family connection, Elizabeth felt terrible. The image popping into her head was a sorrowful one; the dead body now had a name, he now had a face. Elizabeth had only met Mr. Doyle a couple of times when visiting the Helliwell home. She knew her friend would dearly miss him. She wrapped her arm around Alexandrena, pulling her close.

"Why is there so much death? I at times, feel guilty – guilty for being happy and in love, living my life. While my da and mum grieve for their two lassies, and now a dear friend. Then it rains, and it washes all of the sadness and guilt away, and the earth unveils everything new again. I canna explain it. You must think I'm daft." Alexandrena stopped to adjust her shoe, her heel still irritated by yesterday's blisters.

Elizabeth released a small chortle. "It's yer Highland blood, traditionally bound to the earth and the sky, you are." Elizabeth made light of her friend's comment, as she herself was too familiar with the loss of loved ones.

The girls arrived at Scott Lyons Bakery, ready to punch in for their shift.

"What counter are you at today, *Rena*?" Elizabeth shot her a wink. "I think we should honour yer Mr. Doyle and his Irish lilt. From now on, you shall be called Rena."

"Aye, fine, can I call you Liza, then?"

"Absolutely, after all, it's time we shed our formal Christian names and acquire more fashionable ones – you know, something that sounds more titillating. Rena and Liza have arrived for our shift, please pass us our aprons, and baker's caps if you will, Mrs. McLeish," Elizabeth expressed. Her performance flared an uppity tone featuring an Edinburgh dialect.

Both girls laughed. They entered Scott Lyons new women.

# Part Three

*We Send our Boys to War
Only to Become Tattered Men*

## CHAPTER THIRTEEN

# Christmas Day Countdown

*December 1941. Hong Kong Island*

The British and the Japanese prepared themselves for what would be considered Hong Kong's darkest days of battle.

If there could be any sense made out of the irrefutably chaotic predicament the soldiers found themselves in, Nick craved to hear it. Shortly after the disturbing news of the unit of Royal Scots' and Brigadier Lawson's deaths, it had been reported that a platoon of Winnipeg Grenadiers were gunned down at Mount Butler. Just days prior to their deaths, the Grenadiers fought valiantly to recover the mountain, and the Japanese rebounded with great force. They moved quickly and divided their regiments, surrounding the Grenadiers. The Canadians found themselves confined on the slopes of the mountain with limited ammunition. The Japs outnumbered and overpowered them.

It was later said that Major Gresham's unselfish act of bravery and courage would forever be remembered. His pleas for surrender and effort to save his men had no influence over the Japanese; holding both hands high above his head, he stepped out into a blitz of gunfire.

This was the chaos that bore no logic. Nick tried to concede to all its political platforms. He thought back on when he arrived in Hong Kong, sitting in the briefing room studying defence lines and battle tactics. One would have to be naive to think the strategic performances demonstrated on a screen would ever compare to those of a battlefield. Nevertheless, it never really prepared one. War was unpredictable, regardless of tactical training and critical directives. He watched comrades brutally decimated, women and children mercilessly slaughtered, and he solemnly deliberated if any of it made sense anymore.

"Six more days til Christmas," Harry stated as the Company A Royal Scots marched towards the next theatre of operations.

"Aye, and nae fuck'n chance of a Christmas goose!" Charles responded.

"More like a Christmas grenade!" Peter stated. Nick laughed and felt grateful to be back with some of the boys. He hadn't seen some of the lads since the Gin Drinkers Line battle on the mainland. They were all together now for the final countdown. After some brilliant bantering back and forth, the lads remained quiet while they trudged onward. They'd heard it all before – each defence line, each campaign more critical than the last. But in their hearts, they knew this would be most critical. It was a matter of life and death. If Jardine's Lookout and Wong Nei Chong Gap could not be recaptured, and the Japanese remained in control of the centre island, all would be lost.

Nick thought of Harry's countdown: six days til Christmas. Or six days until they were all dead? He shook away his emotional brooding; there was no place for it. Not in his mind nor on the battlefield.

Pie whistled the first few bars and the boys fell into military march. And as if dressed in garb and Glengarry caps, each belted out the final verse of *Scotland the Brave*.

> *Far off in sunlit places,*
> *Sad are the Scottish faces*
> *Yearning to feel the kiss*
> *Of sweet Scottish rain.*
> *Where tropic skies are beaming,*
> *Love sets the heart a-dreaming,*
> *Longing and dreaming for the homeland again.*

And somewhere through the valleys and hillsides of Hong Kong Island marched the Royal Scots in tattered army gear, with little ammunition and empty stomachs. But with hearts full of vigour.

The Royal Scots arrived at Mount Nicholson, east of Jardines Lookout and Wong Nei Chong Gap. They were reunited with a platoon of surviving Grenadiers, who'd made their way west from Mount Butler. The last to arrive would be the Punjabi. Once assembled, the western brigade would prepare themselves for what would be the longest five days of the eighteen-day battle.

The morning of the twentieth found the men rationing stale biscuits and taking inventory on the little ammunition they had. They waited all day to receive magazine rounds and a 3.7 howitzer, but neither arrived. Rab Stewart was taking orders over the wire. "Lads, the Japs are advancing quickly. It's critical we hold our defence lines and push forward to recapture the area."

Nick observed Rab's expression, and it was unsettling to see such angst. Frank caught sight of Nick's unease. "We're nae getting out of this, are we?"

"I don't believe we were ever told we would." Nick felt drained of any hope, and his reply to Frank alarmed even himself.

"Fuck! We dinna need to hear this shite!" Pie hurled his helmet to the ground. The battle had evolved into much more than enemies penetrating defence lines, seizing strongholds, and occupying territories. The atrocious news left the men bereft of speech. Nick felt the bile choke the back of his throat. A group of Middlesex soldiers had been captured near Repulse Bay, south of the island. Their hands were bound behind their backs, and their headless bodies were found by a unit of Royal Scots. Japan's act of warfare became horrifyingly wicked; its genocide surged ruthlessly, without humanity.

The Japanese penetrated through from the northeast and south entries of the island with great speed and efficiency; their aggrandised egos soared, intensifying their combat warfare.

The eastern brigade of Royal Rifles and Middlesex were being pushed farther south of the island, and the number of casualties were staggering. Each time Nick and the boys heard the static voices over the wire they knew it was only a matter of time before they too would be surrounded.

"I hope you lads can swim, because it's the only way we're getting out of this fuck'n mess," Pie commented, twisting at his ammunition belt. "And where the hell is our reinforcements?" He tapped his fingers alongside his belt as if counting the remaining number of rounds.

Pie's action prompted Nick to do the same. He remained crouched in the trench, eyeing his belt, and took inventory. Next to him was John, and like a fall of dominoes, all the boys took stock, with great disconcert. "I'd rather die than be taken prisoner," John expressed to Nick. Nick perceived John's fear and could only nod in agreement.

The heavy bombing was relentless. Each set of reports over the wire was becoming more alarming than the last. North of Wong Nei Chong, a Bren gunner, was hit, killing a captain and officer of the Royal Scots. The Japanese were now in control of the northern shore, and they sieged the line of pillboxes at North Point, killing a unit of volunteers. Jardine's Lookout was lit up like a cluster of Christmas trees, and blazing lights scored through the night sky. The Royal Scots clung to the eastern slopes of Mt. Nicholson, awaiting further direction. The two runners sent to retrieve food and ammunition never made it back. Sadly, Nick knew their fate. And if that wasn't bad enough, the Japanese were ascending the mountain like a colony of angry ants. Captain Ford ordered the men to fall back. They were severely outnumbered.

Their descent down the mountain in the dark was long and arduous. The men were exhausted; they had little water and now no food. The skies opened up and a monsoon rain fell, hard and steady, making the muddy slopes of the mountain treacherous. Nick couldn't see a foot in front of him. *God save them*, he thought. If they encountered a conflict, they would end up like the poor Grenadiers at Mount Butler: fighting until their ammunition depleted.

They settled into their new position at Wan Chai Gap, north of Mount Cameron. Patrick winced, looking for a dry area in the sodden trench to protect his infected feet. Nick crouched between Patrick and John. "Fuck, I think Pie may be right; the only way out of this mess is to swim."

John, still weak with malaria, gave a subtle laugh. "You would have to go without me, lads. I don't have the strength to shite!"

"Five more days, mates!" Harry's parody countdown could be heard above the pound of the rain.

The morning of December 21 was just as dismal as the night before. Heavy fog held the skies hostage, the air was hard to breathe, and the dense terrain paralysed one's movement. The Japanese advanced across the island like a blaze of wildfires, and each time the men altered positions, they invited an affliction of gunfire. Not that Nick believed in miracles, but his mother certainly did. And there was not a better time to conform to her credence, as surely it would take a miracle for the British to defeat the Japanese.

And when the dispatch came from the British sentries posted north of the island that dozens of boats with fresh, invigorated Japanese soldiers were making their way across the harbour out of Kowloon, singing what was assumed to be combat songs, Nick searched his soul for not one miracle, but a thousand. It was determined that close to 7,000 Japanese reinforcements had arrived on the island, prepared to fight and die under their code of the Bushido of the Samurai.

All the men knew; they felt it pulsate through their veins. The heavy, unbreathable air was redolent of blood and desperation, and whether sanctioned in days, hours, or minutes, the inevitable countdown commenced.

Winston Churchill's last call to victory filtrated through the entire Hong Kong garrison: "There must be no thought of surrender; every part of the island must be fought over, and the enemy resisted with the utmost stubbornness. We expect you to resist to the end. The honour of the empire is in your hands."

"Well, lads! It's up tae us. This will be the fuck'n fight of our lives." Pie spat on the ground and adjusted his ammo belt.

Nick patted Pie's shoulder and bellowed out, "We'll no die here, lads! Let's give these Japs hell. Show them what us Scots are made of." He placed his helmet on his head, shook his canteen, and calculated how long the little amount of water might last.

The island would become a death trap, and no one would escape its wrath. The sky blazed with shells and gunfire, summoning the men towards its theatre of killing. Nick heard a panicked squeal, then the gallop of hooves, and one of the Leighton Hill racetrack horses darted past in a frenzied, disoriented state.

❧❧❧

He lay between a mound of dead soldiers, both British and Japanese. He dared not move. The air was stale, and it was hard to breathe. And again he found himself caught in the hourglass of time. He had no idea how long he had been lying in the trench. His right wrist throbbed in sync with the beats of his heart. He knew it was a bayonet gash. He had felt the cold steel blade slash through his wrist, and again as the Jap pulled it out. The darkness of the night and a pile of fallen soldiers had saved his life.

When he was sure the enemy was gone, Nick shoved the lifeless body, and it rolled down into the bloodied mud pit. He signed the holy cross and looked upon the faces of dead soldiers. The last five days of battle had been a massacre. Both the British and Japanese had lost a significant number of men.

Harry Graham's Christmas Day countdown was like a sadistic parody of the twelve days of Christmas, only executed within five. Each day, the atrocities grew more destructive than the previous. The horrors of war screamed out, reaching the heavens. Wounded men's' cries charged the battlefields. Nick had completed the countdown. It was now Christmas Day, and the sky bled red.

## CHAPTER FOURTEEN

## *All That We Had Known No Longer Exists*

*December 1941. Hong Kong Island*

The surrender, as devastating a blow as it was when the official word had been dispatched, was regrettably a salvation for the men. They were beyond exhaustion, both physically and mentally, with ammunition, food, and water near depletion. They had become imprisoned on an island of no escape. Nick iterated Pie's sentiment over and over to the point of madness. "The only way out of this fuck'n mess is to swim."

Christmas Day 1941, the day Hong Kong fell, would be known as "Black Christmas," and it would resonate as the darkest day in the minds of the Allied forces and the Chinese civilians.

Nick and thousands of soldiers were rounded up and assembled on the same docks of the island he had arrived on in March 1941. His once-naive notion of a hasty return home to all that he planned for and dreamed of was stolen in a matter of eighteen days.

Fear and anxiety perspired from the crowd of men. Nick felt lost among all the unfamiliar faces. He had been picked up by an officer shortly after he climbed out of the trench. The Japs had moved on after decimating the Wan Chai Gap area where Nick and his regiment were fighting. Thankful to be alive, he entered Bowen Street Hospital with hundreds of injured soldiers.

Nick sat propped up on the hospital bed, the cold, stiff sheet of dried blood crackling beneath his weight. The nurse instructed him to remain still. "Ye'll nae be wanting the same fate as the last unfortunate soldier who occupied this bed."

The ward and all its occupants moved in slow motion, and a narration played inside Nick's head, revealing each excerpt of atrocities. He did not like what he was seeing. The roaring sound of gunfire and anguished cries bellowed in his ear. Japanese soldiers shouted incomprehensible orders, Arisaka rifles sprayed bullets, and bayonets whirled, splattered with blood. Cries from nurses being raped rang through the corridors.

He didn't know where to look or turn next; there was no set of military orders for this brutal onslaught. After some time, it was evident. The Japanese soldiers were dividing the healthier bodies to one side of the ward and killing the severely wounded on the other. The Japs diligently manoeuvred through rows of beds, prodding, determining who would survive, who would die. A simple, although mad, process of elimination.

Nick, incandescent yet fearful, remained motionless; he had never witnessed such flagitious behaviour. He sat as straight as he could, trying not to divert any attention his way. He kept his left arm hidden under the cold, stiff, bloodied sheet. His open gash on his wrist throbbed, and each heartbeat drummed, spilling a flow of blood. Nick watched a group of nurses trying their best to stay collected, and in all their efforts, try to save as many soldiers as possible.

A young soldier lay in the bed next to Nick. He was still, his breathing erratic, his pensive facial expression staring towards the ceiling. Perhaps the lad was praying. Nick couldn't decipher if his laboured breathing was caused by a wound or from oppressive fear. He tried whispering loud enough for the soldier to hear. "Laddie, what's your name?" Nick was guessing he was no older than nineteen. He had no idea if he was a Canadian Rifle or Winnipeg Grenadier. At this point it didn't fucking matter what the lad was, or any of them, really, Nick thought.

The young soldier turned his head slightly towards Nick. Tears streamed down his dirty, bloodied cheeks, leaving a distinct path to the end of his chin. To Nick's surprise, he answered, although it was a strained response. "And . . . Andrew Reid, I'm from the C Company, Winnipeg Grenadier."

"Nick Massaro, Second Battalion Royal Scot. Pleased to meet you, Andrew."

"Am ... am I going ... to die?" His breathing was strained and shallow.

"Not on my watch, lad." Nick spoke low, keeping his composure. "Where are you hit? Can you sit up?" Nick wanted to slide out of bed and help the lad, but his feelings of apprehensiveness wouldn't allow him. He didn't need a Jap catching him helping an injured soldier; they both would be killed. He would not allow such a careless action to cause him and the lad's death, least of all at the end of a bayonet.

Nick was trying to think fast before the yellow bastards made their way towards them. He vigorously looked around for the nurse he was speaking with. He caught her eye, and she started approaching through the mass confusion of screams, bullets, and bayoneting. "We have tae act fast, soldier, the Japs will be doon this way soon enough. They are showing nae mercy tae the ill or the weak. Those who have superficial wounds are dragged off tae another area of the hospital. Those who have more severe injuries are ... well ... bayoneted – killed. "

Nick reached out and touched the young nurse's hand. "I need you to help this young lad sit up. I'm not sure if he's hit? And I didn't want to draw any attention until I was sure of his wounds." Nick felt compelled and therefore informed the nurse his actions were not cowardice but caution.

"Aye, dinna fash, I'll check him over, but we must move quickly." She folded back the bloodied stained sheet and noticed Andrew had no wounds. The blood was from another soldier. Quickly, nevertheless thoroughly, she checked his chest, abdomen, and groin area – nothing. She then assessed his head and face, and that's when she discovered a long gash behind his right ear. This was the blood source streaming his face. Andrew flinched at her touch.

"It's quite long and could use some stitches. The Japs canna see this wound. If he requires any form of medical supply, they will kill him where he lies."

"Christ! What can I do?"

"For now, nothing. I will tend to the lad's head." With that said, she worked quickly, tearing a piece of bed sheet that had not yet been painted with blood. "Ye must sit up, soldier, ye must look alive," she said, edging

Andrew into survival mode. "He's in a catatonic state, but he'll be fine." Nick detected an Edinburgh dialect.

"My name is Katie, Katie McDonald, and aye, I'm a long way from hame. Scotland . . . Edinburgh, to be exact." Her soft voice yet strong accent caused a flood of warm emotions Nick had not felt in some time, and he gave her a large, brimming smile. Katie noticed Nick favour his left arm. She quickly wrapped his wrist in the same bandage-sheet assembly as the young Canadian and told him stitches would be required when they got the chance.

"Now you both need to sit up and look alive, understand?" Her voice was stern and direct. As she spoke, Nick saw her own fear ascend from her beautiful green eyes. It wasn't long before the Japs made their way alongside their beds. The incomprehensible yelling shook him to the core. He was afraid to look directly into their yellow, slanted, bastard eyes. Nick knew he could hold his own; sitting up was easy, his only injury being the bayonet gash.

He feared for Andrew, as the poor lad still looked in shock. Nick could see a pale-pink colour bleeding through the sheet bandage, which Katie had ever so carefully wrapped. Nick directed his stare towards Andrew. *Keep your head, lad*, Nick thought. He wanted to smile and assure Andrew they would survive – survive at least this encounter – except his instinct about the trigger-happy Japs wheeling their Arisakas led him to believe any interaction would be deadly. He was hopeful that remaining alert would somehow provide Andrew the confidence he so badly needed.

A Japanese soldier pushed Katie to the ground and she fell hard but managed to pull herself up onto another bed that was occupied by an unconscious soldier. Nick followed Katie's movements. Her hand brushed along the soldier's, pale, perspiring forehead, and he lay motionless. *Christ, another young lad, lucky to be eighteen – likely a Grenadier*, Nick thought. Most of the lads from Winnipeg were between the ages of eighteen to twenty years. The eldest may have been twenty-six; they were just boys with little or no experience. He hated thinking the fate of this young soldier.

Suddenly Nick was grabbed by his shoulder and pulled to the ground, and he fell against the Jap before he heard his head smack the floor. A dirty black boot slowly appeared through his blurred vision, with a soiled lace with dirt and blood flopped to one side, untied from its two missing eyes. Nick tried rising, his head still heavy. A hard blow between his shoulder blades rendered him helpless, and he fell backward, as foreign words were expelled overhead. Without knowledge of the language, the intonation was a translation in itself. He remained still and helpless, and exposed. The Jap stood over him, a cunning expression piercing through, a bayonet inches from his throat, edging him to make a reckless move. Nick assessed his assailant. He wasn't much taller than himself: heavier-set, thick neck, fat-faced, large anthracite eyes, unemotional pits staring into Nick's soul.

From his peripheral vision, he watched Andrew being dragged from his bed, and the lad's face was pale and moist with perspiration. Katie was still trying to wake the unconscious soldier. In the pits of hell and fire, she continued to be a nurse. And above all, with passion and courage. He commended her bravery. *The war made soldiers of us all*, he thought. The Jap was quick. He pushed Katie aside, and in one swift and accurate plunge the bayonet pierced through the young soldier's chest. No movement, no sound, although Nick thought he could hear the river of blood as it flowed, soaking the sheet. He bowed his head, and the sting of a cynical reality surfaced and rattled his entire being. "May God be with you, soldier," he said under his breath

Hong Kong had fallen, and the fate of every soldier, every man, every woman and child, was now in the hands of the Imperial Japanese Army.

Nick and none of the British army, were prepared to witness such brutal atrocities. He had heard from another soldier that St. Stephens College, which was converted into a hospital, suffered severely. All the wounded were bayoneted, and all the nurses had been raped.

He held his wrist, and it still throbbed where a dozen or more stitches were applied without anaesthetic. And he thought of Katie McDonald, the nurse from Edinburgh, and prayed she had survived. He never did see her again after the Japanese rounded up the walking-wounded soldiers and corralled them out to Victoria docks, waiting to be ferried over to the mainland. And if the treatment they endured at the hospital was any indication of what imprisoned life would be, then God help them all.

*December 1941. Mainland*

Just days after Japan defeated Britain and seized Hong Kong, thousands of Royal Scots, British, Canadian, and Indian soldiers were ferried off Hong Kong's island, where the battle had ended over to the city of Kowloon on the mainland.

They were placed into captivity at the Shamshuipo British Army barracks, where the Canadians first took up residence on their arrival to Hong Kong. Conveniently, the Japs converted it into what would be the Royal Scots and Canadians first POW camp. The Canadian barracks were in no better condition than the Royals Scots barracks in Victoria on the island. The Japs ransacked through all personal belongings, beds and wardrobes were dumped upside down and sideways, and the Japs pillaged through every item with no regard. Pictures of loved ones, hair ribbons, and good-luck charms lay strewn across the barracks' wooden floor. Nick watched as the poor Grenadier lads desperately searched for their cherished belongings.

Before Nick and his battalion left their barracks in Victoria, he was relieved to find his small red-velvet box. It must have flown across and landed under the toppled bed frame when the Japanese dumped his kit bag.

Not that he was concerned; they were only simple charcoal sketches, but it was odd that they were missing. Hong Kong was beautiful, and in his leisure time before the battle began, he'd enjoyed capturing the spectacular view of the coastline.

When the Royal Scots arrived at Shamshuipo barracks, Nick recognised Andrew among the defeated-looking lot of soldiers. Nick asked how the lad's head was. Andrew, still shaken from their horrific encounter at Bowen Street Hospital on Hong Kong's Island, responded with just a nod. Once they had all settled, Andrew revealed that he had not even completed his sixteen-week basic training. A few other Winnipeg lads spoke up, admitting the same. Another Grenadier nervously laughed as he mentioned most of the boys were completing their training on the *Awatea* as they sailed over, and he then broke down and cried; he was only nineteen. Andrew stated he had been happy at the time to come to Hong Kong. They were told it would be warm, and likely no combat, and it was a great alternative to fighting the Germans in Libya. "The lesser of two evils," Andrew concluded.

It took some time for the men to settle into their once-familiar barrack. It had been their home for months but it was now unfamiliar, and it resonated a charge of defeat throughout. It had now become their captor.

The Canadians had come late to the game, and the men agreed if Churchill hadn't dragged his feet and acceded to have the Canadians arrive earlier, then just perhaps events would have turned. Before the battle, Nick and a few of the lads had debated that if war with Japan was affirmed, it would be indefensible without the support of reinforcements. The Hong Kong garrison was just over 14,000, and it was estimated that Japan's army was triple. Churchill's broadcast rang in the troops' heads: "We must avoid frittering away our resources on untenable positions."

They arrived November 16, 1941, on the *Awatea*, accompanied by HMSC *Prince Rupert*.

The *Don Jose* was to accompany the Canadians, carrying 212 vehicles to support the Hong Kong forces. The fate of the *Don Jose* was undisclosed, at least to the troops. It never made it to Hong Kong until the end of December, after the battle. Some heard it was rerouted to Manila via Australia; others, with acrid emotion, stated that the fucking US Army required the vehicles to defend the Philippines. For the most part, the troops were basically kept in the dark on any official communications. They followed orders, followed commands. That was their position – their rank.

Nick recalled their arrival, and it was quite the spectacular welcome. All came out to cheer: the British Regiments, Indian Regiments, Hong Kong Chinese regiment, Hong Kong volunteer Defence Corp, and the elated Chinese citizens. General Maltby, commander of the British troops and the Indian Brigades, conducted the lead. Hong Kong breathed in a new life. It was evident the Canadians' arrival inspired morale, if nothing else.

Churchill's broadcasts of Hong Kong's defensive positions, or more so, the lack of, promoted propaganda to spread like wildfire. The Japs dropped thousands of pamphlets over the city. The Hong Kong Defence Corp strived to destroy and burn as much of the persuasive material as possible. Nick was usually not affected by the anti-British posters nailed to lamp posts and street signs, or the leaflets blowing aimlessly along the streets among garbage. But when one leaflet caught his boot, against his better judgment, he picked it up and studied it, and it had left him unnerved. It was a cartoon version of Japanese soldiers raining down with AKA rifles upon a pile of dead British soldiers, the British flag aflame. The only application of colour was of the Rising Sun. And in its deep, blood-red disc was a caricature of a Jap soldier's face staring out brazenly laughing.

Now it was that very image that provoked Nick's dispirited consciousness as he sat in the barrack among his comrades, all captive under the Japanese Imperial Army.

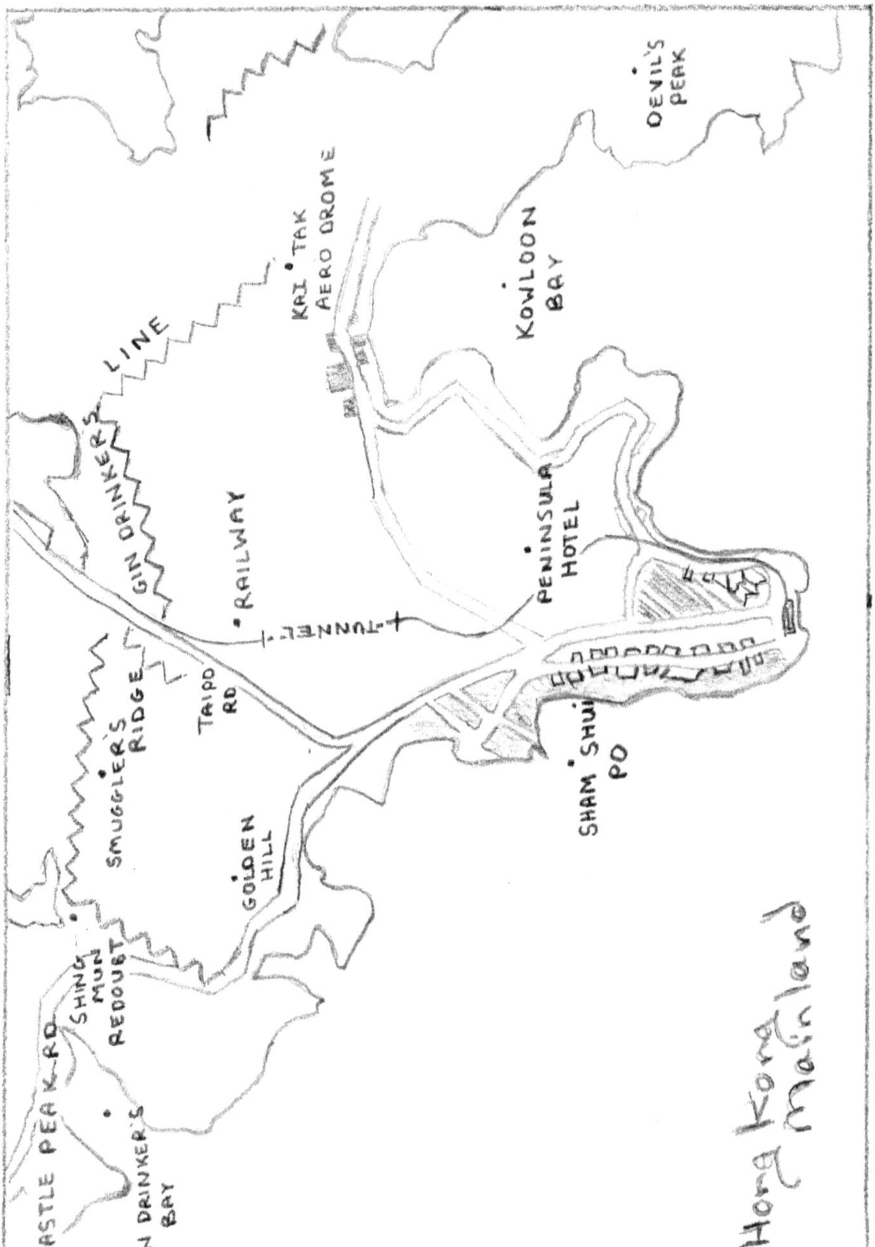
DEVIL'S PEAK
KAI TAK AERO DROME
KOWLOON BAY
GIN DRINKER'S LINE
RAILWAY
TUNNEL
PENINSULA HOTEL
TAIPO RD
SMUGGLER'S RIDGE
SHAM SHUI PO
GOLDEN HILL
SHING MUN REDOUBT
CASTLE PEAK RD
GIN DRINKER'S BAY
Hong Kong Mainland

# THE ROLL OF HONOUR

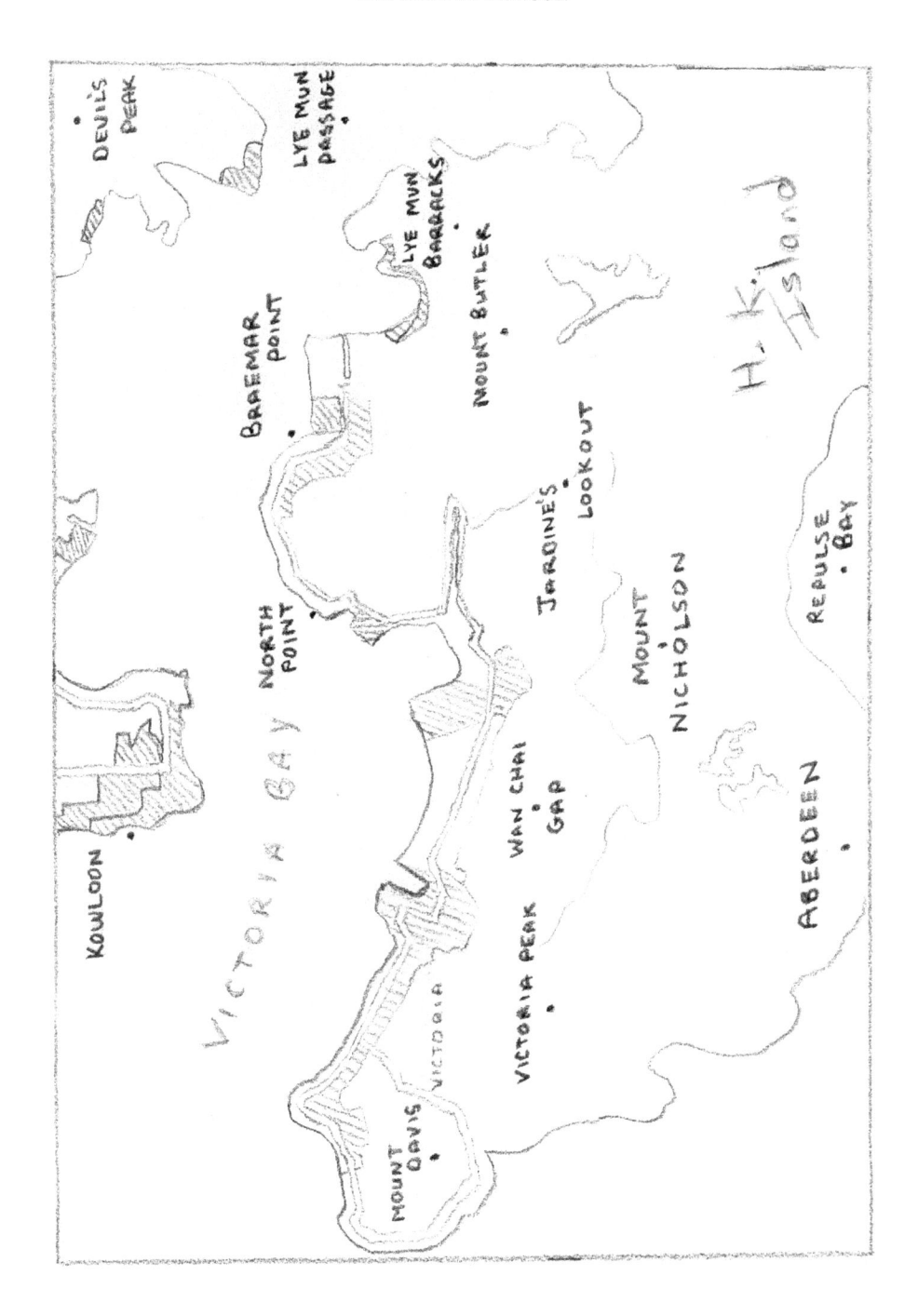

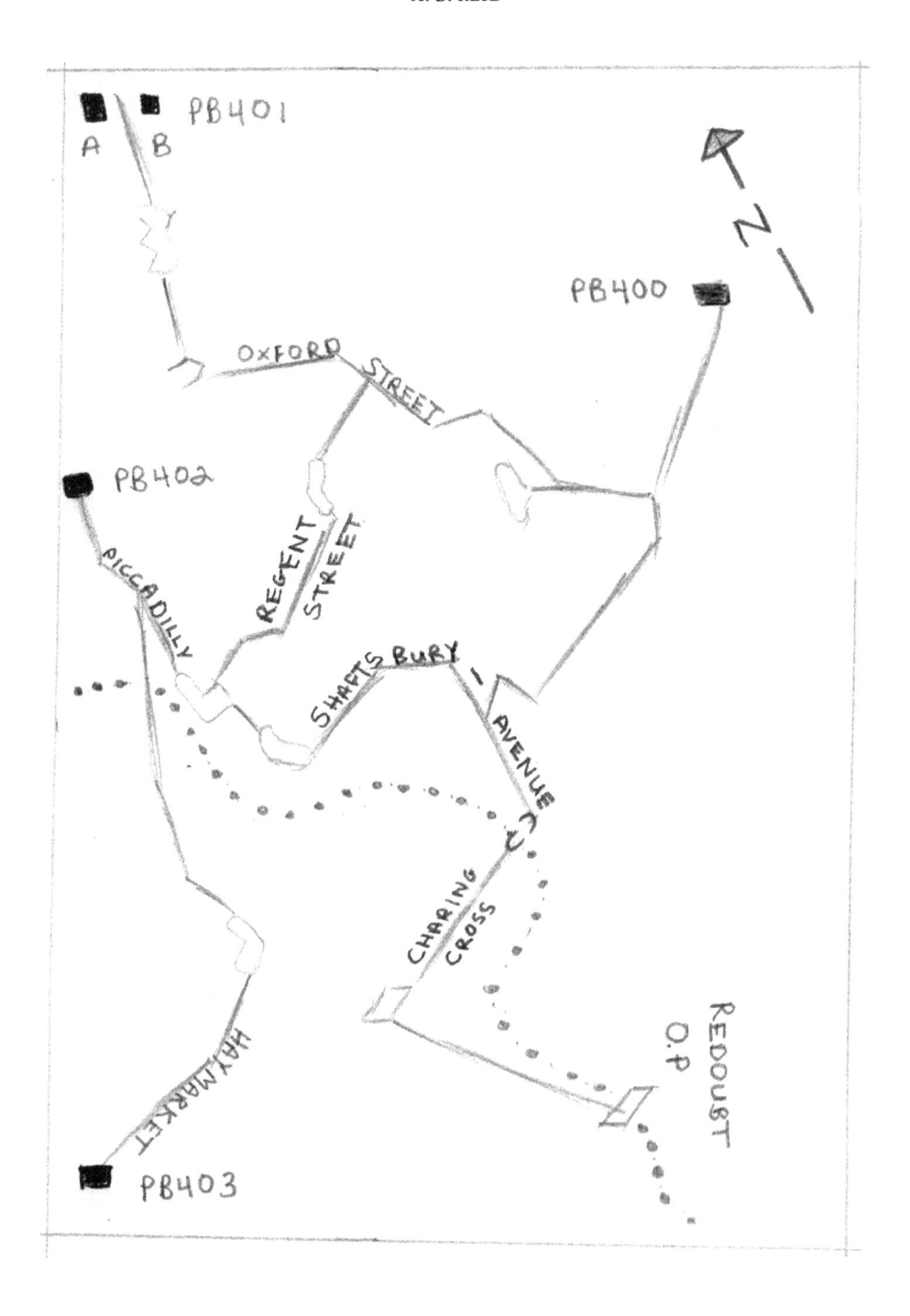

## CHAPTER FIFTEEN

## *Imprisonment*

*December 1941 to September 1942. Camp Shamshuipo, Mainland*

The third blow rendered him helpless, and a numb despair overwhelmed both his body and spirit. His bound wrists ached. He felt each stitch that Katie McDonald had hastily fastened just days ago at Bowen Street Hospital rip open as the Jap guard seized his arms behind his back and threw him to the ground. His vision blurred, and his eyes stung from the salt of the sweat trickling from his brow.

At first, he thought the guard was going to chop off his head and it would hang with the collection at the gates of Camp Shamshuipo. To intimidate the prisoners, the Japs hung the heads of British soldiers on spiked poles. And as the prisoners marched towards their first accommodation of captivity, the bloodied, decomposing heads did just that.

He couldn't understand a word the guards were saying, although their wicked laughs were evidence enough of their barbaric intentions. Before the first blow, he shuttered his eyes in disbelief. So, this was how he would die? He had survived the Gin Drinkers Line battle, the battle on the island, and the deadly encounter at Bowen Street Hospital. Now, just days after Christmas, he would die at the end of a sword, helplessly bound.

The first guard swung the silver blade high. Nick heard it swoosh, breaking the air. He felt it on his lower vertebra, the blunt force rattled his head, and his lower neck pulsated with excruciating pain. He screamed out, "Christ! I'm not dead ... and my head!" Nick's surprised action invoked an uproar of laughter. He looked up to see the guard still holding his sword high. The second blow bounced his head off the ground, his jaws clenched, and he could taste the blood from his tongue. The laughter now resonated in devious tones, and the second guard performing the mock beheading stood beside Nick with his sword encased in its scabbard, anticipating the third strike.

He didn't recognise the soldier that lay beside him. A stream of blood ran from his ears, mouth, and nose, making its red path toward Nick, who turned his head to avoid the soldier's startled expression before he died. Nothing was shocking anymore; witnessing the heinous acts of cold-blooded killings and the raping of nurses at the hospital demonstrated a cruelty beyond comprehension, and grievously this was only the beginning.

Nick couldn't see the activity occurring around him, although he heard the men being ordered to split up into groups by ranks: bystanders to the gruesome play of events. A chap from the Royal Navy was ruthlessly thrown to the ground, landing beside Nick. The same degrading theatrical performance gave way, and there was nothing anyone could do.

Nick saw the guard strutting towards them, carrying something in his clenched hand.

The cynical laughter halted, and the group of guards gathered in a circle, eyeing the sheaf of papers the arriving guard held. A wave of nausea rose so violently that Nick's battered neck pain momentarily surrendered. He recognised his drawings; they were simple charcoal sketches, mapping out the areas of both mainland and Island. One lazy afternoon, before the threat of invasion, he'd drawn the sketches with his remaining piece of charcoal. His once recreational pastime had now raised suspicion.

This was no guard that violently waved the sketched papers in the air above his head. His uniform flaunted his rank. Nick was mercilessly pulled up. "*Kyotskee!*" the one guard yelled, a word the men became quickly familiar with, meaning "Attention." Nick diverted his eyes past Colonel Tokunago's petulant glare. One thing the men learned quickly: don't direct your stare into the face of your oppressor.

The sting of slaps reddened Nick's cheeks, and he felt his blood throb to the surface, his right eye sore and swollen. The guard's left-handed aim wasn't as precise as his right, and each time he reached in to slap Nick's face, he clipped the side of his head and eye socket. After he'd been slapped repeatedly, Nick closed his eyes, succumbing to not looking at all. It was

Colonel Tokunago's resounding voice that caused his eyes to nervously open. The first thing Nick caught sight of was a large vein on Tokunago's neck. It pulsated at each word he bellowed, and streams of sweat poured from his temples.

Nick wasted no time volunteering that the drawings were his; he would not condemn his comrades to an unwarranted punishment. Nick's mouth was dry, and when he tried to swallow, he gagged on his tongue. He thought this was the end; this was his death.

It was the English-speaking guard that redirected his attention. It was odd seeing the young Japanese man with his boyish features and kind face speak English. From their time of imprisonment, they had only been subjected to the Japanese language. And it proved to be boisterous and intimidating.

After a short time, Nick realised the young Japanese guard was the colonel's interpreter. During the interrogation, Nick asked his name. Akito had been stationed in Hong Kong only weeks ago. Nick discerned he was well educated and no more wanted to be here than Nick. Akito, after his introduction, was quick to the point. He asked Nick about the drawings and if there were any other official military maps or documents.

Nick hoped he sounded convincing that the sketches he drew were merely a leisurely pastime and they were not incriminating documents exposing military reinforcements. They were just simple recreational drawings of the island, mainland, and the tunnels of the Gin Drinkers Line. Nothing more.

After what seemed like hours that Akito had been interpreting Nick's vindication, the colonel's temper began waning, and Nick's trepidatious thoughts continued to soar.

Mercifully, the inquisition was abruptly cut short. The men were pushed and punched back into their barracks. The news didn't take long to circulate. A small group of prisoners had escaped, and the Japanese guards, including their colonel, stormed around in a heated rage. Nick's once-perceived perilous sketches lay in a heap on the ground.

Hours had passed, and the prisoners' bodies were soaked through to the bone, hunger and thirst making them weaker, making the severe torture of standing at attention excruciating. John had slid to the ground, lying between Nick and Ian, his face planted into the wet mud. It would only be a matter of time before a guard would come and beat him back onto his feet. The men had been called back out of the barracks and made to stand at attention, and no reasons were given. They merely stood while the afternoon sky unleashed its monsoon.

When the prisoners returned to their barracks, they fell onto the wooden floor, soaked and exhausted, their spirits broken. No food or water had been given the entire time they had been made to stand. The four Canadian soldiers who had escaped the day before were dragged back to Shamshuipo and beaten in front of the British prisoners as they stood in the pouring rain. Before the men were released from their fatigued stance, the Canadians were shot. Their beaten, lifeless bodies were dragged through the sopping mud.

The Japs' intimidating performance prevailed, and the next morning the prisoners stood in line-ups waiting to sign their lives away. Each signed a non-escape clause as they peered up towards the newly added heads of the Canadians.

That afternoon a convoy of vehicles arrived; Nick counted possibly twenty, which he told the boys when they were all trying to peer out the barrack windows.

"Not another fuck'n roll call." Pie's voice wavered, feeling he could not endure to stand again.

"*Hyaku! Hyaku!*" the guard yelled. It was another term the men learned: "Hurry up."

They all fell into positions. General Maltby was at front row centre with a line-up of captains and lieutenants. The remaining prisoners stood behind in rows. They were told the camp was about to be inspected, and all the men were to look healthy and smile, as a photograph was to be taken. The men watched as General Maltby tried speaking with the Japanese officials; however, they couldn't make any of it out. They could only assume the conversation was not in the favour of the British.

The whole charade was wrapped up within an hour. Not one Japanese official entered the barracks to inspect their conditions, nor were any of the sick looked in on. And not one Japanese official paid attention to the hundreds of starving POWs that stood before them. The flashes from the cameras wrapped up the so-called inspection.

Malaria, though still at large, had taken a backstage to the growing number of dysentery cases. The one and only medical officer in Shamshuipo feared that the men's lack of nutrition and lack of medical supplies would be the death of half the soldiers, and they would not be strong enough to fight any epidemic thrown their way. The fear of a diphtheria outbreak was constant. And when the infectious disease veered its ugly head, nearly twenty prisoners a day died. The Japanese refused to administer any medication. It was heinous. Adding to this affliction, the Japanese reduced the twice-a-day rice ration to one. Only the men made to work would be permitted two inadequate offerings. One evening after his work detail Nick learnt that seven POWs inflicted with dysentery had died within minutes of each other. He was outraged. He approached Akito asking him to help set up a meeting with Colonel Tokunago. Something had to be done, Nick thought. He knew the colonel's acts of cruelty and orders to withhold food and medication was against the Geneva Convention's agreement for humanitarian treatment of prisoners.

Akito, with great empathy, convinced Nick that it would be a futile attempt, one that would only put Nick in danger. Akito explained that Colonel Tokunago's orders must be followed and no one is to ever challenge his authority, not even another Japanese guard. He also told Nick that in the eyes of the colonel, the sick were nothing but weak men lying about, not contributing to Japan's work force. This contemptible thought process led to the prisoners' daily death count. And there was nothing anyone could say or do.

The work parties were the worst. Nick couldn't decipher if John being laid up in the prison camp eating one portion of four ounces of weevily rice a day was a blessing or not. At first the prisoners picked out the white wriggling maggots. But after a while they gave up and welcomed the tiny morsels of protein. The second bowl of weevily rice that the working men received at dinner time was no better, it contained some type of unrecognisable slimy greenery. It certainly was not enough to sustain one's frail body to the amount of work the prisoners were forced to perform. If anything, it added to their already problematic bowels and sickly guts.

"This is against the Geneva Convention. It's illegal to subject prisoners to work for the enemy's war effort," Rab complained under his breath. He dared not raise his voice, as a slap away was an over-enthusiastic Jap guard with a bamboo pole.

"Well, so is fuck'n starv'n us!" Pie yelled out, not caring about the consequential blow he received from the long wooden crack. He flinched, then cursed under his breath.

Nick was elated when he arrived at Shamshuipo Camp and saw the Lothian and Edinburgh lads. The trench he had been caught up in during the last five days of the battle had been with a mix of another Royal Scot platoon and a group of Royal Rifles. The death of those lads that he lay among was tragic, yet knowing they weren't from his own unit was a relief. The comradeship Nick and his mates had proved to be their saviour. And when he showed up that day at Shamshuipo, recognising Pie's flame of red hair and blustering grin, as he stood head and shoulders above the rest, Nick couldn't help but smile.

They worked from 5:00 a.m. til 8:00 p.m. each and every day. The first directive was to comb the hills and valleys and clear the dead bodies. They marched out under the scrutiny of groups of guards carrying rifles and swords. The prisoners plodded, pushing broken-down carts, collecting the dead.

It had been nearly three weeks since they were captured, and it was horrendous that the wounded and sick had been left without food, water, or medical attention. Nick choked as he and his work crew came upon their first pile of dead soldiers; there was no recognising any of them, their bodies and faces decomposed. The smell was so putrid, it penetrated through your skin and burned your eyes. Nick pulled his red bandana over his face. It took days on end to clear the bodies, and sadly the Chinese civilians of women and children lay within the heap of death. Among one pile was a dead monkey, and only its fur and thick black pads of its hand and feet remained. Jordie flung the dead animal using a toss of a stick and gave Nick an empathetic stare as he watched Nick pull out a young child. Nick couldn't discern if it was a laddie or a lassie. It was enough to make his stomach retch, and tears streamed and moistened his bandana.

These poignant moments would prove to be the catalyst of many a tormented dream the men would bear for the rest of their lives.

The little humour the men achieved came with much tragedy, and they tried using it to overcome each catastrophe; it was a survival tactic. Pie's uninhibited laugh caused a curious state. A statue of Queen Victoria had been carelessly dumped into a mound of debris and trash. "I have to say, the Japs didna take too kind to the once British queen, something a few of us Scots may have in common!" he said. Some of the lads who supported the Scottish National Party roared with great response; those who did not walked away to the next heap of destruction.

But when a couple of Japanese fighter planes crash-landed on the Kai Tak aerodrome that 800 POWs had worked on daily to repair and extend, well, the entire camp broke into bouts of laughter. With great caution, the working team of prisoners had sabotaged the runway. The celebration was short-lived, but never so needed.

Summer was approaching, and the death toll and the pathetic stuff the Japanese called food was the only thing the POWs could count on. Each day that passed seemed worse than the last. Beatings had increased, and they became common practice; it was as if the Japanese guards were bored, and the sport of torture filled their days.

Akito had made friends with the British. He earned the nickname "Happy." He was pleasant and kind. He did not agree with the prisoners' treatment, and he was bold to share his views with Nick one afternoon during one of their conversations. Akito was no taller than Nick, 5'4" and slim built. He shared many a story of his homeland and told Nick that not all the Japanese people were for the war. He had a family back home whom he dearly missed. He pulled out a folded photograph of his wife and two young children. Nick observed Akito as he longingly admired his photo. "You have a beautiful family, Akito."

On occasion Akito smuggled cans of fruit in for the men. It was a grave risk, and he knew if he was caught it would be the death of him. Still, he couldn't bear to see the men starve while the Japanese filled their bellies with the Red Cross packages that had been dropped for the prisoners.

Civilians also took their chances smuggling food in through the fence to their loved ones, those who fought for Hong Kong's Chinese Volunteer

Defence Corps. Many were shot and killed, and the Japanese weren't particular on age or gender.

It was early evening, and the sun was slowly falling behind the barracks. Nick, just back from a day of work detail, was walking across the yard inside the compound, his body painfully tired and his mind plagued with thoughts of being rescued and returning home.

When he heard her voice, his knees weakened. "Pan! Pan!" He ran to the fence line. He looked upon her beautiful face, searched inside her empathetic large brown eyes, and broke down. "What in God's name are you doing here?" Though he was happy to see her, he feared for her life.

Pan explained she and her friends were sneaking food into the barracks for both the Chinese and British.

"It's atrocious what is happening, Nick. Hong Kong has turned into nothing but an impoverished city. The Japanese have removed all Chinese business signs and replaced them with Japanese names and flags. My people are being beaten into oppression, and there are many spies lurking about."

Nick grabbed Pan's tiny hand through the fence, and he made her promise to stop coming to the camp barracks. "They will kill you, Pan, no questions asked."

Pan gave Nick that same enticing smile she had that night back at the Peninsula Hotel, the night before the battle of Gin Drinkers Line. She reached into her pocket and pulled out a couple of hard-boiled eggs. "Take these, Nick, I will bring more." Nick couldn't convince her otherwise. She was young, and the youth in China were determined not to fall under Japan's dictatorship. She and her friend continued to bring eggs, and Nick continued to discourage her.

The first month of imprisonment found the men being segregated, and their superior officers were moved to Argyle Camp. The Indian battalions had been moved out almost immediately, and their camp location was never disclosed. Rumour was the Japanese were hoping to coerce the Indian soldiers to switch sides and become allies. They were banking on many Indians being indifferent to the British; after all, their country was unfavourably under British sovereignty.

The news of the beheading of Captain Ansari of the 5/7 Rajputs ran rampant through the camps. He was tortured and starved, yet he never relinquished his position or his British alliance. However, there were Indian soldiers who turned, and the Japanese used them as spies. Nick was disheartened to learn his friend Amik Singh had been one. He wasn't totally surprised by Amik's decision; he had mentioned several times that he had no trust in the British. One afternoon while drinking gin slings and making horse race bets, Amik had divulged the story of the slaughter at Jallianwala Bagh, Amritsar, Punjab in India. He was a young boy when he and his father, along with thousands of unarmed Indians, entered Jallianwala to celebrate the Baisakh Sikh Festival and to peacefully protest against the arrest of a number of leaders from India's National Party. During the event and under the direction of the British/Indian party leader Lieutenant General Michael O'Dwyer, the troops opened fire, killing hundreds of innocent civilians. Amik's father was among them – shot and killed in front of him.

Nick learnt that the pathways through a war were precarious and unpredictable. One truly never knew oneself until faced with a controversial circumstance. He didn't judge his friend, or any of the Indian soldiers, though he felt the sting of betrayal.

Nick then thought of his uncle, his mother's brother, off fighting for Mussolini. He certainly could not be judged; he was fighting for his country. The war divided families, friends, and now allies.

Eight months had now passed, and summer was coming to an end. The camp conditions had worsened. Lice and bed bugs now added to the numerous flies and maggots occupying the men's living space. The latrines were a mess, and the men's dysentery was so bad that there was little time to clean in between. Cholera was the latest disease, and it proved to be deadly, pushing the death toll beyond counting. Still, the Japanese gave no medicine. This had all been enough to constitute the cheers coming from the lads when word erupted they were leaving Hong Kong.

There were no details, and as far as Nick and some of the lads were concerned it was all speculation. Jordie heard through the camp's rumour mill that the US and British were closing in and the Japs, out of fear, planned the eviction.

Nick was not only concerned about the possibility of leaving Hong Kong, but he had become very worried about Pan. He hadn't seen her in weeks. Her visits had become less frequent. She had told Nick that the killings of civilians were increasing. One would only need to walk along the street without bowing and a Japanese soldier would either beat or shoot you. There was nowhere for her to flee, not even home to Shanghai.

It was a Sunday morning Nick would never forget; it would remain etched inside his head forever. The rain was heavy, and fog was settling in. He heard the screams, but they weren't the usual screams of men being beaten or men dying: they were high-pitched lassie screams. He raced out of his barrack, and then his heart stopped and he fell against the fence at the sight. He watched in helpless horror. Pan and her friend were bound to a pole just feet away from the prison fence line. They had been beaten ruthlessly. Nick watched as the guard raised his Arisaka rifle and shot them both. Their heads slumped forward, and their bodies dangled. They were left on display for days to deter other civilians sneaking food into the camp.

No amount of training prepared you for the onslaught of war; its landscape of death haunted you. Visions of mutilated bodies and decomposed faces reached out to you in your dreams. Horrific screams pierced through your head. Its traumatic scene was inescapable. Nick fell into a place of despair, and he wasn't sure if he could ever climb out. Deep down he prayed the rumours were true and that they would be leaving Hong Kong.

## CHAPTER SIXTEEN

## *A Shite Send-Off*

*Friday, September 25, 1942. POW Camp Shamshuipo Barracks, Hong Kong*

Fogged clouds of breath hung trapped in the crisp morning air, and a bitter breeze gripped the shivering, garish-looking lot of soldiers. They stood side by side and row by row, dignity and honour still a stronghold in their minds and in their hearts regardless of the stance their sickened, diseased bodies portrayed. Not one man escaped the affliction of wound sepsis, dysentery, beriberi, or diphtheria. The last ten months imprisoned at Shamshuipo Camp was less than tolerable. Adding to the men's infamous list of diseases was now malnutrition. And it would prove to be the most deadly.

Nick stood between Jordie and Pie, and he felt his heart thump so hard he thought it would jump out of his chest. He was assured the other men shared his angst – why such an early *tenko*? The sun had not yet peaked, and the atmosphere seemed less than its usual dark, pitted platform of misery and degradation.

"You must look healthy and be grateful for your stay in Shamshuipo," Happy announced, then added, "Our great lieutenant will honour you with his visit." Once Happy finished his proclamation, the Jap guards made their way between the rows of prisoners, long bamboo poles in hand, slapping anyone who was not standing at attention. Aside from the list of diseases acquired from captivity, the men who had first entered the prison with malaria suffered greatly. Without meds or proper nutrition, they deteriorated gravely. John was a mere skeleton of himself; his body wavered and trembled. Nick grabbed his arm to steady his friend before the guard came casting around to inflict a fury of bamboo. John, with great perseverance, stood through the humiliating roll call.

A long black car arrived with the Rising Sun flapping in the wind; a flag that solely signified destruction and dominance to both the prisoners and Chinese citizens. The driver, once stopped, jumped out, rushed anxiously around to the back of the car and opened the door. Out stepped a vision in white, his pristine uniform decorated in colourful ribbons adorned with silver and gold medals. A samurai sword cradled in a red sash completed the lieutenant's persona.

Pie whispered to Nick, "Jesus Christ, nae liking this, mate."

Nick countered, "You will get no argument from me."

Lieutenant Hideo Wada approached the rows of British soldiers with an air of prestige and formality. Nick watched as the lieutenant walked along the front row, eyeing each soldier with the same look of disdain the Jap guards bestowed on them. Nick's throat became dry, his hands clammy. Sometimes it was hard to decipher the feelings of apprehensiveness or those of pure starvation and disease: it all meshed into one. One thing was indisputable – you could never let your guard down, not for one second.

The lieutenant came to a halt, and as if on command he gave a quick turn and faced the prisoners. He did not direct his stare at the prisoners but through them. Nick's disconcerted feelings flooded his entire being, and his hair bristled along his arms. The familiar sting of an unwanted reality rose from the pit of his stomach, torturing his mind, such as it had that Christmas Day at Bowen Street Hospital.

The lieutenant addressed the prisoners. His hand lay tightly clenched on the pommel of his sword, as if anticipating an altercation, or perhaps resistance: "You will be leaving Hong Kong to a country where you will be well treated, and well fed. Take care of your heatlh."

*Sunday, September 27, 1942*

They stood buck naked, skin hanging loosely over what now felt like old, weary bones. Though luck had struck them this morn, they'd received a double ration of rice, a whopping eight ounces. It was enough to make them feel pathetically grateful.

Nick's stomach turned; the extra ration was a welcome relief from hunger, but sadly it would not last. Even one's stomach had surrendered to the measurement of rationing and its foul sustenance, as its rumbling complaints had long ceased. You couldn't help it; food was constantly on your mind. Unless, of course, you were being beaten, and then you only thought of surviving, praying the assault didn't cause further damage, adding to your list of ailments.

*What I wouldn't give for a plate of my mother's fresh pasta*, Nick thought as he stood looking down at his dirty feet. Two of his toenails had turned black and fallen off. It was the most horrific yet indescribable feeling watching one's exterior deteriorate. Nick glanced over at his comrades. *Christ, do I look as bad as that lot?* With greater scrutiny he couldn't help but consider that they all looked alike, except in height. And of course Pie's red hair still stuck out ablaze.

John leaned in towards Nick, trying to remain upright. "Hold on . . . stay strong," Nick urged while bracing John's frail body.

"What the fuck dae they want us tae dae now?" Pie asked, now irritated.

"Hold your tongue, Pie, I'm nae getting a good feeling about this . . . let's not make it worse," Nick countered in a lowered tone.

Both Pie and Nick turned their heads hearing their battalion captain Rab Stewart conversing with the Japanese official; no doubt inquiring on the naked *tenko*.

There was nothing, nothing any of the men could do, regardless of rank. Rab was slapped hard across the face. "*Kyotskee!*" (Stand at attention!) the official yelled.

A dozen Japanese soldiers clad in white coats and medical gloves strategically stood in a row. The POWs were instructed to gather in groups, line up, and bend over. Happy, at this time, was sweating and anxiously interpreting the process. He stood straight at attention, bellowing orders as commanded.

"There is to be no disease brought to our graceful land of the Rising Sun. You will be given medicine in your arm and a test of your health. You will be treated very good! Good food! And good climate! It's important you take care of your health, always," Happy concluded. For the first time, Nick noticed Happy was not smiling.

The so-called medicine in the arm was an inoculation. For what? The men never knew. Years later, after the war, it was determined the Japanese injection was one of sterilization: after all, to the Japanese, the war was about a superior race and the power of their Rising Sun. The so-called test of health was a glass tube probed up each man's arse. It was a pitiful and grotesque act to witness. The men tried keeping their heads about them after a few of them uncontrollably shit out whatever excrement their bowels had to offer. Splats of shit sprayed out, painting the Japanese soldiers' white coats. It was hard not to laugh; the humour was a welcome distraction from the pain and humiliation the men endured.

No medical records were ever documented or found post-war. The charade of tests was just that – a charade.

The docks at the harbour were crowded with POWs and Japanese soldiers. Frightened Chinese civilians made their way through the impoverished streets to wave farewell to the British army, who fought valiantly to protect the colony and its people. Their fate now would be determined under the tyranny of the Japanese. The memory of Pan and her friend's decomposing bodies tied to the pole would be a vision Nick would never forget.

Dark clouds and a soft drizzle of rain were to be the men's send-off leaving Hong Kong, leaving their ten months of torture, starvation, and humiliation behind. The men were allowed to pack their belongings (all that remained, that is) into their kits and prepare themselves for the journey to what was being called the "graceful land," full of good food and good treatment. Nick adjusted his kit strap. It felt heavier than when he'd first arrived in Hong Kong, though its contents were less, and the strap dug into his shoulder bone, with no muscle or fat to support it. He prayed he had gathered everything of importance needed for the journey, including the tiny red-velvet box his mother insisted he take, *"to keep you safe, my Michael."*

The men's destination was never officially announced. Rumours were they were to be shipped to either Taiwan or Japan. Most of the men were rejoicing, welcoming the news of leaving Shamshuipo Camp, leaving Hong Kong. However, Nick did not embrace their celebratory spirit. The image of a painted Japanese warship haunted him: it reached out to him in his dreams. His mind circled like a caged animal with nowhere to escape, and unsettled feelings of consternation surged once again. Were they ever really absent?

The men were on the move. Nick and Charles guided John, trying to keep him from collapsing. Charles carried both his own and John's kit.

"Fuck, how in the hell do they expect us to climb up these fucking steps?" Charles whinged. John gave a slight gaze at the poor attempt of the assembled rope steps, his stomach cramping, praying he wouldn't shit himself during the climb – that's if he could even make it.

Japanese guards positioned themselves on the dock at intervals of five feet. Their stance was formidable; steely grave faces and black anthracite eyes leered expressionlessly. Long bamboo poles, now an extension of their existence, whirled in the air. Their performance was one of sure intimidation, in case a prisoner tried to escape. Which was impossible! The only escape would be a jump in the harbour, where drowning would be a Godsend – that's if you managed to dodge a shower of bullets.

The sound of bamboo smacking skin hurried the line of feeble bodies along; no matter the effort, it was never sufficient under the scrutiny of the Japs. "*Hyaku, hyaku!*" (hurry up) a Jap guard spat out, in sync with a good landing of bamboo.

Most of the boys in the 2nd Battalion were aboard, apart from Nick, Pie, Charles, and John, who in all his strength could not force the climb. Nick grabbed the rope first and pulled himself up. For his mere weight his body felt heavy, and no energy gave way.

"John, grab my trews and hang tight," Nick instructed. Charles was behind John, pushing his back end up with a thrust of his shoulder while keeping both kits intact. Laughter was heard below, the Japs finding this an amusing sight. "*Damme, damme!*" (foolish idiots).

The disparaging laughter tore through Pie's already oppressed good nature. He tried, he tried hard, but gave way. "You fucking yellow bastards!" His yelling bellowed up the ladder to the deck of the ship where the POWs looked down with grimaces, but hearts full of vigour. Poor Pie took a solid beating. Four over-enthusiastic Japs were just waiting for an excuse (not that they ever needed one) and unleashed a fury of bamboo.

Pie often took a beating, more so for his towering height and mass of red hair. The Japs took pleasure in beating the taller men; their height intimidated the Japs, and it provoked the most violent of beatings. It was a most peculiar sight watching a Jap guard standing on a wooden stool, leering down at his adversary, slapping him senseless. And if a stool was not within reach, the guard had the prisoner kneel, making for a more forceful slap as the guard planted his feet on solid ground. One could not determine if the wicked laughing was worse than the act of slapping itself. And God forbid the blessing of red hair from your homeland, because you were just asking for trouble then. The Japanese believed a deviousness lurked within a man with red hair.

Once all the men were aboard, Lieutenant Hideo Wada welcomed them. Nick was pleased to see Happy was joining them, an ally within the enemy. He hoped this was Happy's ticket home. *Someone needs a fucking happy ending*, Nick thought.

The men were positioned in groups by their commanding officers, and a short briefing took place on how maintaining discipline and conducting oneself in an orderly fashion would be essential during the journey.

The men were pleased to hear that once they were established in their quarters, food and water would be provided.

"Christ!" Nick whispered to himself as he inspected the wooden structures protruding out from the deck; each plank of raw wood was no wider than two feet and just long enough to accommodate twelve men. Each hole was no more than a foot in diameter. This, the men learnt was their latrine. "Hope they're nae excepting us to sit our arses on those contraptions," Rab protested with a quizzical expression.

Ian tilted his head in between Nick and Rab, eyeing the row of holes. "Ye ken, we'll have some clean arses, just like one of those fancy French bowls," Ian stated with a half-hearted laugh.

Pie leaned in, and even bent over, he was a head taller than the rest. "It's called a bidet. And I'll nae be sticking my arse over any part of open water." A slash of bamboo struck all four men simultaneously. The Japs precision was flawless. The men shuffled back into line. Nick's stomach turned, and his hatred turned more.

Each man would have an allotted period to carry out their business, so the instructions specified. Men with dysentery would be allowed to skip the line. Pie cautiously, not wanting to draw attention from the guard, angled his head slightly towards Nick.

"Well, Christ! That's half us lot. When in bloody hell is Churchill going to make a move to get us the hell oot of here? Christ! It's already been nearly a year!"

Nick gave a nod to Pie's remark, but his focus was on Lieutenant Hideo Wada marching up and down, assessing the POWs, his disdaining guise lording. He kept his hands clasped behind his back, and each step he took was precise. Flashes of blinding light danced around the men's heads, piercing their eyes. The sun now appeared, reflecting off Wada's medals, adding to his intimidation. His minions were running around following orders, bowing at every cessation.

There was a total of 1,800 British soldiers aboard the 7,000-ton freighter. Three holds at the bowel of the freighter were to be home until they reached their destination. Orders were being discharged by the British lieutenant commanding officer, he, alongside Captain Cuthberston would oversee the Middlesex Regiment and the Royal Scots Battalion.

John, still holding his own, stood between Nick and Charles. As far as Nick could account, almost his entire unit was on board. There were still men left behind in Hong Kong, but they were to make the next ship, so the men were told.

"The sea will be a warm welcome, Nick, a bit of fresh air is what us lot are in desperate need of," Jordie assessed, then added, "And I'm sure we will experience better food."

Nick wished he could agree with his pal, only he couldn't.

Ian shifted his stance, turning to face Nick and Jordie. "It's good to be getting out of that fucking hellhole. Assuredly, word is out what is going on over here in Hong Kong – it won't be long, and Churchill will be assembling attack tactics and rescue parties."

Soldiers ranked as privates forged through the war with great discipline and purpose. To serve country and king was considered a great honour. The fall of Hong Kong was not only a cataclysmic blow, it was an incessant embarrassment. Fingers pointed in every direction; the blame was merciless. The Japanese were severely underestimated. The once-regarded inferior and sloppy regiments of little, yellow, bandy-legged men with slanted eyes and imbecile-like behaviour defeated the Canadian and Indian battalions. And to the perturbation of the Royal Scots, the entire British army.

Nick's mind toiled over and over. The stretch of the eighteen-day battle played perpetually in his mind. He could only conclude that outside of perhaps the British's arrogance and egotistical behaviour, their defeat was somehow already predetermined. All the odds were stacked against them: first and foremost, the Japanese outnumbered them. The Canadians had arrived late, and over half had not finished their training. And only days before the battle the Royal Scots were posted in a zone of unfamiliar territory, where during preparation half the troops became stricken with malaria. Lastly, they had received no reinforcements and were left to fight alone under the scrutiny of the world.

Hindsight is a dangerous affliction. Its burden heavy, it scourges the mind into persecution. Nick knew he had to free his mind of its tyranny. They fought with passion and courage for their country and king, and then they fought for one another.

The fallacious judgment made on the once considered "impregnable fortress" would see each POW suffer, either by torture, starvation, or death.

The sun filtered through the dissipating clouds as the *Lisbon Maru* pulled out from Hong Kong's harbour.

## CHAPTER SEVENTEEN

## *It's a Long Way to Tipperary*

*September 1942. Leaving Hong Kong*

Before he began his tour with the Royal Scots, Nick had completed a mural for a well-to-do lady. She had a large cottage in the Fairmilehead district, south of Edinburgh. She was born and raised in Aberdeen and came from family money. She married a chap who was the bookkeeper for Alexander Hall & Sons, Aberdeen shipbuilders. Now a widow, she lived in an oversized home, surrounded by paintings of old ships, replicas of ships, and a collection of countless old books about ships. At first, Nick thought her inquiry about painting an old ship on her sitting-room wall was daft. However, once immersed in his composition, his artistic senses became aroused as he watched the ship come to life under his brushstrokes.

When the mural was completed, the lady stood in silence, inspecting each and every inch of the majestic painting. Nick noticed her stoic profile soften, a slight smile surface, and her eyes brighten as she finished her appraisal. "You forgot one item of detail, Mr. Massaro," she observantly mentioned. "Every great artist signs his work." She picked up one of the small paintbrushes. Nick obliged and signed his name in small letters below the base of the ship: Nichol Massaro, 1939. The lady paid him well and thanked him for painting the "fresco," and he overlooked her incorrect interpretation of the technique. Nick modestly smiled and thanked her; after all, she was the customer, and a good-paying one at that.

The picture she asked him to paint had been given to her husband by the shipyard's owner, more or less in payment or trade of service for his love of the old painted relic. Nick learnt the lady's husband was not only obsessed with the *Scottish Maid* but her history. It was the first clipper ship to be built in the Aberdeen shipyard in 1839, and the old schooner constructed out of wood was the first vessel with a raked stem, what was famously known as the Aberdeen Bow. The ship was built for speed and steadiness, and many a route was conducted by means of trade between London and ports of Scotland.

Before Nick began his depiction of the ship, he studied each fragment of the deceased artist's work. A small inscription in the right-hand corner caught his eye: it was the artist's faint signature, *J. Fanner, 1888*.

The sitting room was one of considerable affluence, and it took a great deal of effort not to eye all the contents without appearing intrusive. Nick drew his attention towards another painting, another ship called *Jho Sho Maru*.

"Go ahead, Mr. Massaro, you are more than welcome to study it."

Nick quickly turned, startled by the lady's response. "There is something very haunting about this ship," he expressed.

"Aye, this ship was Japan's first warship, built in 1869 by Alexander Hall and Company. Another one of my husband's favourites. Her first tour was to Japan in 1869 upon her completion, destined for Nagasaki, the capital city."

As Nick continued to study the painting, he couldn't shake the unexplained feelings of consternation.

♣♣♣

It was easy to lose oneself, and Nick watched many a soldier unhinge with madness. Imprisonment affected each man differently. Keeping sane became just as important as any of their other survival tactics. And each morning Nick woke, he prayed for perseverance.

The warmth from the sun caressed his face, and the fresh sea air filled his lungs. As Nick stood on the deck, an unconquerable hunger to survive overwhelmed him. And within that moment, he remembered who he was: not a deteriorating prisoner, but a man with a passion to live. He felt unfettered, regardless of how short-lived. A violent butt struck his shoulder, and he staggered to find his footing. The second blow from the guard's gun pushed him forward, reaching the line-up of POWs waiting to be lowered into the bowel of the ship. *Remember who you are, Nick,* he said to himself. *Remember who you are!*

Before the men entered the holds, the Japanese guards stripped them of their rings, watches, and chains: gifts from loved ones, family heirlooms, pieces of home never to be seen again. Nick held his kitbag tight, thankful his St. Michael was out of sight – tucked away.

Accompanying the 1,800 British prisoners were 800 Japanese soldiers. Their tour of rape, pillaging, and killing in Hong Kong had ended, making way for the arrival of fresh troops.

Nick hadn't seen Happy since the men were ordered to line up and could only assume he was taking orders with great obedience, though with great despair. The three lines began moving. Nick watched as men from the Royal Navy started lowering into the first hold near the bow of the ship. The Royal Artillery troops lowered into the third hold at the stern, and the Royal Scots and Middlesex would occupy the middle – the second hold.

They stood, crammed like sea urchins in a bucket. The air reeked of damp, mouldy steel. The only shed of light peeked in through the hatch, lighting up a small circumference about the rusted ladder, in which hundreds of POWs' faces stared skyward, assuredly contemplating their fate. Promised food and water were served. Not that they expected anything formal; they'd learnt to eat rice using their hands AND eat droppings that fell on the ground, they even ate watery soup prepared in old oil drums. But when the steel buckets fed by ropes descended, the harsh reality on how they were viewed by the Japanese could not have been any more blatant. The POWs were looked upon as nothing less than animals.

It was essential that order and discipline be preserved. Captain Cuthberston was vigilant with his directive. The men stood shoulder to shoulder passing buckets of watery rice, with lumps of unrecognisable meat and a green slimy vegetable, around in an orderly manner, ensuring each man received his share of food and water.

"You're right, Jordie, it's a grade above Shamshuipo standards." Nick swallowed his last mouthful of unpalatable grub. No matter how horrid the food, you ate, as you never knew if it would be your last meal.

"Aye, I told you," Jordie replied with a shake in his voice. "Now, I didna count on such pleasing accommodations."

Nick assessed their surroundings. The walls were shedding a mouldy, rusted layer of steel, and the low ceiling closed in, prohibiting any air circulation. Pie shuffled himself around, facing Nick. "Fuck, ye canna even sit doon. Dae they expect us to stand the entire trip?"

It didn't take long before the damp hold transformed into a sweat room. There were close to 500 men in the hold, and the clamour of voices caused a restive atmosphere.

Captain Cuthberston addressed the men, reiterating the importance of order. "We must remain calm, keep our composure. We are soldiers of the British Army, and it's our duty to carry on with great discipline. Our survival depends on it."

It seemed order and prayer were all the men had left. Their hopes of being rescued and returning home had all vanished. Regardless of the repulsive conditions the camps in Hong Kong had been under, it was familiar territory in which the men remained confident that rescue operations would reach. Relocating to a country of no military intelligence reduced the men's chances of ever being rescued, and escaping assuredly was out of the question. Some of the men felt they would receive better treatment in Japan – surely Emperor Hirohito, under the scrutiny of the world, would prohibit such inhumane treatment.

The men formed groups and assigned rotating shifts to use the latrines and collect some duly required fresh air. Nick, Pie, and Charles helped John climb the iron ladder leading out of the hold. On deck were mainly Japanese soldiers, and the POWs did everything possible to stay clear of their way. Nick caught sight of Lieutenant Wada, who was bellowing at what Nick could best assess was an official of some sort. They were in a heated conversation.

"Best stay away from that, mate." A lad from the Royal Artillery was on deck, waiting for his latrine visit. "That is Kyoda Shigeru, he's the captain of this fine vessel. And from what I've gathered so far, the pair do not get along."

After a few introductions, Nick asked what the conditions were like in hold three. By this time Ian, Jordie, Rab, and Danny had joined the queue.

"It's deplorable, the smell is suffocating, and some of our poor boys afflicted with dysentery cannot make the climb. We've asked for buckets for the poor sods, and we've yet to be given any. The fucking Japs just stand and laugh." Once the line moved, the lad wished Nick luck and made his way to the makeshift latrine.

Before they were shoved back down the hold, Nick noticed the ship was moving at a steady pace, hugging China's coastline. It was only fleeting, but the thought of jumping overboard and swimming to the mainland crossed his mind. He couldn't shake the foreboding feeling trapped inside his gut. It sank further as he made his way back down the ladder.

It was shortly after midnight, October first. Word was they were close to Shanghai and soon would cross the East China Sea to Japan. The conditions had declined horribly, and men had positioned empty food buckets to use as a toilet, as those inflicted with dysentery could still not make the climb. The stench was abhorrent, and to make matters worse men started vomiting; some from the foul, confined air, others from sea sickness. They took turns, allowing groups of men to lie down and sleep, but the stench was worse at ground level. It pervaded the confines of the dirt-packed floor, resulting in further retching.

They carried on with discipline and dignity to the best of their abilities. Nick knelt beside John and wrapped a wet cloth over John's face in an effort to filter the smell. John lay curled on his side. He hadn't made it up to the latrine in over twenty-four hours, and he lay in his own shite, piss, and vomit. The sounds of men choking and heaving were distressing; there was nothing anyone could do. Men were standing, kneeling, and lying, and none uttered a word.

The explosion came out of nowhere, and the ship jolted hard. Men fell and slid through the excrement and piss that spilled from the overturned buckets. It was difficult to see anything outside the beam of light coming through from the hatch, and everything else was dark. Nick faintly discerned black mounds of men's bodies scattered all around and atop one another. Loud screams blared throughout the hold. Guards frantically shoved the POWs who were on deck back into the holds: Patrick and Frank were two.

"Slow doon!" Pie seized Frank's arm. "Slow doon!"

Frank began the commentary, and Patrick finished. It was all the boys could spurt out before the hatches were battened down. They'd been hit: a torpedo had bolted through starboard, hitting the engine room at the stern.

"Christ, the Japs have gone mad! They're no letting any prisoners stay on deck. They're all running aboot screaming." Patrick lost his footing on the slimy dirt floor and as Nick steadied him, he heard Lieutenant Wada and Captain Shigeru above, arguing. Evidently Wada prevailed, as Nick heard the clamp of the tarp as it covered the timber baulks, extinguishing the daylight. Fear tore through his gut and expelled out through his mouth. How long would they last without air?

Captain Stewart yelled out, appealing to the men not to move around, to save energy and breathing air. All they could do was stay still and pray.

It had been nearly twenty-four hours that the men had been entombed in the bowel of the ship with no food or water. One could not describe the fear that raced throughout; it coiled and twisted, wrapping tightly around their lungs and heart. Nick held his breath, listening to the explosion of depth charges and the performance of gunfire from above on deck. And when he inhaled, he gasped upon the little foul oxygen that lingered.

The stench was insufferable, and the men were made to relieve themselves where they lay or stood. The taste of death resided in their mouths and it pulsated throughout their veins at each and every heartbeat. The heat was so hazardous they could feel themselves dehydrate with each drip of sweat. Nick felt his cracked lips split as he opened his mouth to gulp for air, and the bleeding drops tasted like a blessing. He knew if they didn't get out soon, they would die. John was now on his hands and knees and Nick could hear John's stomach constrict each time he drew a breath.

A tapping of Morse code broke through from hold one. The Royal Navy at the bow described the same atrocious conditions as the Royal Scots and Middlesex. The tapping continued, communicating that they'd heard a few ships arrive and the Japanese evacuate. Some guards remained onboard, but that number could not be determined.

The critical news came from the Royal Artillery in hold three. The lean of the ship caused much concern, and it was lodged on a sand bank. The bow remained upright above the water. Gravely, the stern was submerged and men were trying desperately to pump out the water but their weakened bodies were no match against the force of the gushing sea. Nick gave a prayer to the chap he met on deck at the latrine, and then he prayed for them all.

The ship was listing, and panic now set in. It was evident the Japanese were prepared to let the POWs drown. Nick heard a scurry of men climbing the ladder, and alarmed voices called out. A sound of broken timber and the slashing of tarp raised a bolster of cheer, and never was there a more glorious sight than the light of day that broke through. A breath of air took hold. One of the Royal Scots had smuggled a knife onboard, and never was there a better time for its worth.

What transpired next could only be described as a state of sure pandemonium, and at best a ruthless slaughter. The first of the Royal Scots that broke through the hatch were shot by overzealous guards. A second wave of determined Scots overtook the guards and made it to hold one, releasing the timber baulks, and a flood of POWs began jumping overboard. The ship began to move from her perch, and it would only be a matter of time before she sank. The men who couldn't swim were grabbing hold to the next, and others clutched to shared life belts. There had only been a half dozen lifeboats for 1,800 prisoners, and enough life belts to save less than half. The force of the current swept many of the men under, never to be seen again. Nearby, a cluster of small islands posed as a salvation, though the treacherous rocks proved to be deadly, as men crashed to their death.

Nick took hold of a sizable plank of wood and pulled himself up. The jump overboard was unavoidable, as there was no other means of escape. There was no time to think, and he jumped instinctively into the water full of frenzied men. His body performed without contemplation. The will to survive blindly possessed his actions. He only came back into himself when he seized the plank of wood. It was then his body and mind surrendered to the point of sure exhaustion. He was parched, his mouth was as dry as a desert, and while he licked at his stinging, cracked lips, he was tempted to swill down the entire salty sea.

It wasn't long after Nick had secured the wooden plank and managed to pull John aboard that a handful of Royal Scots joined, clinging on for dear life. Ian, Charles, and Jordie were in the mix. They were at the mercy of the current, and bodies, dead and alive, floated by.

It hadn't taken long, just hours after they were first captured and imprisoned at Camp Shamshuipo. The prisoners learnt that the Japanese failed lamentably to conform to any standards of moral virtue, and their deplorable conduct in Hong Kong was nothing short of evil. But this was diabolical!

The sound of gunfire terrorised the wild, thrashing sea of men. Nick watched as the prisoners were being picked off; streams of blood flowed, bodies riddled with bullets plummeting below the surface. Prisoners who tried climbing into the surrounding Japanese boats were ruthlessly thrust back into the sea. Nick and his crew had fortunately drifted away from the Japanese sport of target practice.

There they were, wet, hungry, and thirsty, drifting along the coastline of China. They'd lost all their possessions, all for the clothes on their backs, but were nevertheless thankful to be alive, regardless of the afflictions endured. The sun shone bright, and the warm breeze carried Nick's ditty across the rolling waves. The boys joined in, singing, *"It's a long way to Tipperary. It's a long way to go. It's a long way to Tipperary. To the sweetest girl I know!"*

They were picked up hours later by a Japanese gunboat. The Japanese sailed around for three days retrieving the remaining prisoners from the open water and the cluster of islands. Rumour had it that a few escaped.

The weather changed drastically, and cold, hard rain fell. The men huddled together under leaky tarps. They received only stale biscuits and tepid milk. A few prisoners died before they landed in Shanghai on October fifth. Those that had been separated were once again reunited. Nick was relieved to see Pie and the rest of the boys. Pie hugged John, grateful his comrade survived.

Out of the 1,800 prisoners, 846 lost their lives. The men wouldn't learn until later that the torpedo launched was by an American submarine, the USS *Grouper*. The greatest death toll among prisoners of the Far East was executed at sea. The Japanese ships transporting prisoners never identified their cargo. And after the war, it was determined that one in three who died on the ships were killed by Allied fire.

The prisoners, with great apprehension, had boarded the *Shensei Maru*. Another hell ship, the men claimed. The stench and deplorable conditions proved to be no better than its sister ship, the *Lisbon*. They would now sail across the open sea to Japan.

Nick now found time to rest his mind after the five-day ordeal, and he pushed away the images of the frantic men trying to stay afloat, trying to survive. He then pushed away the images of the dead sinking to their watery graves.

He'd lost everything but his kit bag, all its contents spilled out, including his St. Michael. He could only find solace that his pendant lay in the depths of the sea, vigilantly watching over the brave men who'd unjustifiably lost their lives. And he knew his mother would concur.

He re-tied his red bandana, an article that, unbeknownst to him, would one day symbolise and honour the fallen.

# Part Four

*Far and Awa' - Tis the Twine of Siblings That Keeps Us Near*

## CHAPTER EIGHTEEN

# *Siblings: the Keepers of Our Hearts, Our Souls, Our Secrets*

*September 1934. Edinburgh*

Hannah had entered the kitchen desperate for a cuppa. "Rena. Ye ken I feel daft calling you that."

Rena responded with a grown-up air of pretension. "Well, that is the name I now go by."

Hannah chuckled, grabbing her teacup. "Well, if I call you Alexandrena, would you answer?"

Rena shrugged her shoulders and gave a wary grin. "Perhaps." She poured the tea into their cups and took notice of Hannah's expression when she reminded her sister of the family dinner. "Ye didna forget did you?" Rena asked.

"Aye, I did! Oh, Rena! I canna stay. This is Victor's last night in Edinburgh, and I promised him I would spend the evening with him."

Rena gave her sister a look that only another sister can give when inflicting guilt.

"I dinna ken when I will see him again. He's always running off to Africa, his father is determined to have him enlist into the Royal Navy."

"Hannah, you need to tell Mum and Da of yer plans. Ye havna even brought Victor around. This will kill them both, ye canna keep dodging it."

Hannah knew her sister was right, but she also knew the news would break her parents' hearts. She and Victor had made plans to move to Africa once she completed school. Hannah had tried many times to broach the subject with her parents, but she could never muster up enough courage. And she wasn't prepared for her father's inquisition of a million questions he would impose on her, and more so on Victor.

Victor had taken the news quite well when Hannah informed him that she was not yet ready to introduce him to the family. She did speak with Mary, as her sister had a way of dealing with her father, something Hannah had not yet mastered.

She sipped at her tea and decided she would consult with Mary once Mary and Morogh arrived.

Hannah had met Victor after befriending his sister Grace. The girls met on their first day of university. They had found themselves lost and desperately trying to find their first class. A hasty arrival at the classroom entrance resulted in the girls knocking into each other: books crashing to the floor, papers flying all around, a commotion attracting the austere Mrs. McKenzie, the girls' microbiology teacher.

A couple of months later Grace introduced her older brother. She often spoke of Victor; how close they were, and how much she missed him. Grace's parents lived in Port Elizabeth, Africa, as did Victor. His father was an admiral in Her Majesty's Naval Service. Victor was in training to follow in his father's occupational footsteps. The Ainsworths were originally from Newcastle before emigrating to South Africa. Grace lived in Edinburgh with her aunt, her mother's sister. The first thing the girls shared in common was that both their fathers were from Northern England, and secondly, their mothers were of Scottish descent.

"That's a grand start right there, Hannah," Grace claimed.

Victor was asked to stay in Edinburgh after their aunt's husband's death and assist in the sale of her estate. He found Edinburgh beautiful and decided to prolong his visit, but more so he had fallen for Hannah Helliwell.

Victor had arrived at the university to pick his sister up. Grace was adamant Hannah join them. His car was luxurious, one that Hannah had never seen before. She learnt it was a German model that had cost his parents a pretty pound or two, Victor alleged with a hearty laugh.

Hannah couldn't help herself; she stood staring at him, assessing his strikingly handsome face and his polished attire. He wore a brown herringbone sport coat over a butter-coloured yellow waistcoat, and his tan pants boasted a precise seam. A chocolate-brown wool cap complemented his fair, thick hair. His eyes were the lightest of blue; they looked aqua when captured in the sun. He so resembled his sister.

Sheepishly, Hannah drew her focus away. In turn, Victor was now assessing her. She wished she had put a bit of effort into her grooming this morning. Not to make excuses, but nevertheless, mornings were a challenge. Finding time in the privy between sisters was a task, to say the least. Hannah's jumper could have used a press. She'd known that when she left the house. Already running late, she hated to ask her mother, who appeared to have enough on her hands getting Margaret out the door on time.

Hannah was tall and slender, the second tallest of the Helliwell girls, next to her sister Emma. Hannah took on her father's fairness as well as his height. Her hair was a medium blonde, and when worn down it fell midway to her back. Her eyes were a striking blue, another trait of her father's.

"Well, Gracie, you didn't tell me how beautiful your mate is. I certainly would have been picking you up more frequently." Hannah could sense Victor looking at her as he spoke, but she dared not meet his gaze in consideration of the pink flush rising across her cheeks. His accent was most definitely Northern England. It reminded her of her father's family, who still resided in Yorkshire. She still avoided glancing his way, at least until her high colour wore off.

"Away with you, Victor, don't be embarrassing poor Hannah. How about you take us for a ride? We can stop off at a pub for some lunch and a pint." Grace didn't wait for an answer. She opened the passenger-side door and motioned Hannah to climb in. "I will take the back," Grace said. She jumped in, wasting no time.

Before Hannah realised, Victor was by her side, holding the door open. Duly instructed, Hannah climbed in without a peep.

"Care for a fag?" Victor asked as he held the package towards Hannah.

"No ... no, thanks, I dinna smoke," Hannah replied.

"I will take one." Grace slipped her arm between the two front seats, plucked one, and lit it. "Do take us somewhere special, Victor, we need a reprieve from that cow of a teacher, Mrs. McKenzie." Grace chuckled, then took a deep drag.

Hannah admired Grace's free spirit: she rarely worried about things, like school, homework, what her mates thought. Least of all restrictions. Yet she achieved good grades, was popular among her mates, and knew how to have a good time. Hannah was definitely more reserved and was fighting off her guilty feelings of missing school.

"Discipline and order are paramount in the Helliwell household," Hannah advised her friend when asked to skip classes.

"Of course they are, Hannah, how can it not be with all those bairns? My God, you must feel stifled. You need to break free a bit and enjoy life," Grace responded.

It was easy for her friend, being it was only ever her and Victor. They were accustomed to travel, money, and a particular type of freedom: all foreign to Hannah. Admittedly she felt excited, and she gave way and threw caution to the wind. There was no turning back. After all, she was sitting in a fancy car beside a handsome English chap. Her father should somewhat approve, she thought, smiling.

"Well, ladies, where shall we set our sights on this fine day?" Victor lit his cigarette with a silver lighter. Hannah noticed the engraved initials VEA. She wanted to ask him what the E stood for but was still embarrassed to speak.

They drove along the seaside, windows down, accompanied by Duke Ellington blaring from the car radio. A score of jazz and the sun's warm touch set the mood. A strong breeze danced across the sea, spraying a soft shower of cool mist through the windows, and in unison, they shrilled with delight. Victor pulled into Granton Harbour, destination, the Royal Forth Yacht Club. "We've arrived," Victor said with an air of pretension.

"Oh Victor, how exciting. Come, Hannah, we are in for a treat." Grace grabbed her purse and jumped out of the car. Hannah grabbed hers and fumbled to release the handle. Victor was already by the door, and he opened it and extended his hand. It was soft and warm, his touch tender, and Hannah could feel a warm sensation flood her entire body. She tried not to blush, but her fair skin had a mind of its own.

As they entered the club, the doorman greeted Victor and Grace. It was obvious to Hannah that the yacht club was a common social hangout for her friend and her brother. They sat at a small round table positioned in front of a large window that overlooked the spectacular view of the sea. The clubhouse was beautifully furnished, with tables draped in white linen, centrepieces of crystal vases containing fresh-cut flowers, and tiny crystal ashtrays filled with wooden match sets.

Hannah was taken in with the elegant surroundings, so much so that she didn't notice the two young women standing at the table speaking with Victor. Hannah had only taken a brief look and knew right away they were from wealth. Extravagant clothes, the latest hair fashion, perfectly manicured – even their lipstick was flawless.

Both women ignored Hannah and Grace, their attentiveness entirely on Victor. They were both giggling and stroking Victor's shoulders as they leered over him, each trying to outperform the other. Their strong perfumes caught Hannah's throat, and she coughed unexpectedly. Both girls gave a side glance of offense.

"Ladies, I must tend to my guests, do enjoy your afternoon," Victor excused them ever so politely. "Sorry, girls, just some friends, wanting to check in."

"Oh, please, Victor, they were wanting more than to check in; they could not have been more brazen if they tried." Grace flipped her hand in a show of disgust.

"Let's order some champagne, shall we?" Victor said as he slid his chair back to stand.

He returned from the bar with a bottle of champagne and three glasses. By the time the bottle was empty, Hannah's head was swimming. The club became busier, noisier, clouds of smoke filled the air, and conversations and laughter engulfed her. She felt like she was going to topple. She tried steadying herself and realised she'd hardly eaten all day, which certainly contributed to her state of drunkenness.

"Are you alright, Hannah?" Grace asked as she grabbed Hannah's arm.

"No, I'm afraid. I feel very unsteady."

Victor, also concerned with Hannah's welfare, gathered the girls and escorted them through the crowd of clanging glasses and boisterous cheers.

Outside, the sea air aroused Hannah's senses, and immediately she felt she could breathe and the overwhelming feeling of swooning dissipated. Grace hugged her friend and laughed. "Hannah, my love, you do need a few lessons in champagne drinking."

Hannah never really touched alcohol, the odd time a shandy with her sister Lily, but that was it.

"Come, Hannah, let's get you out of here," Victor said as he led her back to the car. "We can drive along the shore with the windows down, let the breeze sober you up a bit." As they drove, Hannah turned and faced the window, allowing the breeze to wave around her. It was a slight improvement, although she was still a wee intoxicated.

Victor pulled the car over. They had arrived at Portobello Beach, twenty minutes from the yacht club. "Let's stretch our legs, shall we?" Victor stepped out of the car first then came around to Hannah's side and opened her door. "Come, Hannah, my dear, let's walk off your champagne." Victor took her hand and helped her from the seat.

"I'm just going to stay put and have a fag. I'm nae in that much of a rush to lose my champagne," Grace said with a wee chortle.

Hannah followed Victor's lead, and they walked along the shoreline. Victor did most of the conversing. He spoke so eloquently and told her of Africa and how beautiful it was, and the experiences he had encountered in such a foreign land. The safaris and hunting exhibitions, all accompanied by his father. The sailing, he continued, was his favourite. His father owned a large sailboat, and the family shared many adventures along the coast.

"The coastline is stunning. The Indian Ocean engulfs the eastern coast with her warm waters and meets up with the Atlantic at the southern tip, where we've done many a sail to Cape Town. It's intoxicating, Hannah, and I think I would like to one day share that with you." Victor came to a halt, turned, and faced Hannah. He placed his arm around her waist and pulled her in so that her breasts brushed against his chest. Hannah was only a couple of inches shorter than Victor; they almost mirrored each other. Both tall and slender, blonde hair, slim features. Each revealing their bluest of eyes. He leaned in and kissed her, and his kiss was deep and long. His tongue softly parted her lips and gently explored her mouth. She had never been kissed like this. And as nervous as Hannah was, she couldn't pull away, nor did she want to. Victor cupped her chin, tracing his forefinger along her lips, completing his seductive kiss. "You're simply ravishing, Hannah. I must see you again."

Hannah, who rarely said no to her family, agreed with Rena that she would meet up with Victor after the family dinner. However, she did not commit to when she would break the news about Africa to her parents. She sensed Rena's frustration and ignored her sister's sideways glance of suppressed impatience.

Everyone was excited that their sister Mary was coming home. Rena smiled watching her mother bake cookies and cakes, singing and twirling as she pulled each baking sheet from the oven. "My lass is coming hame and she is bringing her bairns. My heart feels it will burst." Rena regarded each one of her mother's blithesome outbursts as harmonious interludes, breaking free from a place of loss and despair. She admired her mother's fortitude, and she could appreciate the importance of each family gathering.

"Lass, would you mind helping oot?" their mother asked Hannah, who gulped her last bit of tea, gave her mother a nod, and grabbed a dish towel.

She nearly dropped the soapy plate at the sound of her brother's voice. "Just in time for some shortbread and a cuppa, I see." William had snuck into the house unnoticed. Brodie's hearing had deteriorated, but his sense of smell remained acute. He slowly made his way through to sniff the new arrival. William gave the old dog a pat on the head before kissing his mother's cheek. "I've brought some socks, hoping you could dae a bit of darning."

"Aye, leave them in the sitting room by my knitting box," Catherine replied, tapping her son's hand as he tried sneaking another cookie.

William had been living on his own for just over a year, though he seemed to be at home more than at his own flat. He was spoilt, no doubt. After all, he was his mother's only laddie. He didn't mind too much being the only male, apart from his father, that was.

He fell in the rank of being born in the middle and he considered himself to have the best of three worlds. The first realm was his older sisters, Jessie, Betty, and Catherine J, and they were all delighted to receive a wee brother. And they all spoilt their wee Willie.

The middle realm, only a few years younger than himself, were Emma and Mary. This realm was not as easy to manipulate as the elder and junior realms. He so found himself dodging this realm, especially his sister Emma; she took no part in his nonsense and did not find it necessary to indulge him. Mary took pleasure in tormenting him and found it amusing to tattle. "William, do leave our Mary alone, why do you upset her so?" their mother would say. A tongue of tease protruded at attention, while crocodile tears vanished as quickly as they appeared. Mary stood behind her mother clinging onto apron strings, provoking her brother's good nature, which the older realm did so perceive.

The junior realm turned out to be the most fun as first and foremost, teasing and tall tales earned giggles and joyful smiles. Eyes alit with enthusiasm viewed in the kaleidoscope of his colourful, changing stories. Rena loved her brother's stories, even though she knew they were just that. "Tell us another rhyme, William," Hannah would request.

"Tell us one of yer jokes that Da would nae like," Lily quietly demanded.

Margaret, too young for tall tales and teasing, toddled around spoilt by all.

William was caught short of sneaking another cookie when Hannah threw him a dish towel. He was close to a protest, but Rena's glare shot him down. He picked up a dripping teacup and began drying it.

"I ran into Robert," William mentioned to Rena, and she passed him a wet plate. "He was heading to the Hibs game. Fine lad, he is."

Rena smiled, agreeing wholeheartedly.

William loved all his sisters. However, he had a deep affection for Rena, though he could never express it in words; it was just there, in his heart. Sometimes his ten-year gap with her felt like it was hundred. And when he would try to speak to her about his plans of joining the regiment, she merely brushed him off.

He caught her by surprise one evening, elbows deep in soapy water with a pile of dishes as high as William Wallace's monument. "Sis, I will be off to explore the world and, if a war should break, I'll be fighting for our country, our honour."

She grabbed the next set of dirty dishes and plunked them in the sink. "Well, how aboot you first start honouring yer sister and help with these dishes."

"A soldier canna be doing dishes . . ." He blethered on while his sister huffed with a roll of an eye. Observing she expressed no interest, he left her to finish the dishes in peace.

He knew his sister had no intentions of leaving Scotland; she was connected to both family and country. Naturally, she would marry Robert Thomson. William liked the lad. He was a hard worker, and Robert loved his sister and would take great care of her.

But little did William know that his own destined path would set him on an unforeseen journey, one he found following his sister Rena. And in the end, most significant.

The afternoon couldn't come quick enough for Catherine. She flitted around the house, straightening settee pillows, pulling at the curtains, settling on open, allowing the sun to light up the room. It was all Rena could do not to laugh. Her mother was staunch with the gatherings; rarely did anyone escape. But she had to admit, here in these rooms were some of Rena's best memories.

A scuffling sound of paws raced through from the hall. John had returned from walking the dog, and Brodie found his way back to the warmth of the fire. "That bloody dug loves his walks, but I believe he loves that hearth even more," John said, laughing as he hung his cap on the back of the chair. "I'll take a cuppa, lass."

Hannah steadied her hand as she poured the tea. Just the thought of divulging her plans made her shake from the inside out. "Freshly brewed, Da."

John's family clock that he'd inherited from his father chimed three times, setting his wife off into a rage of excitement. One by one they arrived: Emma with wee June, and Betty and Percy with their two lads. Lily was working late but hoped to be home before Mary arrived.

It was Margaret who sounded the arrival. "It's Mary and the bairns. I can see them at the gate. They're here!"

Rena joined her mother at the kitchen window and both looked out onto the path leading up to the gate.

"She looks grand . . . she looks happy. Don't ye think, Rena?"

"Aye, Mum. She does indeed."

## CHAPTER NINETEEN

# A Bed of Yellow Roses

*August 1935. Edinburgh*

A year had passed, school was finished, and Rena and Robert's plans of sharing a life together were falling into place. Rena couldn't have been happier. She opened her bedroom window and let the warm evening breeze drift in. She eyed her collection that sat upon the long wooden shelf that her father had built. Each novel was positioned in order of her favourites. Sometimes she switched them up, depending on her mood. She had read them all, more than once. If she wanted to revisit a storyline or character, she read them again.

Leading her collection was the prestigious Jane Austen, and ending, however, with the highest regard was Ann Radcliffe. Charles Dickens, Henry James, Charlotte Bronte, and Mary Elizabeth Braddon were all esteemed between. In careful consideration, she moved Henry James to the end, moving Ann Radcliffe up to second-last position. After all, Henry James was her only American author, though she loved *The Wings of the Dove*. She had received the book from her uncle James, shipped all the way from Canada. A most cherished gift indeed.

As she was preparing to choose a novel, an interruption of weeping came from outside her bedroom door. The ungreased knob turned, making an annoying screeching sound, though it alerted of any intruders. Her mother stood, Margaret beside her with a rubber hot water bottle, tears streaming.

"Rena." Her mother, a bit hesitant of abbreviating her family name, had eventually given way. "Can you take Margaret in beside ye, lass? She isna feeling well. I'm afraid she has another earache and is very peely wally. Perhaps you can read her one of yer novels."

*Of all the nights*, Rena thought. She was exhausted from a long day at Scott Lyons and only wanted to relax. A whole night to herself, that was the plan once she learnt Robert was attending a football match with his mates. And of all nights for both Lily and Hannah to be out too. "Aye, nae bother, Mum," Rena said, resigned.

Margaret always sought out Hannah when she wasn't well. Of course, who wouldn't? Hannah, with her gentle nature and loving manner; no wonder Victor loved her. She would make a grand nurse. This was not only a sister's biased opinion, everyone so declared. The door closed, and Margaret climbed in bed close beside her sister. Rena unfolded her eiderdown and placed it comfortably on top of them both. Most of Rena's novels had been gifts, for birthdays or Christmases, from Emma. Emma always read to her younger sisters, usually in the evening around the fire or in their bedroom when their parents were in great need of peace and quiet.

Rena read each book title aloud, catching glimpses in between for her sister's approval. Margaret snubbed each one with a shake of her head.

"Ye ken, you are a wee stubborn for someone who is ill." Rena reached under her bed, pulled out a parcel, and unwrapped the paper. "Now, you must nae tell Mum, ye ken, she wouldna approve."

Margaret tilted her head to read the title. The hot water bottle fell away from her aggrieved ear. Her eyes grew large as saucers, and a sweeping smile emerged.

Rena smiled, too, watching her sister's reaction. The title was *Lady Chatterley's Lover*.

It was all the rage with the lassies at Scott Lyons. Elizabeth, now known as Liza, snuck the book, considered scandalous, into work. "Rena, the sex in the book is wonderfully dangerous – it will stimulate feelings one never knew they had. I think . . . I myself am in love with Constance Chatterley."

Liza was viewed as eccentric by many; she was free-spirited, fiercely independent, and liberated. She spoke boldly on many subjects, especially sex. She had the most unconventional upbringing. Her father never remarried; it was just the two of them. Charles had a very liberal approach to raising his daughter. She was well educated in and outside of the classroom.

The two had become the centre of gossip. Mirren's mother Maggie was the pinnacle at spreading whispered rumours, like an infectious germ. Rena was pleased when her mother shot down Maggie's cynical view of Liza's father's unorthodox parenting methods one afternoon over tea. Rena gave her mother an indebted smile for defending her best friend's reputation.

Margaret snuggled in closer, placing the water bottle back in its position. Rena opened the book and began to read aloud.

"*Ours is essentially a tragic age, so we refuse to take it tragically. The cataclysm has happened, we are among the ruins, we start to build up new little habitats, to have new little hopes. It is rather hard work: there is now no smooth road into the future: but we go round, or scramble over the obstacles. We've got to live, no matter how many skies have fallen.*

*This was more or less Constance Chatterley's position. The war had brought the roof down over her head. And she had realised that one must live and learn . . .*"

*Monday September 2, 1935*

It was to be the usual stay, perhaps a few days, only to stave off the fever and infection. The house was quiet – too quiet, Rena's mother insisted, when Margaret wasn't home. Home where she belonged, not confined in a bed at Leith Hospital.

Margaret had never fully recovered from her bout of meningitis from when she was a wee lass. Her earaches were notorious, keeping the entire household up during the night. This time was different; Rena could sense it. Her feelings were affirmed when both Emma and Betty arrived, and pensive expressions were exchanged across the kitchen table. Her mother was fumbling to make a pot of tea, her father was in the back garden pacing, his pipe clenched between his stressed lips. William was away on a plumbing job somewhere in the Lowlands and could not be reached. Brodie paced between the kitchen and sitting room, looking for Margaret. The two had become quite close; even he could sense the foreboding climate in the room.

"For the love of Christ, someone let that bloody dug oot!" Betty snapped, "he's relentless." She lit her cigarette, and a cloud of smoke rose to the ceiling. "Mum, what exactly is the doctor saying?" She took a deep drag after her inquiry.

Rena rose to let Brodie out, as she was sure she couldn't bear the answer. Brodie ran past her as she stepped into the back garden. "What's going on in there, lass?" Her father didn't stop pacing, nor did he look in her direction. She wasn't sure how to reply: if she said making tea, he would think it too rigorous. If she said sitting talking, her father would surely lose his temper.

In a houseful of women, talking was everything; it was the greatest healer of all things. Nothing was better than a blether and a cuppa.

"Talking does not fix everything, action does!" her father commanded when the Helliwell lassies were all gathered around the kitchen table.

Rena's mother's riposte was delivered in the fashion only Catherine Johnstone Helliwell could convey. "John, before an action is established, a discussion is most appropriate. You should nae that yerself, being a Cameron Highlander. Besides, you need to talk such things off yer chest. It's what heals the heart – the soul."

John could not and would not argue his wife's declaration. After all, he would have to contend with the Helliwell lassies at arms.

With high consideration, Rena answered, "They are making tea and talking." She thought it best to be curt and to the point. Regardless of what she said, her father would make up his own mind.

Brodie was circling John's legs in a panicked state. Age was catching up with the old terrier. He'd been a part of the family for thirteen years, so how could he not sense such trepidation? "Bloody out the road, dug!" John kicked at the air as he made his way back into the house. Naturally, Brodie followed, panting profusely.

Rena stood alone in the small garden. The air had a familiar chill. She wrapped her arms around her shoulders, pulling them in tightly. Her mother's rose bushes were uninhabited, all but for a single yellow, and it was slowly deteriorating; a few wilted petals lay beneath. All the scented inflorescences had dried and blown with the wind, leaving the lavender stalks bare. Rena's tears welled. She left the garden and all its dying things. *They at least will come back*, she thought.

Hannah and Lily were now among the talking women, with more cups of tea, more prattling. The afternoon turned into early evening. Tea was prepared and dishes washed, all tucked away til the morn. After a belly full of kippers, Brodie had finally settled down in front of the fire. One ear remained perked, waiting – waiting for his Margaret.

Emma had left to pick up June from her mate's house, and she had returned with a tired bundle in need of her bed. "Lass, put the bairn in Rena's room," Catherine instructed, her words sounded drained.

"You mean Rena and Margaret's room?" Rena whispered bitingly. No one heard, though.

The phone rang, June stirred, and Rena jolted upright. As far as she could make out from the moon's faint ray through the window, the small, ornate, gold clock on her nightstand read midnight. She heard two sets of footsteps: her parents, then her sisters.

Her parents left in a taxi. The household was now all awake, except for June. She lay nestled in Margaret's bed, along with Margaret's old, ragged doll, a few rips bound with fresh thread and one eye missing, although still loved and providing comfort.

"There is no use us all being up, ye ken. Mother will call," Hannah said, yawning her last words.

Lily had put the kettle on. "I canna sleep!" she retorted.

Betty came through from the garden with a pail of coal. "A bit cool in here, we are in need of a fire," she stated. Dishes were clanging from the kitchen, and Emma was preparing jam pieces.

*This . . . this is what we do best*, Rena thought. *Under any conditions, particularly a crisis, we function.*

The hours dragged, and still no phone call. Teacups and bread ends lay scattered across the table, the sisters all too tired to tidy. Hannah had fallen asleep at the fire with a textbook in her hand, no doubt studying for an exam. Betty placed a knitted blanket across Hannah's huddled body. "She's awfully tired a lot, is she no?" Betty whispered, not to disturb her sister's sleep.

"Ye ken, she has quite a bit of reading and studying. And after all, it is the wee hours of the morn," Lily replied, releasing a lengthy yawn.

"Outside of all this, I mean." Betty directed her pointer finger in a circular motion, indicating the present circumstances. "She always seems peely wally to me."

"When she is nae studying, she is with Victor, and he is always on the move," Lily replied, tucking her feet under her bum and pulling another knitted blanket from the back of the settee. She continued, "He wants to take her to Africa."

"Africa! What the hell for?" Betty, for the first time hearing this news, was outright aghast.

"To live," Rena chimed in, "he wants her to nurse in Port Elizabeth. There is a new hospital underway. The Ainsworths are donating thousands of pounds to one of its wings. So Hannah explained."

"Bloody hell! Father will not permit such a move, not after losing our Catherine J in Canada. For Christ's sake!" Betty stood, her cheeks a-flame, and not from the fire.

"Betty, do ye have to swear like that?" Emma demanded.

"Aye, Emma, I do!"

*Tuesday, September 3, 1935*

Sheets of steadfast rain swept across George Street, the force of the wind blowing it in sideward. It was hard and relentless. A man walked by the front window, hunched, two hands steady on the shaft of his umbrella, steering the canopy through the weave of the wind. Rumbles of thunder crashed throughout the sky. Brodie jumped and took shelter under the kitchen table, and that crack sounded as if the sky had split.

Mary was drenched, and she struggled to close the door against the wind. She made her way inside unscathed. Hannah came to her rescue with a towel, dabbing her sister's face free from rain, then wiped her tears.

The sitting room was not brightly lit. The curtains were drawn, perhaps to avoid the stormy scene outside, or to prevent the world from looking in. All too familiar with what lay on the other side, Mary knew walking through the entrance would precipitate an unwanted truth: a truth she couldn't bear to endure. Nine years ago, it was Catherine J, and three years ago Jessie and her wee bairn.

Tragic was the loss of both sisters. Jessie's death felt more deep-rooted, not that one could ever compare, but mostly because at the time of Jessie's death, Mary had children of her own, and her maternal empathy bled mercifully for her mother.

She took a deep breath, steadied her tears, and stepped over the threshold. And the world paused. Margaret was absent, absent forever, though her cheeky smile and her teasing manner danced around the room singing, "Ally Bally Bee."

Everyone says time heals, and the reverend even mentioned it in his sermon. *But that's not true*, Rena whispered to herself. Years had passed and her mother still grieved for her two lassies, and now she would grieve for a third.

St. Andrews Leith Church was packed, and some had to gather outside. Everyone had come to say goodbye to Margaret: all her school mates, her swimming team from the Leith bath house, her co-workers from McVitie & Prices biscuit factory. It seemed all of Scotland had come. The abundant attendance deepened Rena's grief, if that was even possible. She sat front-row centre amid her family. William was to her right, Emma to her left. Rena looked around, all the faces steadfast, staring straight ahead, embracing each and every word the reverend delivered. It's losing a bairn that commends such attention.

A boy caught Rena's eye, his dark, thick curls pointed out erratically in all directions, tears trailing his face. She had never seen him before. Rena never really knew many of Margaret's mates, as she always shuffled her wee sister off. "Hang oot with yer own pals, Margaret. Ye dinna need to be chumming me aboot," Rena would command. Something she now sorely regretted.

Outside the church, people stood in clusters, and some approached Rena's mother to offer condolences. Rena's father was not to be found. She tried, on tippy-toes, overlooking the crowds, but nothing. It was a sea of black: black suits, black dresses, black umbrellas. She spotted Lily and Hannah, and they were chatting with neighbours. Mary and William were with another group. She thought she saw Betty, or perhaps it was Emma, their heights almost exact.

She turned quickly, hearing a quivering yet baritone voice. It was the dark-curly-haired lad from inside the church, and he was speaking with her mother. In his hand was a red tin of Jaffa Cakes tied with blue ribbon. Rena made her way over, curious.

"Guid day, mam . . . I mean, sorry, mam . . . sorry for yer loss." Rena's mother was unmoored: she had spent the last days in her bedroom under doctor's orders and some type of medication that made her sleep – too much, Rena discerned.

"My name is Robbie, Robbie Scott. I work at McVities with, or I did, with Margaret. She was going to marry me – in a few years, that is . . . if her da would've allowed us."

Rena smiled. It was obvious this lad was enamoured with her sister.

"The ribbon was Margaret's. I thought you may like it." Robbie nervously handed Catherine the red tin. Rena could see her mother fight back her tears, and she slipped the ribbon off and handed it back to Margaret's young gentleman.

"You keep it, lad, I ken Margaret would have wanted that."

Robbie accepted the ribbon, and he wrapped it around his hand. "That is most kind of ye, Mrs. Helliwell." He gave a slight bow before he bolted off down Easter Road towards the Links.

The rain was tapering, though the sea of black umbrellas remained at attention, all in procession, almost as if a dark cloud was sailing through the street. Yellow roses, Margaret's favourite, and streams of ribbon in her favourite colour, blue, all adorned the glass-covered, horse-drawn carriage.

Rena and Hannah marched behind, hands clenched, holding tight, realising this was their final goodbye to their wee sister. In front were their parents. John had made his way back from wherever he'd made off to. He held his wife close, to keep her from falling, falling from grief, falling forever. They'd lost another, this time their baby, their Margaret. John feared there would be no resuscitation, for this time his wife had lost her anchor. This he knew to be true.

People came and went all day. There was enough food to feed the entire Isle of Britain. Of course, Uncle Jordie and Aunt Lizzie were there; you could count on them in any a crisis. Rena's father's sisters and brother from

Yorkshire arrived, all deeply sad and troubled, their brother losing a third lass, their wee niece, their wee Margaret.

Rena was thankful to see her Uncle Alec and his wife, Iona. They had made the journey all the way from the Shetlands, and it very much pleased her mother.

Catherine's younger brother Alec had moved back to the family farm in Ardersier long after his siblings had left. When his parents passed away, he moved back to the isle with his wife. Catherine hadn't seen her wee brother in years; their embrace was poignant, unyielding. Rena noticed her mother unfetter, if only for a moment. Family had that effect.

The evening was quiet, the house now detached from the outside world. Rena yawned as she tried to find a comfortable position. Brodie, unsettled, jumped from the bottom of the bed, and made his way out of the bedroom. Undoubtedly, he too was lost; disorientated without Margaret's presence.

Mary stirred a bit, then whispered, "You asleep, Rena?"

"No, I dinna think I can," Rena replied, then she sat up. She turned on the small lamp set upon the nightstand between the two beds. "Must you go hame tomorrow, Mary?"

"Aye, Rena, Morogh and the bairns will be needing me, ye ken." Mary threw off the eiderdown and swung her legs around to the side of the bed. "I overheard Da speaking with the doctor. They're both concerned on Mother's recovery. I spoke to Betty, and she will make sure everyone will keep a keen eye and help oot when they can . . . and I will make the journey . . ." Mary paused, cupped her face, and cried.

Rena, still unable to cry herself, wrapped her arms around her sister. "We all are in need of each other, Mary."

Both sisters curled under the covers, entwined within each other's limbs and broken hearts. Margaret's ragged doll lay in between.

Rena, roused by the smell of fried onions and blood pudding, made her way out of bed, leaving Mary still deep in sleep. The fire was blazing, and her father was up cooking breakfast. For a moment everything seemed normal, the way it was just days ago, when Margaret was alive.

"The tea is ready, lass," John turned from the range, wooden spurtle in hand. Tears streamed his face. Rena poured a cup from the pot of fresh brew, sat down, and sipped at her tea.

They both talked at once, and Rena let her father proceed. "I was wanting to say, lass, you will need to be here for your mother, she will be depending on you. I dinna ken how she will survive through this. I'm very concerned, and so is the doctor." John turned away to flip a piece of blood pudding that was starting to stick.

Rena decided not to mention she was thinking of travelling north to Dunnet with Mary. She and Mary had discussed it the night before. Mary had said, "Rena, perhaps you could travel back with me, ye ken, just for a few days. Sometimes it's hard not having the family around . . . in times . . . times like this, I mean. The bairns would love to see you, it's been such a long time." Rena was unsure, but it was something in her sister's voice, a fear almost, a fear that evinced her that Mary could not endure to lose another sister. And perhaps having Rena around for a while would prevent just that. "Sounds grand, Mary, I'll ask Da in the morn."

Brodie budged slightly under the table, his nose turned upright, sniffing at the fry-up of blood pudding. "That bloody dug misses our Margaret something fierce, ye ken, lass." John placed the spurtle on the range, sat down beside his daughter, and began to cry uncontrollably. Rena, sound in her decision, declined to broach the subject of leaving. She knew she was needed at home with her mother, and conceivably, more her father.

## CHAPTER TWENTY

## *Letting Go*

*November 3, 1935. Edinburgh*

"Penny for the Guy! Penny for the Guy!" rang out along George Street. Wheelbarrows and wooden wagons trundled through the cobblestone streets. Old, worn dungarees and a father's once-good shirt padded with strips of rags and old newspapers sat lopsided as heads made out of flour bags with button eyes and imperturbable expressions of stitched mouths bobbed up and down, bringing the characters to life. Effigies of Guy Fawkes filled the street while children yelled out, "Penny for the Guy!"

"Our Margaret loved Guy Fawkes Day. I think it was her favourite time of the year, even more than Christmas," Lily claimed as she poured the boiling water into the teapot. Rena heard her sister but didn't reply. She too knew how much Margaret loved Guy Fawkes Day. She recalled one year Margaret was eleven and adamant that she would create her own Guy Fawkes effigy. "I dinna need any help. I will dae it all on my own." Rena smiled at the memory: Margaret had brimmed with enthusiastic energy while rummaging through their father's old garden clothes.

"Rena, will you have some scones with yer tea?" Lily asked as she filled the cups.

"Aye, Lily, ta." Rena was still unable to cry; it was as though something deep inside twisted her emotions, tangling each thought, each memory, into a tight ball that lay in the pit of her stomach: it remained wedged, hard, painful, with no escape.

Lily sat down, grabbed a scone, and began to smother it in butter. "Rena, remember the year Margaret made her own Guy Fawkes with Da's old garden clothes and the silly face she'd made out of buttons and Mum's embroidery threads? Ye ken, she was sure pleased with herself." Lily looked down at her buttered scone as if in contemplation and instead of taking a bite, she added, "Christ, Rena, I miss her something fierce, it isna fair. She was our Margaret. OURS!" She surrendered her scone, cupped her face, and broke down.

"I remember that night, Lily. The fires were so high they reached the stars. Jessie and Ralph brought the bairns, Ian was balanced on Ralph's shoulders to see over the crowd, wee Catherine Ann was greetin and pressed her face into Jessie's bosom."

"I kent Emma tried taking the poor bairn, as our Jessie wasna feeling well."

"Was she pregnant then?" Rena asked.

"Noo, a few months later, though."

"Oh, aye!" Rena recalled. "Mind our William giving Margaret his old tam o'shanter to place on Guy Fawkes's head. And he told her he must have it back before it was thrust into the fire with all the other stuffed Guys." Rena paused, then took a sip of her tea. "And mind, Lily, Mirren Wilson showed up with her wee brothers and sisters, potatoes in hand, waiting to throw them in for a good bake."

"I dae remember. And ken old Maggie yelling at the top of her lungs, telling her bairns nae tae step close tae the fire." Lily laughed. "And Christ, didn't Da tell her to stop her bloody bleating."

Both girls laughed at that.

"The best, ye ken, was Margaret removing the tam before Da thrust old Guy into the flames and placing it on her head. She sang and danced around the fire. Ye ken, she was daft as a lark. Everyone applauded, Rena. She loved the attention, and everyone loved her."

The door slammed shut, an unintentional act. "The wind isna half picking up oot there. Nearly lost my scarf." Hannah made her way in and bent over to scratch Brodie's ear. He lay sleeping in the doorway of the kitchen. "He does nae move a lot lately, poor old dug." Hannah placed her purse and scarf on the table. "Is the tea still hot?"

"Noo, we are in need of a fresh pot. I'll get it." Lily stood up in preparation.

"We are just discussing the year Margaret made her own Guy Fawkes," Rena mentioned, getting her sister caught up on their conversation.

"Oh, aye, I kent that night very well. Margaret was the bell of George Street. Mind, she stood in her wagon with I think William's tam on, singing her wee heart oot. 'Remember, remember, the fifth of November' . . ."

Their laughter filled the kitchen, which Brodie found startling; he slowly got up and made his way into the sitting room in front of the fire.

Hannah and Lily's laughter turned into tears of grief. Rena, still, could not let go.

*November 5, 1935*

The last of the fires were burning out, and songs of Guy Fawkes had long faded, leaving the streets still and smoky. Rena tossed. She couldn't settle. The house was quiet, and she presumed everyone was asleep. No one from the Helliwell household had attended the evening's festivities. Rena's mother had to retire to her bed early, away from the singing crowds, away from such memories of her bairn being there, partaking – living.

Rena rose from her bed, tired of fighting the fight to sleep. The house was dark, all for the cast of moonlight that filtered in through the kitchen window. She walked past the sitting room and past the dark mound that lay curled in front of the hearth, its fire long extinguished. Quietly she manoeuvred around the kitchen. She pulled together a jam piece and made her way into the sitting room. She curled up in the chair and pulled down a knitted blanket, wrapping it around her legs. Her mind was really nowhere; it was just present, in the room. *The body wakes first*, she thought. *Then the mind; it can be your saviour or your worst enemy.*

She focused on the dark bundle and slid off the chair onto the floor, making her way over. She placed her hand on its side. No up and down movement of breath; the bundle was lifeless. She stroked its wiry black and grey head, both ears drooped back, no longer standing at attention. All the days, all the hours, all the empty moments from the time of her sister's death unleashed like a highland gale. She cried out, "Oh Brodie, you poor dug, I will miss you something fierce. I will!"

Rena placed Brodie in her lap and cradled him, rocking to and fro, crying uncontrollably. "Oh! Margaret! Ye kent how much I loved you, how much I will miss you. Oh Margaret . . ." Twisted emotions and tangled memories emerged; Rena had let go.

Voices stirred, and lights turned on from room to room. It would be another night of broken hearts, tears, and cups of tea, and most of all of family, strength, survival.

## CHAPTER TWENTY-ONE

## *First Footing*

*April 1938. Dunnet, Caithness, Highlands*

When Mary's parents visited, which was rare, it set Morogh's stomach into bouts of spasm. "Yer da will go on and on aboot the lack of running water, the deplorable conditions his bairns are being raised in . . . and by the way, they're my bairns, nae his. And I ken he will say something aboot the mudroom." Morogh had worked fervently on his family cottage before Mary moved in. He wanted her to have all the comforts and amenities she was accustomed to. It made no difference the number of times Mary pleaded with Morogh that those things were not important to her. Nevertheless, to Morogh, they were. He would have given her the world.

Mary kissed Morogh's cheek. "You worry far too much, dinna fash." She kissed him again, this time agreeing. She knew her father very well and would make a point to speak with him.

She was excited about their visit and prepared everything perfectly. Well, as perfect as an old cottage could be. Morogh had renovated it to a great extent, and at least now they had running water. Mary was quite pleased with its almost modern amenities. She finished sweeping fly-away feathers and dried mud out from the small mudroom that Morogh had built off the side of the house. The small room was a great addition for the children's wellies and dungarees.

Alexander and Callum, now eight and seven, made their way in, thick with mud and each carrying a screeching chicken, wings flapping in protest at being roughly handled by two overzealous boys.

"Lads, take these chickens oot of here, right now. I've just swept!" Mary was exhausted, and at this point, she just wanted to sit and enjoy a cuppa. "Where is your da?"

Both boys shrugged their shoulders, laughing as the chickens flapped vigorously to escape.

"Momma, look what I have." Avril, now four, barged in behind her brothers. Her fresh jumper was soiled, and her once neatly placed mass of red curls sprang out in every direction with no signs of the pretty bows that Mary had worked on so patiently to bind her daughter's unruly hair. Her blue eyes gleamed; she had the same crinkle across her nose like her father when she smiled, her freckles not yet prominent. Avril was well pleased with herself; in her hands, she held tightly – perhaps too tightly Mary observed, a black- and orange-spotted newt.

"Oh, for the love of Christ!" Mary blurted.

"Momma, ye said a bad werd," Avril stated as she tried holding a grip onto her wriggling captive. If chickens and dirty children and an undesirable amphibian were not enough, two wet, smelly collies ran into the small, already chaotic, mudroom. Morogh had entered with mud-sprayed clothes and a rueful smile. What could she say? This was her heart, her home. This was where hundreds of years of ancestry howled her name amidst the highland gales.

Mary gazed upon her children. Her daughter was the spitting image of her husband, not her laddies that she'd envisioned all those years back by the seaside in Leith where she and Morogh had promised each other a lifetime of love and bairns. Both her lads had her dark hair and the Johnstone brown eyes. And their cheeky smiles inspired a flood of her own childhood memories, leaving her with a medley of feelings of both gratitude and loss.

Avril gave a wee scream, enough to distract Mary from her musing. The newt was trying to escape, and all three bairns were lit with excitement. She stole a moment before urging Morogh to deal with the children. Her attention was now directed onto the mudroom's door, as it hung slightly off kilter and the large iron hooks were carelessly hammered into their wooden slats. She knew her father would criticise. She could already hear him: "Lass, this room is a bloody muddle. How can bairns tread through this? I'll do a wee repair job while I'm here." Of course, her mother, with great force, would nudge her father. And Morogh would eye Mary with a distressed expression.

"When will Grandad and Gran be here?" Alexander asked, now bored of his sister's wiggling newt.

"Soon," Mary replied as she began sweeping up the fresh mess of feathers and mud.

"Will we get a gift, Momma?" Callum asked.

Her parents hadn't travelled up into the Highlands for close to two years, and that was in 1936, the year after they lost their Margaret.

"You will have to wait and see, Callum."

Avril was now greetin, as Morogh released the newt outside. "Morogh, she's needing to be washed and a clean jumper."

Morogh swept Avril up in his arms, her wee legs kicking in protest. "Aye, Mary, you go rest. I'll tend to the bairns and tidy the rest of the mudroom. Nae bother, all will be grand for yer parents' arrival."

Mary, relieved, made her way into the kitchen, placed the kettle on the range, and sat down. She settled her hands atop her swollen belly and caressed it gently, contemplating if this time it would be a laddie or a lassie. Just a couple more months and all would be revealed. She smiled, excited to announce the news to her father and mother, assured they would be delighted, if not surprised.

Mary had been prepared to announce the news on the eve of Hogmanay, but each time she tried, her words were washed away. A packed house of bairns, drams, and singing outranked. It was the first Mary had been home since Margaret's funeral. It was important to her mother that she and Morogh make the journey home to Edinburgh with the bairns to ring in the New Year of 1938. Her heart ached when she read her mother's letter saying, "A new year, lass, a new beginning." Her mother, with great determination, as well as her own sacrifice, did her best to assuage the emotional afflictions that her surviving children bore each time they lost a sister. Somewhere deep, Mary knew her mother harboured a great fear of losing another child.

The night gave way to new beginnings, no doubt. Mary was elated to see her sisters and brother, and all their bairns. Her breath felt at ease seeing Rena, now the youngest. Mary's disconcerted feelings had lingered for months when she'd arrived home to Dunnet after Margaret's funeral. The fear of loss jounced wildly inside her mind, heart, and soul. She could not bear to lose another sister. When she hugged Rena, she couldn't let go; the hug was fierce, purposeful. It was Robert who came in between. "I dae hope I get such a hug, Mary."

Mary turned her head, and Rena gave a jovial laugh.

"Aye, Robert, of course." She hugged his tall, lanky body, and the smell of fresh shaving cream filled her senses. He was bonnie, no doubt. Mary looked at both her sister and Robert and smiled, thinking what a beautiful couple they made. She did hope Robert would soon pop the question.

The night flew by. The Helliwell house was alive once again. Midnight struck and all held hands, singing "Auld Lang Syne," welcoming 1938.

Mary had looked at Morogh and all the sleeping bairns around the fire and thought *I'll keep my news for another time*. She would let all be.

*December 31, 1937. Edinburgh, Hogmanay*

The new year was to be grand. Everyone was looking forward to welcoming it. Rena's mother was faring well; as well as could be expected, that is. It was important that everyone come home; come home and celebrate Hogmanay.

Rena toiled over which outfit to wear for tonight's celebration. She now had her own room, and it seemed empty and lonely. A picture of Margaret sat upon her nightstand. It was a professional photo sitting her mother had arranged for each Helliwell child. The sepia-toned photograph captured Margaret's cheeky smile and large brown eyes. Not one morning escaped that Rena did not say, "Hello, my Margaret."

"That's it!" Rena, happy with her selection, undressed the coat hanger from which hung a royal-blue dress with a white collar and a tier of tiny pearl buttons that cascaded from its top down to its waistline. She brushed her honey-coloured hair and set the rows of romantic, sculpted waves down, just past her jawline. It was the latest of styles, and thanks to her sister Betty, she was in the trend. She stood in front of the mirror, studying her reflection. She had her mother's brown eyes, but her father's chiselled features.

She was turning twenty in March, and so much had changed within the past few years. She didn't have to convince her mother to stay home in Edinburgh. Margaret's death had saved her from moving to the Highlands to work alongside her Uncle Geordie and Aunt Lizzie. She heard her parents speaking one night when she was in bed. Her father's commanding voice was decisive: "Our Rena is going nowhere. She will stay here, where she belongs. I will not lose another lassie."

Her mother's reply was reserved, yet acquiescent. "Aye, John."

Rena followed her initial plans and worked at a shop on Princess Street, where she was one of four bookkeepers. She still saw her friends now and again, but even their lives had changed. Mirren Wilson's father had died, caught in the pits; they were always the most tragic of deaths. Many widows and fatherless children were left behind trying to survive on the little compensation they received. Mirren got herself pregnant and married the lad. He was a fisherman at Leith Docks. She seemed happy enough, though Rena saw her rarely. Regrettably, good old Maggie still made her rounds to the Helliwell house, to her father's dismay.

Her friend Kitty decided to attend college and take up bookkeeping, the same as Rena. She met an English chap attending Edinburgh University – he was going through to be a doctor or a professor, Rena could never remember correctly. Liza, of course, came around all the time, and the two remained tight. Liza shared that she liked women, something that did not surprise Rena. But she did promise Liza's secret was safe with her. Liza pursued her calling and was on her way to becoming an obstetrician.

Rena's father still spoke of the inevitable war; he followed the news assiduously. Hitler's Nazi Party was now a hot topic. Hitler arrested and imprisoned thousands of Communists and Social Democrats and their leaders, along with any other radicals. Opponents of the Nazi Party were set up in concentration camps. The most horrific rumours were about the number of Jewish citizens being murdered right out in public, in the streets.

The Spanish Civil War was raging. And Hitler and Mussolini allied to support General Francisco Franco, the Nationalist leader of Spain, to overthrow the Spanish government. Hitler sent his German Condor Legion aerial combat unit made up of BF-109b, JU87, and He11 dive bombers. Within that same year of 1936, Hitler mustered troops and stormed into Rhineland, a direct contravention of the Treaty of Versailles. He then turned to Austria. Austria's chancellor appealed to the League of Nations but to no avail. Austria was quickly seized, like pulling a pacifier from a bairn's mouth.

Japan, somewhat behind the limelight of Germany, but just as deadly, had seized Shanghai and Beijing all within the same year. And in December of 1937, the Japanese Imperial Army stormed into the capital city of China, Nanjing. Their actions were nothing less than that of pure annihilation. They slaughtered and butchered thousands of civilians, including children. Monstrous acts of rape were performed on both women and young girls, bayonets were used in the most grotesque methods of violations.

They said the Qinhuai and Yangtze Rivers ran red with blood. Next, the Japanese conquered Inner Mongolia. By May 1938, Japan extended its war into south China. The Brits feared Hong Kong was next.

Each time Rena's father apprised the family of the world's mad events, she fought hard to push them into a place of darkness. She couldn't fathom how any human could treat another human with such brutality.

"Rena, Spud is here, hurry round, lass," Rena's mother called out to her room. Robert Thomson was now referred to as Spud, named after his own creation, the hearty potato scone, which proved to be a good seller at the shop. It became a fun poke from his mates, but the tattie name stood.

Rena pulled out a set of earrings. Red veins of iron oxide, representing blood, ran through the dark-green jasper gemstones, a most precious birthday gift from Robert. She did a final inspection of her honey-coloured waves and the tiny, teardrop-shaped bloodstone birthstones. Robert had informed her that tonight would be special. And both his parents and his sister Meg, and her husband, Sandy, would be attending the festivities.

The table was a mound of food. The heavenly smells mingled through the air, inspiring yet another family memory. William, now married, arrived first, with his wife, Susan, and their wee bairn, Margaret. Margaret had just turned one, and she was the sparkle in William's eye. It took some time, Rena thought, to call this wee one Margaret, but somewhere behind those chestnut-coloured eyes, her own sister's gleamed.

Betty and Percy arrived shortly after. Nicol, eleven, and Ronald, now eight, were almost as tall as the adults. Margaret played shy when the boys bent over to greet their wee cousin. Next to arrive were Lily and Jock. They had been married a couple of years and nicely settled with their firstborn, John William, named after his grandad. Though, he was referred to as Ian (Scottish Gaelic origin). He was just weeks old and his pudgy face and soft auburn hair made everyone coo and make soft noises. Curiosity made Margaret forget her shy disposition, and she toddled over towards the wee bundle.

Hannah, who was flying solo because Victor was in Africa for a fortnight, came out of her bedroom dressed in a sharp cream suit, her hair now cropped with the same romantic waves as her sister Rena. Betty smiled, pleased at her creative masterpieces.

Hannah made her way over to Lily's bairn, picked up the sleeping bundle and kissed his forehead. "Welcome, wee Ian, to yer first Hogmanay."

A burst of energy with red cheeks and blonde-bobbed hair ran from the front door into the kitchen. June was now six, and she was excited to see her cousins and meet her new one. "June, you didna take off yer boots, do get back here," Emma called out. The request was lost among laughter and screaming bairns.

Rena watched as her mother hugged each child and each grandchild. This was positively what her mother needed, she thought. She knew Jessie's bairns would not be present, and it broke all their hearts, but it was what it was. Well, that's what her father so asserted.

The last arrivals were Mary and Morogh, and they burst in like a flock of bleating sheep. Alexander and Callum ran in first, yelling that they brought blowers and whistles. Morogh entered with a sleeping Avril heavy in his arms. Mary came after with a travel case in one hand and a bag of goodies in the other. Rena made her way through the crowded room. She stopped and smiled at her sister. The feelings were mutual; they hadn't seen each other since Margaret's funeral; their emotions overwhelmed. Rena embraced Mary, whose hug was tight, unyielding, fierce. "I miss you, Rena," Mary whispered. Robert made his way over and interrupted the two.

The Helliwell family clock struck midnight, hands were held, and *Auld Lang Syne* belted out. Hugs and kisses were offered and received, everyone stepping over bairns curled and sleeping by the fire. Rena took heed of Mary's expression and sensed her sister wanted to announce something. But the buzz in the room was energetic. She observed Mary's eyes as her sister scanned the room, her warm smile landing upon Morogh. Rena would make certain to find a private moment with her sister before the night ended.

Robert called the room to silence, but his soft voice held no weight against the Helliwell clan. A loud, roaring voice commanded attention. John Helliwell called order to the house. "Now, laddie, you may proceed."

Robert sheepishly smiled and gave a nod. First, he cleared his throat and looked around the room at the family he had entered into, a family he respected and loved. His father and mother stood with quizzical expressions. His sister Meg gave a tight grin, her eyes enlarged while she waved her hand. "Go on then, Spud!" she finally gasped out.

"Right then." Robert turned towards Rena, bent down on one knee and pulled a tiny, gold-covered box from his shirt pocket. He took her hand and looked up into her eyes. He was nervous, Rena could tell. His hand was shaking. "Rena . . . I mean Alexandrena." He was trying to be formal. "Ye ken how much I love you, we've been sweethearts since you were sixteen and myself nineteen. Would you do me the honour and marry me?"

The room was silent, the most it had been all evening. Rena looked around the room and eyed her father. "Right, lass! The lad has asked my permission. Get on with it, give him your answer." Her father stood proud, tugging at the corner of his waistcoat, a most distinguished habit.

"Robert, ye ken I will."

Robert opened the box and pulled out a gold band with a solitaire diamond. He slipped it on her finger and kissed her hand, then he stood and kissed his wife to be, long and hard. The family roared. John and Robert's father handed out tumblers of whiskey. John stood centre. "I'd like to raise our glasses to this fine young couple and wish them a life full of happiness, a business of success, and a houseful of bairns."

All cheered and raised their glasses. He continued, "Oh! And let's not forget our 'First Footing' was a tall, dark-haired lad with a piece of coal and a parcel of black bun. We are truly blessed. Thank you, Robert."

Robert Senior stood next, and his wife, Margarie, made her way over to her son and her daughter-in-law to be. "Rena, Mr. Thomson and I were both surprised, ye ken. I dae think Meg and Sandy was in on it, though. We are so happy tae bring you into our family, lass."

"If my wife is done talking, I can proceed." Robert Senior shot his wife a wink along with a cheerful smile. "Rena, from the day you and yer wee sister Margaret came into our shop, I kent Robert had fallen for you." He fell silent, and he hesitated to finish. He had mentioned Margaret – how heedless of him.

It was Catherine Helliwell who broke his uncomfortable silence. "Mr. Thomson, dinna fash, we all talk aboot our Margaret, that's how we keep her close, ye ken. You are family now, and I thank you for mentioning our lass."

"Thank you, and please call me Robert."

Catherine nodded and directed him to continue.

"Our lad never stopped talking aboot you, and we are most proud to welcome you into oor family."

With that, the house was raised with more cheers and drams of whiskey.

Rena and Robert snuck outside. The sky was clear, and the moon was full. It lit up the back garden. The ground was lightly covered with a dusting of soft snow. You could hear the hum from neighbours all around, singing and setting off whistles and blowers, bringing in the New Year, 1938, a new beginning.

"I love you, Rena." Robert bent slightly, pulling her in close and tight. He then lifted her off the ground. One shoe fell off, and she giggled. He kissed her long and hard, his tongue exploring her mouth. They felt as one, untouched, unharmed from the uncertain state of the world everyone had found themselves in.

"I love you tae, Spud. I was hoping you would be asking soon, ye ken, we canna keep dodging our ... ye ken ..."

Robert laughed and responded with a slight tease in his voice, "Our what?"

She moved slightly closer into the weight of his hips. "Ye ken, Spud ..."

He laughed and kissed her again, his tone softened. "Rena, I kent these last couple of years have been tough, with Margaret's death and helping oot your mum. I promise you, I will look after you, and if that means looking after yer mum, I will dae that tae."

Rena broke down, and tears streamed her face. She licked both the happy and sad salty substance from the corners of her mouth. "I ken that, Spud, that's why I love you so." They hugged, and Rena fiddled her foot back into her shoe. Large snowflakes danced slowly down from the sky covering them both in a veil of white. It was a beautiful ending to a most memorable Hogmanay.

Robert and Rena

## CHAPTER TWENTY-TWO

# *The Black Dress*

*Edinburgh, 1938*

It was all Rena could do to get through their vows. Robert insisted they postpone the wedding. She couldn't bear the thought of choosing another date, let alone all the planning that accompanied the change. It was enough she surrendered her white satin gown of Chantilly lace and pearl buttons for a layered lace chiffon dress of black.

Liza had taken her shopping along Princes Street, and they ducked into a woman's apparel shop. When the shopkeeper asked the occasion, Liza whispered in the lady's ear. Rena couldn't hear what was said. She was only thankful her friend was there, helping her once again. They left the shop, each carrying a parcel under their arm.

It was hard to imagine that making a trunk call could be so exciting, not to mention convenient. The operator connected the long-distance call with a most professional tonality. Rena could hear the operator asking to confirm that a Mary McIntosh was on the line. It was scratchy with a bit of an echo, but Rena could hear her sister's reply. "Aye, this is Mary McIntosh. Hello?"

"Mary, it's Rena, can you hear me?" A click sounded as the operator disengaged her line.

"Aye, Rena." The evolution of not having to book a long-distance call between the operator and the receiving party made reaching out favourable and impromptu; of course, if the receiving party was in earshot of the phone ring.

"I canna talk long. I only have a few shillings for the call." Rena could hear her nephews and niece shouting in the background.

"You better speak up, Rena. Enough! Morogh, shoo these bairns oot of here, I'm on the phone with Rena." Morogh's muffled voice faded, as did the children's. "Right, Rena, you were saying."

"Robert and I have picked a date to be married, Friday, August twenty-sixth. I ken yer due with the wee yin come end of June. But if there is any way you can make it, Mary. We both, Robert and I, that is, would love to have you attend. Liza is standing in as my best maid. I couldna choose from my sisters, the decision was tae hard."

There was silence. For a moment, Rena thought the call was disconnected, which was a common occurrence, especially in the northern part of the Highlands.

"Mary?" Rena called out a little louder.

"Aye, Rena, I can hear you. I canna promise, but I will try." A few general inquires on bairns, health, and how their parents were keeping bounced back and forth.

"I will call you again, Mary, closer to yer birthday. We all are thinking about you, do take care." The static was building on the line, her sister's voice was waning, and she could barely make out the last few words before the call was dropped. Rena was sure Mary had said how much she loved her and that she would see her soon.

Robert was handsome, and he wore a dark-grey suit with a matching waistcoat and a crisp white shirt and matching grey tie. A white carnation with sprigs of heather was fastened to his lapel. His thick, dark waves were greased back, accentuating his soft, dark-brown eyes and long lashes. On his left wrist he wore his father's watch, an inherited heirloom that befell too soon. Rena held his hand tight, and he squeezed back in reply.

Robert assessed his bride. She was beautiful. He assumed all grooms viewed their brides that way; nevertheless, he couldn't stop himself from eyeing her entirely, in front of everyone, including the minister.

Her dress, her second choice, was exquisite. The underlay was a brocade lace of cream, and its only visibility was a small panel at the front that peeked out and trailed from its Peter Pan collar down to her mid-shin. The outer layer of the dress was of black chiffon lace, two satin lapels draped open just enough to view the cream brocade accentuating her breasts. Its bodice formed around her waist then draped down just over her hips, trailing to her ankles. The long, black-laced sleeves exposed her porcelain skin. Her elegant black headpiece sat tilted, tiny cream flowers beaded along one side of a black mesh veil. It swept down over her face, just under her chin, giving a sense of mystery. He took an indulgent breath as if he meant to breathe her in. Deeply. He gave a slight smile, and she tightened her grip.

They were married in the Church of Scotland on George Street. The chapel's lighting was dim; nonetheless, the sunlight radiated through the stained-glass windows, offering, if nothing else, a glow of warmth. The minister's voice rang in echoes. His words bounced around the walls and were caught in the high ceiling. Rena never heard a word he had said. She held Robert's hand tightly. Her grief was numbing. She was simply going through the motions.

Robert was insistent, and he advised Rena that his father's heart attack would not change their marriage date or plans. Rena felt otherwise, but nevertheless, Robert maintained the wedding stay on schedule. Robert Thomson Sr. had died a month after Hogmanay. It was a shock to everyone, as he seemed so fit and lively that night at the Helliwells'. That was the last time Rena had seen her future father-in-law. She seldom saw Robert after his father's funeral. The shop required attending to, and so did his grieving mother. Catherine Helliwell stopped in as much as possible to offer help wherever she could.

"Spud, we can postpone the wedding or reduce the venue, ye ken, I won't mind," she had said. Rena was standing at the counter in the bakeshop, looking through the pane of glass at the baked goods. Robert had just filled the top shelf with a fresh batch of black buns.

"Rena, my da would not have wanted us to change our plans." He stood up, brushing pastry crumbs off his baker's apron. "My mum agrees, Rena."

"It's just I feel . . ." Rena wasn't sure how to compose her response. Robert came out from behind the counter and took her in his arms. He held her close. "Aye, Rena, I ken." He kissed her softly on her forehead. "We will get through this. Just give me time to settle my da's business and help my mum. But I promise the wedding will go on. Nae more talk of it."

Rena gave a nod, not entirely agreeing that the wedding should go on, but in agreement: people did get through losing loved ones. It was a condition she was too familiar with. She kissed Robert's cheek before leaving and reminded him of the family dinner on Saturday. "It's a big day for my da," she concluded.

*Saturday, June 18, 1938*

Rena had cut a dozen yellow roses from the back garden, each one perfect, just at the burst of opening. Her father had at first insisted the old rose bush be dug out, discarded, a husband's course of action to save his wife from a constant reminder of what was lost. "John, I will nae let you remove that rose bush," she had said. "Its absence will nae stop me from thinking of my lass. Its blossoms embrace me, it's all I have left."

Rena placed the bouquet under her nose and breathed in the perfumed fragrance – breathed in her Margaret.

The day was beautiful, not a cloud in the sky. The sun beamed through the streets and back gardens. Her mother was in making the tea. Rena placed the bouquet of roses in the centre of the table, finishing off its presentation for the family gathering.

It was to be a day of celebration. John Helliwell was retiring from his position as a merchant engineer at the Leith Docks, a decision that was not easy for the robust, energetic sixty-seven-year-old. He did claim he would help out now and then when the men needed an extra hand. It was time, he said, as they all were seated around the table.

"I'm happy for you, Father. You can tend to your gardening and rose bushes and catch up on your reading," Lily remarked.

"And ken, drive Mother mad." Emma poked at her father.

"Aye, lass, that he will, but I have enough chores for him to keep him oot of my hair," Catherine replied with a chortle.

William laughed. "Aye, you women never give peace, always something you need us men to dae."

"Aye. William, are you speaking from experience?" his mother asked. "And by the way, where is your wife?"

"Ken, she is pretty busy, but does send her best."

"Well, lad, I'm glad you brought wee Margaret. I'm sure we shall see yer Susan soon enough."

Emma and Lily exchanged a quick, doubtful glance. Rena caught it but knew the timing was inappropriate to ask.

"Right, let's plate our dishes," Catherine ordered. The smell of baked finnan and haddie and roasted potatoes filled the entire house. A bowl of steaming neeps draped with butter, and a fresh loaf all lay waiting for a hungry household. Lily had just fed wee Ian, and he lay fast asleep in his pram. June, now old enough, joined the adults at the table. She sat beside her mother, Emma, waiting to dig into the thick fillets of fish. Wee Margaret fussed about the house, curious at every stop. "Shh, dinna wake the wee yin," William whispered out to his daughter, who was tumbling around the pram.

"Nay bother, William, Ian could sleep through a war," Lily claimed.

"I thought Hannah and Victor would have been here by now. They are always late," Catherine said with a hint of impatience. "Betty and Percy and the lads will be here after tea. They are driving doon in Percy's new car." Catherine did manage to smile at that. "Their hair salon is quite successful."

"So it should be, it's the only one in Aberfeldy," John retorted.

"Haud yer wheesht, John. They've worked hard," Catherine replied with a stern tone. "I'm only saying . . ." He was cut short by the thud of the front door.

Hannah and Victor made their way in, Hannah apologised for their tardiness, and both squeezed in a seat at the table. "Please, Mrs. Helliwell, it's my fault we are late. Business keeps me quite tight." Victor gave a sincere nod and turned his head toward John. "A big day, Mr. Helliwell. I wish you much happiness in your retirement." Victor understood Hannah's apprehension at introducing him to her family. And when she did, they were polite and welcoming, but he could feel their angst; it hung in the room, thick like coal dust. He was well aware of Hannah's parents' tribulations and proceeded with caution at each family event.

It's not that John didn't like the lad – he was a well-educated chap, following in his father's path to becoming an admiral in Her Majesty's Naval Service. And he was English. John was, however, opposed to him taking his lass away from Scotland, away from home. More so, moving her to South Africa, a country in turmoil, something he and his wife agonised over.

Victor, with great consideration, thought it necessary at each family gathering to offer updates on the progress of South Africa in securing its successful future. It was hard to get a word in sideways at the Helliwell table, but he had learnt one had to jump in loud and incessant. "South Africa is seeing some fruitful ventures in her economy."

"Pass the haddie, will you, Rena," William asked as he stretched his arm across the table.

Rena picked up the plate and held it out. "Pass me the tatties," she countered.

Robert, discerning Victor's apprehension, gave him an encouraging stare, persuading him to be assertive and carry on. He couldn't help but feel embarrassed for the chap. He too at one time could relate to Victor's position of being the odd man out. The Helliwells were a strong force to be reckoned with, something Robert had learnt to orchestrate through.

"I say! The economy is booming, General Motors are assembling close to forty-five cars a day." Victor, after appreciating Robert's support raised his voice over the family's requests of passing dishes. "Plus, Cadbury Fry's factory is growing, creating hundreds of new jobs."

There was a moment of silence, and it was almost uncomfortable. It was John who spoke next. "Well, I'm sure that will keep my lass safe, cars and chocolate being the pinnacle of events."

Victor thought carefully, and he was not sure what to say next. He didn't want to insult Mr. Helliwell or cause any unease, especially in Mrs. Helliwell. The family had already been through so much loss and grief. He understood their anguish about Hannah moving to Africa.

First, Victor gave a slight laugh, trying to ease the inflection of Mr. Helliwell's remark. "Well, you are quite right there, Mr. Helliwell." He shuffled in his seat in effort to collect himself and felt Hannah rest her hand on his lap in reassurance. "I can assure you, Mr. Helliwell, South Africa is seeing more and more anglophile supporters, and the fight against fascism is paramount. And if I may add, which is quite confidential, I will be working with Admiral Guy Halifax. He was appointed director of the South African Naval Service. Our mission is to oversee and convert a flotilla of fishing trawlers and whaler ships into military vessels. We are not naive about what is happening in Germany, or Japan, for that matter. South Africa will be diligent in maritime control around the cape and in coastal patrol." He felt quite confident in his delivery and hoped this eased Mr. Helliwell's consternation.

"I'm not concerned about South Africa's political position or their plight for an anglophile union. I've fought in the African wars and the Great War. No one is safe from a country's warfare of destruction. No one!" John abruptly stood and excused himself to the sitting room. Victor felt defeated. He would never gain Mr. Helliwell's trust or convince him of his daughter's safety.

"I'll make tea. You lassies clear the dishes. Victor, we know you love our Hannah. It's not that that we question or fear." Catherine patted Victor's shoulder, then turned towards the range.

*Saturday, July 2, 1938*

Rena had popped into the bakeshop on her way to work. She wanted to remind Robert of their last-minute details for the wedding. The sign read, "Closed," and the blinds were pulled down. She stood in the back room, leaning against the baker's wooden table. Robert was pulling trays of baked goods from the oven.

"Ye ken, my mum has told me tales of being a young lass herself in Ardersier, helping her father bake. It was some of her fondest memories. Mind, I was named after my grandfather, Alexander Johnstone. We didna travel often up to the Highlands, there were too many of us, but my mother would go up with one or two of us at a time. I still remember my grandfather and my Grandmother Jessie. I was nine when they died."

Robert placed another tray of pies into the oven. "They both died when you were nine?"

"Aye, it was quite sad for the family. My Uncle Alec was the last of the children to stay behind. He and his wife lived on the farm with my grandparents until they died, that is, then they moved to the Shetlands. It was a blessing he was there, so my mother had said."

"Oh, aye," Robert agreed, preparing another batch of pastry.

"I remember my grandfather's wake. He was spread out on the table, dressed in a gown of white: his white hair and long beard were groomed to perfection. A posy of lavender lay tucked in the hold of his hands and each eye covered with a pence, to pay the ferryman to enter St. Peter's gate. So my granny declared. I touched his beard, ken I was frightened to approach him; he looked as if he was only sleeping, and at nine it was a very scary experience. I had never seen anyone dead before. My mom's Uncle Erik stood outside the cottage. He was dressed in full Highland garb, playing the pipes." Rena giggled, and Robert gave her a quizzical look.

"Och, I'm no laughing at my dead grandad. Only the memory of me at nine, standing by the body, waiting for his spirit to fly out the door. Which my grannie was sure she saw depart."

Robert gave a relieved nod.

"Ye ken, us Highlanders are very superstitious."

"Oh, I ken that, not sure what I'm getting myself involved in." Robert gave a jesting chuckle.

"My grannie died nine days after my granddad. I kent my mother was torn tae bits. She headed back up to Ardersier straight away. She said her mother died of a broken heart and that she couldna bear to live without her husband. My da said that was absurd, ye canna die from a broken heart, only a heart that isna working correctly."

"I can believe yer mother didna take light to that," Robert replied.

"Yer right there, she spoke a few curt words, said something aboot him fending for himself and all the bairns while she was gone to the Highlands. Something like that, I canna recall, ye ken it was years ago. Odd I'm thinking of all that now."

Robert rested the hot tray on the wooden table and grabbed Rena in his arms. "I couldna live if you died, Rena, and I do believe I would die of a broken heart."

"Don't be daft, Spud," she said, though she smiled.

"I canna wait for us to spend the rest of our lives together and run our own shop. Something my da always spoke aboot." He pulled her in closer, running his hands down her back, then over her bottom. He squeezed, the same time kissing her earlobe, then her neck, and she gave a slight sigh. Her hand cupped his face, and she kissed him deeply.

"I love you, Spud."

The shop was coming to life, the blinds were raised, and the sign now read "Open."

"I will see you tonight, Spud, after I call our Mary. Ye ken, she is due any day." Rena blew a kiss as she made her way out of the shop and through the line of anxious customers.

She felt it impossible to be any happier. It was a passionate feeling of sure bliss; something she hadn't felt in a very long time. Robert was her world, her everything. She thought of his heartfelt belief when he commented that he couldn't live without her. Truth be told, she couldn't live without him.

The wedding day was fast approaching, and she was busy with last-minute purchases and errands. She headed towards Princess Street to hit a few shops before returning home to call her sister.

Rena didn't make her phone call. She arrived home to find her mother and father sitting at the kitchen table. It was the silence that was unbearable, its bottomless pit expelling a humming sound of emptiness. Her father stood – his approach seemed reluctant, he bore an expression of deep anguish. It was familiar; she recognised it. Her eyes shifted to her mother, who hadn't moved, her head hung, her cheeks wet, her face old, tired. Rena cried out, "No! Oh God, no!" She kept her face hidden in her father's chest, and he held her as long as he could. She cried out again, sliding down to the floor, into the pit of emptiness.

Mary Grant Helliwell McIntosh died July 2 at 6:15 pm. She had suffered the same affliction her older sister Jessie had during childbirth: mitral stenosis. Both Mary and her infant son died during the cumbersome delivery. Her heart gave out, though the doctor did everything he could to save both mother and child.

Those were the words Rena heard her father say, but how could she begin to even believe? She couldn't make sense of such tragic words; they were words she did not want to comprehend.

It wasn't that long ago, April 13, to be exact, that she had called Mary to wish her a happy birthday. Mary had turned twenty-six, and Morogh was having a small party for her. Rena could hear the laughter and her nephews' and nieces' voices in the background. They were happy, singing. Her sister was alive. *Oh my God!* Rena thought, *poor Morogh! Poor bairns! Oh God! My poor mother.*

The funeral was in Leith, at the same church as Margaret's was. Morogh brought Mary home, home to be buried, alongside her sisters, Jessie and Margaret. "She belongs hame. I had her and loved her, now she's gone, my Mary, my heart. She's gone, just like my mother." Morogh was inconsolable. He rambled on at the church and back at the house. He blamed himself, said he couldn't live without her. How could he tend his bairns? His grief was overwhelming.

His brother Maxwell attended the funeral. He offered Morogh and the bairns to stay in Edinburgh at his home with his wife, at least for a few days. Morogh refused. He would stay the night at the Helliwells', then take his bairns back home, where he could feel Mary's presence.

*Friday, August 26, 1938*

Robert lifted her veil, and she shifted her bouquet of twenty-four white carnations, embellished with green ferns, off to her side. He kissed her lips, then her cheek. He kept a tight grip on her hand. The organist began to play. Rena recognised the song, but the name escaped her. The pipes blew out a haunting sound, each note louder than the next, its allegro tempo circling the chapel. She wished the organist would stop.

The reception was small. Rena's friends Liza, Kitty, and Mirren took over and prepared the Helliwell's house with fresh flowers and set the table with food, beer, and champagne. Robert's sister Meg had brought the wedding cake. One professional photograph was captured, and that was inside the church. And it was only of Robert and Rena. She lay her white-glove-covered hand in his, safe and guarded. Both had managed to smile.

# CHAPTER TWENTY-THREE

## Broken Hearts and Shattered Pieces

*November 1938. Edinburgh*

Rena spread the white linen tablecloth out and over the dining table, pressing it with the palm of her hands, trying to flatten out the middle crease that persistently stood erect running down its middle. It was one of her mother's, and when Catherine had gifted it to Rena, she had instructed her on how to care for it. Each corner displayed an embroidered posy of lavender. "You must take great care in the washing and the pressing of it. It was a gift from my Grandmother Johnstone," Catherine informed her daughter when she handed over the box.

Rena smiled as she unpacked each assorted item and found a home for them. A wooden sideboard ran across the entire length of the tiny kitchen, where she placed a teapot and a set of cups. Next in line, she filled a clay vase with an assortment of wooden spurtles, and she laughed to herself. As her mother always declared, "Ye canna never have enough spurtles." The other items consisted of cake plates, a butter dish, a matching milk jug, and an array of cutlery, odds and bits that didn't match, but it was nevertheless a good start to Robert's and her new home. It was a tiny flat, just around the corner from her parents.

Robert knew she did not want to live far away, and it was an unsaid condition. And of course, there was the persuasive stare Rena's father gave Robert when he had mentioned finding a suitable home. "I'm assured, lad, that you will not be taking our lass too far from her mother." He had to admit when John Helliwell discharged an order, especially using his Yorkshire accent, one listened. Not to mention the tug on the corner of his houndstooth woollen waistcoat. Robert wanted to chuckle when John pulled at it but gave way.

He had asked his wife why her father performed such a gesture during his discoursing. Rena merely laughed. "He just does, Spud."

Rena unpacked another box labelled "books and picture frames." She sorted through her collection of classics, placing them on the shelf her father had built when she lived at home. Robert had fastened it on the wall beside the fireplace. She allowed her fingers to lightly stroke each worn and frayed binding, tapping her finger on *Lady Chatterley's Lover*, thinking back on the evening she read the book to Margaret. How delighted Margaret had been. She loved all the scandalous bits and pieces. But most of all, Margaret had loved her time with her sister.

Rena wiped her tears and moved on to the last few items at the bottom of the box. Unsure where to arrange them or which room to place them in, she decided on the picture of Margaret, the one she kept by her nightstand when she lived at home. She hugged it against her heart and with a solemn breath, whispered, "You will stay right here." Rena placed the framed picture beside the row of books. She grabbed the next frame and smiled as she unwrapped the tissue. It was Robert's and her wedding photograph. One would have never known the grief that was so concealed. Both looked handsome, and their smiles were tranquil, untroubled. She placed it on the mantel, and as she did, a bundle of pictures fell loose from an envelope and fell to the floor. After collecting them, she sat down and shuffled them into a pile of tidiness.

She hadn't the courage to view the photographs; each face would cause her sorrow and heartache, awakening memories of a time in which her sister was alive. It felt like an hour, but it was only a few brief minutes, and her decision was sound. She turned the pile right side up and ventured through each sepia-toned, matte-finished memory. Some corners were torn and folded. And the dull white scalloped edges indicated hours of handling – hours of viewing. Morogh had stipulated in his letter that he had plenty of pictures of Mary and the bairns. His pal from Dunnet had taken up photography and was hoping to become a professional photographer for the new photojournalistic magazine called *Picture Post*. He added that her father would greatly appreciate the magazine, with its liberal, anti-fascist opinions.

His closing remarks were sensitive, fragile, almost careful: "I miss her, Rena, and often I think I'd rather die than live without her. It's my bairns that keep me upright. They're all I have left. Come spring, I will bring them to see your parents. I ken how important that is to both." His signature bore a soft calligraphy, in contrast to the tight cursive writing of what had to be a most arduous letter for him to compose. Rena could see where his tears had spilt, blotching the letters M, r, and g of his name.

"Christ!" The tap on the door startled her. "It canna be that time already?" she uttered aloud, carefully placing the letter and photographs back in the box. By the time she reached the kitchen, Lily had made her way in with a parcel of what smelled like homemade soup.

"Lamb and lentil," Lily announced as she pulled the sealed pot from the brown paper bag. "I kent better to bring bread or baked goods." She laughed. "Spud being a baker and all." She took off her coat and handed it to Rena.

"I see I'm the first here. Lovely flat, Rena, it truly is." Lily walked into the living room and assessed the contents of half-unpacked crates scattered across the floor.

"It's getting there. It does nae feel like hame."

Lily peeked into the box on the chair and then quickly turned her head towards her sister. "It will, Rena, just give it time."

A play of laughter blustered through the front door, expelling into the living room. The scent of fresh cold air wafted in behind Betty and Emma. Both carried on like a couple of mad magpies, blethering on about how the conductor was flirting with them both as they climbed onto the tram car.

After their lunch of Lily's soup, Rena's basket of crusty homemade buns, and raspberry fern cakes, compliments of Robert, Betty pulled out a bottle of port.

"A gift from Percy. A friend of his brought it back from a Spain trip. He says it's quite exquisite and expensive." Betty gave a chortle and asked Rena to fetch some tumblers, then added, "unless you have a few crystal schooners lying aboot." Rena came back to the table with tumblers, ignoring her sister's inquiry about which glass a fine port should be drunk from.

Betty poured the remaining port, distributing it evenly into the four tumblers. They retired to the sitting room, feeling relaxed and slightly intoxicated. Their conversation was light, noncommittal to anything cumbrous. At times it was safer that way. They discussed the weather and what winter would bring: more rain or perhaps snow. How miserable Lily's lad Ian was during his teething episodes, and that she was glad to leave him with her in-laws for the evening. Betty boasted how clever her laddies were at school, which didn't surprise the Helliwells. Emma announced that she and Charlie had set a wedding date. Rena, with great pride mentioned that Robert's long hours at the bake shop were paying off, and sales were steadily increasing. The sisters raised their glasses and toasted to the stillness of untroubled moments that had filled the room.

The girls finished their last swallow of port in silence, their minds in unison, thinking of Hannah. Afraid to be the first to mention the unthinkable. Lily spoke first, and it was a slight distraction, only in avoidance.

"Mum and Da are nae happy aboot William's talk of separation." Lily was holding her silver lighter while she was talking and pacing. She then lit her cigarette and sat down on the floor and crossed her legs. She leaned back against the sofa and inhaled deeply. Rena quickly grabbed an ashtray and, like a curling stone, threw it across the hardwood floor, its delivery precise, arriving at Lily's bent knee. "Ta, Rena," Lily responded.

"Well, I will say, I think our brother is daft leaving Susan. And I believe it's for another woman," Emma stated, lighting her cigarette.

Betty stood, arching her back, her hands placed on her narrow hips. "Da is certain it's Susan leaving our William, because of the other women. And delivered in the style only our da can disseminate, he called him a bloody fool."

Lily tapped the long ash from her cigarette, then added, "Tis sad, regardless. What's upsetting our William more, ye ken, is that his wife calls wee Margaret Margo. Apparently, she never liked the idea of the wee yin named after a dead sister." The four fell quiet, immersed in their own thoughts.

Rena broke the silence. "This will nae help our mum. She does nae need this trouble, ye ken. Not with Hannah ill in the sanatorium."

That was it said; the words unleashed. Each unendurable word hung suspended in the confined space of the sitting room. The whole family skirted around Hannah's diagnosis. It was tragic – it was impermissible. Consumption was running rampant in Britain. It plagued the congested areas of Scotland. Hannah had spent the last couple of months in and out of the Royal Victoria Hospital in Edinburgh, an institution founded by Robert William Philip, a physician specializing in the treatment of tuberculous. And once she completed her convalescence and was strong enough, only then could she come home. Hannah's entire world was put on hold; she no longer could nurse, which broke her heart. Victor was in Africa more than he was in Scotland. She missed him terribly, and her friend Grace.

Rumours of war were now becoming a real threat. Germany and Japan were running amok, unambiguously under everyone's noses. Victor wrote as much as possible. His station with Her Majesty's Naval Service was now critical, and he could not disclose any pertinent details, only that he missed Hannah and would come to Scotland as soon as he could. His sister Grace was also summoned to South Africa, along with their aunt. The hasty move of the Ainsworths concerned John Helliwell greatly.

Victor apprised John of a few internal affairs, although John did not require such information to perceive the inevitable. "War is brewing," he so promulgated. Catherine had long surrendered, combating her husband's words of war, her heart shattered with the loss of her lassies. And if her grief gave the impression it could spiral no further; her Hannah's diagnosis gripped her soul and pulled it into depths of despair.

Like a bee flitting from one floret to the next, collecting just enough pollen before moving on, their conversations emulated as such, each sister afraid to hover too long on a specific topic, one that would sting.

"Is Liza a lesbian?" Betty asked.

"Betty! What an insolent inquiry," Emma retorted uncomfortably, looking sideways towards Rena.

"It's no an inquiry, it's a direct question." Betty shifted her austere gaze from Emma, softening it as it landed curiously on Rena.

"Well, I will say, it's quite a cheeky question." Lily, now keen on the answer, asked, "Though is she, Rena?"

Not that her friend cared what people thought of her sexual orientation. Liza had asked Rena to keep it quiet only due to the classification of people living in Leith. "They are simple living people, Rena, fisherman, miners, labourers. I would be the talk of the town," Liza explained before she packed up and moved to London.

Once confirmed that Liza liked women, and with the sisters' vow of secrecy, their interest turned to Liza's intended profession. All agreed she would make a fine obstetrician.

Rena pulled a bottle of bubbly from the icebox. "It was a wedding gift and I was going to save it, not sure for what as Spud loves his pints and drams, nae this lassie's drink, as he so calls it." Rena gave a wee chortle. Lily gave the tumblers a rinse and went back into the sitting room, finding a seat on the floor among her sisters. They formed a circle around the box of pictures. Rena suggested they should sort through the pictures, and each choose the ones they wanted. The first few were old, the edges brittle. Carefully each photograph was circulated. They studied the timeless photos; one was of the girls' grandparents, Alexander and Jessie Johnstone. Another was of their grandfather on his own, standing in the doorway, leaning to one side, his hand wrapped around his suspenders. Beneath his white beard, there appeared to be a slight smile. Another was of their mother and their uncles: James, Donald, Geordie, and Alec. The picture had faded, but their facial expressions were quite distinct.

"Mum said this was taken just before James and Donald left Scotland," Rena said as she passed the picture on. The sisters examined the faded photo, inspecting the group of family members all standing in a row, accompanied by a few collie dogs resting in between their feet. All seemed cheery, except for Donald.

"Mum's brother Donald is no half dour," Lily mentioned, lifting the picture closer to take a better look. "A bonnie lad, though," she said, handing it to Emma.

"Do you see a likeness in these lads and our William?" Emma asked.

"Oh no! Not at all. Our Willie is a Helliwell through and through," Betty responded with a snigger. They all laughed.

"You may want this photo, Emma," Rena suggested as she handed it over. It was a picture of their sister Margaret holding a two-year-old June.

"Ta, Rena." Emma studied it, then reached for a tissue.

Rena handed two photos to Betty. "Here is lovely photo of you, Betty, wearing a shell necklace, and another of your two laddies in their kilts." The next three pictures were of their sisters, Hannah, Jessica and Catherine J. Rena placed them on the floor side by side so they could all view them together. A moment of silence passed, each sister immersed in her own thoughts.

It was Emma who spoke first. "Catherine J looks smashing in her dress and silk bow. She was so beautiful."

It was a hesitant gesture, but nevertheless, Rena reached in and removed the pile of pictures Morogh had mailed. The first few were easy to view and made the sisters smile with escaped moans of oohs and aahs: they were of Morogh and Mary's laddies standing among a few sheep, with dirty dungarees and tartan caps. The next was of Avril as a wee lass wearing an oversized bonnet, her eyes barely peeking out from under. "This one catches my breath," Rena said as she held the picture of Mary dressed in a woollen houndstooth jacket and silk scarf. "She just had her hair cropped, and she looks smashing." Mary was sitting holding her daughter Avril, who was bundled in a woollen winter jacket with a hooded collar of white faux fur.

"Isn't Avril the bonniest bairn. Will you look at that smile," Lily said as she took the picture from Rena.

A few other pictures were passed around. There was another of Morogh and Mary, standing in their kitchen, arms entwined. Morogh was kissing Mary's cheek. The next was just of Mary. She wasn't staring directly at the camera but somewhere else, unaware she had been caught on film. The sisters clambered together, almost on top of each other, for a closer look. In the background was a birthday cake and Mary's gaze appeared to be on it. Her expression was tender, beautiful. Her eyes gleamed, filled with content and happiness.

Lily handed out the last few tissues from the now-empty box as the girls released their muddled emotions, tears welling in response. "This was her twenty-sixth birthday." Rena choked on her words. "I talked to her that day . . . on the telephone. That was the last we spoke."

The pictures lay askew across the floor. The only sounds were gulps of bubbly, a soothing rush of comfort and solace.

"Why are we doing this to ourselves?" Betty announced as she stood, trying to shake away the sadness.

"Because it's what keeps them alive and in our hearts. Never to be lost. That's what Mum says," Rena concluded.

The rest of the evening was spent navigating through broken hearts and picking up shattered pieces.

Nichol and Ronald Ormonde

Betty Ormonde nee Helliwell

Jessica Mitchell nee Helliwell

Alexander Johnstone

Margaret and June

Mary and Avril

Hannah Helliwell

Catherine J. Helliwell

# Part Five

*Everything I Hold So Dear
Seems Lost*

## CHAPTER TWENTY-FOUR

# *Its Nae Better Here Than There*

*October 1942. POW Branch Camp 9-A, Amagaski, Japan*

Nick wasn't sure of the day, only the month. The journey over seemed like a long ongoing nightmare. Once the ship pulled into the Nagasaki harbour, a group of Japanese boarded; their attire of white coats and face masks left Nick dubious of their intentions, recalling the glass tube charade before leaving Hong Kong. This group of impersonators carried a chrome cylinder with a long hose and nozzle. "What the fuck is this?" Pie groaned.

The men were at the point they could suffer no more indignities. Yet here they stood in front of an assembly of oscillating Japs, spraying them down with some type of disinfectant; another layer stripped from their being.

Nick shook his head, spitting the toxic-tasting substance from his mouth, then he thought of the warship *Jho Sho Maru*, built in his homeland. And now here he was, in that very city – a POW. He spat again, this time spitting out the taste of betrayal.

They all formed into groups, waiting to be transported to the nearest train rail. That was what one of the interpreters had instructed. Nick never did see Happy again; either he was one of the casualties when the *Lisbon* sank, or he was picked up by a cargo ship. Nick hoped for the latter. John was looking worse for wear, and he hadn't mumbled a word as he stood leaning against Danny. Peter gave a sombre look towards Nick and shook his head. They all knew their comrade was dying.

The train doors opened, and orders were blasted for the men to pile in. Japanese civilians had now gathered, curious. Nick expected jeers and hateful gestures, but there weren't any. Most stood with expressions of empathy, others looked horrified. Nick could only imagine what the lot of them must have looked like. A small girl stood clutching her mother's hand. Both were dressed in the brightest of colours, and the blue and red kimonos were the prettiest things Nick had set his eyes on in a long time. The mother surveyed the group of POWs with a pitying stare. When her gaze landed upon Nick, he turned his head, his embarrassment overwhelming. Before he climbed onto the train, the little girl smiled at him, waving her hand.

Hours had gone by, and they received only one tin cup of tepid water and a bowl of rice with some type of meat; it was putrid. "I stand corrected. The food here isna any better than in Hong Kong," Jordie announced. Small, tense sniggers bounced around the train car. The rest of the journey was quiet, each man entombed in his own thoughts. When they arrived at their destination, Amagasaki, they were greeted by what Nick perceived as a domineering group of guards. Their devious grins were enough to intimidate the shite out of anyone. "*Kyotskee!*" bellowed one guard. He yelled it again. It wasn't until the English-speaking guard called the men to attention and commanded them to salute did the men fall into order.

A scowl-faced, middle-aged Japanese with beige pants and jacket approached the men. He peered out from under his sweat-stained beige cap, dark anthracite eyes surveying the prisoners. Mitsuzo Inagaki would be a name the men would never forget.

He addressed the men in Japanese, and his interpreter ran behind, delivering the ordinances of the camp. They learnt they would be made to work twelve- to- fourteen- hour shifts, and their job would be breaking up pig-iron and feeding the hot furnaces. A very important job, the interpreter made clear. Two meals a day would be administered, and those that became ill or injured would receive one meal only. Each would receive their own *tatami*, what the Japanese called the thin, straw sleeping mats. The latrines, or the *benjo*, were a couple of rickety sheds without doors that stood just yards away from an old warehouse, which just over 200 prisoners would be expected to call home. Each prisoner would have their own three-foot space to reside and sleep in.

Nick assessed the grounds, and they were desolate and depressing looking. Two large steel vats were centre-stage of the camp. Nick stared at the rusted tanks with an unsettled choke in his throat.

When the instructions of bowing and saluting to their new commander had ceased, the men entered the wooden, anaemic-looking building. At the door was a pile of thin shrouds; they didn't constitute being called blankets. Winter was approaching, and this would be their only means of warmth. Rab picked up the first and drew it to his face. He choked and shook his head. "Christ!" The stench was foul.

Morning came early; roll call, or *tenko*, was 5:00 a.m. sharp. The men were prodded and poked with bayonets. And if you forgot to bow, you were slapped in the chops. A forced series of exercises were performed, then a small serving of watery rice with lumps of – well, the prisoners weren't actually sure what it was, but they ate it anyway. This was their first day of slave labour at a steel foundry for a company they would later learn was called Otani Heavy Industry Factory. They marched out of the camp as Commander Mitsuzo Inagaki waved his bayonet as if conducting a symphony.

John was determined too ill for such a laborious job; instead, he was made to work in a nearby rice paddy field, knee deep in mucky water, bent over planting long green shafts. It would be his first and only day of farming the land for Japan's war effort.

John Findlay did not wake that morning when *tenko* was called. The slight mound of what once was a young and vibrant man lay lifeless beneath the stench of a rancid slip of material. This was the men's first ordeal of losing a comrade in the Japanese POW camp. They all stood speechless, their minds tormented, their hearts broken. Without forethought, Nick bent over and removed John's soiled, damp socks. Nick visualised John's riddled, diseased, exhausted body falling onto his mat, pulling his socks over his cold, wet feet. He wasn't sure of his intentions with the woollen pair; only that he needed something to represent John's existence here with the men.

The quick prick caught his hand when he placed the socks in his kit bag. Pinned to the inside of the brown army bag was a darning needle. How it remained in place all this time was a surprise. It wasn't until that evening, after their insufferable day at the iron factory, when he fell onto his woven mat and wiped his forehead with his bandana. He lay visualising the two guards without humanity dragging John's body away. Within that moment he was inspired to design his tapestry.

With little material to work with, he improvised by using his regulated red bandana. He became very resourceful at obtaining threads off the other prisoners. And after his daily toil at the steel foundry, he whiled away the little free time he had by putting his artistic skills to use. He began to embroider the crest of the Black Watch, symbolising the Royal Regiment of Scotland. Above the crest he stitched the words "Anglo American Japanese War," below he placed the year as 1941, when the battle began, and 1942 representing the year they'd arrived in Japan. He darned the "2" of the year in red, with intentions of changing the date, depending on the year the war ended. Below he stitched: "A Company 2nd Bn. The Royal Scots R.R. To the Officers and Men Who Fell Defending Hong Kong." The last inscription was in Latin: *Nemo Me Impune Lacessit*, meaning "No one provokes me with impunity."

Then, he laboriously unravelled John's woollen socks into strands of yarn. And he made a vow to honour each man in his Company A that died in the camp.

Respectfully, he named his composition "The Roll of Honour." And the first name he embroidered was his comrade's, his friend, John Findlay.

The work at the factory was horrendous. It was a continuous assembly line of undernourished, anorexic men heaving pig iron into furnaces at blazing temperatures. If you got too close, your hair, eyebrows, and lashes singed off within seconds. The melted steel was collected into large vats waiting to be processed. The guards added to the men's daily misery. Smacks and punches could be heard against skeletal bodies: either you weren't working hard enough, or you happened to be the recipient of a guard's bad mood. Most of the guards were former Sumo wrestlers; their girth, to say the least was intimidating. One guard named Verasaki was a slight man with a kinder disposition, and he spoke some English – impressive for being a farmer. He often distracted the other guards when one of the prisoners had to stop and take a breather.

It wasn't guaranteed the men would have a day of rest. It was all dependent on Commander Inagaki's mood. Pie, with great caution warned the men, "Nae lik'n the feel of this, lads, something is up." Patrick, Rab, and Harry stood in a circle eyeing the guards as they cleared a large ring just outside the commander's hut. Charles and Nick arrived, curious of the activity.

"What's going on here?" Charles asked. Harry replied with a shrug of his shoulder. Shortly after all the POWs had been summoned to form a circle around the cleared, dirt-packed wrestling ring, it was announced that instead of work, they were invited to partake in some recreational activity. That's what the interpreter called it. Mitsuzo Inagaki's cunning laugh bellowed over the gasping groans as each prisoner was savagely thrown to the ground. Pie was the first chosen opponent, no doubt because of his height and blazing hair. He had been a target in Hong Kong, and he would receive no different treatment in Japan.

After Pie had several rounds with three of the guards, he lost his temper and sucker punched one in the face. This would be the first time the POWs witnessed the use of the two rusted steel vats standing in the middle of the camp filled with water. Pie was held down in the deep tank, and each time he came up, his eyes bulged as he gasped for breath. This continued for an hour. Once satisfied the redhead had learnt his lesson, each guard kicked Pie as he lay on the ground unconscious. The men stood paralysed and quiet, witnessing what would become known as the "water treatment."

Other forms of abuse were the box and bamboo treatment. There was not one POW who escaped either of the barbaric tortures. The box, with a few drilled holes, lay close to the *benjo*, and if the despicable act of being entombed in a 4x4 box was not enough, the stench from the latrines would be enough to kill you. Some POWs spent days in the box, no matter the weather conditions.

The bamboo treatment proved to be worse. Your limbs grew numb, and spasms of twisted pain rendered you helpless. There were a couple of variations. The first one had you kneeling on bamboo rods, your kneecaps numbed almost immediately, and another bamboo rod was placed behind the fold of your knees. You were pushed to lean back with the weight of a pail of water on your thighs. Your misdemeanour from not bowing, not saluting, or staring too long into the face of the guards determined the period of time you remained in the immobilised stance.

The second found you standing with your arms stretched above your head, holding a bamboo rod, each end holding a pail of water. While standing, the guards took turns slapping or punching your face. If you lowered your arms, the cruel drill repeated.

The first time Nick was strong-armed into the bamboo treatment, his bony thighs cramped immediately upon kneeling, spilling the pail of water. He was beaten senseless, and he woke in a pool of his own blood. The guards left him on the ground the entire night. The prisoners were not allowed to move him or tend to his punched, beaten face.

It was now Nick's turn to fight, and the one wrestler called Snake Eyes, a name the prisoners gave him on account of his predatory leer, grabbed Nick and threw him into the ring. Nick knew this would be the fight of his life. He was the same height as his opponent. The only thing he had going for him was his weightless body, and he used it to his advantage. The two hours that Nick outmanoeuvred the fat, sloppy guard had proven successful. Snake Eyes couldn't take hold of Nick; he stomped his wide, fat feet on the ground like a bull ready to charge, beads of sweat streaming off his body. Nick could smell his rage. Finally, the out-of-shape sumo guard fell over, his girth heaving relentlessly. The prisoners cheered and yelled out Nick's name. Then Commander Inagaki stood, slowly stretching his arms above his head, and gave a wide yawn. He closed the matches down and ordered everyone to retire for the evening.

Back in the warehouse, the lads sang Nick's victory. "That is worth a day of fags, mate!" Donald claimed, reaching into his bag of cigarettes.

Ian chimed in, "You can have my dinner ration tomorrow."

Pie, who lay on his mat, battered and blue, wheezed out, "I will buy you a bottle of the best scotch when we get hame!"

"I will hold you to that, Pie!" Nick countered with a celebratory grin.

The men settled in for the night. It had been the most satisfying event they had experienced in a very long time. They all fell asleep feeling content, battered or not.

Nick felt Snake Eyes' eyes all over him; the guard's facial expression expelled a searing hate. Nick thought it best to stay clear of him. The bad-tempered, mean-spirited guard had been outperformed by a POW, a white man, something that had brought great shame on him and his code of Bushido.

The heat inside the steel foundry was hazardous, but the guards were instructing the POWs to turn out double the amount of pig iron. "Something must be up," Donald said, throwing the broken iron into the furnace. The fumes rose to the ceiling, shedding a cloud of steel dust so thick that the men choked and gagged. Nick wiped his steel-gritted tears from his eyes.

The men never saw anything of real value leave the factory, though they were well aware whatever they were producing was towards Japan's war effort. On occasion, and when a guard was not close by or watching, Nick and a few of the lads would slow down the production line by sticking a piece of pig iron into the machinery.

One morning in particular, they caused such a disturbance that the factory had to be shut down for an entire day. Both Nick and Pie heaved two large pieces of pig iron into the heart of the machine. Within minutes it spat, choked, and came to a grinding halt.

Commander Inagaki made an appearance, stomping and yelling. He ordered the prisoners to line up and had the guards strike each POW with the butt of their rifles. The prisoners stood, and through blood-streamed faces, triumphant smiles emerged.

The catalyst for the morning's revengeful sabotage had been in the name of their comrade Arthur Paton. Arthur was a quiet chap and was duly obedient when the guards poked and prodded him.

He had broken down one evening on his mat next to Nick's. "I canna go on, Nick . . . I'm going mad. We will never be rescued, and this trying to survive is fuck'n rubbish!" Nick could see Arthur's tears stream down his cheeks. "Ye ken, my lassie was with child when I left Scotland . . . I will never see my bairn. That I know, Nick, I feel it every day I'm in this God-forsaken country." Nick tried appealing to Arthur, using every possible notion he could conceive. And he actually thought he'd gotten through to his comrade. But just days ago, before Nick and Pie threw the iron rod into the mechanical workings and obstructed the machine, Nick discovered just how downtrodden his pal's emotional state was.

Arthur refused to rise for *tenko* and line up for work duty. It took two guards kicking and punching his face, stomach, and groin. They shoved him and threw him, and when they locked him in the 4x4 box, they pissed upon it. Arthur didn't make a sound, not even when they beat him. And on the third day, when the guard unlocked the box, the lads knew their comrade would forever be silent.

Arthur's body was thrown into a broken-down wagon, and when the guard trundled it away, it fell over and out several times. The men stood not as prisoners but as Royal Scots 2nd Battalion A company. They stood at attention and saluted the fife soldier's body until it was no longer in eyeshot.

That evening, when they had all made it back to the warehouse after a gruelling day of standing with no food or water while the guards repaired the machine, Nick sat on his worn mat, needle in hand, embroidering the letter A.

The next morning started like any other: *tenko*, a weevily bowl of four ounces of rice, then a gruelling series of exercises that half the men could not even perform until they were smacked into conformity. Out of all the devised practices to maintain one's health, the Japanese considered a rigorous workout was far more beneficial than a nutritious meal or an administration of medication.

When the prisoners arrived at the foundry, the machinery was running at top performance, but the guards' moods exhibited a spiteful rancour. Nick felt Snake Eyes breathing down his neck. The men knew each morning they rose could be their last. Nick believed this would be his. He cautiously worked around the furnace, eyeing Snake Eyes every move.

It was one careless moment. The steel arm swung over the vat of blistering, melted steel, and dangling from its end was Nick. His unease had caused the heedless slip. The clamp that carried large pieces of steel to be dropped into the vat had caught the end of his sleeve. He was trapped.

Snake Eyes kept his hand on the lever of the steel arm and lowered it just enough that Nick's feet dangled mere inches above the blistering swell of liquid death.

Without haste, Nick took hold of the clamp with his other hand, closed his eyes, and drew a deep breath. It was the screaming from his mates that forced him to open his eyes. They all stood staring up at him, encouraging him to hang on. The guards were laughing. And at best, Nick discerned they were making bets.

That night he lay curled in the foetus position, and he thanked God, Jesus, and the Virgin Mary. Surely it had taken the mighty trio to save him. An hour had passed, and the cheers from his comrades had turned into a disheartened silence. Finally, when the guards grew tired of Nick's courageous endurance, the steel arm swung out of harm's way. The solid land inflicted a shock of pain throughout his entire body. When he regained consciousness, he found himself inside the warehouse on his bamboo mat, with half the lads peering down upon him.

Mercifully, Nick grinned and uttered, "I need a fag!"

It had been almost a year. They'd been moved twice to other sub-camps, yet the POWs were made to endure the march to the steel foundry, no matter the distance.

More names were added to Nick's Roll of Honour; the deaths were from starvation and being riddled with disease. Red Cross parcels had become far and few between. And those that dropped were quickly seized by the guards; the prisoners never benefited.

That summer of 1943 welcomed a troop of Canadians, and when Nick recognised Andrew Reid from the enfeebled group, he ran up and grabbed the young lad. Andrew and the Grenadiers were in no better shape than Nick or the other prisoners. Things had increasingly grown worse in Hong Kong. Andrew informed Nick that murder and rape of the Chinese civilians continued. The once beautiful, established city had been turned into a squalid, impoverished Japanese district.

## CHAPTER TWENTY-FIVE

# A Tear Away from Heaven

*December 1943. POW Branch Camp 9-A, Amagaski, Japan*

"Nick, are you asleep?" whispered Jordie.

"No, nae yet, I'm trying to fight off going out for a piss," Nick replied.

"Listen, Nick, I'm hearing some fucked-up shit. We are tae be moved to another camp within the week, and the men that are tae weak to make the travel are tae be shot, or worse."

"Well, Christ! Jordie. That's the lot of us."

"Aye, I ken."

"Jordie, the Japs need us to work the iron factory. They'll nae be so eager to shoot us. Our work is essential for their genocide war," Nick said, though he knew the Japs were very cavalier in their killings. "And Christ, if we do move, that will make three camps this year. We can always pray for a step up." Nick was trying to make light.

"I dinna think I have the fucking strength for another move." Jordie coughed, his lungs full of iron dust from the furnaces. "We've been in this fuck'n country for over a year, and we've heard nothing!"

"I ken, pal. The yellow bastards believe they've won. Christ! I'm starting to believe they have," Nick replied.

Jordie snickered, then coughed again. "The land of the rising sun, my arse!" He budged from his side into a sitting position. "Well, I dinna think I can sleep now, throw me a match. I need a fag."

Nick reached under his mat, grabbed the matches, and tossed them. "Christ, I may as well go for a piss." Nick stood and assessed his work. He'd almost completed the Black Watch's patron saint, Andrew. He took one final look upon the apostle's threaded face and said, "I hope you're listening to all our prayers." He secured the embroidery needle along with its thread, and once folded, he wrapped his red bandana in an old shirt and lowered it into the hole that lay hidden under his mat and a loose floorboard, safely out of sight from the Japs.

Nick shuffled his way to the door of the dilapidated warehouse, following the moonlight's gleam through the gaps of the deteriorating wooden planks that neglectfully hung from the ceiling. There was only one large window in the makeshift building the men called home.

He opened the door, stood out on the tiny stoop, and relieved himself, grimacing at the end of his urination. The pain, at times, was unbearable; the end of his penis was fire red. He was always cautious and tried cleaning it as best he could. *Be thankful, so far no blood*, he thought. He made his way back inside and walked towards his worn bamboo mat. Faint moans permeated all around: men in pain, men dreaming, men dying – one never knew.

Endurance became common practice; if you woke in the morning, you were thankful. As the day lingered and the burden of heavy work, starvation, and torture engulfed you, you prayed for a quick death. Nick approached Andrew's mat, bent over, and patted the lad's leg. "How are you tonight, Drew?"

A faint reply surfaced. "Tired. I'm tired of trying to live . . . yet I'm afraid I will not wake if I sleep." Andrew's breathing had weakened tremendously over the last twenty-four hours.

Nick squeezed the boy's thin, bony leg. "Drew, you canna be that lucky to leave us sodden lot in this beautiful establishment." Nick tried to ensure his reply was light. But in his heart, he knew his friend might not see morning.

Death was nothing new to the men. They tried to view it with a complacency bred of a hard familiarity. It became a survival tactic, just like any other of their training.

Andrew, not alone, suffered with what was commonly referred to in the camp as Changi balls (scrotal dermatitis). His condition had worsened, his skin was burning, and it began to peel up between his thighs into his scrotum and penis, leaving him susceptible to infection, which was already apparent from his high fever. And as if he could bear more, he was stricken with an insufferable, stabbing, hot pain that ripped at the soles of his feet, setting them on fire.

The lack of food, nutrition, and medical attention took the lives of many. The Japanese gave no medicine, nor would they permit extra rations of food or water for the sick. The Japanese did not tolerate illness or weakness. "Stay healthy," was an ambiguous phrase the men heard all too often. Andrew had become a mere skeleton of himself, his youth, his life, stolen.

If there were one commonality the men could attest to, they would all eventually suffer the same afflictions. Electric feet was one. Seeking relief would be a fair runner-up. Some would immerse their feet in ice-cold water to relieve the insufferable hot stabbing pain. Unfortunately, the impulsive action led to no more than an exchanged tormented feeling of ice shards piercing through one's skin, subsequently requiring the solace of heat, a vicious cycle to say the least.

If one could find the lighter side, or appeal to the antidote of humour, it helped lessen the atrocities, if not only for a moment. This was something with which the Royal Scots were gifted.

It became common sight, men jumping up and down or running around in circles, while some broke out in song, making their agonising stomps into a jig. A chorus of "Stop Yer Tickling, Jock" belted out across the compound, alarming the Jap guards.

> *Will you stop yer tickling, Jock!*
> *Oh, stop yer tickling, Jock!*
> *Dinna mak' me laugh so hearty,*
> *Or you'll mak' me choke.*
> *Oh, I wish you'd stop yer nonsense,*
> *Just look at all the folk.*
> *Will yer stop yer tic-kle-ing, tic-kle-ic-kle-ing.*
> *Stop yer tickling, Jock!*

Electric feet amusingly became referred to as "Happy Feet." Most POWs suffered from the affliction, from one degree to another. And even years after captivity, surviving POWs continued to experience sharp, electric pains dancing through the soles of their feet. The nerve damage was permanent.

Nick lay back down, trying to find the most comfortable position his eighty-nine-pound skeleton frame could conform to. He slept on a bamboo mat accompanied by an old, worn blanket that was frayed and nearly transparent. No warmth did it ever give, but he'd grown attached to what little coverage and comfort it bestowed.

"Nick, do you think Andrew will make it through the night?" Ian asked.

"For his sake, I hope not." Nick shifted his body slightly to relieve the sharp pain that pierced his hip. He closed his eyes and his mind and prayed for his comrade.

Mornings arrived with never enough sleep. At first wakening, there was an unidentifiable moment; it faded between moments of reality and fantasy, confusing the mind. Dreams became your only escape. If you were lucky, you dreamt of home or a loved one. Many a night Nick's dreams lay trapped in between what was real and what was not. And as the months dragged on, he found himself waking mostly in the depths of turbulent nightmares.

There would be no work at the steel foundry today. Depending on Commander Inagaki's mood, the POWs would be granted a day reprieve from their fourteen-hour shifts. The day started like any other. A series of regimented exercises were imposed on the soldiers: running on the spot, jumping jacks, push-ups. It was a humiliating sight to behold – rows of skeletons cloaked with ragged cloths hanging from their bones, hanging from their soles. Thin arms flapping up and down, not enough to stir a draft. Electric feet hitting the dusted ground, inflicting waves of shock, alerting the brain that a life still existed, alerting the heart to a life that was missed.

The day of so-called rest continued with the cleaning of latrines and living space. And a favourable task among the men: the eviction of the four-legged tenants. Sometimes a fat-infested free rat would constitute a good meal. The odd time the men would set a small trap outside of the warehouse to catch tiny birds; it was not enough to sustain them, but any amount of protein was welcome.

## THE ROLL OF HONOUR

The December morning air was chilly. The sound of men stirring grew as another day of hunger, sickness, and degradation subjugated them. Nick awakened accompanied by a burning ache at the base of his neck. He rose slowly. Each morning there was a reminder of the mock beheading the Japanese guards had subjected him to during imprisonment at his first camp, Shamshuipo, in Hong Kong.

The cool, damp air did the sick and dying no favours. Quivering bones rattled, searching for warmth from the first ray of sunlight beaming through each crack and crevice of the warehouse walls. Small moans and familiar coughs arose, a subtle reminder . . . *yes, you are still here, still alive.*

Nick rubbed the base of his neck while he stretched his body as long as it would reach. He made his way over to Andrew and noticed he hadn't moved, not even the slightest. Arms and legs remained curled inward, hugging his body in the same position Nick had left him in at nightfall. Nick crouched down, placed his hand on Andrew's shoulder, and was astonished when a current of warmth replied. "Drew, lad, you made it. It's morning."

"Nick, I . . . can't feel my legs . . . I've pissed all over . . . I . . . I can't get up." Andrew tried turning towards Nick, his words faintly spoken.

"Dinna you worry, I will help clean you up, and will find something for you to eat and drink." Nick would look to trade a few fags for any type of food he could come by. Bartering became common practice. You traded to survive or traded to die. Some soldiers would only smoke cigarettes to suppress their appetite and hoped for a quicker death. Red Cross airdrops became less frequent, and even when they had been abundant during the first year of imprisonment, the POWs received few or no parcels. The Japs either kept the goods locked up or would sell them off to the highest bidder. Smiley, a middle-aged Japanese camp officer, was famous for trading supplies with the POWs, dependant on his mood. The men had nicknamed him Smiley as his facial expression always bore a smile, which did not jibe with his ruthless nature: barked orders and bamboo smacks were all conducted under an ignoble smile.

"Don't bother yourself, I can't eat . . . just sit with m . . . me." Nick sat alongside Andrew and what was left of his tiny, declining frame. By this time, the men had already left the warehouse to start their daily toil of survival. The air was still chilled, as was the silence. Andrew lay on his side, curled into the foetal position, a position that many men found comfort in as it was once a sacred place of immunity. Nick rubbed Andrew from the nape of his neck to the bottom of his spine to offer warmth and comfort. He felt each bone protrude, each surfaced vertebrae, as if no skin or muscle lay between. Andrew was taller than Nick by at least four inches. Yet as Nick guarded over him, he thought how much smaller he looked. Then he thought of all the men, and how they were all shrinking, withering away from existence.

Andrew tried to speak, but his weakened condition prevented him. Nick very well understood Andrew's trepidation and prayed he would slip away before the Japs made an impromptu camp inspection. Rumour was that the Japanese used the bodies of terminally ill soldiers for medical experiments.

## CHAPTER TWENTY-SIX

# *Prayers, Mourners, and Saints*

*December 1943. POW Branch Camp 9-A, Amagaski, Japan*

The POWs' casual chatter outside of the warehouse eased Nick's nerves. The signal was that the men would cease talking if the guards were approaching.

It was an unspoken ritual that the soldiers remain close by, act normal (whatever that was), and not draw any unwanted attention. The fear of death had long passed; it was the fear of *how* you could die that evoked the men's trepidation. Thoughts of being beaten to death or left for days in agony without medication or proper nutrition became a constant state of play. It was considered a blessing if you died within the warehouse walls with a companion at your side.

The men performed many common practices, and praying became the most essential.

Andrew's breathing became laboured. Nick remained close, offering as much warmth and companionship as he could. "You're a tear away from heaven, lad," Nick whispered into Andrew's ear. Andrew had used this citation at the end of his nightly prayers.

Every night, Nick, once he'd finished his Guardian Angel Prayer (which took him forever to choose, or even remember, for that matter), performed the sign of the holy cross. Then he lay quiet while Andrew finished his Presbyterian prayer: "May we be secure in your loving protection and serve you always with grateful hearts. We ask this through Jesus Christ, your Son who lives and reigns with You and the Holy Spirit, one God, forever and ever, Amen." Andrew then fell silent, only for a moment. His last citation was voiced with conviction: "I am a tear away from heaven." Silence again.

Nick knew without seeing his face that the lad shed his tears in the dark of the night. He was not alone; hundreds of young soldiers would cry in the night and die a thousand deaths. This young lad, far from his homeland, Canada, clung to Nick for security, not that he was weak or cowardly, only because he was human. When the deprivation of everything vital to surviving is stripped from your being, and your days and months and years are subjected to acts of brutality and demoralization, your being falls, your soul is lost. Then it's at that pivotal moment, without even realizing it, you choose to survive – or choose to surrender. Andrew, for as long as humanly possible, chose to live.

Camaraderie was essential to survival. The Japs tried to break every element of both body and soul. They greatly underestimated and were nescient of the brotherhood among the battalions. Nick hated that Andrew would die in this shit hole, the only surroundings he'd known for the past year. He would die – die without knowing a life of love and children. The lad would never experience the touch of a woman or feel her naked body next to his. Andrew had confessed to Nick that he was a virgin and begged Nick not to tell the other lads. "They will make fun, mock me."

Nick always replied the same: "Drew, you are not the only virgin in this war, though you may be the only one admitting it."

Andrew came from a strict Presbyterian background, and he told Nick stories of his childhood and how tough and rugged farming life was in Winnipeg for a young boy. Education was not paramount. He had joined the army to travel, find adventure, and fall in love with exotic women from all over the world. Andrew certainly was not the only young naive lad who had the same taste for an unfortunately false adventure.

When the sting of reality bites its way through your flesh and imprisons your soul, all that you thought you escaped from becomes your anchor – your home. Nick spoke to Andrew telling him to think of his homeland, his farm.

Nick's Guardian Angel prayer was one he'd heard his mother, Christina Massaro, use on occasion. And many a night he lay awake thinking of her, his family, and everything he fiercely missed.

A small shrine was assembled with a collection of anointed instruments; a mother's set stage to perform her service to Christ and his mother, the Blessed Virgin. A print of Sandro Botticelli's *Madonna Adoring the Child with Five Angels* hung encased in an gaudy, ornate frame. The print had emigrated to Scotland along with the Massaro family.

How she loved the Renaissance period and its artists. Botticelli was her favourite, Michelangelo a close runner-up. And of course, what Italian did not love the work of Vasari? *"Se potessi riempire la mia casa con tutti I loro besslssimi dipinti"* – "I would fill my home with all their beautiful paintings if I could," Christina professed. She loved that her son took an interest in the arts and proudly claimed his talent at each and every chance.

Nick was ten when his mother secretly purchased two books: *Michelangelo: A Record of His Life Told in His Own Stories and Papers*, translated and edited by Robert W. Carden in 1913. The second was *The Life of Giogrio Vasari: A Study of the Later Renaissance in Italy, 1911*. She saved for them, then wrote to her brother Antonio in Florence to post the books for her son, "*Il Bellissimo artista*" – the beautiful artist. When the package arrived, she swore Nicholas to secrecy. "This is our secret, *capisci?*"

The shrine was an old dresser, small enough to slide inside the hallway closet. The instruments were two fake-gold candlesticks draped with dried clumps of wax, arranged on either side of a small, red-velvet box with a golden clasp. A rosary lay placed atop, carefully. All were anointed by Father Andrea from St. Mary's South Leith Church. Positioned on the floor lay a piece of burgundy velvet material folded over several times, enough to make the kneeling bearable. Two faded knee prints validated hours of prayer, confession, and repentance. After all, thirteen bambinos were in need of saving and guidance into a good Catholic life.

When Nick finished his prayer, he would think of his mother kneeling in her closet on the worn piece of burgundy fabric, candles lit, rosary wrapped tightly around her small, aging hands. He knew she not only prayed for him, but for a tiny soul that slept with Madonna and her angels. Nick never knew his brother Michael. Michael was only six months old when Christina fell pregnant with her fourteenth: Nicholas.

Christina was small in stature, barely five feet tall, with the tiniest frame. It was inconceivable but most impressive that such a small woman had birthed fourteen children without any complications or intermittent miscarriages.

However, she found this last pregnancy draining, and she prayed for an uncomplicated birth. The loss of her son Michael was not one through absent prayers to a saint but through the unintentional act of an exhausted pregnant mother. Nick never heard the story from his parents; nevertheless, he did from his siblings when he was seven. Not that he was frightened of his mother, but the authenticity of the story itself did unnerve him.

Large kettles of boiling water filled the old tub in preparation for bath time. The worn relic lay positioned in front of the fire hearth. The evening breathed of chaos, mounted dishes, piles of unattended homework, bairns playing and running about. The older girls assisted their mother while their father minded the shop. Christina was exhausted and her mind seemed scattered, less focused. She just wanted to push on, complete the nightly chores. Her mind wandered, envisioning a hot cappuccino while sitting quietly by the fire. Perhaps tonight, Saint Gemma Galgani, the Virgin of Lucca would be her audience. She was in desperate need of relief of aching feet and an unforgiving, aching back.

Michael, now nine months, was crying and hungry. Christina lifted him in preparation for his bath. She slipped off his wet nappie, his chubby legs kicking in protest. Her breasts, heavy with milk, would find no relief until her baby suckled. The old tub had accompanied them from Italy. Christina desired a more modern tub, larger with a smoother finish – a cleaner look. She lined the old sheet metal bottom with terry cloth to save chafed bottoms and avoid slippage.

The tub's level of hot water had been reached, and the commotion remained steadfast. Christina placed her baby in the tub, hot steam seized her hands, and a shrill scream echoed throughout the small family room. Her body shook, her heart missed a beat, her mind focused. She hastily reached back into the tub to remove the baby, and as she did, little Michael turned over, immersing his face and body into the scalding water.

The tragic death of Michael Massaro was rarely discussed, and although Nick was baptised Nicholas Massaro, his mother frequently called him Michael. Christina had not lost her wits, as many had discerned, nor did she confuse her newborn with the child she had lost. It was a mother's means to navigate through her grief. Nick became accustomed to what he considered his angel's name. His mother justified her belief by affirming, in broken English, "My Nicholas, our Michael, he sleeps with the blessed Virgin and all the angels. I see him forever in you." It seemed like a heavy burden to carry for a young boy, though Nick could never question his mother's edicts; after all, she had high counsel with the Blessed Mary.

Nick's father, Francis, dealt with his grief by working countless hours, and he relied on the older children to help. Once Nick became tall enough to reach the ice-cream counter, he joined ranks. His two older brothers, Jimmy and Philip, ran the shop at night. One thing was indisputable: Francis Massaro made the best ice-cream in Leith.

Nick didn't mind his hand in helping out, although his passion was art; in his spare time he loved to draw and paint and was hoping to attend the arts program at Edinburgh College. He also worked part time as a terrazzo mason worker to pay for school. Dinner conversations were always the same: his father spoke of business and shared his idea of opening another ice-cream shop. And he made it quite clear his children would play an intricate role.

Nick remained quiet, focusing on his plate of pasta smothered in fresh grilled tomatoes and olive oil. Surely his brothers would be better suited; already Jimmy was cranking out ice-cream just as good as his pop. *Yes, Jimmy,* Nick thought as he spooned the pasta into his mouth. He knew his father was eyeing everyone up at the table, inviting the conversation. And, as always, his mother would save him. With all good intentions, her conversation began in English, however broken and slow. Frustration prevailed, a roll of the tongue, and her statement ended in Italian, trailed by "*capisci.*" That particular evening her message was delivered directly to her husband, full Italian style, hand gestures and all. There would be no talk of business at the family table – dinner was for eating and enjoyment. Nick raised his head and smiled at his mother, and she responded by cupping his face and kissing his forehead. "My ... ah ... Michael, my bellissimo boy."

Nick was stationed in Africa when Mussolini announced Italy's support and alliance with Germany. He was appalled to learn of the atrocities back home and was greatly concerned for his family's safety.

The Italians in Leith suffered tremendously, and their community turned their backs on them. Violence and looting broke out, and angered crowds paraded the streets throwing bricks and rocks, smashing windows, damaging numerous Italian businesses.

"Must we now endure violence in our streets? Is it not enough we're subjected to dirty jeers and racial jabs?" Francis vehemently expressed while closing the flat's sitting room window to block the defamatory threats bellowing out from below.

"I will pray . . . pray extra," Christina replied in broken English. For what else could a mother do?

"Pray all you want, Christina. It didn't help poor old Mr. Demarco."

"Traitors! Mussolini wops! Greasy dagos! Go hame, yer nae welcome here!" yelled a woman with a bairn tucked under her arm. She stood out from the crowd. Francis looked down onto the street from their sitting room window, watching as bricks and objects flew through the air targeting shop windows. Fires were set ablaze in the middle of the street. He caught her eye, the young woman holding her bairn, and he recognised her. She lived along Junction Road, and she frequented the shop for a soft vanilla cone. Christina always gave the wee bairn a lick of ice-cream from a spoon. Yet, there she was, standing brazen as ever, screaming discriminatory jibes, and her wee one smiling, soft pink cheeks aglow, fat fingers jammed into her mouth, all tucked under her bonnet; her first innocence stolen.

Francis's heart sank. These were people he'd grown to know and love. He spent afternoons in his ice-cream shop discussing horse races and bookie bets and playing chess. His wife, Christina, handed out Italian home remedies to local families whose bairns suffered from a bronchial chest. Never in his thirty years living in Scotland had he ever missed home, missed Italy, as he did that very evening. He was thankful his wife knelt tucked away praying with Madonna and all her angels, as he knew this would have torn through her soul. The hateful fear that bred throughout Leith was inconceivable.

On June 10, 1940, Mussolini's declaration of war on Great Britain changed the lives of all the Italo-Scots in Leith. Winston Churchill ordered authorities to "collar the lot" of so-called "enemy aliens." His impetuous mandate proved only to provoke violence, hysteria, and paranoia. Sadly, and unforgivably, hundreds of Italian men were deported back to Italy. On July 2, they were forced onto the *Arandora Star* and shipped off. Tragedy struck when a German U-boat launched a torpedo, destroying the ship and killing "the lot."

Francis and his family, fortunately, came out unscathed, the mobs died down, and fires were extinguished. News travelled fast, such as the fires the night before blazing through the Italian neighbourhoods. Looting and fires swept through Edinburgh, Abbeyhill, Dalry, and Portobello. Italian-owned cafes and ice-cream shops were pillaged of all goods, leaving windows smashed entirely out. Francis was deeply concerned for his old friend Galletta, who owned the local barbershop just down the road from Francis's ice-cream parlour on Henderson Street; he had heard it was completely demolished.

The most disturbing news, which shook the Italian community, was the death of eighty-two-year-old Guiseppe Demarco. He and his wife owned a cafe shop on the High Street in Portobello. Two young men entered the shop and began threatening the old couple: they swore, spat, and began to throw goods from the shelves. They seized Mr. Demarco by his throat and beat him to death with his own stock of glass bottles. The whole time his wife watched in horror. Unable to call for help and save her husband, she stood, helpless. The last thing Mrs. Demarco heard was, "You filthy wop," before she was battered with the same glass bottles that killed her husband. Her injuries were severe, and miraculously she survived. The two young men were arrested, along with a bag of stolen money from the cash register.

A community mourned.

# CHAPTER TWENTY-SEVEN

# A Simple Scottish Ballad

*December 1943. POW Branch Camp 9-A, Amagaski, Japan*

Without mercy, the winter wind blew, finding its way through the warehouse's dilapidated structure of boards. Andrew shivered and tightened his tiny frame, and Nick continued to rub his back and speak of his homeland. Nick had never been to Canada; therefore, he could only describe Andrew's home and farm by his friend's own portrayal. Both had spent hours sharing stories of their families, loved ones, and homes. When Andrew first shared his stories with Nick, he ended with an invite, asking Nick to visit him after the war. "My mother will cook you a grand meal . . . steak, potatoes, corn, all off our land."

As Nick lay next to Andrew, he studied the boy's face; it had become grey and sallow. His once youthful-looking eyes were now hopelessly lost. Nick's heart weighed heavy, and his tears fell on Andrew's shoulders.

The warehouse door blew open. Jordie and Danny were ushered in alongside a cold breeze, and it coiled throughout. Andrew shivered, clenching his teeth. "Nick, the lads are asking what we should do about the Christmas concert tonight?" Danny asked.

For the past few days Nick's focus had been on Andrew, and he had forgotten the Christmas concert. "Aye, I forgot. No worries, lads, we'll still perform."

Jordie and Danny knelt beside Andrew, and Jordie placed his hand on Andrew's shoulder. "We'll sing our hearts out for you tonight, lad." The three fell silent, and their stares held; by tomorrow, an empty space would remain throughout and within.

One could not help but count – count the days, the weeks, the months, the years. It became a constant, counting days to die or days to survive. At times, neither seemed significant. One only counted.

Nick was now counting in years. It was his third Christmas in captivity. Commander Inagaki allowed the men to celebrate their Christmas beliefs. This year, for whatever reason, the commander gave the men Christmas Eve and Christmas Day off. It was news the men were delighted by but they were also suspiciously cautious.

Last Christmas Nick and a few of the lads had decided to put on a Christmas Eve performance to break the mood and hopefully lift spirits. As promised, this year the same Christmas celebration would be conducted.

The night air imposed a most unwelcoming chill, and the long warehouse was packed with huddled, shivering men, all had gathered to unite and celebrate.

A platform was constructed from an old door and two litter bins. It was set up across the back wall. The concert was about to begin. Weeks of practice would now come to stage. First up, a few Australian lads sang a rendition of "Silent Night." When they'd finished, the applause was subtle, not the boisterous reaction they'd received the previous Christmas. Next up was a mix of a few Canadian and Australian lads belting out "Auld Lang Syne." The first line, "Should auld acquaintance be forgot, and never brought to mind," tore through Nick's heart, and he was sure it did for all the lads this Christmas Eve. Death was not new to the men; they had watched many of their comrades fall ill and die or be tortured to death. The loss of their young Canadian friend that morning resonated with the men on a different level than any other death; however, at the time they couldn't discern the difference.

After Andrew had died in Nick's arms, all the men took turns watching vigil over the young soldier's body until an officer was found to conduct the service. Nick felt compelled to say a few words before the officer finished his closing prayer:

"To our friend, our comrade, our young Winnipeg Grenadier, Private Andrew Reid. You've travelled a long way from home, lad, and your short time upon this earth will not be forgotten. You will not only be remembered as a prisoner of Japan, but as a brave young soldier with a big heart and a kind smile. I do see you on your farm, riding that old mare. How stubborn and unwilling you said she was. Though you never gave up. Just as you never gave up being a soldier. You grew up hard and fast from the young lad I met on Christmas Day in Bowen Street Hospital. You grew to be a man, a good man, a man your mother and father would be proud of. In my heart I know you are riding that old mare through the long golden wheat, far away from this hell pit." Nick paused to collect himself, as he felt choked. He cleared his throat and softly concluded, "Andrew, you are no longer a tear away from heaven. You are now hame."

Once the ceremony was finished, Andrew's body was unceremoniously trundled away in a trailer towed by a bicycle.

The warehouse was still, silent, aside from the assembled choir continuing the last chorus of "Auld Lang Syne." No audience member joined in, and there was not so much a cheer as the lads reached the finale: "And we'll tak a cup o' kindness yet, For Auld Lang Syne." An Australian soldier came to a quick attention once their singing ceased, and he raised his hand and saluted. "To Andrew, our mate, may you be in the heavens, away from this God-forsaken place."

Again silence fell. The only audible sound was of wooden matches striking to light cigarettes, adding to the already smoke-laden room.

It was in that silence the men realised it was more than death that caused their indifference, their apathy. The soldiers would be entering into their fourth year of captivity. While they revelled in their weekly practice in efforts to perform a special Christmas concert, their attention waned. Their thoughts were of home. The lads gazed in the direction of the platform, but their eyes did not rest there; their focus lay beyond, staring blankly, each man immersed in his own thought.

Nick felt the same qualm, his mind reeling with the same trepidations: *Will I survive, will I ever see my family, my homeland?* With great perseverance he shook away his tormented emotions, and he jumped out of his seat and rallied a few lads. "Jordie! Danny! Rab! Get your tartan on. We are going to perform for these boys in the style in which they deserve." The

Royal Scots jumped up, following Nick's command, and hit the platform. The audience stirred in a curious state.

"Now, my fellow comrades, we are going to show these fucking Japs just what us Scots are made of. A lot of you won't know this number, as it's not a Christmas carol, but a simple Scottish ballad." Nick hummed the first few bars. The four stood atop the stage, muffled up against the December cold in their threadbare uniforms. A transformation occurred, and passionate voices sang in andante. It wasn't prisoners in tattered khakis that performed that night, it was four Royal Scots in tartan trews, and they belted out "My Ain Folk". The song was vaguely familiar to some, although completely unknown to others. But the effect was the same.

*Far frae my hame I wander but still my thoughts return*
*To my ain folk over yonder in the sheiling by the burn*
*I see the cosy ingle and the mist upon the brae*
*And joy and sadness mingle as I list some auld world lay*
*And it' oh but I'm longing for my ain folk*
*Though they be but lowly pure and plain folk*

*I am far beyond the sea but my heart will always be*
*At home in dear old Scotland wi' my ain folk*
*A bonnie lassie's greetin' tho' she tries tae stay the tears*
*And sweet will be our meeting after many weary years*

*How my mother will caress me when I'm standing by her side*
*Now she prays that heaven will bless me through the stormy seas divide*
*And it' oh but I'm longing for my ain folk*
*Though they be but lowly pure and plain folk*
*At home in dear old Scotland wi' my ain folk*

The men's eyes lost that faraway look, the corners of their mouths uplifted, the smoke-laden air was alive again. Their indifference had now passed. They still thought of home, their mothers, fathers, sweethearts, and wives, but their thoughts were put into words by a song. A feeling of peaceful contentment and a sense of security had settled over them; they felt in closer contact with their loved ones. The remainder of the evening progressed with lifted spirits.

# Part Six

*Beginnings and Endings; They All Seem Muddled.*

## CHAPTER TWENTY-EIGHT

## A Promise of New Beginnings

*December 1938, Edinburgh*

Rena drifted in and out of sleep, and the soft cooing of the wood pigeon outside the bedroom window was like a lullaby. Robert moaned, turning his lanky, taut-muscled body inward, wrapping both arms and legs around her. She let out a small sound and shifted herself closer, positioning her bottom in the fold of Robert's hips. She could feel the hard urgency of him against her. He nuzzled his head in the crook of her neck, kissing her tenderly, from her nape to her earlobe. He paused there and took a deep breath while roaming his free hand along the contour of her hip, pulling her in closer. "Ye sound like the pigeon, ye ken. All soft and cooing," Robert chortled with a heavy breath.

"My da calls them culvers." Rena circumvented Robert's reach as he tried lifting her nightgown. "Spud, I have to get up and get dressed. Besides, I think you should be well worn oot from last night." Robert lay back, stretching the full length of his body, placing his hand under his head. His black waves of hair laid sprawled out against the white cotton pillowcase. He wanted to respond that here in Scotland the bird is simply known as a pigeon, a large one at that, not a culver. But she always got defensive when it came to her father, even in jest. So, he let the English-named bird be just that.

He watched her rise and reposition her nightgown. He loved watching her in the mornings. Her honey-toned hair was a mess of waves, and it bounced gently just above her shoulders, soft and loose. Her soft brown eyes flitted with a sense of innocence. No one would ever know the loss that lay deep within, encompassing her heart. But everyone around George Street, perhaps the whole of Leith, Robert thought, kent the tragic losses the Helliwell family had endured. Helliwell was not a common name in the area, and John's reputation exceeded his own self-importance. And he was bloody proud of it.

"Who will be there this evening?" Robert asked, now rising himself to dress for work. He had hired a young lad to open the shop and prepare the morning bake. It gave him at least a bit of a lie in to spend more time with his wife.

"I am certain Emma and Lily. I'm hoping William. Not sure of Betty, she says Percy has been quite ill." Rena sat on the edge of the bed pulling her stockings on, fastening them to the clips of her garter. "Hannah seems better. Mum says she has a wee bit of colour. She's been home a couple of nights now and it will do her good to have us around."

"I don't have to come, Rena, I can leave you be with your family," Robert said, bending down and kissing the top of her head. He took in the smell of rosehips, the scent wafting out from her hair.

"You are my family, Spud." Rena took his hand, implying that he sit next to her. When he did, she said nothing. She only sat, tucking her hand beneath the expanse of his. He knew she felt safe feeling the weight of it, supporting, bearing all her shattered pieces that lay lost in the fractured places of her heart.

"I'll call if I'm late, then," Robert offered. "We are busy with all the Christmas baking. I've convinced Meg to help oot." He laughed. "Ye ken, she wasna too pleased, but thank God her husband convinced her."

"Aye, Sandy is a good man and a wonderful brother-in-law." Rena jumped, startled by the thud of the flap of wings hitting the pane of glass as the pigeon a.k.a. culver took flight.

Rena arrived at the gate the same time Lily did. Perhaps their recollection differed, and the years in between formed a discordant memory, each orchestrating their own score through the family crisis. Nevertheless, subconsciously, the black wrought-iron gate dressed in thick, twisted, bare branches gripped the sisters. It had been twelve years, springtime, and the ivy vine then had flaunted a mass of green. It was the day they'd all learnt of Catherine J's death. Rena could no longer remember her sister's face; she could only visualize a likeness perhaps to Jessie, but even her dark eyes and striking features had long faded. Mary, she thought, would be the closest in likeness, and she fought hard to keep her sister's image in her mind. And when she felt she was losing it, she sorted through Morogh's pictures. "There you are," Rena would say to herself. Afraid to lose it, like a misplaced gem.

Lily spoke first. "Ye mind Hannah belting oot 'Three Craws' that day?"

Rena grinned, thinking of the exact same thing. "Aye, I think she has the best singing voice oot of the lot of us." Rena opened the gate and let Lily pass through first.

"We fought that day, Rena," Lily said, her grip tight on the gate.

"Lily, we all fought, that's what sisters do." Rena felt that same pang; sometimes it was like a cramp gripping at her chest. Her fights with Margaret were silly, infantile-like. She tried hard to think of the fun times. But she had to admit some of her best memories were of the silly squabbles she and Margaret had.

"That's why I took off and left yous all behind. Hannah and I fought over oor lunch boxes. I kent she had mine, she grabbed it in the morn. I tried telling her, she wouldna listen. I kent it was daft, but she made me so angry. And then I got pissed at Mary and told her I would walk hame with my mates." Lily released her grip on the gate, folded her hands toward her face, and cried.

"Lily, it's alright. She's hame. If she wasna well, the doctor wouldna have discharged her." It was a guarded statement. Lily knew it, and Rena even knew it before she delivered it.

Tuberculosis, commonly referred to as the consumption, was causing havoc within Edinburgh's health establishments. Research was at the forefront, and the Royal Victoria Hospital was paving its path. Hannah's symptoms were latent; they lay dormant, but for how long? No one knew, not even the doctors. The X-ray images proved to be of poor resolution, leaving doctors frustrated and exasperated. Sputum tests were frequently required; however, they were only effective if the patient had active symptoms. Sanatoriums became the hideaway for convalescence. Hannah had her share of visits in and out over the past few months from the time of her diagnosis. Light treatment or phototherapy (artificial light therapy) was the most prevalent practise. Initially, hospital wards were erected for recovery. Most homes were overcrowded with large families, and the fear of further breakouts led to the increased number of hospital admittance. A shortage of beds in rural-area hospitals was a serious issue; only patients who had advanced stages would be allowed admittance.

Hannah, at least, was home, and all any of the family could do now was hope that she was on the road to recovery. Her diagnosis had been a shock. Looking back, they'd all thought Hannah seemed peely wally. They all discussed it, her sisters and brother. Betty more so, as she stated it several times. But she was told to hauld her wheesht, as their mother did not need to hear such things. Rena's father's antidote was a hearty meal or a dram. He was always insisting Hannah eat more.

"You need some sustenance, lass." Rena could hear her father's persuasive tone, expelled in his Yorkshire dialect, which was emphasised during such circumstances. Then the tug of the waistcoat. Rena did wonder if her father was conscious of his action. He must be. It was most intimidating.

The sound of laughter caught Rena and Lily as they entered the house. The smell of haddie and chips lingered pleasantly in the air. Rena's mother was busy in the kitchen, darting back and forth between the range and the table. Her apron was dusted with fish batter, her mound of dark hair, streaked now with grey, was loosening from its bun. Rena could see particles of powdered batter throughout it.

"Mum, slow doon a bit. Lily and I can help oot, ye ken." Rena grabbed the set of plates from the sideboard and began setting the table. Lily grabbed the cutlery and tumblers.

"Thanks, lassies," Catherine said in a very worn voice. She sat down, wiping her hands on her apron. "I'm awfully tired."

"I can see that," Lily replied, wiping a dusting of batter from her mother's cheek.

"Mum, go in and sit with Hannah and William, Lily and I will finish up in here then join you." Rena stated it sternly, otherwise she knew her mother would argue.

William's laugh was deep, his banter brilliant. Rena and Lily could hear their brother and sisters' laughter billowing out from the sitting room.

"Tis exactly what she needs, William's patter," Lily claimed.

"I think we could all use our brother's patter," Rena said with an earnest expression.

When their work was done, both girls joined in on the private party William and Hannah were having, and of course the recent addition, their mother.

"Well, look who the cat dragged in." William laughed as he stood to hug his sisters. "Yer both in time to cheer our Hannah up."

"Looks like yer doing a fine job yourself, brother." Rena embraced him, whispering in his ear, "Is she okay?" William gave a nod, but Rena was not too sure how to interpret it. She glanced over her brother's shoulder and eyed Hannah. *She looks well enough,* Rena thought. Hannah had caught her sister's gaze and gave a smile. Rena quickly altered her sharp, concerned expression into a tender one.

William excused himself out to the back garden to help their father mend the coal shed. "Don't be too long. Tea is almost ready," Catherine demanded. "Yer father has been mending that bloody coal shed for over a fortnight. He's driving me mad, ye ken."

Lily glanced at Rena with a commiserating expression. Their father, now retired, didn't have the sea to sail off to during a crisis. Apparently, the coal shed had become his asylum.

The six of them sat around the table enjoying the battered fish. Rena's mind drifted, thinking back to all the family gatherings that had taken place. It was hard not to think of those who had passed. They were everywhere, their voices and faces still lingered within the walls of their home, and each meal evoked a treasured memory.

Rena watched as Hannah tried to bite into her thick fillet of fish and laugh at the same time. William was telling a joke and his punch line was on cue with Hannah's intake of food. Laughter filled the kitchen. It may have only been a brief moment, but it was long enough for everyone to relinquish their worrisome thoughts of Hannah's condition.

Tea was finished, and Lily offered to help their mother with the dishes. William joined their father out in the back garden, where John could smoke his pipe. Emma never arrived, as she said June had caught a cold, and she'd thought better of having her around Hannah. To Rena's surprise, Uncle Geordie and Auntie Lizzie declined, as both bake shops were bustling with Christmas orders of cakes and bridies.

Rena was actually glad for the small gathering; it would give her some alone time with Hannah. The two had retired to the living room, leaving Lily and their mother on clean up.

"I'm feeling much better, Rena," Hannah said, hugging the knitted blanket around her shoulders. Rena sat closer, eyeballing her sister's expression, trying to decipher if she was telling the truth or not.

"How is your flat coming?" Hannah asked, wanting to change the subject. "I must visit again, perhaps before Christmas," she stated, placing her hand on her sister's. "I can't wait for Victor and I to be together, ye ken, living as a couple. I do miss him. I just received his letter, he and Grace are coming to Edinburgh for Christmas. I'm bursting, Rena, I love him so much." Hannah coughed a little into her blanket. Rena gave her a look.

"I'm fine Rena, I'm on the mend."

Regardless, Rena offered her a hot cuppa.

"Och, will you stop, I said I'm fine. Just sit and blether with me. I miss that the most." Hannah smiled and unfolded the letter, excited to read it aloud to her sister.

> *My Dearest Hannah,*
>
> *First I want you to feel my kisses, imagine them, warm and long. On your eyelids, across your cheeks to your beautiful perfect nose. Then to your sensuous lips. I will reside there the longest.*

Hannah paused, and her eyes danced as she looked at her sister. "Rena, isn't he exquisite!" She read on.

> *I can't describe how much I desire to be with you. Each passing day I miss you more. I will spare you the official naval duties I am assigned here in Port Elizabeth to perform. They are nothing compared to what I would like to do with you when I return home.*

Hannah lowered her voice at that piece, and she beamed, her smile radiant. A rush of blush crept across her cheeks. Rena could feel her sister's happiness; it flowed out from everywhere. She knew that very feeling with her Robert.

"Oh, this is my favourite bit." Hannah resumed:

> *I will be home December 24, in the morning. That's when my train will arrive into Waverley Station. Be prepared, I have purchased you a most beautiful gift.*
>
> *Until I hold you in my arms.*
>
> *Love Victor.*
>
> *PS. Grace sends her love, she can't wait to see you.*
>
> *PPS. Please give my regards to your mother and father.*

Hannah held the letter to her heart then raised it to her lips and kissed it. "I'm overjoyed."

"I'm so happy for you, Hannah, honestly I am. Christmas will be brilliant." Rena turned in closer to her sister. "I have something I must tell . . . tell someone I mean. I'm not certain, but . . . well . . . ye ken. A woman knows. It's deep . . . maternal." Rena raised her brow, hoping Hannah would catch on. Hannah stared at Rena with a slightly perplexed expression. Rena raised both brows, amplifying her eyes like saucers.

"Oh Rena, what wonderful news," Hannah shrieked out.

"Shh, I have not yet told anyone, not even Spud."

Lily shouted through from the kitchen, inquiring what the commotion was. Both girls laughed and said it was nothing.

"You have to promise not to say anything to anyone. I'm very early, just missed one cycle. But I had to tell one of my sisters. And I wanted it to be you," Rena explained, keeping her voice to a whisper.

"Oh, I promise, Rena. You must announce it at Christmas, you must." Hannah hugged Rena with great intensity. "It will be a wonderful holiday." She sat back, still holding Rena's hand, smiling. Rena studied her sister's face, her eyes. She did look happy, and healthy.

Christmas was two weeks away. Rena wasn't entirely sure if she was pregnant and was still hesitant to tell anyone else, even Robert. She wanted to be sure. There were so many girls who thought they were, then found out they weren't. Or worse, lost the baby early in their first term. Rena knew she could not bear to explain either possible outcome. It was enough of a struggle being cordial while simulating a smile when asked how she was keeping or coping. Each sister's death precipitated such behaviour in neighbours, friends, even people she didn't know. She knew they meant well. But what they didn't realise was it disturbed the pit.

The bottomless pit of emotions, they lingered deep, and they were fragile when told a simple word like "Sorry" or asked a subtle question like "How are you lass?" or "How's yer mother? She must be heartbroken." The customary code of etiquettes remained in an incessant state of apologies, with gentle touches across shoulders and arms. She didn't blame her mother for not wanting to leave the house. She didn't need the outside world to remind her what she had lost.

## CHAPTER TWENTY-NINE

# *Our Hearts Can Bear Nae Mair*

*December 1938. Edinburgh*

She almost blurted it out. It may have been the champagne, or just the sincere feeling of comradeship. Liza had travelled home from London to spend the holidays with her father. Mirren and Kitty accepted Rena's afternoon invitation for a girls' gathering, first and foremost to see Liza, and second to christen Rena and Robert's new flat. It had been a while since the four girls had gotten together, and either party could not get a word in edgewise. Mirren, who was noticeably pregnant with her third, blethered on about being a mum and how exhausted she was. And that her nipples were the size of Jaffa Cakes. The three girls laughed and politely declined when Mirren offered to show them off.

Kitty appeared to be madly in love with her professor boyfriend and admitted she was fortunate to find a fellow with such great status. Rena hugged her friend and told her she was too hard on herself and she deserved such a chap. And more so, he was very lucky to have such a grand lassie.

Liza, of course, spoke about the field of obstetrics and its medical progress. And that the future held promise in saving many women's lives during difficult births.

Rena stood sound through all the conversations of births, breastfeeding, oversized nipples, and the latest in pain relief drugs during labour, and did not waver. She still had not told Robert.

The afternoon flew by. Two bottles of champagne and a plate of steak and kidney pies were devoured. Bellies were full, friendships rekindled. Mirren and Kitty left first. Hugs were exchanged and the promise of getting together more often had been made. Mirren, almost out the door, gave a quick mention that her mother Maggie hadn't been successful catching Rena's mother at home. Rena pretended she did not hear, though she could hear Liza behind her give an intense snigger.

Liza toured the sitting room, assessing the knickknacks that were randomly placed here and there. She eyed the collection of books, then picked up the picture frame of Margaret. She held it to her chest and smiled at Rena. The girls had made a pact years ago, the day after they found Cian Doyle dead by the seashore. The day they shed their birth names, the day they became new women. They were on their way to work, Scott Lyon's Bakery, and both agreed, if preferred, they would not need talk of such things; the death of loved ones or the pain that lingered. A promise of strength and solace would always remain, and if chosen, words would or would not be spoken. Liza placed the picture frame carefully back on the shelf, turned, and embraced Rena. They stood silent for the longest time, arms entwined, exchanging each other's deepest of emotions, without words.

Robert bustled in, catching the two off-guard. "Am I interrupting?" he said with a chortle.

"Don't be daft, Robert. Come give me a hug," Liza replied, making her way over to him.

"You look grand. Running your own business agrees with you," she claimed.

"Well, I have my wee wife to thank for that. She keeps me quite in line, she does." Robert gave a wink Rena's way. The three laughed.

Robert and Rena insisted Liza stay for tea, and she accepted with no hesitation. She was glad to spend as much time with her friend as possible.

After tea and another bottle of champagne, Robert stood, stretching, and gave a lengthy yawn. "Sorry, lassies, I must head for bed. Christmas orders are flying in, and I must be up early." He hugged Liza goodbye and excused himself to bed.

"You have a fine man there, Rena."

"Aye, I ken."

"Nonetheless, he is very lucky to have you," Liza voiced with a strong accord.

After a few exchanges of small talk Liza announced she must be setting off to catch the last trolley. "My da will be waiting up. We haven't properly spoken." Liza slid her coat on and adjusted her hat and scarf. "It's a wee nippy oot."

"It's been a grand day and evening, Liza. I've missed you so," Rena expressed.

Liza took Rena in her arms, drew her tight, and kissed her cheek. "I too, Rena, have missed you. You know how much I love ye." Rena did know, without the words having being said.

*Friday, December 16*

A loud knock reverberated throughout the entire flat. Rena jumped out of bed, stubbing her toe on the nightstand. "Bloody hell!" She grabbed her housecoat, feeling the chilled air linger in the bedroom, and cursed Robert for not having his key. He had only just left for the shop and the sun had not yet peaked. "Coming! I dinna ken why ye dinna have yer bloody key. I was in a deep slee—" She heaved the door open to find her father standing there.

"Get dressed, lass, Hannah's in the hospital and your mother needs you."

There was not time to think. Still dazed, she rooted through her wardrobe and dressed quickly, favouring her throbbing toe.

"Hurry on, lass," her father urged.

The morning's crisp air was biting, and it awoke all her senses, her mind now focused on Hannah. She wasn't sure what to expect when they arrived at the house. Her father hadn't spoken a word as they ran down George Street. "God," she gasped, surprised she could hardly keep up with him.

It was only her mother at home sitting by the fire. She wasn't dressed and she looked dishevelled. Rena ran and knelt at her mother's side, taking her hands.

"She's been there since the wee hours of the morn, lass, I can't get her to move, or talk, for that matter." John placed another piece of coal on the fire. "I called the doctor, he will come round as soon as he can."

"Mum?" Rena pressed her mother to answer. "Mum?" she pressed again.

Her mother didn't budge, not even an acknowledgment of her daughter's presence. Rena pointed her finger, directing her father into the kitchen.

"Hannah took a turn for the worse just around midnight. Your mum heated a bowl of hot broth. But Hannah couldn't . . . couldn't. Oh Christ, she's no well, Rena!" Her dad slid down onto the kitchen chair, burying his face between his hands. She stood, almost paralysed, her mind racing. She stared down at her father's tilted head, and she noticed a small bald spot, just on his crown, a few grey hairs circled within.

"Christ, Rena, snap oot of it, focus!" she uttered.

Emma arrived promptly after Rena's phone call. They both managed to get their mother into bed. The doctor had come round and gave her a sedative. He had nothing left to say; he had visited their mother each time she lost a daughter. Words were pointless, and he could only prescribe her a piece of escapism. John left shortly after the doctor's arrival. He arranged a taxi to take him to Colinton, a suburb in Edinburgh where Hannah was admitted into City Hospital.

"Did you call William?" Emma asked.

"Aye, he was up and already gone to work," Rena replied. "Let's wait a wee while before we call Lily and Betty."

"Alright, Rena, only a wee while, though."

The two sat quietly, nursing their cold tea. The fire's flames reached out like arms, and a wave of shadows darted all around. Rena became entranced with the flickering warm colours; they were hypnotic. She then heard singing and laughing. And here they all were, just like they had never left. Each sister's silhouette pirouetting around the room. And for the first time in a long time, she could see their faces, as clear as the stars in the sky.

*Monday, January 2, 1939*

"Five out of ten . . ." That's what her brother William whispered in her ear. Rena took his hand, and she could feel him tremble. Out of all the sisters, Hannah admired William just that wee bit more. She was the first to laugh at his jokes, and she defended his daft actions. She would not let any of the family speak crossly of his failing marriage. That was their Hannah: tender, caring, passionate. Always with a smile.

Those were a few of the words the minister used to describe her. He ended by saying, "Our community will mourn the loss of Hannah Midgley

Helliwell. We've lost one of the Lord's lambs. A family has lost a daughter, a sister, an aunt. Our community has lost a fine nurse."

Hannah died at City Hospital Wednesday, December 21 at 8:35 a.m. She had spent a week in the infectious disease ward as the complications of her TB worsened. John was by his daughter's side. When he arrived home that afternoon, he walked past his wife and his five remaining children, entering the sitting room and leaving them all in the kitchen. He sat down in his reading chair and broke down. If the loss of one child was not enough to bear, losing two within six months was an unfathomable affliction.

Hannah was laid to rest alongside her sisters at Rosebank Cemetery on Pilrig St, Edinburgh. Her name was inscribed on the same stone as her sisters. Catherine J was listed first, age twenty, and the inscription under her name read "Died at Toronto, Canada (her body never brought home)." Her name was followed by Jessie, age twenty-nine, Margaret, age fifteen, then the word "Also" was engraved above the name Mary, age twenty-six and now Hannah, age twenty-two. Each name displayed a tragic awareness – *Our hearts can bear nae mair.*

The streetlight shone in through the bedroom window, and large snowflakes floated down in soft spirals. Two wood pigeons nestled in tight, looking like one giant bird with two heads, their tail-feathers pressed tightly against the windowpane. For a moment, the world seemed undisturbed, perfect.

Rena lay awake, staring out the window, her mind nowhere. She was just physically in the room, a place of consciousness she was too familiar with. She didn't want to move and wake Robert, but she felt restless. She slipped out from under the eiderdown, grabbed her slippers and housecoat, and quietly made her way out of the bedroom. She made a pot of tea and snuggled into the sitting-room chair, and she managed all this without lights or loud noises.

Her mind raced, each thought desperate to reach the surface first. It was the image of Victor that prevailed; he was truly broken, he fumbled at every point. He and his sister had already left Africa, and he knew nothing of Hannah's passing until he arrived. Rena had opened the front door, and at first his presence surprised her, then she realised it was December twenty-fourth. She had to break the news, and it was like reliving Hannah's death all over again. He did everything that was expected: he fell apart, he cried, he hugged Rena and wouldn't let go. It was his sister Grace who led him away by his arm. Rena noticed Victor carrying a small parcel wrapped in red cellophane paper and laced with gold ribbon. She knew what lie within, and under her breath she said goodbye to Victor, then she said goodbye to the gift, which symbolised a promise of love and marriage. And as he walked away, she watched her sister's world of hopes and dreams vanish into fragments of only a yesterday.

She thought of her mother and all the family stories she had shared, stories of her childhood, her memories. And her father – well, he always laughed and said he had never wanted bairns, only to travel the world as a Cameron Highlander. Rena couldn't help but wonder, did her parents now think of all these things? Their choices, their chosen path. It was a question surely everyone asked themselves at pivotal moments in their lives. She knew it was daft to even think such things. Her parents could have never foreseen such an altered path. It was all tangled and twisted with grief. Would they have chosen differently if somehow they knew? Of course, she would never ask. Her thoughts became uncontrollably mindless. She shook her head in an effort to think sensibly.

Robert turned on the sitting-room light, and it startled Rena out of her mismatch of thoughts.

"What are ye doing oot here in the dark?" he asked as he draped his warm arms around her from over the back of the chair.

"I couldna sleep, my mind and body are both restless."

"Come back to bed, it's bloody cold in here." Robert took her hand to pull her up.

"First, Spud, I have something I must tell you." Rena pulled him down, so he was kneeling on the floor in front of her. Their hands entwined on her lap.

"I wasna sure, then losing our Hannah, I . . . I . . ." Her words hung, and tears streamed down her face. Robert gently wiped them with the touch of his fingers. Before he met Rena, she had already lost two sisters. He only ever knew them by the way of family stories. He'd now been with her for six years, and during that time she had lost another three.

He realised there were no magical words, no course of action to put things right. One thing he knew to be true was the love he possessed for her was unyielding. He would die for her. And to Rena, that was enough to save her.

Robert couldn't hold back his tears. He was excited but careful, and he knew Rena's feelings were running amok. He placed his head on her lap and kissed her warm, sacred place, where inside a wee one flourished.

"If it's a lassie, I want to name her Catherine."

Robert cupped her face. "Aye, Rena."

It was an ending, it was a beginning, and they all seemed muddled.

## CHAPTER THIRTY

## *War, War! It's Here, There, and Everywhere*

*May 1940. Edinburgh*

It was unsettling times. John Helliwell's prophecy of a second world war had come to fruition, much to his regret. And each day people lived on pins and needles. Catherine Helliwell was a regular at St. Andrews Church, and she joined the Red Cross and helped support the war effort. She prayed and knitted socks and hats for all the unfortunate bairns in Leith. It had been nearly nine months, and Britain's state of war showed no signs of an end.

That Sunday morning, September 3, 1939, began like any other Sunday morning. People went to church, prepared grand breakfasts, tended their gardens, searched for clams along the seaside. Rena and Robert popped into the Helliwell household at 8 George Street for Sunday tea. Catherine had attended church and was already home to greet her daughter, son-in-law, and her new granddaughter, her namesake.

John sat in his chair holding the wee one. Catherine Johnstone Thomson was born Saturday, August 12, 1939. Innocently, she came into the world unaware her presence would have the ability to heal broken hearts and inspire new beginnings.

"She is the bonniest bairn I've ever set my eyes on." John beamed ear to ear, cooing down at the sleeping bundle. This new little light of life had filled their hearts and brought a sundry of joyful feelings that had been absent for a very long time.

Catherine entered the sitting room with a plate of scones. She placed her free hand on Rena's shoulder and squeezed it. During her daughter's pregnancy, Catherine felt like she drew a deep breath and only exhaled the moment she learnt of the successful delivery and that both daughter and grandchild survived. The fear of losing another daughter was irrepressible.

John interrupted his wife's and daughter's laughter. He didn't hear what Robert had said, but obviously it was in good humour.

"Shh! Catherine, turn up the radio." John glanced at his family clock that sat on the mantel above the fireplace. The time was 11:15 a.m.

Prime Minister Chamberlain's broadcast was devastating, the news quickly expelled from the crackling speaker. However, its content lingered in the air, reluctant to settle. "This country is at war with Germany." The prime minister's voice was assertive, though clearly shaken.

The sitting room remained quiet, all but for wee Catherine waking and releasing a slight newborn noise. John patted the bundle. "Now, now, wee lass." His pensive stare remained on the old clock.

♣♣♣

Wee Catherine had just learnt to pull herself up, her chubby legs stiff and straight, holding tight to the cushion of the settee. Her free hand was mercilessly plunged inside her mouth, rolling to and fro, over what Rena assessed were swollen teething gums.

"Is there nae something you can give the lass, Rena?" Robert asked, swooping down to pick up his daughter. He held her high in his arms, and she squealed with delight.

"Spud, she's just finished her porridge. I wouldna be so . . ."

"Och, she's fine. She can spit up all she wants on her da, can't ye, my wee lamb?" He swung her again, high to the ceiling. Another chorus of delight sang out. "Rena, did you hear that? She said Da." He brought her into the kitchen, folded in his arms, and he was smiling proudly. "Did you hear her? Say it again: Da, Da." Robert's soft brown eyes flitted under his lush dark lashes. His expression was one of pure joy and admiration.

"She has yer eyes, ye ken that?" Rena turned from the sink and dabbed the corners of her daughter's mouth where a stream of drool was steadily hanging.

"Aye, that she does." Robert kissed his daughter's rouged, chubby cheek. "Even her wee cheeks are aflame." He rubbed his fingers across them, giving his wife a concerned eye.

"Spud, she will be fine. All bairns go through this." Rena reached in and collected her daughter. "I promise. Now you must be getting to the bakery. Lily is dropping wee Ian off. She has a job interview and has asked me to mind the lad."

"Alright, Rena, but you will call me if her gums worsen or she comes across a fever?" Robert's expression bore a grievous concern. He stroked his daughter's dark, wavy hair. "You promise, Rena?"

"Spud! I promise! Stop being daft. Now off with you." Robert threw on his tam and offered one last disquieted glance. Rena refused to rise to her husband's last-ditch effort to stay home and mind their daughter. Instead, she gave a wave of her hand, insinuating he depart.

The door had shut, and Rena sighed a tad of relief. She placed her daughter in the highchair and positioned a cool, wet cloth inside Catherine's crinkled pink, moist hand, where lines and folds had appeared due to the intense gnawing. "Here, wee lamb, this should save yer hand." Rena kissed the crown of her daughter's head, smiling, while she smoothed Catherine's thick dark waves, undoubtedly a trait from her husband. "Well, I will say this, lass, yer da loves you tae bits."

Lily arrived through the door like a highland gale, tossing a bag of toys and books on the table. "I should nae be long, Rena. When I return, we'll have a cuppa and a blether." She ruffled Ian's mass of auburn hair. "Now, Ian, you listen to yer auntie."

"Good luck, Lily," Rena hastily squeezed out, before her sister departed.

Rena sat at the kitchen table, watching her three-year-old nephew pull out his toys and offer his cousin a wooden horse. Catherine only wanted to shove the horse's head into her mouth. Ian grabbed it, saying, "No," though he showed her how to pull it with its rope. Catherine giggled as the red wheels carried the horse around the sitting room.

Rena was frying up a batch of kippers when her sister returned. Catherine had nicely settled down for a nap, and Ian was quietly playing in the sitting room.

"Rena, I ran into a few lassies down in George Square, and they talked about joining the Edinburgh Women's Defence Corps. The Home Guard does nae allow women, which is absurd. So they've come up with their own forces. Bloody brilliant, it is. I'm thinking of joining." Rena didn't answer or turn from the range; she kept flipping the smoked fish, staring out the window. She wanted nothing to do with the war, and she tried avoiding everything about it. But it was here and there, it was bloody everywhere. It hung in windows, blackening out light. It lay across back gardens and car parks in piles of sandbags. Makeshift bomb shelters replaced garden swings and hammocks. It even flaunted itself at your front door, where fire extinguishers and gas masks hung, reminding you that the world out there was not safe.

She recalled an afternoon outing with her father on Princess Street, where advertisement signs hung shamelessly at every post, each store window competing for one's business. "Purchase your bomb shelter today. The best blackout curtains sold here. Fire appliances and equipment, all reasonably priced. And let's not forget, you can't live through a war without official broadcasts and entertainments. Radio will be indispensable: Get yours today, prices starting at £7."

Then there were the curfew hours. It was prohibited to be out after the blackout time. Regulations were posted everywhere, listing the new orders of dos and don'ts. Even the media had its spin; newspapers published speculative warnings, exhorting an already unsettled and anxious country. One paper published an article stating that having a lit cigarette outside during blackout hours could breach the new order of regulations. Rena's father laughed at that one. "Lass, we are already a target, living by the seaside along the Firth. The Huns don't need a lit fag to find us." However, his wife made him smoke his pipe upside down when he was in the garden.

Paranoia and fear rushed through Edinburgh in waves of hysteria. Some people wore their masks in the streets (just in case). The fear of poison gas attacks ran rampant. Again, Rena's father, the voice of reason and fact, claimed that the German Luftwaffe did not have the capability of delivering such an attack as gas, only bombs.

What did concern John, though he chose not to share it with his wife or children, was the lack of bomb shelters around the city. Despite the efforts of churches, halls, and storage spaces vigorously converted, the newly constructed shelters were only large enough to accommodate a third of the city's population. What aggravated him even more was the number of trial air-raid sirens. "Christ, we'll never know if we're being bombed or not. Folk are already becoming complacent."

Rena watched her father's mannerisms as they walked home. His gait was severe and unforgiving. "Da, I'm sure we've learnt something from the first war and are duly prepared."

"I wouldna count on that, lass," John countered, tugging at the corner of his waistcoat.

"Rena!" Lily's loud blast brought her back into the room, leaving her father's declarations of war behind.

"Sorry, Lily. You were saying?" Rena shifted the frying pan off the range and plated the kippers.

"I was talking aboot joining the Edinburgh Women's Defence Corp. I think Emma may be interested too. Are ye keen?"

And here it was, right in her kitchen. "War . . . war, that's all anyone talks aboot!"

Lily, taken back, remained quiet.

"I'm sorry, Lily. I'm just tired of it being a constant in our lives. From food stamps to running into bomb shelters every time an air raid siren blasts. I think I will go mad." Rena flopped herself into the chair, feeling defeated.

To lighten the mood, Lily advised her sister she got the job at Woolworth's and was excited to start. Before Lily packed up wee Ian and departed, Rena agreed to help mind Ian.

"Between Mum and I, we will watch him, Lily. Dinna fash."

Rena knew Lily didn't need luck to get the job. The workforce in Edinburgh was mainly women, as most men were off at war, including Lily's husband. Rena prayed each night that Robert would not be called upon. He wasn't a military man, and he never showed an interest in joining any of the Scottish regiments. Therefore his admission over tea that evening unnerved her deeply. It rattled her to near deafness. She asked him to repeat it, then again.

"Spud, you canna, you just canna!" Robert tried to calm her, reassure her. He promised to be safe.

"It might no even happen, Rena. Yer getting upset over nothing." He had reached for her arm, but she pulled it away. Each dish she removed from the table flew into the sink. He thought he heard one break, although he knew better and said nothing. When she finished flinging the dishes, he broached the subject, this time exploiting her father.

"Even yer da said all men could face conscription. Just like in World War One."

"I dinna bloody care what my da said!"

"Rena, I'd rather volunteer than be forced, ye ken that." He tried to be delicate in his delivery. "And yer poor brother, he spent all his years wanting to join a regiment, and because of the slightest ailment, he canna. And here I am, healthy and able to fight for my country."

"Spud, yer helping oot here, in Scotland, yer a member of the Warden services. We still need men here. And I can tell you, my mother is very relieved her son has a hearing impairment."

He watched her tears well and rush down her flushed cheeks. "You have a wee lass, Spud. Ye canna leave her."

Out of all the reasons, it was that one that shot him down. He took Rena in his arms and held her tightly until he could feel her entire body ease. It wasn't just the war, he knew that. His wife's fear of losing loved ones lay embedded deep within. He reached down and kissed the tip of her nose, then her lips. He kissed her hard, and she responded with great ferocity. It took him a bit by surprise, though he didn't stop her.

It was more than passion that drove the sure intensity of their lovemaking that night. He wasn't sure if it even was his wife. She had come undone, opening all her deep and sacred places, releasing her pit of emotions. Robert felt each one, and when they finished making love, she clung to him, kissing him softly, but spoke no words.

Robert knew he would not leave her – he couldn't.

## CHAPTER THIRTY-ONE

## *And the World Went Silent*

*June 1940, Edinburgh*

Summer arrived and offered some solace. It swept in like a warm breeze and the touch of a sunny day. The month of June kicked off with blowers, streamers, and birthday cake. Rena's niece June turned eight, and it was a grand reason for celebration. Emma had bought a brand-new camera and was eager to try it out at the party. The first snapshot was of their mother standing beside June, outside the front of the house.

At first Catherine resisted, saying, "Lass, I'm a mess, I've been in the kitchen all day preparing dinner and cakes."

Emma laughed and insisted her mother get in the photo with her granddaughter. "You look like fine, Mum." The second was of their father John, one arm wrapped around wee Ian and his other hand pointing out towards Emma, coaxing his grandson to look at his auntie for the photo. The day offered a moment of reprieve after learning the disturbing news of Germany capturing Paris and Italy's declaration of war on Britain. Rena honestly thought the world had gone mad.

Rena and Emma entered the house to make tea, leaving the remainder of the family in the back garden to carry on with the celebration.

"I'm thinking of sending June north. Train schedules are being arranged, evacuating the children north into the Highlands." Emma didn't sound convincing explaining all the details to her sister. Rena listened to Emma's hesitant words, "My lass will be safe . . . I know it's the right thing." Emma was unconsciously twisting the corner of the tablecloth tighter and tighter, binding it into a cone shape.

"You dinna have to send her, Emma," Rena said as she reached across the table, filling her sister's teacup.

"Betty offered us to come up and stay with her and the laddies in Aberfeldy. But there is an encampment of German prisoners just up the way from her, and . . . well," Emma floundered, ". . . it may not be safe."

"Are any of us safe, Emma? Christ, the whole of Edinburgh is running around with gas masks and expressions of fear riddled across their faces. Mirren told me her mother Maggie piled sandbags inside her flat . . . INSIDE, Emma! Mirren says when she and the wee yins visit, they have to clamber over the bags to get into the sitting room."

"Da always attested the woman is bloody daft!" Emma replied with a chortle and slightly less strain in her voice.

"Betty may just need you, Emma. Ye ken she still struggles a wee bit." In February, just two months after they lost their Hannah, Betty's husband died. TB was still a prevalent threat, and Percy had been battling the disease for nearly a year. The depth of tragedies demonstrated no prejudice or mercy in the Helliwell households. Its revolving door rotated from one tribulation to the next. Rena at the time was pregnant and normally would have enjoyed the train ride north, though her first trimester was, well, to say the least, a sickly one. She told Robert that his morning fry-up of kippers would have to wait until she gave birth, and even afterward she contemplated yielding to its distinct, fishy smell.

The jostling train car made her stomach flip inside and out, and she had to keep a paper bag in reach. And the poor car attendant was run tattered, fetching Rena pots of tea and oatcakes. They were the only substance that settled her unwavering queasiness.

Rena stayed a fortnight with her sister, and she minded the lads while Betty sorted out Percy's funeral arrangements and established that she would carry on the hair salon business independently.

"I ken, Rena. But I've already taken a leave from work to visit Betty. They'll nae be so keen if I book off more days; especially now during a war." Emma hummed and hawed. "She's now eight. I think she will fare well. All the neighbourhood children are leaving." Emma still did not sound convinced. She shifted the conversation, leaving her decision undetermined. "I ran into Getna Massaro. We popped in at her father's shop for ice-cream. It was disgraceful what happened to the Italians in Leith. Thank God her father's shop wasn't vandalised. Whereas the death of that poor shop-keeper in Portobello was just heart-breaking." Rena recalled the tragic story. It only took one broadcast announcement and her country turned into a frenzied pit of hate. Leith became fearful of the same Italians they had lived and worked alongside with for decades.

"Getna told me her brother Nick is to be stationed in Hong Kong. He's somewhere in Africa right now, with the Royal Scots. She says her mother is beside herself with worry."

Rena gave her a quizzical glance.

"Aye, ye ken Nick Massaro. He and I dated for a wee bit."

Rena gave a nod in recollection.

"The Massaros are worried sick about their family in Italy. Seemingly Getna's uncle, her mother's brother, is fighting for Mussolini." Emma started unravelling the cone-shaped corner of tablecloth, her mind now distracted away from her own concerns.

Chamberlain's broadcast of war had been like someone propelled a football into the air. It soared mercilessly, spinning and whirling. And when it landed, everyone was disoriented and terrified. The same day of Chamberlain's announcement, September 3, 1939, King George VI delivered his grave speech, provoking great concern: "There may be dark days ahead. And war is no longer confined to the battlefield."

Rena asked her father just what that meant. However, he did not reply; he remained quiet, patting his sleeping granddaughter.

Within the first few days of the devastating broadcasts, over one million children, pregnant women, and the infirm were evacuated to either the countryside or abroad. Rena felt trapped between the spinning and whirling, not eligible for either evacuation category. She was no longer pregnant, and her daughter was only a month old. Regardless of the qualifying classifications, Robert did not want either out of his sight, and neither did her father.

*Sunday, July 13, 1940*

Rena was looking forward to having a full Sunday dinner. Of course, being in the middle of a war, food items could be scarce, so one had to improvise. She was thankful her husband was a baker, and he could turn any type of meat into a decent pie. She asked her brother William to join them for dinner. William was devastated he didn't qualify to become a soldier. It was all he had spoken of growing up. He felt he had let everyone down: his mates who were already off fighting, his country, and more so, his father. And to add to his turmoil, his separation had not been an easy one, causing his wife to deny him access to his daughter. It was a tangled mess that he did not want to burden his mother with. Rena became his sounding board – not that she minded, as she loved her brother.

It had been just the three of them, besides wee Catherine, and she was already down for the night. William had played her ragged. She had fallen asleep in his lap.

"She's a grand wee bairn," William said, catching a tear from his cheek.

Rena picked Catherine up and carried her to bed. "Aye, William," she said, not wanting to say much more, as she was sure her brother's heart was bursting for his own lass.

When she returned to the sitting room, Robert had poured a dram. He raised his glass and toasted to good health, happiness, and for the bloody war to end. The three clanged their glasses and downed the single malt.

The rest of the evening was light conversation about family members and friends. Emma was still indecisive about sending her daughter north. Betty was faring well, but busy with the shop. Lily was hoping Jock would be home soon on leave.

"I have a wee bit of news," Rena pipped in. "I received a letter from Morogh. He sent me a few pictures of the bairns. He's been working with the Scottish government. They've asked to use his land to grow crops and help supply food during the war." They all nodded, agreeing this was a good distraction for their brother-in-law, who still struggled without their Mary.

"I ran into yer friend Mirren. Christ, she's bloody pregnant again." William laughed out.

"I ken, she comes aboot often for tea," Rena replied.

"That reminds me, Rena, a letter came from England," Robert mentioned, rising to fetch it. Liza had been keeping Rena apprised of the war activity in London. It was an area everyone agreed would likely take the brunt of a German attack. Rena feared for her friend's safety. She accepted the letter and tucked it in her apron. It would be a read for the morn with tea.

The evening was closing, and William almost forgot to mention his news. "Mum had the opportunity to meet both king and queen on their visit here last week. After their hospital tours of visiting injured soldiers, Mum's Red Cross group welcomed them at the church for lunch."

"She never mentioned it," Rena replied, surprised. "I'm dropping Catherine off tomorrow while Kitty and I attend the movies. I'm sure she will tell me all aboot it then."

"Aye, sure she will, Rena. Princess Elizabeth is to arrive sometime next week. She is looking forward to that," William mentioned, placing on his cap. "A grand night, Rena." He reached in and kissed her cheek.

"Spud, I hear the Hibs may play next week. We should catch a game."

"Aye, sounds grand," Robert replied.

Rena opened the bedroom window. A warm breeze drifted in, and she inhaled the earthy scents of summer and the seaside. She climbed into bed and wrapped her arms around Robert, kissing him. He pulled her in tightly, kissing her gently across each cheek. He arched her body while his lips travelled from her mouth to her breasts, savouring each taste of her. She let out a small moan, and if it were even possible, she drew herself closer, wanting to climb deep inside him. A small cry interrupted any further intimacy.

Robert rolled onto his back and laughed. "I'll get her, Rena." He was up and out of the room before Rena replied. She drew the sheet over her body and lay still in a haze of love and contentment. She could hear Robert in the next room singing his rendition of "Katie Bairdie" and found herself peacefully drifting as he sang each verse to a giggling Catherine.

*Thursday, July 18, 1940*

Kitty had asked Rena to the movie house. However, Rena had forgotten she promised Lily she would mind Ian that evening. Robert planned to catch a football match. The friendly games were few and far between but a good distraction from the war.

Rena's mom eagerly agreed to take both grandchildren for the evening. "Lass, I will be fine, ye ken I've raised ten bairns." Catherine gave her daughter a wry grin.

"Mum, I'm no questioning yer skills. It's just these two are a handful."

Catherine laughed and hugged her daughter. "Ye worry tae much, lass, yer da will be home later. And Spud said he should be home for tea. Go and enjoy yerself."

Rena gave her mother a heartfelt hug. She turned towards her nephew. "Now Ian, dinna give yer grannie any grief." Next, she kissed her daughter's head and tapped her on the behind. "You tae, wee lamb."

Rena met Kitty at the theatre, and both were looking forward to catching up.

"Christ! There better nae be any air raid sirens tonight. It'd be nice to get through an entire movie," Kitty stated while they purchased their tickets.

There were no sounds of an air raid siren, but the commotion at the back of the movie house sounded as if there had been one. Henry Fonda's character, Tom Joad from *The Grapes of Wrath* had just been released from prison and was walking across the big screen when loud gasps and screams coiled throughout the aisles and seats. Crowds of panicked people pushed and shoved to reach the exit.

Rena lost sight of Kitty among the chaotic shuffle, and she found herself trapped among a group of women who were frantically yelling the name Julie. Rena's heart raced, and she couldn't make sense of all the madness.

Once outside, she eyed through the frantic crowds of people. Everyone was running here, there, and everywhere. She had not expected to see her father, as she was still searching for Kitty. He stood still amid the panic-stricken crowd.

The world stopped, and his look bore a familiar, unwanted expression of despondency. "Lass . . . you must come . . . " He couldn't finish the words, and he struggled while trying to take her hand. She pulled back with great resistance. It was Emma's hands she felt behind her, gripping her shoulders.

"You must come, Rena," her sister said softly but with urgency.

Rena followed in a deaf march as the world around her played out in silence. The street – her street, the one she grew up on, reached out to her in mournful gestures. Its chaotic mess was suffocating. Ambulances were parked just buildings away, a surge of white coats and Red Cross uniforms oscillated back and forth as if they had a purpose. Spectators with contorted expressions peered her way, mouths in motion, and still she could not hear. Outstretched hands brushed along her arms and shoulders. She pulled away, wanting to run. Then suddenly, without warning, she heard a clap of wings, and two wood pigeons took flight. They soared out from the piles of debris, high into the sky, breaking through the mounds of dust and dark clouds. Rena watched as they flew towards the sun's last beam of light.

She wasn't sure how long she had been sitting there. She was frantic to find her daughter, and when she stood, a man in a white coat delicately positioned her back to the ground. He tried asking her questions, but the world was still muted; she then noticed a group of people clear a path. Wee Ian was wrapped in a blanket in some women's arms, his auburn hair full of debris. Her heart sank seeing Emma and her father running towards her. Behind them, a nurse followed, carrying a crying, bundled blanket. Rena struggled to stand; her world exploded. She fell against her father's chest, and this time she did not let go.

She heard the words, but they didn't make sense. Emma's hands were wrapped around hers, gently telling her what Robert had desperately willed her to say. It was tragic enough to hear her mother was found in her chair by the fireplace. She'd been knitting and both needles pierced through her hands. "They said she died instantly, Rena."

It was the words her sister spoke next that destroyed her. Robert had been in the kitchen when the bomb hit. The entire building collapsed, and he became trapped under the range and a pile of debris. The emergency services worked tirelessly to dig him out. Emma was able to make her way through. She was by Robert's side until he died. He clung to her hand, tears streaming, and had said, "Tell Rena I love her. I'm sorry for leaving her, she must forgive me. Tell her to look after our wee lamb."

In the distance Rena heard deep sobs, and it made her tremble. She covered her ears and wished they would stop; her heart could bare nae mair. She then realised the cries were hers.

There is a moment between sleep and awakening. There are no real thoughts. Existence is a glimpse away. Within that moment a warmth embraces you, it's euphoric. Then reality plunges deep within your being, your soul. As if underwater, your body pushes you to the surface as your lungs cry for air. Your mind awakes, your body awakes. It's within that moment you realise that everything you tried to suppress has rattled you back.

It had been all over the news: Edinburgh had suffered its first civilian casualties. Leith was an easy target positioned along the seaside. News reports determined the German Luftwaffe had broken through the sky without warning. Its first bomb struck numbers 8 and 13 on George Street. A three-year-old boy was lifted from the rubble by a local woman. A wee lassie around one-year-old was found in her pram. Fortunately, the hood was left open, which shielded her under a pile of wooden planks that fell against it in a crisscrossed formation. Seven civilians were killed. Rena's mother, Catherine Helliwell, and Rena's husband, Robert Thomson, were two.

Catherine Helliwell nee Johnstone and June

John William Helliwell and wee Ian

## CHAPTER THIRTY-TWO

# The Handsome Stranger

*1941, Edinburgh*

It wasn't easy picking up these fragmented pieces. Rena didn't think she ever could; it was hard enough breathing. Her family had always been everything, and those that remained had become everything.

Betty travelled home. After all, she too lost a husband. She didn't treat her sister in a namby-pamby fashion. Both Emma and Lily thought her harsh, and when they brought it to Betty's attention, Betty defied them gravely. "Rena needs to find her strength. She canna hide in the hoose and drown in tears of pity. She has a daughter to raise. And Christ, our father, he's nae better." Emma tried intervening, but it was pointless. Betty was resolute about how this family crisis would be handled. "I ken how she feels, I lost Percy. But I had to pick myself up. I'm thinking of our sister, our Rena. Christ! if she does nae pull through this, we will lose her too!" Her stance was intimidating, her Helliwell steel-blue eyes stared unnervingly.

William gave heed before he spoke; however, he was no more successful than his sisters. Betty shot them all down. "We are in the middle of a bloody war. And we're all at risk of being bombed, starved to death, or worse. I'm saving our sister so she can save herself and that wee lass of hers." Betty's eyes welled with tears, but she stood her ground. And they all agreed to save their sister.

Shortly after the attack, Rena and her father had moved into a flat on Granton Terrace in Edinburgh, away from Leith. Neither could bear living close to the horror of the bombing and everything they had lost. The unfamiliar space represented nothing of family, love, or laughter; its small surroundings felt barren, providing, at best, shelter. Its dull beige, freshly painted walls offered only hopes of a new beginning.

Almost everything had been destroyed during the explosion. And each new piece of furniture and dishware arranged in the flat felt like a betrayal. All that once was would never be again.

Rena sat on her bed, which was one of the items she'd moved from Robert's and her flat. It was there she could still feel and smell him, and it was there she would desperately search for him in her dreams. She didn't take everything, only what she thought necessary: Catherine's crib, her mother's kitchen items, her book collection, the shelf her father had made, and the box of family pictures.

Once her siblings finished helping with the move and left, she sat alone in the unfamiliar bedroom holding a photo of Robert cradling a newborn Catherine in her parents' garden on George Street. She traced his smiling face with her finger, and then she felt herself fall back into the bottomless pit.

John settled his granddaughter down for the night and made himself a tea. He had heard Rena crying earlier but thought it best to leave her be. He felt lost on how to help his daughter, as he too was mourning.

When he entered the bedroom, he saw she lay sleeping, curled up like a wee bairn, her cheeks dampened with tears. He sat beside her and pulled the photograph from the fold of her hands, placing it on the nightstand. Gently he covered her with the blanket and ran his hand through her hair. "My Alexandrena, here we are, lass. Left to face the world with all that we've lost. I promise you, you and wee Catherine will always have me." He wiped his tears on the back of his hand, gave her one last pat, then left his daughter to sleep, hoping she would find solace within a world of peaceful dreams.

Rena couldn't face her childhood friends. Mirren and Kitty came around and tried desperately to get her out of the house. She made excuses, blaming her father, saying he was fragile and couldn't be left alone. Mirren, with nothing but good intentions, mentioned this to her mother. And, when old Maggie arrived at their front door with her intolerable, demanding attitude, blethering on about how she intended on stopping by regularly to cheer John up, she got the shock of her life. John, for the sake of his wife, had always kept his composure around Maggie. This time, he was adamant he would not become the pinnacle of that women's gossip. Rena actually felt sorry for her, standing at the door, mouth gaped open, while John unleashed years of restrained sentiment. And unbeknownst to John, the old bird did cheer him up. She snorted and snuffed and stomped, and as she walked away, she yelled, "Yer nothing but a bloody limey."

It had been the first both had laughed in a very long time; they laughed so hard that wee Catherine started to giggle, and Rena realised she hadn't heard her daughter laugh since that evening Robert sang her the "Katie Bairdie" song. She picked her daughter up and hugged her fiercely. John joined in, wrapping his arms around them both.

It was during breakfast. Her father came through from the bedroom, placing a stained and tattered box bound with ribbon on the table. The seams of the lid were unglued, no longer fitting securely. Rena could smell the smoulder and debris from the destruction of the bomb. Its smell twisted at her stomach, making her want to retch.

John's fingers tapped on the lid as if contemplating what he should say. "This is for you, lass. It was your mother's," he said, sliding the box towards her.

She waited until her father was out for his walk and Catherine down for a nap. It took her a moment to release the ribbon; she wasn't sure what to expect. The first thing that caught her eye was her lost bloodstone droplet earring. Robert had given her the set for her birthday before they were engaged. She was frantic when she had lost it and didn't have the heart to tell him and thank goodness he never noticed or asked. Her mother must have found it before Rena and Robert moved out and then forgotten all about it.

She shuffled through the pictures. There were some of Mary's bairns. Morogh, bless his heart, was diligent in sending his mother-in-law pictures of the bairns. Her mother was delighted each time she received them. There were only two pictures of Jessie's bairns, and that was when they were wee. It broke her mother's heart not to see her grandchildren. It was all she had left of her lass, she would say.

There were dozens of letters, and Rena didn't know where to begin, so she picked them randomly. Some had return addresses, and she started with Australia. The letters from her Uncle Donald were light, a great deal about sheep and Australian herding dogs. He always signed off with, "I love and miss you." The next grouping of letters was from Canada. Her Uncle James wrote often. One letter in particular caught her eye. The opening sentence drew her in.

"Catherine, I've tried writing several times to your husband, and he will not reply. I'm convinced he has not shown you or mentioned any of my letters. He only wrote to me once. And I carry the guilt of that letter around with me every day. I know he will never forgive me for the death of your lass."

Rena placed the letter down and allowed herself to breathe. She could not continue. When stacking the pile, she noticed a piece of tissue at the bottom of the box. Its once-white colour had paled to yellow, and it crumbled to her touch. She stared down at the sepia-toned photograph that lay hidden all these years. And now, in the thralls of her own sorrows, she thought of her mother and regarded her as nothing less than a pillar of strength and admired her courage. Not only did her mother survive each loss, she'd endured the worst of unspoken tragedies a mother should: losing half her children. "Five out of ten." William's words hung. Rena prayed, asking God for her mother's fortitude.

She studied the photo of her sister Catherine J, dressed in what looked like an expensive dress. Her dark hair lay long and neat below her shoulders. Her face was angelic, her eyes closed, her expression lifeless. How heart-breaking, Rena thought, that this would be the last image her mother would have of her daughter: lying in a coffin.

The war was everywhere, no one escaped its wrath. The blitz that hit London was horrific. It wasn't enough Rena had lost her husband and mother, she had now lost her best friend. Kitty delivered the dreadful news. London had been under severe attack for months, and the Germans were incessant in their bombing. Liza was out in the street helping clear dead bodies when a German bomber spiralled down, blasting the city and everyone in it. Rena visited Liza's father, Charles, and both broke down, embracing each other. Another casualty of war, another shattered piece.

Emma meant well, and to appease her sister, Rena agreed.

Rena stood in a brand-new dress, a dress her sister Betty had insisted she purchase. "You will knock them dead in that number," Betty said.

"Don't be daft," Rena replied.

She felt awkward at first and out of place, but she promised Emma she would accompany her to the dance. She fingered the bloodstone earring that hung from her lobe, feelings its cool, smooth stone. She was grateful her mother had placed it away for safekeeping.

People were staring at her. Was it because they knew who she was, the widow from George Street? Or perhaps her sister was correct, and the red-velvet number drew attention. Its elegant fabric hugged her body, and there was barely room to move. She'd lost quite a bit of weight and felt frail. But when she gazed at her image in the mirror that day in the shop, she felt alive. "There you are, Rena," she whispered under her breath.

The music was loud and lively, and cigarette smoke hung throughout the air. Dancers were jiving and swinging. She politely declined the many invitations to dance; most were from soldiers on leave. She thought it far too soon and a betrayal to Robert.

She'd lost sight of Emma, and then felt anxious. Her eyes darted back and forth until she spotted her sister on the dance floor. It came on suddenly, without warning, and its brief clutch crippled her. "You can't hide from the world, Rena," Betty had told her when she first declined Emma's offer to attend the dance. But Robert was everywhere, and she couldn't hide from the fact he was dead. She had tried before her sisters and brother forced her out into the world of the living. Everything reminded her of Robert. And seeing her sister dance with the dark-haired handsome stranger was a mournful reminder of something she no longer had.

They must have been talking about her, because once the music stopped, Emma pointed her way, and the handsome stranger gazed directly towards her. Before Rena and Emma left the hall, Emma informed her that that was Nick Massaro. "Ye ken, I told you about him. He's with the Royal Scots and is leaving for Hong Kong." Before Rena made her way to the door, she turned and gave the Royal Scot a warm smile. And hoped he would not be another casualty of war.

*Hogmanay, December 31, 1941, Edinburgh*

She wasn't really up for it, and like everything else, she felt like she was surviving (she couldn't call it living) through the motions. It was William who convinced her.

"Rena, we need to laugh and find a bit of happiness. It's been well over a year since..." William could not bring himself to mention the bombing; they all had learnt to skirt around it. Rena didn't entirely disagree with her brother's sentiment. Hogmanay had always been important to her family. It represented new beginnings and letting go of painful endings.

But a party? She didn't think she had it in her. Both she and her father struggled just to plod through their days. "It's no fair to Catherine, Rena. She needs to be around her family." Again, she didn't disagree. It was when her brother mentioned their mother and how she would have wanted them to carry on with tradition: "We all need a new beginning, Rena," William lastly evinced.

"Let me speak to Da," Rena replied without committing herself. It was safer that way.

She had become an expert in dodging social events, and when Betty warned her that her friends Kitty and Mirren would eventually tire and lose heart, she gave way and invited them for tea. Perhaps her brother was right; her sister had been. The visit with her friends felt familiar, enjoyable, and most of all, safe.

She invited everyone, though her father raised an eyebrow when she mentioned Uncle Geordie and Auntie Lizzie. "Da, we have not seen them since the..." She too struggled to say the word. "Uncle Geordie has been a big part of our lives, and Auntie Lizzie."

"I'll not be taking my pipe to the back garden."

Rena laughed and hugged her father.

"What's that for, lass?"

"Because you are yer old English stubborn self again." She kissed his cheek. "And ken I love it!"

Robert's mother, Georgina, was thrilled about the invite. "That is grand, lass. Meg, Sandy, and I will be there." Rena felt guilty for not visiting Georgina more often, for she too lost Robert, and the only tie remaining was her granddaughter.

It wasn't the same, and everyone felt it. It would never be again. Their journey through those turbulent years of loss and grief taught them how to survive, and they were bestowed a strength they never knew existed. With fierce tenaciousness and unconditional love, they pulled together and saved each other.

The flat on Granton Terrace was packed, and once everyone arrived and eager greetings were exchanged, it shed its still and sombre beige-painted walls and breathed a new life of family and laughter.

It was not intentional, but she caught herself studying each family member. She wasn't sure what she was searching for; perhaps it was reflections of a thousand yesterdays. She remembered what William had said at Hannah's funeral: "Five out of ten." She had to shake that off. She recalled one morning entering the house shortly after they had lost Hannah. Her mother was in the kitchen baking, a fury of flour and butter had become her escapism, her new drug. The pain of loss and grief kneaded into each fold of the dough. Her mother had been crying but stopped when Rena appeared. "Mum, dinna hide your sorrow on my account."

Catherine paused, her dark-brown eyes wet with tears. "Aye, lass, I ken. There are times I struggle . . . I become so lost in my grief, I fear I wilna find my way back." She resumed pounding the dough. "You bairns are all I have left, and I must stay with the living."

Looking back on that morning, Rena realised her mother was right, and she too would have to learn just that.

Her daughter had become her saviour, and hearing her giggle made her smile. Wee Catherine sat on the floor encircled by her cousins while they tickled and teased her. Ian, now four years old, hadn't spoken since the bombing, and the odd expelled word resulted in a painful stutter. The doctors told Lily and Jock that their lad suffered great trauma from the explosion, although in time, he would regain his speech. Betty's laddies, Ronald and Nicol, who were now in their early teens, were chastised for teasing their cousin and his speech impediment. June, Emma's daughter, at the age of nine, appeared all grown up and took charge of all her cousins. Betty chortled and commented that her niece's firm governing nature was a trait no less than that of her mother's. Emma concurred, smiling. She raised her sherry glass, and they all laughed.

"Where is that brother of ours?" Lily glanced down at her watch. "He said he would be here by seven. It's well past." The sisters were happy for William, as he recently became engaged and seemed truly happy. He still could not see his daughter, and like everything else, he learnt to bury it deep in his heart and move on.

"Oh, he's keen on making a grand entrance, our Willie," Betty said with a wry grin.

"There is no reason for tardiness. Rena has worked hard to put this party together. I will grand entrance him!" John stood tugging at the corner of his waistcoat. Everyone stood quiet. It was Lily who couldn't restrain herself; her laughter was infectious, and within minutes the entire household was laughing. John only surrendered a smile, though it was enough for his family to ascertain that John Helliwell was back with the living. The evening carried on with stories of family and embellished tales. Rena's heart tugged when Georgina and Meg shared stories of Robert as a wee lad. She managed to smile, realising this was what they too desperately needed.

"I can tell you one thing, Rena – our Catherine is the spitting image of her da," Meg proudly claimed.

"Aye, Meg, yer right there," Rena agreed.

William made his grand entrance, although alone. He apologised for running late and explained his fiancée was under the weather and sent her regrets for missing her first family party.

"How ill can she be?" Betty's intonation did not go unnoticed. Everyone had the same concern, questioning the validity of William's excuse. He saw it on all their faces.

"Well, Christ!" William cleared his throat. "Aye, well, if you must ken, Ruby is pregnant, and she canna keep her head oot the bowl." It was a cheery silence, and not a long one by any means. Drams were poured and toasts of congratulations circled the room. William grinned from ear to ear. "Now, if it's a laddie, which we think it is, he will be named in the traditional manner – John William Helliwell."

John raised his glass and patted his son's shoulder. "Good form, lad, good form."

The New Year would prove to be one of new beginnings. Lily and Jock announced they too were with child. Lily hoping for a wee lassie, claimed she would not be short on choosing a lassie's family name.

Warm-hearted chuckles were interrupted by Lizzie. Through all the family adversities, poor Lizzie still sought diversion. "That is grand, Lily. But what if it's a wee laddie?" Lizzie, not wanting to linger long on names of dead lassies, gulped at her sherry nervously. Rena noticed and could only sympathise with her aunt's awkward manner, for she too had lost loved ones: her nieces and a dear sister-in-law.

"Norman," Jock cut in, saving Lizzie from further discomfort, "that will be our laddie's name." He smiled towards his wife, and Lily nodded in agreement.

"*Slàinte mhath.* Cheers to two laddies!" John raised his glass, finished his scotch in one swallow, and cleared his throat. "We've not had an easy journey, and each time we lost a lassie, we lost a part of ourselves. Your mother's strength is what saved me, it saved our family. I could not have survived without her." He paused, looking upon his five remaining children. "Now, we don't have her, but we do have each other. And your mother would want us to look after one another." Lily topped off her father's drink before he finished his tribute. "Let's raise our glasses to those who are sorely missed. May they live on in our hearts forever." John downed his dram, then tugged his waistcoat.

Rena snuck out to the garden shortly after midnight, leaving the household to welcome in 1942 singing the first chorus of "Auld Lang Syne." She needed a moment of solitude. She slid her hand inside her coat pocket and felt the unopened envelope her Uncle Geordie had slipped her way when her father wasn't looking. "Lass, it's from James. He mailed it to me after the news of the bombing. He didn't have your new address and wasn't sure if your da would accept the letter." She thanked her uncle and tucked it inside her coat pocket that hung at the back door. She didn't need her father to find it. It would unsettle a fury of emotions that had long been buried.

Party horns and blowers could be heard from the surrounding flats. Rena thought back to the New Year's Robert asked her to marry him. She never imagined she could be happier than within that moment, and outside of the birth of their daughter, she hadn't been. The night air chilled through her coat; it had begun to snow. She hugged her arms inward and looked up, watching the large flakes gracefully fall from the sky. She reflected on the message Robert left Emma before he died, and she allowed herself to cry, "I canna forgive you, Spud! I just canna. You promised you would never leave me." She drew a deep breath, wiped her tears, and with conviction looked to the heavens. "I can promise, I will look after our wee lamb."

She heard Emma calling out to her. They were about to cut the fruitcake that Meg and Sandy had brought. "Aye, Emma, I will be right in." She was heedful her sister wanted to speak with her in private. A household that always spoke of battles and wars and family clans fighting in the Highlands became muted by a single German bomb. Perhaps in years to come stories would be revived, and someone would tell the tale of the devastation on George Street.

Emma, cautious of the topic of war, took Rena aside and in a hushed voice advised Rena how concerned she was about her friend Nick Massaro. The horrific broadcast reached the entire world. Hong Kong had fallen Christmas Day, and panicked families tried to learn the fate of their loved ones. Getna informed Emma that her mother had locked herself in her closet of worship and refused to come out. The Massaro family had no news about Nick; they didn't know if he was killed in action or taken prisoner. Emma was beside herself. Rena hugged her sister and promised they would speak after the evening closed.

Before Rena returned inside, she thought back on that night at the dance, and the warm smile the handsome stranger had given her. She prayed for her sister's friend, that he remain safe and would make it home alive.

Robert and wee Catherine Thomson

Alexandrena (Rena) Thomson nee Helliwell

# Part Seven

*A Destined Path*

## CHAPTER THIRTY-THREE

## *A Bomb Away from Freedom*

*August to September 1945 POW Branch Camp 9-B, Amagaski, Japan*

The men were losing heart – losing faith. They merely existed within a shell of skin and bone. Survival seemed to be a losing battle. They desperately searched for that peaceful contentment they had once found that Christmas Eve 1943, where four Royal Scots lifted their spirits by singing a simple Scottish ballad, making them think of home and loved ones. But each death in the camp slowly washed away everything they desperately clung to.

Nick found himself awake most nights; sleep did not come easy to an undernourished body, as it twitched with hunger and pain. At times his neck was so sore he couldn't hold up his head. His feet were charged with electric stinging, and his transparent skin stretched over his protruding rib cage. It was a slow, demoralizing death, one he was sure would find him soon.

One night he couldn't sleep at all. His mind roamed back to when he was a wee lad standing in his pop's ice-cream shop. He pictured his father proudly smiling while he taught Nick how to make ice-cream. He thought of his mother when she presented him with the books she had sent for from Italy. Her tiny hands cupping his face and telling him in broken English what a talented artist he was. Then his sisters and brothers appeared, their faces seemed so real that he reached his hand out as if to touch each one. It was the face of his sister Getna that lingered the longest. He lay with tears streaming.

He thought of Andrew dying that Christmas Eve. He then thought of Jordie, Danny, and Rab belting out, "My Ain Folk." Names that had now been added to his Roll of Honour, his comrades, his mates, that died a slow and miserable death. Nick bowed his head and sang, "I am far beyond the sea, but my heart will always be at hame in dear old Scotland wi' my ain folk."

And in the darkest corners of his mind, he pulled that memory he held so dearly. Her red velvet dress had now faded, blurred by tones of grey. She seemed farther away from his touch, yet her warm smile lured him to survive.

The alleged news was incessant, and it raised the men's hopes. Each time a US plane flew over the camp, the men shouted; those that could, jumped high as if to touch the skies. "We're close. I can feel it in my bones," Charles said. He bore a smile so broad you could see his infected gums where once a set of teeth had resided. Most of the men had lost teeth; some pulled their own to relieve the pain from the decaying dentin.

Nick wanted to believe Charles, but it was almost as if he was afraid to raise such hopes. They had to be close to winning the war. *Christ! We all can't die here*, he thought. He said, "Charles, when the troops come marching through that gate, then I will fuck'n believe it." Charles gave a nod and left it at that.

It was mid-August, the days felt long and hot, and many of the prisoners couldn't continue hauling pig iron. Some worked in the paddy fields, others lay in what was considered the "recovery room." The prisoners called it the "death pit." Both Frank and Harry were there. Nick and the lads snuck food in as often as possible. It had only been a few days since the two Glaswegian soldiers surrendered their sickly bodies. Afraid of having their rations cut, they had persevered through the daily slave labour until their dying bodies fell over in the insufferable heat of the foundry.

The men plodded along, usually singing or telling tales, anything to get them through their fourteen-hour days. Today was absent of the usual banter or ditty. The four and a half years of imprisonment now felt like a lifetime. Loved one's faces had faded, the smells of home had long ceased, even the simple thing of colour was lost among the dreary confines of the camp. The guards had even grown tired of their post, making their moods unbearable and beatings became more frequent.

The men's weakened conditions led to careless activity working under the weight of the iron. Patrick Munro could hardly stand. Nick noticed him waver, and as Nick grabbed him, a large steel vat came crashing down on top of Patrick.

That night was unbearable. Nick and a few lads restrained Pie to the ground. "I will fuck'n kill those yellow bastards!" Pie yelled. Even skin and bone, he had the strength of five men.

They all heard the deafening screams, and they could do nothing. It was total madness. Patrick's arm broke under the weight of the steel vat, and when they marched back to the camp, Patrick was taken to the recovery room. Rather than administer medication or try to set the arm, the Japs simply sawed it off. The men sat on the dirty warehouse floor, helpless, listening to the cries of their comrade. Come morning, Patrick had died.

Nick knew Patrick's family; they lived in Leith. If he made it out alive, what would he tell Patrick's mother?

The following night Frank MacLeash died when his starved body surrendered.

As the prisoners stood at the gate saluting the bodies of Patrick and Frank, Nick eyed the Jap guards as they unmercifully towed them away. Nick had stopped seeing the Japs as men during his first year of imprisonment; now, he stopped seeing them as human beings.

On August 15, before the US troops stormed in, the crackled announcement circulated the camp and the prisoners began gathering, eyeing the guards and Commander Inagaki as they stood attentively, listening to Emperor Hirohito's recorded voice. The Japs' usual impassive expressions mutated into ones of incredulity. It wasn't until Veraski stood on the wooden table outside the commander's hut that they learnt the news. "Our great emperor has, with great consideration, decided to effect a settlement of the present situation by resorting to an extraordinary measure." The men looked at each other, baffled, then looked back at Veraski. "The war is over. You are now free," Verasaki said before he bowed. He walked towards Nick, shook his hand, and broke down and cried.

What happened next was completely unbelievable – incomprehensible. To the prisoner's surprise, most of the guards lowered their rifles and swords and bowed. Astonishingly, Snake Eyes had been the first to relinquish his. A few ran out of the camp, including Commander Inagaki.

Some prisoners lashed out, though most were too weak to inflict any real damage. Nick watched Pie and a few others push and shove the remaining guards onto the ground. Some picked up the swords from the mounted pile and threatened to behead the guards right there and then. It was like the final act of a bad play.

It was all too much to bear. The news was overwhelming. American planes filled the skies, and Red Cross parcels dropped down like it was Christmas morning. When the US troops walked through the gates, it was like the prisoners had shed four and a half years of oppression for deliverance. They dropped to the ground, they yelled, hugged, and cried.

The camp was now occupied by US troops, and the looks on their faces were beyond shocked. "Christ! What the fuck have these nip bastards done?" one US soldier ululated.

The American soldiers combed through the camp, horrified by each and every inhumane living condition they came across. And after witnessing the ghastly state of the incapacitated POWs in the so-called recovery room, they too imposed a violent threat towards the Japanese guards. Nick knew harming the guards would not absolve them from their immoral reign of terror; it would only serve as a moment of retribution. The hate that lingered within Nick's soul scared him. He just wanted to leave this strange country and head home.

He appreciated the Americans' avenging actions towards the Japs, though their encounter had only been a glimpse. They would never truly understand what the men endured, for they had never reached the depths of emotions as each POW had.

And when the final scene played out, the men for the last time walked out through the gates of hell at Camp Amagasaki. They didn't march in a tattered procession of dying men, they walked out free, side by side, singing "God Save the King."

Two bombs had saved their lives; that's what the US troops contentedly reported. The first bomb, referred to as "Little Boy," dropped on Hiroshima on August sixth. The second bomb, "Fat Man," dropped on the city of Nagasaki on August ninth. And as the men travelled through Hiroshima, it shocked them into silence. Thousands of burnt, smouldering bodies lay scattered all around the scorched ground. The city looked as if it had been disembowelled.

All the buildings were demolished into piles of incinerated rubble. Charred tree trunks reached out from the ground as if pointing to the heavens. The smell was of an evil death; it drifted inside Nick's mouth and nose, choking him, and he turned his head away from the horrific sights.

When they reached Nagasaki, they witnessed the same atrocities. It seemed surreal that the liberated prisoners had returned to a city in which they'd first arrived as prisoners to now celebrate their freedom and prepare for their journey home.

*September 1945, Nagasaki*

The docks were flooded with prisoners: British, Indian, American, Australian, and Chinese. All liberated and free, waiting to head home to their loved ones. It was the most compelling scene one could imagine. Nick and the lads learnt that there were camps all through Japan. To see all the survivors gathered, waiting to leave their four and a half years of imprisonment, was inconceivably overwhelming. Songs from their homelands filled Japan's skies. The atmosphere was energetic.

The ship that Nick and a few hundred men boarded was headed to Hawaii; there, their convalescence would begin. Some walked on, others were carried on in stretchers. Harry Graham was one, as he had outlasted the death trap. Still in a weakened condition, he gave a slight smile when Nick grabbed his hand saying, "We're going hame, pal, we're going hame!"

They were not the same men leaving Japan as they once were nearly six years ago, arriving in Hong Kong. Their feelings were indescribable. This was the day they had all dreamed about and spoken about. They were showered, shaved, clothed, and fed. Nick cried as he stood under the hot water. It was the best thing that he had felt in years. And when the first sip of hot tea passed over his lips, it brought him one step closer to home.

As they stood on the ship's deck, Pie wrapped his arm around Nick's shoulder, pressing him in close. "I dae believe I owe ye a fine bottle of scotch."

Nick smiled and countered. "Aye, pal, ye do."

Walking to the bow of the ship, Nick stole a moment for himself. Peering over the railing, he spotted a pod of dolphins surfing the swell of the wake. They twisted and turned and glided effortlessly; how free they looked. It made him realise how much he had missed. He thought of Scotland and wondered how his homeland had survived through the hardships of the war. He thought of his mother. Certainly she would be shocked by his appearance. He smiled, picturing her in the kitchen making all his favourite foods. Afterwards, he would indulge in his pop's ice-cream. And maybe his father would ask him about being a POW, and maybe Nick would tell him. He then thought of Alexandrena Helliwell. Perhaps he would look her up.

He tilted his head, breathed in the entire world, and yelled, "I'm going hame!" He then pulled out his red bandana and traced his fingers over the threaded names he had so carefully and respectfully embroidered. He thought of each comrade in his unit, each Company A Royal Scot 2nd Battalion that died in the camp, and he spoke the last verse he had stitched. "No one provokes me with impunity."

After the war, it was determined the death rate of prisoners of the Japanese was six times higher than those held in German camps.

## CHAPTER THIRTY-FOUR

## An Unforeseen Journey

*Edinburgh, 1946*

The tram car was heading down Ferry Road, Rena was making her way home to Granton Terrace. She had just settled into her seat and opened her book when she heard someone whistle, but when she turned to look, there was no one she recognised. She continued reading her book. "Emma! Emma! it's me, Nick!" Rena looked up at the breathless stranger standing beside her. He was smartly dressed with tartan trews and waistcoat. He removed his Balmoral cap, and his ocean-blue-coloured eyes gave an apologetic glance. "I'm sorry, I thought you were an old friend of mine."

Rena gave no reply, only smiled.

"If you don't mind me asking, by chance, are you Alexandrena Helliwell, Emma's sister?"

"Aye. I mean I'm Rena Thomson, but yes, one and the same."

"I know you ... I mean, I met you. Well, we weren't formally introduced. I saw you at a dance with Emma before I was stationed in the Far East. Please don't think me forward. You saved my life."

Rena laughed at the handsome stranger's attempt at flirtatious flattery.

They'd spent the rest of the afternoon at Nick's father's ice-cream shop. He'd succeeded in persuading her to join him, contending it was the best homemade ice-cream in Leith. It was one of the most enjoyable afternoons she'd had in a long time. They talked over two bowls of ice-cream. And Rena had to admit it was the best she'd tasted.

She knew Nick was familiar with her family through Emma, and he expressed his condolences about the bombing. Rena felt no need to speak further of Robert, though she told Nick all about her daughter. Rena was cautious about asking too many questions and sympathised with Nick's apprehensive responses. Perhaps he too had learnt to bury his afflictions. She respected that there was more to Nick's portrayal of being a POW than he let on. He kept it light and spoke mainly about the exotic foreign countries he had travelled to. Her father had told her that most soldiers from World War One came back broken men, never speaking of the atrocities they witnessed. She wondered if Nick would ever relinquish his demons. Those discussions would perhaps be for another day; today was about laughing and living.

Nick offered to accompany her on the tram back into Edinburgh. Before she accepted, a petite older woman dressed in black stood at the counter. Her grey braid lay perfectly bound atop her tiny head. Rena smiled and couldn't help but mention that his mother looked like she was still from the old country. Nick laughed and agreed, then explained that a piece of Christina Massaro's heart remained home in Italy. Needless to say, Rena understood; her heart would always belong to Scotland.

She detected a few English words, as Christina randomly plopped one here and there, although she spoke too quickly. Rena surrendered smiling and hoped she was nodding accordingly.

Nick graciously interrupted his mother. "She's inviting you for dinner, Rena. And she will not take no for an answer."

"Tell her aye, I would love that."

Christina understood and cupped Rena's face. "Bella . . . Rena, you come." Before leaving the shop, Christina wrapped her tiny, aging hands firmly around Nick's face and plunked a long kiss on the crown of his head. "My a Michael."

Rena took notice of Nick's smile, and it was warm and tender; he truly admired his mother. Rena couldn't help but wonder how relieved Christina must have been when her son came home safe and alive. She had to ask, but Nick merely responded, "The story of my brother Michael is for another day."

Rena and Nick found themselves inseparable. They spent as much time together as possible. They got to know each other's friends and family members. Every Friday night they hit the dance hall. Some nights they cleared the floor, and their dancing was brilliant. They jived and fox trotted. Their harmonised steps performed to an audience within themselves. Each dance step triumphantly diverted worlds of loss, hopelessness, and imprisonment. Above all they held each other tight, moving as one, their hearts soaring to a celebratory crescendo.

Rena adored Christina and Francis Massaro, and they adored her. They fussed over Catherine and spoilt her with all the ice-cream she could eat. Getna and Emma were happy that their sister and brother had found happiness and love after enduring the vicissitudes of war.

John Helliwell had his own opinions and concerns, and was quite blatant about it when his daughter broke the news she was re-marrying. "Where will he live?"

Rena poured the tea and sat down across the table from her father. "With us, of course."

"And what of our lass?"

"Da, Nick adores Catherine." She tried keeping her tone equable.

"She'll no call him father! Robert Thomson is her father." Rena didn't want to argue. The past six years it had just been the three of them, and she knew her father was struggling with the idea of another man entering their home and their lives.

They were married on November 23, 1946, nearly a year after Nick had returned home from months of convalescence. The weeks leading up to their wedding day had left them both disconcerted and utterly tattered. "There is only one resolution, Rena. And I say we inform both families."

Rena knew Nick was right. There would be no appeasing either party any other way. "The whole thing is daft! Christ, we've just survived a war," she said.

"Then it's agreed! I did not suffer beatings, starvation, and near death for four and half years to be told where we can and canna get married."

Both families assumed the ceremony would be conducted under their respective religions. And while stern discussions of churches, ministers, and priests whirled around, Nick and Rena informed the families that there would be two services, the first at the Catholic church and the second at the Presbyterian. Not much more was said.

*Edinburgh, June 1954*

They say a soldier's road to recovery and reclamation is a long and onerous one. It took Nick months of convalescence to regain his health and to feel like a man again. The prisoners had been made to feel less than animals, worthless. He bore the scars both physically and mentally. They would last him a lifetime.

After deciding what he had packed in his suit case would suffice, he closed the lid and gave the top a tap of his fingers, as though still in contemplation. *This is it*, he thought, his plans were in motion and there was no turning back. He gathered his remaining items and pulled them off the bed. Even now, years later, his discipline training in becoming a soldier was not so easily forgotten. He stacked his cases and boxes in an orderly fashion on the floor.

He laid out his tapestry across the bed and read each name aloud, honouring the men he'd fought beside and had been imprisoned with, men who died as POWs.

Before he was to leave Scotland, he was asked to present his embroidered red bandana to the Royal Scots in Glencorse at the Glencorse Barracks. There, the Roll of Honour would tell its tale and commemorate the soldiers of the A Company 2nd Battalion Royal Scots. It was to be a night of remembrance to the fallen and a celebration for those who survived.

He held his "soldier's release book," and just reading its contents flooded him with a surreal mix of emotions. The front cover identified him as "N. Massaro – Army No. 3063670. Rank: Private. Ex-Prisoner of War, Far East." Before placing the remaining documents in his army bag, he scanned the number of medical conditions he was afflicted with during captivity and the remaining few he would continue to endure. He did not forget the promise he made himself the day the POWs were freed: If he made it home alive, he would never forget the passion he struggled with each day to live. And foremost, he would live his life to the fullest and never let the stain of war afflict him again.

Whether it was fate or destiny, they never questioned one another. And when Nick described his dreams of her during imprisonment, she gave him the same warm, heartening smile that inspired him to survive. And that day, when he ran down Ferry Road chasing after the tram car, he never imagined mistaking Rena for her sister Emma would change his life forever.

He knew that emigrating was a good decision. A new beginning was what he so desperately needed. To him, Scotland had changed. The war had changed everything and everyone. South Africa was his first choice; however, Rena, with great disconcert, said she couldn't, that dream had once belonged to her sister, Hannah. Canada was agreed upon. It was a vast country, and its opportunities were immense. He knew Rena was hesitant, but he also knew she needed a new start. She herself was surrounded by too many ghosts. He loved her the moment he saw her on the dance floor before he was stationed in Hong Kong. And now he loved her daughter. It took wee Catherine time to call him Dad, and when she did, his heart rang like a large church bell. He worried he would never have children of his own. There were many cases of sterile POWs, either from vitamin deficiency by way of starvation and disease, or from the obscure injections the Japanese had administered.

He felt it a great responsibility and honour to care for and raise another man's child. He promised Rena he would give the lass the world. He also promised Rena's father.

John Helliwell pulled no punches when informing Nick how important his granddaughter was. "He is a man not to cross," Rena warned Nick. And Nick gravely agreed.

*July 1954*

They were to set sail for Canada in two days on the MV *Georgic*. Checklists of items and clothing ran through her mind, and she was hoping nothing would be left behind. She'd never been outside of Scotland; well, perhaps England, when visiting her father's people. But never off the British Island. Her stomach turned and twisted. Nick had been all over, to countries she had never heard of. And after what he'd been through, this move was a promise of new beginnings.

Then there were the goodbyes. Her sisters and brother threw Nick and her a bon voyage party. That's what her sister Betty called it, anyway. *Christ,* she thought, *I'm not going on vacation. I'm moving, leaving Scotland, leaving hame.* But she smiled, and everyone hugged and made promises to write. Her brother, now married with bairns, spoke of one day coming across to live. She gave William a smile in response, thinking she could be back within the year. Her stomach still twisted.

The most difficult goodbyes were to the ones that were already gone. Nick dropped her off at Rosebank Cemetery; he didn't go in with her, nor did she ask him. He knew she had to do this alone. She placed a bouquet of yellow roses in front of the first stone, which bore her sisters' names. She hadn't visited the gravesite since her mother and Robert were buried. She never found the courage or the strength. She did, however, return to bury her father.

It had been difficult watching her father, a once strong, vibrant man, become sick and ill-tempered towards the end. He only wanted her or his granddaughter. He would yell out from his bed, needing them. There were nights he yelled out for his wife; other nights he called out to daughters that had long been dead. Mostly, he cried out for Mary. It broke Rena's heart and pushed her own emotions to the edge. Then there was the guilt. She had dedicated these past years to caring for him, yet when Nick mentioned moving to Canada, she couldn't bear the thought of leaving her father.

She thought he was asleep and their voices low enough. But Nick was startled by her father's loud response and promised Rena that he would not mention Canada again. John's voice reverberated through the flat: "You two will not be taking my granddaughter out of Scotland! Rena, get the hell in here!"

Months had gone by, and Rena never spoke of leaving again. Her father settled, and to him, the world seemed right again. The night he was dying left her conflicted and confused, and as much as she wanted a new beginning, she was scared to let go of the past and everyone in it. And as if that had not been enough, watching her daughter struggle to say goodbye to her grandfather broke her heart. She'd asked Nick to sit with her father until she helped Catherine get into bed. It had been a long night, and the hour was pushing midnight. Preparing the pot of tea was instinct, highly appropriate in any crisis. She carried the tray through into the bedroom. Nick didn't have to say the words. Rena looked upon her father's face and she let go.

She stood at the cemetery, overwhelmed with emotions. She hoped she was making the right decision for her daughter and herself and that the dead would approve. She laid another bouquet of roses by the second stone and swept her fingers over the etched words. "In Affectionate and Loving Memory of Catherine Johnstone, aged sixty-one years. Wife of John Helliwell. Also, Robert Thomson, aged twenty-five years. Husband of Rena Helliwell. Both killed in enemy action, 18th July 1940." It had been decided by both Rena and Robert's family that because the two had died together that they should be buried together. And that one day Rena would join Robert and be together for eternity. The family plot consisted of two headstones, and below the ground, her sisters, mother, and husband, and now father lay. Rena's heart ached, she was leaving them all behind.

Her eyes filled with tears. "I love you, Spud." She paused, swallowing the choke in her throat. "I can promise you, I will look after our wee lamb." She drew a deep breath and continued tracing the words with her touch. "John W. Helliwell, who died 13th February 1954. Aged eighty-three years."

"Goodbye, Father." It was all she could do to stop herself from breaking into the shattered pieces that she had struggled so hard to pick up and put back together. Even her happiest of memories found sadness.

Her daughter's voice caught her attention. She'd arrived by Rena's side, hugging her mother's shoulders, scanning the stones where almost an entire family lay. An entire life of stories and songs of love and pain. Rena thought of her mother and how important her family was – her family circle, she would say. "I will always miss you, Mum," Rena whispered.

"I wish you would have known your grandmother, lass."

"I do know her, Mum, you've kept her in our hearts."

"And your father, Catherine. I promised him."

"Aye, Mum, I will." They both stood silent. Catherine spoke first. "Are you ready, Mum? Da is waiting in the car."

Rena turned to her daughter. "Aye, Catherine, I'm ready."

## Nick Massaro

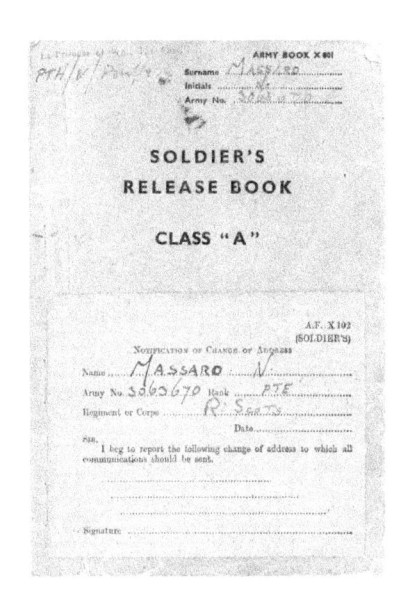

Alexandrena Thomson, nee Helliwell

Catherine Thomson, age 9

# EPILOGUE

*Canada, October 12, 2002*

Memories can be discordant: one's subconscious can contrive multiple twists and turns, all influenced by a simple touch, a specific smell, or a faint feeling. For Rena, ambivalent feelings haunted her. At times, without warning, they mercilessly took hold, rendering her powerless and vulnerable.

They had been her formative years, and regardless of one's lifetime, memories were not easily forgotten, only perhaps slightly altered. All Rena's plans, methodically laid out, began a journey of their own, twisting like branches of an old tree, each influenced by the elements that surrounded it.

Somewhere in the distance, in a foreign land, a life once lived had travelled its course.

Rena lay in a clean, firm bed. She heard voices no louder than a whisper, much the same as her mother and father sitting in their family room sipping tea, quietly discussing the events of the day, laughing softly at something one of the bairns had said, or a subtle weep and shed of tears on bairns that were sadly missed. Distinct were the faces, youthful in appearance: her mother's stoic look, her expressive Johnstone dark eyes narrating her family stories. Her father's warm smile, blue eyes alit, wearing his favourite waistcoat, proudly dressed, sitting reading his paper.

Was that a wink?

*Aye, it was, lass.* She thought she could smell his pipe.

There you are, Spud, how handsome you look, it seems like a lifetime ago.

*Aye, Rena, it tis.*

At times I missed you fiercely. You left me too soon. I grieved for you desperately.

*Aye, I ken, Rena.*

Your daughter is beautiful, you would be so proud of her. I wish you could have known her as she grew.

*Aye, Rena, she has remained in my heart, as you have, always.*

Rena's thoughts drifted, her memories travelling back and forth throughout the years. She felt serene but unaware of her surroundings. The voices continued, keeping in muted tones, but making sure a presence was known. Struggling to stay in the present, she focused on the voices, ever so familiar, yes, voices from loved ones. This voice was new, a more recent addition, one with formality but comforting, for it was in her home tongue. It brought a cessation to her subconscious journey.

"Your mother is in no pain. We are doing everything we can to keep her comfortable. Continue talking, she can hear you. I will be back this evening. If you need me, the nurse can reach me."

"Thank you, Doctor," Catherine said. "May I ask what part of Scotland you are from?"

The doctor smiled. "Edinburgh."

"I thought that. My mother is in good hands."

Catherine ... Catherine. Rena heard her daughter's voice.

Like the pages in one of her classic novels, the years turned over. A life, all well-read, composed of plots and climaxes. Alas, the anticipated epilogue was a page away. A reprieve is necessary before a new book begins. There is the time of mourning and contemplation. It is most vital between stories, most vital for grieving. You require time to digest the story. Endings are hard to let go.

Rena's stories unravelled like her mother's entwined collection of yarn, knitting a composition of colours and formation. An heirloom designed of cherished memories and family antecedents descending to her children, grandchildren, and great-grandchildren, and even perhaps to her great-great-grandchildren. The once devised journey of motherhood was influenced by unforeseen elements, twisting like a branch, forming its own.

Rena had one child – a daughter. Catherine Johnstone Thomson. Her heart, her piece of Scotland, her piece of *hame*.

A soft kiss brushed her forehead. "I love you, Grandma." Rena momentarily struggled for recognition of the voice. Then she felt a warm hand upon her shoulder.

"The boys send hugs and kisses." The boys – her great-grandsons, Robert, Erik, and Nicholas, of course – my lovely laddies. The voice was Angela, her granddaughter.

Rena felt his touch, the warmth of his hand, a hand older in years, though familiar. A gap once perceived as a hundred years had come full circle, a moment embraced. "Oh, my bonnie Rena, what will I dae without you, my bonnie Scottish thistle." Tears fell from William's eyes. He lowered his head towards his sister, kissed her brow, and smoothed his fingers along the side of her cheek, his tears steadfast. He whispered, "Oh my Rena, here we are, far from hame. We have lived a lifetime. You are going hame, lass." With a broadened accent, he began to sing a familiar rendition of "Bonnie Banks of Loch Lomond," a song his sister sang back in Scotland as a wee lassie.

*By yon bonnie banks and by yon bonnie braes*
*Where the sun shines bright on Loch Lomond*
*Me and my true love were ever wont to gae*
*On the bonnie, bonnie banks of Loch Lomond*

*Ye'll tak' the high road and I'll tak the low road*
*And I'll be in Scotland afore ye*
*But me and my true love will never meet again*
*On the bonnie, bonnie banks of Loch Lomond*

The room fell silent, aside from deep sighs and crinkling tissue. Tears spilled from Rena's eyes, streaming from their corners. Like the dawn of a dream, the surface of awakening, Rena realised where she was: a hospital far away from hame. Scotland. She had lived almost a whole life in Canada, a good one, she thought.

In the distance, beyond hushed voices and sad faces, a whistle sang a familiar tune, and it made her smile. In tartan trews and Balmoral cap, he smiled back. Through war and death and atrocities, they had rescued each other: they learnt to survive, they learnt to laugh – to live again.

*May I have this dance, Rena?*
Aye, Nick.

*Me and my mother, Catherine Johnstone Reid nee Thomson at Rosebank Cemetery, Scotland. October 2018.*

## AUTHOR'S NOTES

Stories change throughout the years; some are altered, and some remain the same. These are stories that my grandmother Alexandrena (Rena) shared with me, stories of her family before and after the war in Scotland.

John and Catherine Helliwell did lose five daughters. Their causes of death, and the dates and times, are accurate to their death certificates. Their stories are close to truths, with of course some embellishments.

The bombing of George Street in Leith is accurate to the date, time, and the deaths of my grandmother's mother, Catherine Helliwell, and my grandmother's first husband Robert (Spud) Thomson. They were two of the first casualties of war in Edinburgh.

My grandfather didn't talk much about being a POW. At times he'd share a story or two, and when he did, you sensed the raw emotion. It resonated through from his voice, it settled deep within his blue eyes. His tales were shocking, beyond belief, almost. It was truly incredible how any of the POWs survived.

I was fortunate that my grandfather had kept his war records. Transcripts, documents, and letters from ex POW's who were members of "The Royal Scots Association". Soldiers who shared their stories from the Battle of Hong Kong to the labour camps in Japan. All of these helped to assist me in sharing my grandfathers story. It was an emotional journey, to say the least, and it's something I can now share with my children, and grandchildren.

To keep the authenticity of these records, the Japanese words/commands used by the guards in the camps are spelled in the manner in which they were recorded in the original documents.

He lived his life to the fullest and loved each and every aspect of it. We were blessed to have him as our grandfather, and our children were blessed to have such a wonderful great-grandfather. Everyone who knew my grandfather loved him.

My grandmother missed Scotland dearly and visited often. She always spoke of moving back *hame*. In the summer of 2005, my mother, Catherine Johnstone Reid nee Thomson, my sister Valerie, and my brother David took both my grandparents' ashes to Scotland to be buried in the family plot at Rosebank Cemetery in Leith. Their ashes were buried together. I know my grandmother would be happy to be laid to rest with her family and her first husband Robert Thomson.

We also took my Great-Uncle Bill's (William Helliwell) ashes home to be buried in the same cemetery, in a different location, with his wife Ruby. His eldest son, John Helliwell, and our family arranged the voyage of ashes.

Our family in Scotland arranged a smashing celebration of life. It was a great send-off I know my grandparents would be proud of.

## THE TAPESTRY

Out of respect to the families and the Company A Royal Scot 2nd Battalion POWs who died in my grandfather's unit in Japan, I did not use their names on the "Roll of Honour." The names of the characters in my novel, are fictional. However, the events from the battle, the hell ships to the prison camps in Japan, and the experiences of abuse and torture are from true events.

It was lost, and then it was found.

Before my grandfather sailed to Canada, he was asked to bring his work of embroidery to Glencorse barracks, and there the Royal Scots would honour their fallen and celebrate the surviving. The celebrations left my grandfather a little inebriated, and afterwards he couldn't recall the whereabouts of his tapestry. With no time to backtrack, he left for Canada. It wasn't until years later he decided to hunt it down. Still a member of the Royal Scots, he asked to have an advert placed in the *Scottish Patriotic Magazine* called *The Thistle*. Below is a snippet of that advert.

A Lost Souvenir

"In June 1954, just before he emigrated to Canada, Nick Massaro took the prized possession to Glencorse, intending to offer it to the officers' mess. At the depot he was taken to the sergeants' mess where he showed off his souvenir and was entertained so royally that he got no further and remembers no more until he found himself on a No. 16 bus going homeward, without his embroidery. Busy with his preparations for emigration, he made no effort then to retrieve it. But in 1983, on holiday from Canada, he went back to Glencorse and with the help of a corporal tried in vain to find his embroidery. He concluded that it must have been removed from Glencorse by the Royal Scots when the regiment gave up its depot there. Nick Massaro is now making an effort to recover it in order that he may donate it to the museum. If anyone can remember seeing this kenspeckle piece of embroidery at Glencorse or elsewhere..." The readers were invited to contact a name and address disclosed in the magazine.

In August of 1991, printed in the Royal Scots Association Newsletter, it was reported that Nick Massaro's Roll of Honour had been found and it would hang at the sergeants' mess at Fort George, Inverness. My grandfather was elated, to say the least. It had been thirty-seven years that he had thought of the whereabouts of his tapestry.

What's extraordinary about this story is my third cousins (or fourth, I can never keep it straight!) To keep it simple, these lads are the sons of Ian Dow (The wee lad in the house bombing), his mother being Lily Dow, my grandmother's sister.

My cousins served as Royal Scots, and after the Gulf War they were stationed at Fort George. It was there that my grandfather's tapestry had been found in a frame in the attic. The Royal Scot Museum traced down its history. My cousin Kenny Dow had come across it and learnt it was his great-uncle Nick's. The historical piece has travelled to West Germany, Colchester, and Edinburgh.

After the amalgamation of the Royal Scots with the "King's Own Scottish Borders" my cousins Kenny and Leslie Dow retrieved it before it went back into storage. That same year we took the ashes to Scotland, my cousins presented my mother (Catherine) with her father's piece. Today it resides with our family, a keepsake of our grandfather.

Nick Massaro shoulders the Knapsack he carried in the Second Word War.

The year Emperor Hirohito died, January 7, 1989, caused mixed emotions all over the world, especially for the British, Indian, and Canadian veterans who'd survived Japan's tyranny of war.

In February 1989 my grandfather was interviewed by both local newspaper and radio broadcasts. He and thousands of aging veterans, British and Canadian, were outraged by Canada's Prime Minister Brian Mulroney's decision to send the governor general and trade minister to Japan during the week of Emperor Hirohito's funeral.

The article in the paper quoted my grandfather in saying, "I harbour no animosity to the Japanese people. Yet I will neither forgive nor forget the militarists of half a century ago. Above all, I hold Hirohito responsible. We were there, we went through their savage treatment. They beat us, starved us, stabbed us to death, they watched us die day by day. We shall never forget. Sending representatives from Canada is a slap in the face to each British and Canadian soldier who fought, were imprisoned, and lost their lives."

The president of the National Prisoners of War Association and many veterans agreed with my grandfather's views.

My grandfather, not alone, received no reparations. The former POWs of Britain rallied together to fight, not only for compensation but recognition for each day they were subjected to forced labour and torture. He worked effortlessly writing letters, keeping in touch with the Royal Scots and the British Government. And finally, in the year 2000, after years of fighting for what some referred to as "The forgotten people," the Ministry of Defence announced that each surviving veteran or widow would receive a "Debt of Honour" of £10,000.

Unfortunately, my grandfather had passed away by then. My grandmother received the payment with a heavy heart, knowing that her husband never lived to see his accomplishments.

My grandfather died peacefully on May 3, 1995, surrounded by his family.

"Lest We Forget"

Printed in the USA
CPSIA information can be obtained
at www.ICGtesting.com
JSHW020012181123
51886JS00011B/17

9 781039 169463